I0523357

THE COGSMITH'S DAUGHTER

ALSO BY KATE M. COLBY

The Desertera Series

THE COGSMITH'S DAUGHTER

DESERTERA BOOK ONE

KATE M. COLBY

BOXTHORN
PRESS

The characters and events portrayed in this book are fictitious. Any similarity to real persons, living or dead, is coincidental and not intended by the author.

Copyright © 2015 Kate M. Colby

All rights reserved.

No part of this book may be reproduced, or stored in a retrieval system, or transmitted in any form or by any means, electronic, mechanical, photocopying, recording, or otherwise, without express written permission of the author.

Published by Boxthorn Press

New Haven, CT

ISBN-10: 0-9967825-0-8

ISBN-13: 978-0-9967825-0-0

Library of Congress Control Number: 2015914399

Cover design by Damonza.com

Editing by Red Adept Editing

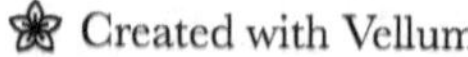 Created with Vellum

To my parents,

*Thank you for trusting my ambition
and never saying that writing isn't a real career.*

1

*A*ya Cogsmith awoke, as she did every morning, to the croaking of the mechanical frog next to her bed. Reaching across the pile of blankets and pillows, Aya grabbed the frog between her thumb and forefinger. If she didn't pick him up first thing, he would hop all the way across her room in five leaps and run into the wall. Aya didn't have the money to fix him again.

Riibbuuuutt.

She rubbed the frog's smooth metal belly with her free hand, keeping her fingers clear of his still-jerking legs. She peered through his side to examine his center cog, ensuring its nine golden teeth were connecting properly with the other gears. She listened carefully to his croaks, counting the seconds between them and trying to gauge the volume.

"You're sounding older every morning, Charlie."

Aya turned the winder on his back, and Charlie's legs slowed their jerking. He let out one final croak before going still. Aya placed Charlie back on the floor next to her bedding and watched him as if he might move again. She remembered when she was a little girl—how she would jump out of bed and hop along the floor behind Charlie. When she caught up to him, she would grab him with both hands and frog-leap back into her bed. There, she'd either let Charlie hop along the blanket until he got caught in the pillows, or she'd place him under the covers, holding them high over him like a tent, and let him hop around in his froggy cave.

After a few minutes of this, Aya's father would peek his head in through the door and tell her to let poor Charlie rest. She would sigh until her father mentioned whatever warm breakfast he had prepared. At which point, she would unwind Charlie and place him back on the floor next to her bed.

Aya yawned and patted Charlie's head with her forefinger. "At least I've still got you, buddy."

Charlie didn't move, which she took as a sign that he wouldn't leave.

Aya stretched her arms out wide, wincing slightly at a twinge in her lower back. Even after ten years, her body refused to adjust to sleeping on the floor with only pillows for cushioning. She got up and walked to her window, relishing the feel of the warm morning wind on her face. The window was about six inches wide, installed when the hovel's previous owner put his fist through the wall during a fight. Aya had covered the hole with scraps of red fabric from her favorite skirt. A carpenter had ripped the skirt one night at work, and she couldn't bear to let the silk go to waste. If the skirt hadn't brought her any dignity in its life, maybe it could bring her misshapen window sophistication in its death.

The streets of Sternville were relatively empty, meaning that the men were still at work pumping the wells, and the women were either tending their children or sleeping off their nights' works. Aya craned her neck to look over to the palace. The sun hovered just above the starboard railing, meaning that it was not yet lunchtime. She looked the other way toward Kalinda and Jasmine's hovel. She couldn't see anyone moving behind the windows, and there was no smoke from a fire.

Good. I won't be the last one to the wells.

Aya crossed to the other side of her room and opened her old steamer trunk. The brass buckles and hinges were still cold from the night air, and they groaned as she lifted the lid. She pulled out a plain brown dress with matching corset, a green cloak, and her tough leather shoes. If she intended to walk all the way to Bowtown for water, her slippers wouldn't do.

Once dressed, Aya went into the hovel's small common room. Dellwyn was not there, but Aya heard faint snores coming from Dellwyn's room. She crossed the common room quietly, lifting her cloak so it wouldn't rustle on the dirt floor. The common room held a wooden table, two chairs, a storage trunk, a basket of dried cacti husk and tumbleweed for kindling, and an iron wood-burning stove. Aya knew they were lucky to have the stove, as most of the girls and families in Sternville only had fire pits—one of the many perks of Dellwyn gathering noble admirers at work.

Atop the table sat a five-gallon glass jug and a black urn. Aya opened the urn's lid and reached inside, wiggling her fingers around in the ashes until they found their target: two gold coins. Aya pulled out the coins and dusted the ashes from her fingers back into the urn. While treating her father's remains like a safe made Aya's skin crawl, his urn was the only place Madam Huxley didn't search when she accused Dellwyn and Aya of skimming from their earnings.

Aya tucked the coins between her corset and the side of her left breast. Carrying anything in her pockets was too dangerous. When she'd first come to Sternville, she had learned that lesson the hard way, losing over a dozen gold coins to grubby-handed children before she reached the Rudder. She grabbed the glass jug and placed the leather strap tied to its handle over her shoulder. It wasn't much, but the strap helped distribute the weight across her body.

Aya opened the hovel's door and was instantly greeted with a gust of hot air and dust. She pulled the hood of her cloak over her hair and face, tucking in her brown curls and trying to shade her already tanned skin from the sun's unforgiving rays. She couldn't afford to get dirty, as her next bathing allowance from Madam Huxley wasn't for at least two more weeks. She knew the long walk to the other side of the palace would make her sweat, but she could wipe most of that off with her cloak, and Dellwyn still had some wildflower extract from Lord Derringher that she would let Aya borrow to freshen herself up.

Strictly speaking, Aya didn't have to walk all the way to the other side of the palace for water. Each of Desertera's four towns had their own wells. Sternville, her village at the rear of the palace, had one not five minutes' walk from her hovel. The water was a bit muddy, but it wasn't any worse than what she would find in Bowtown. However, the neighborhood children liked to stand over the Sternville well and spit in it, racing to see whose saliva could reach the water first. Instead of stopping them, the wellmen turned the children's game into a gambling one, and when they were drunk enough, they imitated it with piss.

To the west of the palace, Portside also had wells. The village was home to the merchants and traders of Desertera, and they had a crude filtration system to clean the water for cooking and other crafts. However, they weren't too polite to the wellmen's wives and ladies of the Rudder from Sternville, and they made a point to charge Sternville residents an unfair price to use the well. Likewise, Starboardshire, the eastern village and home to the lesser nobles, had several wells. Aya would never have dreamed of seeking water in Starboardshire. Even if she could have afforded it, the guards would have never let her across the border—even when her father, the only cogsmith in Desertera, had been alive.

Therefore, Bowtown, all the way to the northern side of the palace, was her best option. Bowtown housed the agricultural district's farmers and gardeners. Like Sternville, it was a poor neighborhood, but they at least respected their water and other people, no matter what village they came from. And of course, the Bowtown wells were the only other ones Aya could afford.

As Aya walked through Sternville's crooked streets, a few children poked their heads out of their doors. Aya glared at each of them, hugging her jug tighter to her chest. Near the Sternville-Portside border, six children tumbled out of their tent. Aya recognized them instantly. They belonged to Mrs. Jack Wellman, and they were the most ill-behaved litter in Sternville. Aya picked up her pace, but the oldest rushed toward her, waving his arms to get her attention. He was about thirteen, just old enough to begin understanding what Aya was and that he would like to be a part of it in a few years.

"Miss Cogsmith! Won't you stop and say hello?"

The boy motioned to his five younger siblings, and they all swarmed Aya's legs. The three girls tugged at her skirts, while the two boys reached into her pockets.

"Where are you going?"

"Why are you walking so fast?"

"Miss Cogsmith, will you play with us?"

"Why is your jug so big?"

"Miss Cogsmith, why are your pockets empty?"

Aya did not answer—to answer was to encourage. Instead, she raised her eyes to the palace and trudged onward. When she reached the anchor line between Sternville and Portside, the children released her skirts and ran back to their tent.

As Aya approached the palace, she felt her mouth go dry with thirst, and she wondered if the structure shared her longing for water. It had been built as a ship, but it now sat buried up to its propellers in sand. Over the years, the metal itself stayed intact, while its color slowly oxidized from black to brown in the sun. The name of the ship, Queen Hildegard, had faded as well, leaving only the letters H-I-D-E on the palace's port side. Beyond the letters, the side of the ship contained rows of windows, meant to let sunlight wash over the top floors and glimpses of sea life sneak in the bottom ones, and a large door and drawbridge, meant to release weary travelers into a safe port on land.

Aya let her eyes wander from the railing at the top of the palace, all the way down the chain to the anchor at the edge of the village. The borders were all marked by the chains of the anchors, one at each corner of the palace, cast down when the water level first began to drop, back when the people on the ship had hope for finding a fertile new home.

As a child, Aya used to start at the Portside-Bowtown anchor, placing her hand on the chain and running as far as she could before her fingertips could no longer reach the links. She'd imagine that she could climb up the anchor lines and swing herself nimbly onto the palace's deck, ready to guide the ship on its next adventure, like Queen Hildegard in the stories her father used to tell her. His tales about the palace were far better than those espoused by any of the street preachers and, as Aya had learned, much more romantic than the palace itself.

~

"OUR PEOPLE DIDN'T ALWAYS LIVE in Desertera, Aya." Papa pulled her onto his lap. "Once, hundreds of years ago, our ancestors lived in a beautiful, lush land—a land filled with grass and trees and lakes and rivers. There were rolling hills, open meadows, and flowers, all kinds of colorful flowers."

"Was there still sand?" Aya brushed a few grains from the hem of her skirt.

"There was but only at the edge of the ocean and in places far away. Our land had fields and cities. Oh, the cities, Aya! They were built from metal and stone, with buildings as tall as the sky. All the machines ran by gears and cogs, like the gizmos in my shop, and there was enough water and steam to power every single one. More than that, there was enough water and steam to power entire cities, whole countries." Papa swept his hand in the air, pointing at all the gadgets.

"What happened to it all?"

Papa sighed. "Do you remember what I told you about the Gods?"

Aya nodded. "There is a kingdom above our heads, a whole world of gods in the sky. The Almighty King and the Benevolent Queen were married, but then the Almighty King forsook their bed for another goddess's. The Benevolent Queen was so sad that She cried. She cried so much that Her tears fell down to our world and flooded everything."

"That's right. It rained for decades, and our ancestors built a great steam ship to carry them through the Benevolent Queen's tears."

"The Queen Hildegard*!" Aya clapped her hands.*

Papa smiled and patted her head. "Yes, Aya. The Queen Hilde-gard*, named after the mortal queen who ruled when the great flood happened."*

Aya scrunched up her face. "But Papa, if the world was all water, why is Desertera so dry?"

"After the Benevolent Queen cried all Her tears, She got mad—so mad that the heat of Her anger dried up the world and made it into a desert."

"Without water, the ship got stuck on land and became the palace."

"Exactly." Papa leaned forward. "Then the Benevolent Queen took the Almighty King's power and banished Him deep below the soil. When She did that, She saw the mortal world had become a desert, and She felt guilty for what She had done to us, Her children. So She appeared to our king and offered to help us."

"But the world is still desert. Why didn't She save us?"

"Well, She discovered that our king, just like the Almighty King, was sharing the bed of a woman who wasn't his queen. This angered the Benevolent Queen, and She cursed the mortals, swearing that we will never again know our beautiful world of water and land until our royals learn honesty and fidelity."

Aya's brows furrowed. "But King Archon is good, isn't he? No one speaks ill of King Archon. He must be good."

Papa motioned for her to stand and looked her straight in the eyes. "That's right, Aya. You must never speak ill of King Archon or Prince Lionel or the queen, no matter who holds the title."

"I won't, Papa."

"Good." Papa smiled and squeezed her shoulders.
Aya pursed her lips and tapped her chin. "Papa?"
"Yes?"
"Why did the Almighty King want a different bed? Was his too stiff?"
Papa chuckled. "Something like that."

❧

"Miss? Are you lost?"

Aya jumped. A guard stood a few feet away from her, his face and body covered in dust. Aya blushed, realizing that she had wandered into the shade of the palace, where the guards were stationed. The guard stepped toward Aya, and a gust of wind blew down the side of the palace. Aya tugged her hood closer to her face to avoid the specks of dirt within the wind. The guard ignored it, taking bigger strides.

"No." Aya curtsied. "Please, excuse me."

The guard frowned, looking her up and down. "You know Sternville whores aren't supposed to travel this close to the palace. You can walk around the edges of the city or through it, just like everyone else."

Aya did know this. The only people allowed to walk in the shade of the palace were merchants and traders delivering goods and, of course, guards and nobles. When Aya was a child, the palace hadn't had such tight security around its perimeter. However, as King Archon's brides kept being seduced by mysterious men, and even some women, the king thought it best to increase security and keep out any wandering adulterers. Aya didn't blame him. It must have shattered the king's ego to know that nearly every woman he had ever married would rather bed a vagabond than him. Personally, she thought it served him right.

"I'm sorry, sir." Aya lowered her eyes. "I'm trying to get to the Bowtown wells. My jar is very heavy, you see, and I wanted to walk the shortest route."

"Why can't you use the Sternville well like the rest of them?" The guard spat at the ground.

"It's filthy."

"And that bothers *you*?"

The guard stepped closer to Aya and smiled, revealing clods of dirt between his yellowed teeth. Aya turned her gaze away from his mouth and searched his uniform for some sign of his patronage. Each lord rotated out his personal guards to watch the palace perimeter. If this man was from the right house, Aya might be able to get through. Sure enough, he bore a welcome patch on his shoulder: a red square dissected by two crossing lines, a white vertical bar and a black horizontal bar. Lord Collingwood. Dellwyn's most loyal customer.

"Yes, it does bother me. It also bothers my housemate, Dellwyn Rutt."

"Dellwyn, you say?" The guard's eyes shifted from side to side.

"Yes. Dellwyn Rutt, who I believe has done many a noble service for your Lord Collingwood and his men. Perhaps even you?"

"And this water you're fetching, it's for Dellwyn?"

"Of course." Aya smiled.

The guard took a step back. "Forgive me, Miss…?"

"Miss will do."

"Yes, forgive me, Miss." The guard placed his hand over his heart and bowed. "Please, let me escort you to Bowtown."

Aya shook her head. "That won't be necessary. However, if you could signal down to your comrades to allow my passing, that would be quite helpful to Miss Dellwyn and me."

The guard nodded. He waved his left hand and placed his right thumb and forefinger between his lips. Upon his sharp whistle, the other guards turned. The guard pointed at Aya, her jug, then down to the bow of the ship. The other guards clapped three times in unison to indicate they understood. Aya smiled at the guard, repositioned the jug higher on her hip, and continued around the side of the palace.

As she walked, Aya admired the smooth seams along the palace walls. The craftsmanship was solid on the outside, and she knew that the inside matched its functionality with luxury, rivet for rivet. She wished she lived back in those days of excess her father used to describe. She would have loved her own shop, where she could build more frogs like Charlie and tinker with the numbered circles. *Clocks.* Her father told her that they used to tell the time, that people numbered the hours by the hands of clocks instead of the angle of the sun or stars. He'd also told her how, on the inside, clocks were made entirely of cogs and gears, the movement of each one spurring movement in the next. If even one piece got out of place, the entire clock would stop working. He had said their family used to work on these clocks and other devices from the steam and machine era, and that was where their name originated: Cogsmith. Aya's father had taught her a little craft, enough to fix Charlie and the few other machines in their household. Before he died, her father had been an expert cogsmith, the only one left practicing the ancient art in Desertera.

Aya did not know as much as her father, but she knew enough to admire the rivets that held together the walls and had, long ago, kept the palace from sinking. Maybe. It was a nice story, but she didn't know how much of it she believed any more. A few people still held true to the sea myths, especially in Bowtown, but everyone Aya knew was too busy working—or enjoying her work—to care much about bringing back the ocean.

As she made her way to the bow of the ship, the guards watched Aya closely. The final guard held out his arm to stop her. "Will you require return passage?" He licked his lips.

Aya knew she wouldn't be able to walk alongside the palace again. Not for free.

"No. Thank you."

She'd have to wait for Lord Derringher's guards to be on duty to take the shortcut again.

Aya walked straight out from the bow of the ship into Bowtown. The wells were directly in front of the palace, in the very center of the village. Unlike Sternville, which contained only shabby wooden hovels and fabric tents scattered across the dirt, Bowtown's houses were arranged in curved rows, as if the ship were the world, and Bowtown's rows of houses marked the arc of the sun around it. Each house had a fenced area behind it, where the farmers grew whatever crops they could, mostly cacti, grains, and wildflowers. The farmers on the edge of town raised livestock—goats, sheep, chickens, pigs—the descendants of the animals taken aboard the ship during the flood. The ancestors had brought horses, too, but they were all kept in Starboardshire by noble families and used for status over nourishment.

A few Mrs. Farmers bowed their heads to Aya as she passed. They sat in front of their houses, plucking the needles from cacti and tossing them into tin cans. The older women's hands were tough and leathery, spotted with calluses earned from needle pricks. The younger women's hands were soft and pink with little specks of red or scabs where the needles still punctured their flesh. Aya would have taken a million cacti needle pricks over her entire body in place of the ones she received every night. But it couldn't be that way for her— farmers only married other farmers' daughters—and unfortunately, when her father died, there had been no other cogsmiths to take her.

Aya smiled and returned the women's nods. She weaved her way through the rows of houses, finally reaching the open square with the wells. It was late enough in the morning that she didn't have to wait in line. She walked right up to the wellman and held out her jug. He took it and bounced it in his hands.

"Five gallons. Two gold coins."

Aya held her cloak together with one hand and fished the coins from her corset with the other. The wellman raised his eyebrows, but he didn't say anything. He uncorked the jug and fastened it to the well's chain. Turning the crank in even circles, he lowered Aya's jug down into the well. Every year—almost every week, it seemed—it took longer for her jug to reach the water. Eventually, she heard the distinct gurgling sound of water pushing air from her jug. When the sound stopped, the wellman spun the crank in the opposite direction until her jug reappeared. He put the cork back in, and Aya exchanged the coins for the jug. The water inside was murky—a consequence of coming late, after everyone else's containers had stirred up the sediment at the well's bottom.

"Thank you."

The wellman nodded, and Aya turned to head back to Sternville. Instead of returning to the palace, she followed the line of houses extending from the wells back to the Bowtown-Portside border. Even if the anchor and its chain had not been there to mark the border, Aya would have seen it immediately. Portside's streets were arranged in a rigid grid pattern with every building perfectly parallel to the palace's western side. She followed the anchor chain to Baker Street and turned.

Not only was Baker Street the most direct way back to her and Dellwyn's hovel in Sternville, it was also the location of several bread and pastry shops. Aya had been hungry when she awoke, and after lugging the full jug back home, she would be famished. As she strolled past the shops, the aroma of fresh baked goods wafted from the windows, and Aya's mouth watered. She and Dellwyn didn't get treats often, but she hoped that she could milk a bit more of Lord Collingwood's influence. Aya searched for his crest on the shops' doors, and about halfway down the street, she saw the familiar red square with the black and white cross. Before entering, she readjusted the jug on her hip and used her cloak to wipe the sweat from her face.

"Good morning." Aya tried to sound cheerful. The baker had her broad back to Aya, and her hands were wrist-deep in the tub of dough she kneaded.

"Good morning, love. I'll be right with you."

Aya braced herself. The moment the baker saw her in her plain clothes, without a wedding band, she would know what Aya was.

The baker turned around. "Oh! I'm sorry. I really am, but I can't sell to you."

"I know." Aya sighed. "But I saw the insignia on your door, and I'm hoping that you could *donate* to me on behalf of Lord Collingwood."

The baker raised her eyebrows. "And to whom would I be making this donation?"

"Dellwyn Rutt."

The baker put her hands on her hips, creating white marks on her dress. "You, cogsmith's daughter, are not Dellwyn Rutt."

Aya blushed. "No, but I live with her, and I am here to fetch her breakfast."

"And I am meant to trust *your* word?"

Aya straightened. "Well, you can either take my word, or you can have a word or two with Lord Collingwood."

The baker wrinkled her forehead, causing flour to sprinkle from her crown to her nose. "Very well, then. You may have those rolls on the windowsill. They're yesterday's, so I can't sell them anyway."

"Thank you." Aya took the rolls and stuffed them in the pockets of her cloak. She hoped Mrs. Jack Wellman's children would be inside when she returned. She didn't want to hide the rolls down her dress.

The baker sighed and brushed the flour from her face. "I'm sorry for what happened to you, love. It really is a shame to see you like this."

Aya shrugged and left the bakery without another word. If

any of the merchants had truly felt bad for her, they would have offered to help after her father died.

As her consolation prize, Aya rode Dellwyn's skirt-tails and bartered for favors with her name. Being a woman of the Rudder was shameful, but it did have nice benefits when one fell into favor with the right lord. Aya understood why men adored Dellwyn so much. She had beautiful dark skin and brilliant white teeth. Her figure was plump, but her waist looked slim in comparison to her ample bosom and wide hips. In contrast, Aya had tanned skin, the color of the Desertera dirt, and while her figure was also curved in proportion, her breasts and hips came in a much smaller size. As one lord had put it— pretty to look at, but not much to play with. While this did sting her ego a bit, Aya didn't mind being considered boring. As the nobleman had said, she was pretty enough to attract sufficient clientele to pay her debts, but not enticing enough to be visited several times a night. She, at least, had never had trouble walking after work.

As Aya had hoped, Mrs. Jack Wellman's children were nowhere in sight when she crossed the border from Portside to Sternville. Lord Collingwood's guard, however, was still on duty, and she saw him watching her from the other side of the anchor line. Aya ignored his gaze and tried to walk home in a dignified fashion, which was becoming increasingly difficult under the weight of the jug. Luckily, her hovel was only a few minutes from the border, and when she pushed open their door, Dellwyn was waiting to grab the jug from her.

"What were you thinking?" Dellwyn cradled the glass jug in her arms so Aya could untangle herself from its leather strap. "You know it's my day to fetch water."

"Yes," Aya groaned, rubbing her shoulder. "But I also know

how busy you were last night, and I assumed you needed the rest."

Dellwyn twisted her lips, but she didn't say anything more. She set the jug on the table, which wobbled under the weight.

"Speaking of which," Aya continued, pulling the rolls out of her pockets, "your name is worth more than a dozen gold coins."

Dellwyn's eyes widened. "Where did you get these?" She took one of the rolls from Aya, running her fingertips over the smooth top before taking a large bite.

"From a bakery in Portside. I saw Lord Collingwood's badge on the door and thought I'd test his affections for you." Aya pinched off a chunk of her own roll and popped it in her mouth. The bread was somewhat chewy, but it still tasted sweet and melted against her tongue.

"I wish you wouldn't have." Dellwyn took another bite of her roll. "Once word gets back to him about this, he's going to feel I owe him."

Aya swallowed her bite slowly. "Then you'll probably be mad that I used your name to take the palace route to Bowtown, too."

Dellwyn gasped and tossed a piece of her roll at Aya. It fell into the folds of her cloak, but Aya fished it out of her lap, tilted her head back, and dropped it into her mouth.

Dellwyn laughed. "You're lucky I enjoy bedding him. If you'd used Lord Derringher's name, I really would be cross with you. That poor man has no idea what to do with his hands."

"I will never understand how you enjoy any of it." Aya bit her lip. "Every single client makes me sick."

"That's because you never learned how to do it for fun. It's different when you do it for yourself."

Aya shrugged. Dellwyn was probably right. Before working at the Rudder, Aya had never even seen a man naked. She took another bite of her roll.

"You know what Duke Aster told me yesterday?"

Aya shook her head.

"The new queen was crowned last night. Finally. Apparently, the bishop wanted to wait at least a month to do it, given that Queen Isadona barely lasted three months from marriage to funeral pyre."

Aya rolled her eyes. "Long live the queen."

Dellwyn scoffed. "Fat chance of that. I wonder why they all run so quickly into other men's beds. I mean, King Archon isn't the most attractive man in the world, but he's not an ogre or anything. Surely he's not so repulsive that it's worth losing your head for a better bedding."

"Maybe his hands are as clumsy as Lord Derringher's."

"Or maybe his pecker is—"

Aya held up her hands. Dellwyn smiled and shut her mouth.

"Maybe it's just a side effect of the curse," Aya offered. "There hasn't been a devoted royal couple since before the great flood. Maybe they can't be faithful anymore."

Dellwyn scoffed. "You don't really believe that fundamentalist garbage, do you?"

Aya shrugged.

"I'll tell you what it is." Dellwyn pointed toward the palace. "*They* know that people out here still believe all that religious nonsense. And they also know that it is all made up. The second there is a faithful royal couple, all the common people will start asking about rain. And when the rain doesn't come, it will prove that their gods and goddesses don't exist and that the world is just a burnt crust—the way it always has been and always will be."

Dellwyn stuffed the last piece of her roll in her mouth. She retrieved two tin cups from the trunk next to the stove and poured them each a glass of water. "If you ask me, King Archon needs to suck up his pride and accept that his wives are going to sleep with other people. He can hold as many trials as he likes and sentence every one of his queens to death, but it will never scare the next one off adultery. There's no point in keeping that law around, not in today's world."

"He'll never do that," Aya whispered. "He's killed better people for less."

Dellwyn slid Aya's water cup across the table, careful not to disturb the urn. "So he has." Dellwyn lifted up her cup. "To never becoming queen!"

Aya smiled, clinking her tin cup with Dellwyn's. "To never becoming queen."

2

At sunset, Aya and Dellwyn left for work. Aya wrapped her cloak tightly around her. While everyone in Sternville knew what she did for a living, she didn't like to flaunt her corsets and high-slit skirts to every peeping wellman. Dellwyn, on the other hand, didn't bother holding her cloak closed. She strutted through the dusty, winding streets of Sternville, letting her stocking-clad legs emerge from her cloak with each stride. Aya looked everywhere but at Dellwyn.

As they approached the propellers in front of the Rudder, a knot tightened in Aya's gut. She imagined those propellers spinning, slicing through ice-cold water, and she couldn't decide whether she would rather be aboard the *Queen Hildegard* as it sailed away or jump into the blades' path. She remembered the first time she saw those blades, so tall and wide, looking as if they could cut through the sand and spin again at any moment. They made her sick then, too.

⁓

"Excuse me?" Aya asked one of the women leaning against a propeller blade. "I'm looking for the Rudder. Is this the way inside?"

The woman looked Aya up and down. She crossed her arms over her chest, pushing her breasts up in the process. "Honey, you'd best turn around. This is no place for little girls."

"I'm not little. I'm thirteen."

"Is that so?" The woman chuckled. She crinkled her nose and pointed in between the two bottom propeller blades. "Right through there."

Aya hesitated and peered through the gap. Pitch black. As she walked, Aya placed her left hand on the propeller blade the woman leaned against, as if to keep it from moving and chopping them both to bits. The woman placed her hand over Aya's. "If you walk in there, there's no coming out."

Aya stared up at the woman. She would have been beautiful with her bright, blond hair and blue eyes, if it weren't for the purple bruises and red splotches dappling her face and neck.

Aya's lower lip trembled. "I don't have anywhere else to go."

The woman sighed and looked out over Sternville. Aya followed her gaze. The village was dark, save for the orange glow of the fire pits. The woman removed her hand from Aya's. "I'm sorry."

"Me too," Aya whispered.

Squaring her shoulders, Aya walked into the Rudder. She hadn't known of the place until her father died. After his funeral, she'd overheard some of the merchants' wives say that it was the only place in Desertera for orphaned girls. And Aya was an orphan now.

At first, the Rudder didn't look so bad. The entire room was made of metal—walls, ceiling, and floors. A tall, wooden podium stood near the center of the room with a large book open on top of it. An even taller woman stood behind it counting coins. The woman was thick, but she had pulled in her girth with an emerald corset, worn over a black dress. Her hair was red, like the sun just before it slipped below the earth, and it was gathered in a curly, frizzy pile on the top of her head. Thick black makeup lined her green eyes, and Aya thought they looked like charred timbers burning under her fiery hair.

As Aya approached, the woman looked up. "Can I help you, child? Come to fetch your father?"

Aya took a deep breath. "My father is dead."

"Ah." The woman snorted. "Your mother, then? Older brother or sister?"

"My mother is dead, too. I don't have any siblings."

"So you're an orphan?"

Aya nodded.

The woman cocked her head to one side. "No family at all?"

"No, ma'am."

The woman stepped out from behind the podium. "And why are you here?"

Aya laced her fingers and looked down at her feet. "The landlord kicked me out of my father's shop. I heard this is the only place for orphaned girls in Desertera. No one else will take me in."

The woman huffed. "Well, I'm not sure that I want you either. How old are you?"

"Thirteen."

"Thirteen! I couldn't let you touch a man. It'll be three years before I can make any money from that little mouth of yours. Why should I feed it?"

Aya's lips parted, but she couldn't find any words. She didn't know exactly what women did at the Rudder, only that the people who visited—mostly men—seemed to like it very much, and the people who didn't visit—mostly their wives—didn't like it at all.

After a moment of silence, the woman sighed. "Let me look at you." She motioned for Aya to step closer. Once she came near enough, the woman grabbed Aya's chin, turning her head from side to side. "Well, you have a pretty face. Show me your teeth."

Aya curled back her lips. The cracks in them deepened as they stretched, and she winced, hoping they didn't bleed in front of the woman. Aya hadn't drank hardly any water in the last two days.

The woman bobbed her head. "A bit yellow but straight. That's good." The woman ruffled Aya's hair. "The brown isn't exceptional, but you have beautiful, soft curls. Bouncy, too. Men like bouncy."

The woman put her hands on Aya's shoulders and ran them down her body, stopping to squeeze her breasts and then her hips. Aya straightened her back and crossed her arms over her chest.

"Have you bled yet?"

Aya's eyes widened, but when the woman's face remained stern, she nodded.

"When did you start?"

Aya felt her face reddening. "About a year ago."

"Fine." The woman gestured across Aya's chest then from her head to her feet. "You may yet gain a few inches here and there. Not that petite is bad. We could use another girlish lady."

Aya didn't answer. She tried to spy the exit from the corner of her eye. Maybe it wasn't too late to turn and leave.

"And you have no family? No uncles or aunts, no grandparents or cousins, no one at all who will want you?"

Aya shook her head. The woman squatted down to Aya's level and stared directly into Aya's eyes. Aya noticed that the woman's green eyes were watery, and faint wrinkles extended from the corners like cracks in the sand. The woman reached out and took Aya's hand in hers and gave it a gentle pat. "Very well then. My name is Madam Huxley. I run the Rudder."

"Aya Cogsmith."

"Cogsmith, eh?" The woman chuckled. "I heard about what happened to your father. The last mechanical tradesman gone by royal order. No wonder no one wants you."

Aya bit her lip and looked down.

Madam Huxley touched Aya's shoulder. "I'm sorry, sweetheart. I didn't mean it like that, but I see now why you are here. There's no room in civilized society for a traitor's daughter—guilty or not."

Aya nodded. She didn't want to talk to Madam Huxley anymore. Her stomach growled, and her feet ached.

Madam Huxley straightened. "Right. Let's get started."

She took Aya's arm by the elbow and guided her into a hallway and through a thick, iron door. Inside the room, there was another girl, maybe three or four years older than Aya, seated on a bed. She had rich, black skin and the straightest hair Aya had ever seen.

"Aya," Madam Huxley began, "this is Dellwyn Rutt, our ladies' maid. Dellwyn, this is Aya Cogsmith, your replacement."

Dellwyn glanced up from the stockings she was mending. Aya held her breath, waiting for recognition or judgment to cross Dellwyn's brown eyes. If she knew anything about Aya's father or his death, Dellwyn didn't show it. "Yes, Madam."

"Dellwyn, you will show Aya her duties. Aya, you will be responsible for cleaning up the rooms after use and attending to our ladies and guests as necessary. Dellwyn will teach you." Madam Huxley paused so Dellwyn could nod her assent. "Good. I shall let you two get acquainted."

Aya stayed in place as Madam Huxley turned to leave the room. However, before Madam Huxley closed the door, she turned back to address the two girls. "Oh, and Dellwyn, now that you are no longer our cleaning girl, I will be booking you priming appointments. I expect to you to be waiting in Room G at sunset to get Lord Collingwood ready for Alisa."

"Yes, Madam," Dellwyn replied. Madam Huxley shut the door. Dellwyn looked at Aya, as though waiting for her to speak.

"Priming appointments?" Aya asked. "What are those?"

Dellwyn sighed. "Let's begin with where we store the mop."

❧

As Aya and Dellwyn walked between the propeller blades, Aya placed her hand on the one to her left, pinching it in her fist. Nothing in the main room of the Rudder had changed in the last ten years—other than Madam Huxley's face, which now held a few extra wrinkles. A man stood on the other side of the tall podium, waving his hands in the air, his voice threatening to reach a dangerous level. "Are you protesting the word of an earl? The Earl of Cornsworth has been married for twenty years, and I know for a fact that he is a regular client of yours!"

Madam Huxley held up her hands. "I'm sorry, Lord Bernstein, but we simply cannot provide our services to married people. You know the law—adulterers, both the offending spouses, or in this case, the offending spouse and the unmarried concubine—shall be executed without mercy. Surely you don't think that I, a respected businesswoman, would so blatantly defy the law. We only serve the unmarried."

Dellywn laughed. Madam Huxley and Lord Bernstein's heads snapped around. Dellwyn bit her lip to contain a smile and scurried off to her room. Aya, on the other hand, stayed put. They all knew the routine, and with Dellwyn scampering off, Aya would have the honor of being the bearer of good news.

"Aya." Madam Huxley smiled, her voice rising to a high, feminine lilt. "Could you please escort Lord Bernstein out the back exit? Door M. I would hate for his reputation to be threatened if someone saw him leaving from the propellers."

Aya nodded and looped her arm through the nobleman's. He huffed but allowed himself to be pulled away. When they were out of earshot of the common room, Aya stopped.

"I apologize for your alarm, Lord Bernstein." Aya gestured to a door on their left marked with a letter M. "I am sure Kalinda will do everything in her power to ensure that you are well compensated for your emotional distress."

Lord Bernstein raised his eyebrows, staring down at Aya as if she had just proclaimed it was raining. "Won't Madam Huxley be angered to learn I am being served?"

"Oh, you don't understand." Aya spoke softly and quickly, attempting to soothe Lord Bernstein and relieve herself of his company. "Madam Huxley was simply acting. You see, we cannot allow the royal guard to catch wind of our operations here. If King Archon knew, every employee in this establishment, along with every person who has signed the guest book, would be executed—you included. I assume you signed in at the desk?"

"Yes." Lord Bernstein arched an eyebrow. "The Madam insisted on it."

Aya smiled. "Good. Then we are happy to serve you in exchange for your discretion."

Lord Bernstein shifted his eyes from door to door. Aya couldn't tell whether he was upset that he had been duped into leaving evidence of his transgressions or relieved that he would be served after all. She stepped in front of him and opened the door to Room M, motioning for him to enter. He frowned then walked past Aya without another glance in her direction.

"Have a lovely evening," Aya crooned, shutting the door with a loud *thwap*. She heard Kalinda giggle, and she hoped the nobleman had jumped at the noise.

Aya continued down the hallway to her own room, Room V. There were twenty-six rooms in all, one for each letter of the alphabet. They were assigned to the employees by seniority and clientele with the longest-lasting and most-requested person in Room A. Currently, Room A was held by Alisa, who had been in Room G when Aya came to the Rudder, and Room B was held by Augustus, the only man working in the establishment. Dellwyn had worked her way up to Room E, and she intended to be in Room C by the end of the year.

Despite being a full lady of the Rudder for five years, Aya still worked in Room V, but she didn't mind. This meant that she spent most of her evening alone, and when she did receive a client, he didn't take up much of her time. Of course, she sometimes received merchants who delighted in bedding the dead cogsmith's daughter as some sort of cosmic payback for her father being more successful than them. She even received the occasional woman. While these visits were less invasive, she didn't like them. Much like poor Lord Derringher, she simply didn't know what to do with her hands.

Before Aya even seated herself on her bed, a loud knock issued from her door. She threw her cloak onto the chair in the corner and patted down her curls. Two more knocks came from the door, their strength causing the brass hinges to vibrate against the iron frame.

"Come in," Aya called, trying to keep her voice low and smooth, despite the nerves creeping up in her chest from the rush and the noise.

The door flung open to reveal a large, muscular man with black soot caking his bearded face and hands. He wore a loose-fitting white shirt, also stained with soot, and plain black trousers, straining against his already-present excitement. A blacksmith, no doubt. They were always dirty from the forge.

Aya smiled demurely and moved to close the door. As she reached his side, the blacksmith extended his arm and grabbed her by her corset laces. "Where do you think you're goin'?"

Aya took a deep breath, allowing her hand to slide up the man's arm and caress his shoulder, her fingers kneading into the tight muscle to relax him. He shook his shoulder, sending her hand flopping uselessly to her side.

"I'm just going to shut the door. Madam insists on the privacy of her guests."

The blacksmith jerked the laces of Aya's corset, causing her to stumble back a few steps. He grabbed her around the waist and stared down into her eyes. From this angle, Aya smelled the char and sweat on his skin, and she knew the grease from his hands must be staining her corset.

"Forget the door. Get to work."

Aya opened her mouth to protest, but the man slid his arms up her shoulders and pushed her down. She hit the floor so hard that her knees bounced off the metal before landing in place. Pain jolted through her kneecaps, and Aya grunted through clenched teeth. Her legs shook from the pain and her hands trembled from nerves, but she said nothing. With aggressive customers, Aya knew her only option was to remain silent and do exactly as instructed. For whatever reason, these rough clients did not want to be seduced. They needed to feel powerful, and the sooner Aya gave them that power, the sooner they left her in peace.

As the blacksmith unbuttoned his trousers, Aya began to count. When she had to fumble her way through seduction, her job could take hours. But in most cases, when her client only required compliance, she rarely had to count higher than a thousand.

One. Two. Three. Four.

~

As the door slammed shut behind the blacksmith, Aya leaned against her bed and pulled her knees to her chest. Her stockings lay haphazardly on the floor like two lifeless snakeskins. She shifted through the folds of her skirt to reveal her bare knees. Already her blood pooled under her skin, creating large, purple bruises on either kneecap. Gently, Aya reached one hand up to her neck and another to her hip. Both areas felt raw, and Aya guessed she would be sore from the blacksmith's grip for at least a full day.

Aya allowed her head to fall back against the mattress and her eyes to shut. She took deep breaths, feeling the pinkness drain from her flushed skin and the muscles in her legs and back relax with each one. She had no concept of how long she sat like this, or even if she was awake the entire time. After a long while, Aya became convinced that she would not have any other clients for the evening. She went to fetch her cloak and heard a soft knock on her door.

Silently cursing her luck, Aya seated herself on her bed. She remembered a piece of advice Dellwyn once gave her, about setting the tone for the interaction, and she lay down on her side, hoping to avoid any more stress on her knees. She propped her head up with one arm, using her free hand to adjust her corset and push up her small breasts as much as they could be lifted. She tousled her skirt, making sure to expose the full line of her naked leg. First impressions, Dellwyn had said, could work wonders.

"Come in," Aya called, arching her back as the final touch.

The door opened to reveal a man she'd never seen before. He appeared much richer than Aya's usual clientele of wellman and merchants. He wore a three-piece suit made entirely of purple velvet and embroidered with gold filigree. Atop his head sat a matching top hat with a wide black ribbon wrapped around it. His eyes were beady and obscured behind small, round glasses.

"Aya Cogsmith?"

Aya pushed herself upright. Her clients were not supposed to know her name. In fact, even the seediest merchants, the ones who'd despised her father and paid extra to be assured of her identity, didn't say her full name.

"Yes, my lord?" She slowly curled into herself.

"Oh, good. I am in the right room." The man closed the door behind him.

"A fan of my father, were you?" Aya knew the quip could get her slapped—or worse—but she didn't care. How dare this man use her family name before he bedded her.

"What? No." The man placed a gloved hand over his heart. "Please, dear, cover yourself up. I'm not here for any of that nonsense."

Aya sat up and pulled the folds of her skirt over her legs. She swept her hair to the front so that her curls hid her cleavage. The man walked over to her, slipped a white glove off his hand, and extended it to her. "I'm Lord Ulberion Varick, the Marquess of the Stern. You may call me Varick."

Aya reached up, placing only her fingertips into his hand. "Hello, Lord Varick." Aya spoke carefully. "I'm Aya Cogsmith, but it seems you know that."

"Just Varick, please. And yes, I happen to know a lot about you, Miss Aya. You see, I live right up there." Varick lifted up his ivory walking cane and tapped the ceiling, "At the very top of the palace's stern. I watch over Sternville and its inhabitants."

Aya allowed her gaze to drift from Lord Varick to the ceiling and back down. As she examined his suit, she nearly scoffed. He didn't watch over Sternville too closely, or he would have been ashamed to wear something so lavish in a poor woman's presence.

Lord Varick smiled. His teeth were pointed. "I realize you

may be a bit shocked by the nature of my visit here. Shall I explain myself more precisely?"

Aya squinted. "Please do, Lord Varick."

"Ah, ah! Just Varick, thank you." Varick pointed to the bed beside Aya. She scooted over to allow him to sit next to her, wincing as her knees flexed. She kept her shoulders square and her hands in her lap. Varick's intentions seemed to be truly conversational, but she wasn't going to create any opportunities for the interaction to turn physical.

Lord Varick kept his distance, but he leaned toward her, as if they were two little girls swapping secrets. "My dear, Miss Aya, you and I have something quite horrible in common."

Aya turned her head ever so slightly to look at Varick out of the corners of her eyes. Sharp pain shot through the right side of her neck. "And that is?"

"We both had the people we loved most in this world murdered by the king."

Aya's eyes widened, and she turned her whole body to him. "What are you talking about?"

"Your father. King Archon ordered to have him executed after he failed to repair Prince Lionel's mechanical pet bird. Did he not?"

Aya's body jerked, and she gripped her skirt. She looked around the room, as if someone might be spying through peep-holes. "How do you know that?"

"My dear, everyone knows that. Your father was the last cogsmith in Desertera. His death was a huge scandal."

Aya shook her head in short, harsh twitches. When she finally answered, she did so cautiously, emphasizing every sylla-ble. "They know he was executed for treason, nothing more. Who told you about the bird?"

Varick tapped his forefinger against his nose. "I have my sources, Miss Aya. You'll find that, while the prince's bird may be broken, there are plenty of other birdies in the palace who love to chirp—for the right price."

Aya pursed her lips, keeping her green eyes focused on Varick's face. So this Lord Varick was a businessman of sorts, dealing in secrets. But what did he want from her? Aya took the obvious bait, hoping for some clarity. "King Archon killed someone you loved?"

Varick took off his top hat, placing it in his lap. "I am not sure I would say 'loved,' as I still love her very much. But, yes, he did. The late Queen Isadona was my daughter."

Aya cocked her head to the side and narrowed her eyes. "Forgive me, Varick, but King Archon didn't kill Queen Isadona. She committed adultery, and in accordance with the laws of Desertera, he sentenced her to death. If anything, she killed herself."

Varick smirked. "The way your father killed himself by refusing to aid the royal family?"

Aya felt her stomach knot, and she crossed her arms over it. "I see your point. Go on."

Varick scooted closer to Aya. "Surely even the common people have noticed that King Archon seems to go through a lot of queens."

"Well, yes, we have. But you can't blame him for his wives committing adultery." Aya paused and studied Varick's face. He had wrinkles around his eyes and forehead, but when he held his face still, it smoothed out like a stone, patiently waiting for her to pluck it from the sand. Aya considered that day with her father, the thoughtless and merciless way King Archon had given the order. "Or can you?"

Varick smiled wider. "That's it, Miss Aya. Think like our noble king."

Aya rubbed her temples. "If you're telling the truth, and Queen Isadona did not willing commit adultery, she must have either been raped and wrongly accused or framed in a crime she didn't commit."

"I can assure you, my daughter was not violated."

"Then she was framed."

Varick sighed. "All it takes is one pronouncement, and no one questions a thing. Adultery! Treason!" He raised his top hat and twirled it.

Aya felt the blood rise into her chest, spreading a fire from her bosom up her neck into her cheeks. Her hands balled into fists. "King Archon is trapping the queens into adultery. The strange men wandering the palace, the vagabonds climbing up the anchor lines—it's all him. He's framing them."

"Yes, Miss Aya, he is. And as he is the only judge on all crimes, there is no one to stop him."

"But why?" Aya held out her hands, as if an answer would fall from the ceiling into them. She could rationalize a cruel king killing a craftsman—but a king killing his queen? What kind of man orchestrates the death of the woman he has sworn to love?

Varick rolled his eyes. "Why do powerful men do anything? Because he can. It's a game to him. He seduces a beautiful young woman, and once he is sure of her affections, he frames the queen in adultery to make room for his new pet. When she begins to bore him, or worse, discovers the truth of how the previous queens died, he secures her replacement and orchestrates her betrayal."

Aya turned to Varick and grabbed his hand. The words flew from her mouth before she could stop them. "Surely you're not the only one who knows. Don't other nobles realize this? What he's doing is treason. He must be stopped!"

"Yes, he must." Varick squeezed her hand. "My daughter, my beautiful, naïve daughter loved that sick man. I begged her not to become his queen, but she didn't listen. Isadona never would have betrayed King Archon. That's when I knew. When I heard that my sweet, innocent Isadona had committed adultery and would be executed, I knew Archon must be to blame. Isadona was all I had left—her mother had already departed this life—and Archon stole her from me."

"What does this have to do with me? Why can't you get

together with the other noblemen? The queens' families? Surely they have just as much reason to hate the king as I do."

Varick sighed. "That is true, Miss Aya. They certainly do. But the noble families are afraid to speak out against the king. King Archon is smart and has left no proof of his crimes. To accuse him without proper evidence would be treason. In order for his true nature to be shown without a speck of a doubt, we must prove he is framing the queens."

"But why bring this to me? I'm a—" Aya shook her head. "You know what I am. I can't help you."

Varick rubbed his thumb over her hand. "Miss Aya, you are the only one who can help me. King Archon has harmed you the same way he harmed me. He remembers his wrongs to the noble families, knows each of their members by name. But you—you were a child from Portside. As harsh as it is, the king will not know your face. You are the only person who can help me catch him without being suspected."

Aya raised her eyebrows. "And how do I help you catch the king?"

Varick scrunched his nose. "Well, my dear, I need you to seduce him for me."

Aya jerked her hand away from Varick's and bolted from the bed. "Excuse me?"

"Do not worry. I have it all planned out." Varick reached out to take her hand again. Aya did not let him. "I will take you in as my ward and give you a proper introduction into noble society. Under my protection, your presence in the palace will be safe and unquestioned. You will live in the stern and engage with the nobles. You will seek out private audiences with King Archon, and at every one, you will gain his fancy. Eventually, he will be overcome by his attraction to you, succumb to his lust, and orchestrate the betrayal of his new queen. When he does, we shall ensure witnesses are present, and he will be executed for his treachery."

Aya crossed her arms. "And let's say I go along with your

game. Won't I be executed right along with the king for playing his mistress?"

"Oh, no, my dear! You would not actually commit the adultery. I don't believe the king ever does. Otherwise, why get rid of the queen? No, you simply need to seduce him so that he wants you badly enough to repeat his pattern. This way, you shall remain innocent."

"But King Archon presides over all criminal trials." Aya nearly laughed. "Won't he clear himself and have me, and probably you as well, executed for treason?"

Varick wagged a finger. "Certainly not. The king's guilt will be unquestionable when witnessed by the appropriate parties. As for his power in the trial, you will have to trust me when I say that he will not have a word in his sentencing or yours."

Aya paused, letting Varick's plan sink in. Assuming Varick truly could keep the trial out of King Archon's control, all she would have to do would be make the king desire her enough to commit treason against the queen and secure witnesses for his confession. On the surface, it seemed easy, but as Aya thought about her time at the Rudder, her stomach churned.

"Varick, I would love to help you. Truly, I would. But I'm telling you, I am terrible at this profession. I can name a dozen other women in this establishment who would do a much better job than I ever could. The king deserves to die, but I fear I do not have the talent to get him killed."

Varick grinned and shook his head, as if Aya were an obstinate child. "That may be so, but you are not understanding me, my dear. I *know* you. I have discussed your employment history with Madam Huxley, and I know your every flaw with men. And yes, while some of your fellow courtesans may be more skilled in the art of seduction, I could never trust them to stay loyal to me, not when the possibility of being queen is dangled before them. But, you, Miss Aya, you have a fire within you that they cannot match. You have the ultimate motivation, one I know I will not betray me."

Aya uncrossed her arms. "And what is that?"

"Revenge."

Varick took off his glasses, unleashing the full force of his dark eyes on Aya. She shuddered. She would be lying if she said she hadn't fantasized about taking revenge on King Archon. She'd had a hundred day dreams in which she'd cut out the king's tongue before he could give the order, or she'd sneaked into the kitchens and poisoned the entire royal family's meal.

But now, now that Varick said the word so matter-of-factly, Aya's whole body tensed. Even if she could seduce King Archon, did she want to put her own life at stake by playing the adulteress? Did she trust Varick's word? Did she want to lower herself to the king's level and damn another person to death?

Aya shook her head. "I'm sorry, Varick, but I can't help you."

Varick stayed seated for a few moments. When it was clear that Aya had nothing else to say, he rose and headed toward the door. He placed one gloved hand on the doorknob before turning back to her. "If you change your mind, Miss Aya, my guards are on duty every night this week. They will happily escort you up to my estate."

"That won't be necessary." Aya tried to speak firmly, inclining her head to show her sincerity.

Varick smiled, showing all of his sharp white teeth. "If you say so." He moved to leave her room, but before he closed the door behind him, he turned back to face her, peeking through the narrow space between the door and the wall. "I shall see you around, Miss Aya, whether or not you see me."

With that, he departed, leaving the door open the width of his face.

3

———————

*A*ya and Dellwyn left the Rudder a couple hours before sunrise, when the night was at its darkest. This time, Aya and Dellwyn both wrapped their cloaks tightly around them, attempting to keep out the cold breeze. After a few moments of walking in silence, Dellwyn put her hand on Aya's arm and stopped. "Is everything all right?"

"Yes," Aya lied. "Why wouldn't it be?"

"Because you haven't said a word to me since I came to get you, and now, you won't look me in the eyes."

Aya made a point of aligning her green eyes with Dellwyn's brown ones.

"Aya." Dellwyn gripped her arm harder. "Did you have a bad customer? Did someone hurt you?"

"Not any worse than normal." Aya gently tugged her arm out of Dellwyn's grasp.

"You remembered your tonic, right?"

"Yes." Aya rubbed her tongue against the roof of her mouth. The bitter taste still lingered. "I have no concerns about being with child."

Dellwyn began walking again. "Then what is it?"

"I...I had a strange customer. He was a high nobleman. Wanted to talk."

Dellwyn raised her eyebrows. "Talk? What about?"

Aya glanced from side to side. "I'm not sure if I should tell you."

"What do you mean?"

"I don't want to put you in danger."

Dellwyn stopped, this time, putting both her hands on Aya's shoulders. Aya tensed, wincing as her shoulder muscles pulled at the sore places in her neck.

"Aya, if something dangerous is going on, you definitely need to tell me. I don't want you trying to deal with something bad alone."

Aya considered Dellwyn carefully, watching her plump cheeks and dark eyebrows close in around her eyes. Dellwyn had been her closest, and only, friend ever since Aya came to the Rudder that first night. Dellwyn had always looked after her, helping her hide mistakes from Madam Huxley, taking rough customers off her hands, and giving Aya extra coins on nights when she didn't have any customers. Dellwyn was the only person Aya had ever spoken openly to about her father's death.

"Not here," Aya whispered. "I'll tell you when we get to the hovel."

The moment they arrived, Dellwyn sat down at the table and motioned for Aya to do the same. Aya sat, gritting her teeth as her aching bum hit the chair.

"Spill," Dellwyn ordered.

Aya divulged every detail of her encounter with Lord Varick, from his ornate attire to his theory that King Archon had orchestrated the deaths of his queens, to his surprising knowledge of the circumstances of her father's death. When she finished, Dellwyn took a deep breath. She poured them both a glass of water, sliding Aya's across the table to her. Aya cupped the glass in her hand, but she didn't drink, staring at the water as its sloshing settled.

"Let me make sure I have this right," Dellwyn began. "Lord Varick is the late Queen Isadona's father, and he is convinced that King Archon is trapping his wives—Queen Isadona included—into adultery. Therefore, to avenge his daughter's death and save the future queens, he has come to you to help him seduce the king and prove his treason. And he expects you to help because the king killed your father."

"Yes." Aya hoped she sounded more confident than she felt.

"And you turned him down?"

"Yes?" Heat bloomed across Aya's cheeks. She took a sip of her water. It felt grainy on her tongue. "Do you think I did the wrong thing?"

Dellwyn sighed. "I don't know. That's a lot to digest." Dellwyn paused to take a drink. "On one hand, of course you can't do it. I'm sorry, but you're not the best seductress. Even if you were, if you got caught in adultery by the wrong person, you would be executed."

Aya nodded.

"Then again, King Archon did ruin your life. I mean, you were a merchant's daughter—the last cogsmith's daughter. You had a chance at a business, at a respectable marriage, at children, even. And the king took all of that away from you. I wouldn't blame you if you wanted to kill him." Dellwyn clenched her fists. "Plus, if he really is using that bullshit law to get his wives executed, someone needs to stop him."

"Yes. He needs to be stopped. I just don't know if I can do it. Like you said, I would be putting my life at risk."

Dellwyn reached across the table and placed her hand on Aya's. Aya's tan skin looked unusually pale under Dellwyn's dark hand, but she wasn't sure whether that was entirely the contrast in skin tone or because all of her blood had gone to her face and chest again.

"Honey, look around you. Are you really putting much at risk?" Dellwyn lifted her eyes to the ceiling. "Is any of *this* even worth living for?"

Aya let Dellwyn's question hang in the air between them. She had never thought of her life in that light. Sure, she was miserable, and sure, she couldn't imagine living the rest of her life this way. However, she had never thought about a way out; she just lived one day at a time and accepted her fate. She hadn't realized that Dellwyn was miserable, too. Dellwyn—with the dozen admiring clients and cheery smile and love of sex. If Dellwyn, who was born into this life and thrived in it, didn't think it was worth living, what did that mean for Aya?

～

Aya felt someone gently nudge her shoulder. She rolled away and swatted, but the nudging persisted. It couldn't be time to wake up. Charlie hadn't croaked yet.

"Rise and shine, sweetie!" Papa sang in her ear.

Aya rolled toward him and cupped her hands over her face to shield herself from the light. However, when she opened her eyes, it was still pitch black. Only the lantern Papa had placed on her dressing trunk lit her room.

"What's going on?" she mumbled, digging the crust from the inside corners of her eyes.

"How would you like to go to the palace today?"

Aya sat straight up. "The palace? Can we really?"

"Of course, we can." Papa put his fists on his hips and puffed out his chest. "King Archon's guards were just here. It seems Prince Lionel's pet bird is broken, and they need the best cogsmith in all of Desertera to repair her."

"Papa." Aya laughed and poked his chest. "You're the only cogsmith in Desertera."

Her father's chest deflated, but he kept his back straight and his smile wide. "Exactly. That's why I'm the best!"

Aya chuckled and rolled her eyes.

"Now, come on. Get yourself dressed and to the breakfast table. King Archon expects us there in an hour."

"Are you sure it's all right that I come?"

Papa nodded. "Of course. I asked the guards, and they said it would be fine. They're going to find a butler to take you around to look at the ship's interior. You can see every inch of it and tell me how you think it was made."

"I'll give you a full report." Aya smiled. Papa moved the lantern to the floor and went back to the kitchen. Aya dressed in her nicest, and only, silk dress. She put on her cleanest black shoes and pulled her hair back into a low bun to contain her wild brown curls. When she was finished, she went over to the other side of her bed and picked up Charlie off the floor.

"Too slow today, buddy," she joked, loosening his winder so he wouldn't wake up and hop into the wall. "Don't worry. I'll tell you all about it."

Instead of placing Charlie back on the floor, Aya took him to the corner of her room. She couldn't figure out why, but her stomach felt queasy at the idea of being so far away from him. Normally Aya was just in her father's shop or down the street running errands. Sliding her fingers along the edges of the floorboards, Aya felt for the loose one. She pried it up with her nails and nestled Charlie in the small hole beneath the floor.

"I'll take you out the second I get home."

Aya pressed the floorboard back into place, feeling the churning in her stomach switch from nerves to grumbling hunger.

Aya and her father ate breakfast quickly. Aya had a thousand questions about the palace, and she tried to ask them between mouthfuls of eggs and bacon, but Papa kept telling her to eat and wait. When they left the house, Aya's interrogation started anew. She asked Papa all about the craftsman-ship of the palace, if the inside would be made of the same metal as the exterior. She asked about Prince Lionel's bird and if it was crafted the same way as Charlie and if Papa really thought he could fix it.

"I will certainly do my best."

Aya took in the length of the palace. The sun was beginning to rise over the sand, and she watched the ship for any reflection of the light. She saw a faint glinting toward the bow, right above all that remained of the *name, Hildegard. The letters H-I-D-E and the curve of the R illuminated in orange sunlight.*

The guards called up to their fellows working the drawbridge, and it lowered for Aya, her father, and the merchants' delivery boys who were expected at the palace that morning. Aya had watched this ritual happen several times from the edge of Portside, but she had never gotten to be part of it before. She stood on her tiptoes, craning her neck to observe the bridge's mechanism. Papa smiled down at her and readjusted his grip on his toolbox.

As the bridge reached the ground, Aya and her father gave the main guard their names and were ushered inside. The palace was even bigger than Aya expected. They entered into a wide, open room with dark green iron columns holding up the ceiling. The walls were lined with doors, some iron, some wood, each one presumably going to a hallway or an even bigger room. Castas, the cobbler's delivery boy, had once told her that the palace was like a maze. If you took even one wrong turn, you could be lost within it for days. Seeing all these doors now, Aya understood what he'd meant.

In the middle of the room stood a line of servants: maids in cloud gray uniforms with crisp white aprons and butlers in black suits with white shirts and gloves. The maid and butler on the left-hand end of the line stepped forward to greet Aya and her father.

"Master Cogsmith." The maid extended her hand for Aya's father to shake. "Thank you for coming on such short notice. Prince Lionel is absolutely distraught at the malfunctioning of his dear Penelope."

Papa smiled and patted his toolbox. "It's no problem at all. I'm happy to help however I can."

The maid nodded.

"And you must be Miss Aya Cogsmith." The butler placed his hands on his knees to squat down to her eye level. It was a bit insulting, given that she was thirteen, but then again, she was rather short.

"I hear that you would like a tour of the palace. Is that correct?"

Aya grinned. "Yes, sir."

"All-righty then." The butler returned her smile. "How about I show you around, and in a few hours, we'll go to Prince Lionel's quarters and check in on your father?"

Aya looked at her father. He motioned for her to go. "I'll see you soon."

Aya tapped her temple. "I won't miss a single detail." The butler, who introduced himself as Alfred, took Aya all over the palace. He showed her the engine room, a cavernous space filled with hundreds of dormant machines that Aya could envision glowing and growling. He guided her through all the back corridors, some of which were so skinny and twisty that they made her lungs feel tight. Alfred even took her up to the very top of the palace, to the deck, and led her through the greenhouse. Inside, the greenhouse air was so full of water that it fogged the glass panes of the walls and softened the harsh sunlight. Aya had never seen so many green plants or such brightly colored foods. Alfred informed her that most of them were called fruit, and they could only grow in the special temperature and thick moisture of the greenhouse. Aya salivated at the thought of all that color touching her tongue, but before she could sneak a bite, Alfred led her back out to the deck.

Near the edge of the palace's deck, Alfred walked Aya along the line of lifeboats so she could examine the frayed ropes that still strapped them in place. He allowed her to stand on top of one of the spools that wound an anchor chain, and she held her arms out to her sides, enjoying the breeze on her damp clothes and skin. From the spool, Aya could see all of Starboardshire, with its tall houses and flowered horse pastures, to her left and all of Sternville, with its hovels and smoke-covered tents, to her right. Until she had a hawk-eye view, she had never realized the stark contrast between these two villages, and she promised herself that she would be kinder to the wellmen next time she fetched water, as anyone living in such conditions could surely use more kindness.

After a few hours, Alfred kept his word and led Aya to Prince Lionel's chambers, where her father was attempting to repair his pet bird, Penelope. Aya had heard that Prince Lionel was about her age. She'd started to notice boys her age and a bit older, and she wondered if looking at the prince would make her blush the way she did whenever she spoke to Castas.

As they neared Prince Lionel's chambers, Aya saw a tall, thin man pass through an ornate double doorway. He wore thick, velvet robes and the tallest top hat Aya had ever seen, embroidered with a golden pattern of interlocking cogs and jewels of all different colors: rubies, emeralds, sapphires, amethysts. Everything about his face was sharp—his crooked nose, his blue eyes, his pointed black beard.

Alfred tapped her shoulder then pointed after the man and mouthed "the king." Aya patted her bun, her fingers finding a stray curl to tuck back into place. Alfred winked, and they walked together to the double doors. Before they entered the prince's room, Alfred held his arm out and stopped. Aya bumped into his outstretched arm, startled.

"Father!" A boy stood in the middle of the room, clutching a smaller version of the king's top hat in his hands. His white cravat was rumpled, as was his brown hair, which kept flopping over his eyes as he moved his head back and forth. The prince. "Master Cogsmith says he can't fix her, Father. He says that she is broken beyond repair."

King Archon stepped toward Aya's father, who stood opposite the prince, holding a mechanical bird in one hand and a screwdriver in the other. Papa swallowed as the king approached. Aya could see Papa's throat tighten from the doorway.

"Is this true, Master Cogsmith?" King Archon spoke slowly, softly, as if he had never struggled to be heard in his life.

"Yes, Your Majesty." Papa's voice cracked. "I have tried everything I can think of, and she just won't come back to life. Her heart cog is chipped. One of the teeth has broken completely off." Aya's father pulled back the bird's wing so King Archon could view the broken cog, but the king kept his eyes on the cogsmith.

"I see." King Archon raised his chin. "Do you not have a replacement at your shop?"

"Unfortunately, I don't. Her inner cog has nine teeth. That is extremely rare, as most mechanical animals operate with eight or ten."

"Could you not make one?" The king towered over Aya's father. She moved to cross the room, but Alfred kept his arm stiff, blocking her path.

Papa shook his head. "I'm afraid I cannot. Much like the bookbinder and his parchment, I am limited to the old-world relics we already have. I do not have a proper mold for the metal."

"And you refuse to try?"

"I, well, I could try, but—"

The king held up his hand, and Aya's father fell silent. King Archon went to Prince Lionel and placed his hand on the prince's shoulder. The prince shuddered under the king's touch.

"It seems Master Cogsmith refuses to fix Penelope, Lionel," King Archon crooned. "Does this hurt you, Son?"

Prince Lionel clenched his teeth. The king had his back to the door, and Aya could not see his face or actions, but judging by Lionel's face, both royal men grew more upset by the second.

"Does it cause you pain, Lionel, that the cogsmith denies your request?"

Prince Lionel looked at the ground. "Yes, Father."

King Archon turned and grabbed the bird from the cogsmith's hand, throwing it across the room. Penelope shattered against the wall, her broken pieces cascading to the floor like the rain that never lasted. Aya froze, feeling as if she were watching the scene from outside of her body, unable to move.

The king stood in front of Aya's father, looking down at him. "And what do we call them, Lionel, people who hurt the royal family?"

Papa dropped to his knees. "Please, Your Majesty. I will figure out how to—"

King Archon held up his hand, and again, Papa quieted. "Lionel?"

"We call them traitors." The prince's voice cut through the air, flat and emotionless, and jolted Aya out of her trance.

"No!" she screamed, lunging forward. Alfred grabbed her around the waist and pulled her to the ground.

King Archon glanced in Aya's direction for only a second before returning his gaze to his young son. "And what do we do with traitors, Lionel?"

Prince Lionel looked at the wall. Alfred clamped his hand over Aya's mouth. Her wide eyes landed on her father's bent frame. He was looking back at her, tears brimming around the edges of his green eyes. As Papa opened his mouth to speak, King Archon grabbed him by his collar and lifted him to his feet.

"Lionel! What do we do with traitors?"

Prince Lionel looked at the cogsmith. His eyes watered, too. "We execute them."

Aya barely heard the prince's statement over the beating of her heart. She fought against Alfred's arms, but he held her firm to his chest. King Archon smiled and patted the prince on the head with his free hand.

"Guards!" King Archon cried. Two burly men rushed past Aya and Alfred and bowed before the king. "Take this man to the dungeons. He is to be tried for treason!"

The guards latched onto Papa.

"Alfred!" King Archon called.

The butler released Aya and scurried to the king's feet. "Yes, Your Majesty?"

"Search through his toolbox. Look for a golden cog with nine teeth."

Alfred opened Papa's toolbox and rifled his hands through the contents. "No gold, Your Majesty. Only a few bronze gears."

King Archon huffed. "Send my guards to his shop. Search every nook until you find the cog I seek. Confiscate anything that may be of use to me."

Aya didn't understand what the cog mattered to the king now. He had destroyed the bird. Perhaps he intended to find one to use as evidence of Papa's treason. Before Aya could think about it further, the guards dragged Papa past her.

"No! Please!" Aya lunged at the guards from her seated position. One of the guards kicked her, knocking her back onto her bum. Aya winced, stopping for only a moment before scrambling to her feet.

"Papa!"

"Aya!" Papa shouted back. He struggled against the guards, but they were too strong. Papa stayed locked between them. "Be good, Aya. Please. I love you."

"I love you, too!" The words came out in short gasps. Aya could barely see Papa's figure through her tears as the guards dragged him away. King Archon came out of the room. He strode by Aya without a glance. As Aya stared at the back of his retreating top hat, the gears in her mind clicked into place.

"Your Majesty, stop! Please! I know the cog you seek! I can bring it to you! Please!"

King Archon kept walking.

"Please, Your Majesty! Spare my father! I can fix the bird!"

King Archon turned and stormed back to Aya. She recoiled, clutching her arms against her chest.

"Stupid girl! Your father is a traitor, and your lies cannot help him now. He will face trial for betraying his king, and if you're not careful, you'll join him."

Aya clutched the king's robes. "No! Please, no!"

King Archon ripped his clothes from Aya's grasp and strode away. Aya watched the king go until he passed through a door and slammed it shut. She looked in the direction of Papa and the guards, but they too were gone. She glanced back to Prince Lionel's chambers. Alfred had gathered her father's toolbox and carried it to her. She snatched it from him, cradling it against her chest as if it were a wounded animal.

Aya looked past Alfred to Prince Lionel. The prince stood in the same place, looking at her with tear stains on his cheeks. He didn't say anything, just stared at her with hollow eyes. Aya wanted to scream at him, to run into his room and drive her father's screwdriver through his stone heart. The prince had said the words. He had cowered before his tyrant father and issued Papa's execution.

Everything was a blur after that. Alfred's gentle grasp lifting her to her feet and guiding her back to the drawbridge. The stares of the merchants, the whispers of their wives, the innocent laughter of their children as she walked home alone. The creaking of her broken front door, hanging by a single hinge as she pushed it open.

King Archon's guards had ransacked her home. As Aya walked through the house, she saw through hazy vision the stray pieces of metal scattered around her father's workshop, the overturned tables in the living area, the dustless spots on the shelves where mechanical animals and ancient machines had rested. She went to the corner of her room, stepping over discarded bedsheets and feathers from her ripped mattress, and pried loose the floorboard. Reaching inside, she felt the cool metal of Charlie's body against her fingertips, and her tears fell harder as she scooped him up in her hands.

Aya reached her pinky finger inside his body. A lump swelled in her throat as her finger connected with Charlie's heart cog. She searched her *brain for the name, finally stumbling upon it in a memory of her father fixing Charlie at the dinner table. The vortric cog. A golden, nine-toothed cog—the last one in Desertera.*

~

"No!" Aya awoke to her own screams. For the second night in a row, she had dreamed about that day. She clamped her hand over her mouth, fearful of waking Dellwyn, only to recoil. Her hand was hot and slick; in fact, her whole body was drenched in sweat, her nightdress plastered to her skin. She wiped her hands on her blankets before reaching across the floor and picking up Charlie.

Her room was dark, barely illuminated by moonlight. Still, she lifted Charlie above her head and peered through his gut. Even though she couldn't see inside, she knew that at the center of his core, right behind his open jaw, was a golden vortric cog, the one her father had told King Archon didn't exist.

More than anything, Aya wished that she could ask Papa about the cog. She'd never understood his motive in lying to the king. Did Papa really think that Aya valued Charlie more than him? Was it meant as an act of rebellion, one small way to thwart the king's desires? What if King Archon had some sinister purpose for the cog, some evil plan like the one he'd hatched to get rid of his wives? Even after ten years of thought and her new knowledge from Lord Varick, Aya still didn't know.

But she knew one thing. She'd had nightmares about that day for ten years. She'd been reduced to a life of poverty and abuse. And Papa, for simply being incapable of fixing a bird, had had his head chopped off at the prince's word. She was done.

Aya threw off the covers and jumped up. She reached into the bottom of her dressing trunk and pulled out the blue dress she'd worn to the palace that day. It didn't fit her anymore, but she'd kept it as a way to cling to the last morning her life had felt right. She unwound Charlie so he wouldn't stir, wrapped him up inside the dress, and tucked him away under her other clothes.

She didn't bother putting on a proper outfit. She grabbed her green cloak, threw it over her shoulders, and slipped on her leather shoes. As Aya passed through the common room, Dellwyn stuck her head out her bedroom door. "Aya? Why are you awake? Where are you going?"

Aya didn't answer. Dellwyn was smart. Her questions were either rhetorical or would be very soon. Aya ran the entire way to the palace. As she approached the stern of the ship, the sky began to glow pink over Starboardshire, signaling the beginning of the new day. She stopped in front of the guard stationed near the propellers, hoping he truly served Lord Varick.

The guard was an older man, his hair and mustache the color of salt. He looked down at Aya with kind eyes as she gasped to catch her breath. "Miss Cogsmith?"

Aya couldn't speak, so she nodded.

"I serve Lord Varick." He pointed to the badge over his heart: a black diamond with a purple eye at its center. "Please, follow me."

The guard escorted Aya through the propellers into the Rudder's common room then down the hallway to the back exit, the one that led into the palace. Aya had never used it before, because she had never had the need—or desire—to reenter those halls. The exit door opened to two staircases, one leading down, which Madam Huxley had told the girls would guide them to an underground tunnel that went all the way to the Sternville well, and one leading up to the inhabited parts of the palace. The guard took the latter.

Aya followed him up several flights of stairs and past various doors, until finally, they reached the top of the staircase and stepped through the door into a wide hallway. The bright lantern light and glossy, marble floors told Aya that they had entered a part of the palace frequented by nobles. As the guard rushed her through the corridor, Aya saw old paintings and stone statues fly by in the corner of her eye. The guard stopped Aya in front of a black metal door with a purple eye painted on it.

Aya didn't wait for the guard's permission. She pounded her fist on the door in time with the anxious beating of her heart. When she didn't hear any movement behind the door, she knocked again, harder. This time, she heard a faint rustling over the sound of her own blood pumping. The door swung open to reveal one of the palace's gray-clad maids.

"Miss Cogsmith." The maid had a smile in her voice and on her lips. "We've been expecting you."

Aya remained silent, saving her words. The maid led her through a hallway with walls made of dark wood and decorated with oil paintings of the world before the flood: pictures of cobblestone streets with machines that carried people, metal buildings taller than the palace, and spherical ships floating in the sky. At the end of the hallway was a large sitting room with two leather couches facing each other and an intricately carved wooden table between them. A fire burned in a stone fireplace, its smoke escaping through a chimney that extended out from the exterior of the ship's walls. Below the chimney was a wide balcony, whose faded gray railing matched the top of the palace. Aya wondered how she had never noticed this balcony protruding from the ship.

Lord Varick stood on the balcony, smoking a wooden pipe. Despite the maid's requests for her to stay put, Aya walked past her and out to the balcony. She stepped right up to Lord Varick's side, her knees wobbling only slightly when she looked down at the specks she knew to be tents. He exhaled a thin trail of smoke and smirked at her. "Miss Cogsmith."

"I want my own shop. In exchange for helping you expose the king, I want my own cogsmith workshop in Portside."

"Excuse me?" Lord Varick raised his eyebrows. His eyes remained hidden behind dark glasses, despite the fact that the sun had not yet risen.

"I will not go back to the Rudder." Aya squared her shoulders. "I want to resume my life in Portside."

Varick took a long inhale from his pipe. He looked at Aya thoughtfully before exhaling in short round puffs. "Anything else?"

"Yes. The shop—I want it to be my father's. I don't care who owns it now. You will remove them and give it back to me, along with the tools and machines that were seized when my father was arrested."

Varick extended his hand. "A fair exchange, Miss Cogsmith."

Aya grasped Varick's palm. "Good. Now, let's kill the king."

4

———

"And here is your room."

Aya looked past Lord Varick's gesturing arm and into a bedroom off the main living area. The room itself was larger than her and Dellwyn's entire hovel and at least half the size of her father's shop. Wood paneling lined the bottom half of the walls, and the upper half was painted a rich purple, like the iris on the estate's door. Iron beams stretched across the ceiling. Lanterns hung from the corners and from where the beams crossed in the ceiling's center. The room only contained four pieces of furniture—a bed, a fainting couch, a steamer trunk, and an armoire—but they were large enough that the room did not feel empty.

"Thank you, Lord Varick. This is very generous."

"Oh, it was no trouble at all. I always keep this room made up."

Aya stepped into her new bedroom. She turned to ask Lord Varick why he had his staff keep up the room when he was the estate's only resident, but she stopped herself when she saw the distant look in his eyes. Isadona. Aya pressed her lips together. She knew how painful questions about the past could be. After a few moments, Lord Varick looked up, his gaze snapping to Aya as if he had forgotten she stood there. "Get some rest, my dear. We'll sort out the details of our plan in a few hours."

"Thank you, Lord Varick."

Lord Varick held up his forefinger. "*Tsk.* Just Varick, please."

Aya smiled. "Thank you, Varick."

Lord Varick strolled away without closing the door, so Aya did it herself. Alone in the room, Aya realized that it was much colder than the living area. She walked over to the bed, noticing that a nightdress and thick robe had been laid out for her. Aya changed out of her old nightdress and cloak and into the new garments. She crawled into the bed, the thick purple comforter and fluffy pillows enveloping her in warmth.

Despite the lushness of the bed and the lingering exhaustion from her nightmare, Aya couldn't sleep. She lay awake worrying and wondering what today would have in store for her. She worried about Dellwyn, who had no doubt surmised Aya's whereabouts. She fretted about Madam Huxley, about whether she knew the purpose behind Lord Varick's visit to Aya and whether she would hold Aya's job at the Rudder in the event this plan failed. Most of all, she stewed over her memories of the king, wondering how she would ever act the seductress to a man who made her throat fill with bile.

At midday, a knock sounded on Aya's door. Even though she was still awake, the sound made her jump. She much preferred Charlie's raspy croaking.

"Yes?"

"Miss Cogsmith? It is Mrs. Lemot, the maid."

"Come in." The door creaked open, revealing Mrs. Lemot's round face. Aya hadn't noticed her pink cheeks and wispy gray curls before. She looked kind.

"Lord Varick asks that you meet him for lunch in the living area in ten minutes."

Aya liked Mrs. Lemot's voice. It was deep and soft, the way

she'd always imagined her mother's voice. "Thank you, Mrs. Lemot."

"He has prepared a dress for you. May I bring it in?"

Aya nodded and sat up in her bed. Mrs. Lemot entered, cradling a black garment bag in her arms. "We believe it should fit you, but if it does not, I shall find you another."

"Thank you."

"Would you like me to help you dress, Miss Cogsmith?"

"No." At Mrs. Lemot's blush, Aya added, "Thank you, but I can manage myself."

Mrs. Lemot placed the garment bag on the fainting couch, curtsied, and left the room.

Aya shuffled out of bed and untied the garment bag carefully, as if a venomous snake lurked inside. Aya's eyes widened. By a dress, Mrs. Lemot meant that Lord Varick had arranged for an entire ensemble. The garment bag held a black velvet dress with a wide neckline to expose her collarbones. There was also a purple under-bust corset, already laced, with brass buckles on the front.

Once Aya had dressed, she looked down the length of her body. As her fingers skimmed over the fabric, Aya wrinkled her nose. The harsh blackness of the dress made even her tanned skin look sickly pale, and the velvet pulled across her petite curves in unflattering lines.

As Aya entered the sitting room, she affixed what she hoped was a pleasant smile on her face. When Lord Varick saw her, he burst into laughter. "Oh, my dear Miss Cogsmith, you look absolutely ghastly in that ensemble!"

Aya picked at the side seam of her skirt. "Is it really so terrible?"

Lord Varick put his hand over his heart. "Forgive me. I meant no offense. Please sit, dear." He gestured to the couch across from him, and Aya sat, her spine straight as a corset stay.

"Let me try again," Varick offered. "Miss Cogsmith, I apologize for adorning you in such a monstrosity of an outfit. However, for the ceremony today, I regret that you must wear my house colors, which always make for outrageous attire."

Aya breathed a sigh of relief. "Ceremony?"

"Ah, yes. Phase One of Operation Kingly Entrapment. The ceremony today honors the new queen, Queen Zedara. A few days after the coronation, the king and queen invite the noble families to pay respects and give well wishes to the new queen. You shall accompany me to this ceremony, and I shall introduce you to the royal couple as my ward, an orphan whom I have taken in out of the kindness of my heart. Partially true, of course."

Aya raised her eyebrows. "I suspect we will not be using my real name?"

"Certainly not." Lord Varick tapped his walking cane on the floor. "While I'm sure Archon would derive a perverse satisfaction at pursuing the orphan of one of his victims, the truth of your parentage would cause too much attention and suspicion. No, my dear, you shall be an inconspicuous Aya Wellman."

"If I need to be hidden, why debut me in such a public way at all?"

"Well, as you know, the palace's inhabitants are closely monitored due to the unparalleled amount of lustful heathens sneaking in to seduce the queens." Lord Varick rolled his eyes. "Therefore, I must introduce you to the nobles so they do not question your presence among us. Besides, I do have a few allies who need to know you."

Aya felt her face light up. "When shall I meet them?"

"Oh, my dear, you cannot. I simply cannot risk you mistaking an enemy for an ally or vice versa. You must be guarded. Act pleasant to everyone, but do not trust a soul in this palace. Even the people who I deign to call friends may betray me if King Archon offers the proper reward."

Before Aya's smile faded, Mrs. Lemot entered, carrying a

silver tray full of bread, meat, and colorful balls like the ones Aya had seen long ago in the palace greenhouse. Lord Varick motioned for Aya to eat, so she picked up one of the balls, a purple one, and cautiously bit into it. Her mouth watered as the food's juices washed over her tongue.

"A grape," Lord Varick supplied. "More generally, they're all fruit."

"It's spectacular!" Aya popped another grape into her mouth.

"You've never tasted fruit before? Truly?"

"Never." Aya covered her mouth with her hand to hide both her half-chewed grape and her frown. "I saw it once—the day my father died, actually. A butler took me on a tour of the palace while my father tried to fix the prince's bird. Alfred let me see the greenhouse, but I wasn't allowed to taste any of the fruits."

Before Lord Varick could express his pity, Aya picked up another ball, a dark red one, and popped it into her mouth. This one had a smaller, harder ball in the center. It hurt her teeth to try to chew it. She did not know whether to swallow it whole or spit it out.

"Expunge it, my dear." Lord Varick held out his gloved hand, and Aya delicately dropped the ball into it. "That was a cherry. The hard part is called a pit." Lord Varick shook his head, balling his hand into a fist. He beat it softly against his kneecap. "I'm so sorry, my girl. For everything he's done to you."

❧

"Are you ready?" Lord Varick held out his arm to Aya.

"As ready as I shall ever be." Aya placed her hand on the inside of Lord Varick's elbow and took a deep breath. They stood outside the large metal doors of the throne room. Lord Varick told her they had once been shiny copper, but over time, they had aged to a pale green. Aya imagined her face matched the doors. While she'd felt comfortable and confident in Lord Varick's rooms, now that they were here, a few dozen feet away from King Archon, she felt as if she might faint.

Lord Varick motioned to the guards, and they opened the doors. The throne room was filled with nobles—dukes and duchesses, counts and countesses, lords and ladies. There were more noble families than she realized; they nearly outnumbered the merchants in Portside. Aya couldn't even see the thrones through the piles of curls and smokestack top hats. Varick led her over to the side of the crowd. From there, she finally spied her target, seated in the center of the room, alongside his newest bride.

King Archon looked almost exactly the same as he had when Aya was a child. The only change was that gray now speckled his pointed beard. Even in his seated position, the king still appeared tall and lean. He wore the same gold-decorated top hat with the cog pattern. Most unnerving, his blue eyes still pierced through everything he watched. From his perch, King Archon scanned the crowd, and when his gaze washed over Aya, she felt as if she'd been splashed with well water.

King Archon's eyes did not linger on Aya. In fact, she wasn't even sure whether he had looked at her at all or if he had simply been staring through the crowd. Lord Varick squeezed her arm and gave her a questioning look. Aya nodded. She was all right, really. If anything, seeing King Archon and his evil eyes again reinvigorated her. It reminded her how he had glowered at her as she'd begged for her father's life.

"Shall we greet Her Highness?" Varick asked.

"Yes, let's."

As they weaved their way through the throng of nobles, Aya examined Queen Zedara for the first time. She appeared to be only a few years older than Aya—in her late twenties, perhaps. King Archon was old enough to be her father. Poor thing. Queen Zedara had golden hair and soft, pale skin, but her lips and cheeks were bright pink. She practically glowed, as if she were the one creating the sunbeam, instead of the skylight high above her head. While Aya was not petty enough to worry that the queen was prettier than her—she had defeated those demons when she'd met Dellwyn—Aya worried that the queen's beauty might make her job difficult. After all, why would King Archon ever desire her when his queen looked like a desert wildflower?

Varick stopped them at the base of the thrones. There were four small steps elevating the royal couple above the rest of the crowd. Varick bowed low, and Aya attempted her best curtsy, trying to remember how she'd been taught as a child. Her dip was fine, but her rise up was a little awkward with the stiff corset, and Varick had to gently press upward on her elbow to help her.

A small man stood to the right of the thrones holding a golden goblet, both his hands wrapped around the base of the bowl. He wore a tall, pointed hat and plain white robes. After Lord Varick and Aya finished their bows, he stepped forward with the cup and cleared his throat. "Your Majesties, Lord Varick, Marquess of the Stern."

Lord Varick bowed again. "Your Highness, allow me to humbly welcome you into your new role. I am sure Desertera will flourish under your compassionate guidance and radiant beauty."

Queen Zedara smiled, but King Archon remained frozen. His cold eyes kept darting between Lord Varick and Aya.

"Thank you for your kind words, Lord Varick. I know it must be difficult for you to see me where your daughter once sat, but take comfort that she is in a better place, where temptation can no longer touch her," Queen Zedara replied.

"Thank you, Your Highness," Lord Varick said. "You were

a wonderful friend to her, despite her crimes. I know you cared for her greatly."

Queen Zedara looked down at her lap. "I did. Of course, I cannot imagine your loss as her father."

"It has been difficult," Lord Varick said.

"And this must be the young lady?" Queen Zedara raised her head.

Aya blushed and looked at her feet.

"Yes, Your Highness." Lord Varick placed his hand on Aya's back, cuing her to step forward. "Allow me to introduce Miss Aya Wellman."

Aya curtsied—this time smoothly and without assistance. "It is a pleasure to make your acquaintance, Your Highness. Thank you for allowing me to attend your special day. I am honored to be amongst those to greet my queen, and I wish you many long years on the throne."

Aya wasn't sure from where her eloquence had emerged, but she hoped it sounded proper. Varick looked at Aya with wide eyes and a sideways smirk. She had to purse her lips to keep from smiling.

"The pleasure is all mine, I assure you, Miss Wellman." Queen Zedara tilted her head to the side. Aya shifted her eyes to King Archon, but she still felt the queen's gaze on her.

"Your Majesty." Varick turned to the king. "Please allow me to congratulate you on your beautiful bride. I am certain she is the most splendid creature Desertera has ever seen."

"That she is." King Archon grinned, running a finger over the back of Queen Zedara's hand. "With your dear daughter a close second, of course."

"You're too generous, Your Majesty. Only the noblest king would speak kindly of traitor like my daughter."

King Archon inclined his head before turning his expectant gaze to Aya. She drew in a sharp breath. This was her moment. She imagined the king's blood splattered on the floor, hoping the rage gave her a rosy glow, and the joy made her eyes sparkle.

"Your Majesty." Aya curtsied. She clasped her hands together, squeezing her upper arms gently against her chest, making sure to bend over a little too far to expose an ample view of her décolletage. A classic Dellwyn move. "I am...I want..." She didn't know where to begin. Whatever did a girl say when trying to seduce her father's murderer?

"Yes, Miss Wellman?" King Archon's voice cut through Aya's thoughts, as sharp and gravelly as she remembered. It grated on her eardrums.

"I am speechless," Aya offered. "I am so grateful for Lord Varick's generosity, for it enables me to be in your presence. This is an honor that the people of my village never dream of, and I cherish it."

The corner of the king's thin lips raised in the faintest hint of a smile. "You are most welcome in this palace, Miss Wellman. Please enjoy yourself."

Aya gave another quick curtsy. She felt like a towel whipped up and down by the breeze.

King Archon motioned to the small man. "Bishop, please."

"Will you drink?" the bishop asked. The golden goblet clinked against his ring-clad fingers as he presented it to Lord Varick. Lord Varick took it, slipping the stem between his middle and ring fingers. He raised it to the queen and then to the king. "To your beauty, Your Highness. And to your long and prosperous rule, Your Majesty."

The royals bowed their heads. Lord Varick put the goblet to his lips and took a drink. He handed it to Aya, and she held it in both hands as the bishop had. She peered inside, relieved. It was only water.

"To your new life, Your Highness. And to your compassion and generosity, Your Majesty."

Again, the royals nodded. Aya sipped the water. As the

tangy flavor hit her tongue, her mouth puckered. She handed the goblet back to the bishop.

"That is the strangest water I have ever tasted!" Aya licked her lips.

King Archon mirrored her gesture. "It is salt water, Miss Wellman."

"Salt water?"

"Yes," Lord Varick chimed in. "The great ocean was made of salt water. Whenever we gather in the palace to celebrate a new king or queen, we drink salt water to remind ourselves that, one day, our noble royals will once again lead us over the great ocean to a bountiful land."

"Well then, my king." Aya smiled. "Perhaps I should have toasted your navigation skills."

King Archon chuckled and winked. Queen Zedara rolled her eyes.

"Will Prince Lionel be joining us?" Lord Varick asked.

"I'm afraid not," Queen Zedara replied. "It seems he is a bit under the weather this afternoon."

"Poor chap." Lord Varick shook his head. "I am sure he will feel better by next week's ball. After all, it is not like an eligible prince to forgo an opportunity to socialize with young ladies."

"I certainly hope His Highness feels better soon," Aya said. "I would like to meet him."

"I am sure he will be delighted to meet you, Miss Wellman," King Archon drawled, looking Aya up and down. Aya's shoulders tensed. If the king were going to recognize her, it would happen now, as he admired her for the first time. When King Archon's eyes completed two passes over Aya without showing any recognition, she released a long breath.

Lord Varick cleared his throat. "Your Majesty, I am afraid it would be rude of us to steal any more of your time. Again, Your Highness, my congratulations and best wishes."

"And mine as well," Aya added. "It was lovely to meet you both."

Queen Zedara smiled, her lips pressed firmly together.

"Until we meet again," King Archon said, staring only at Aya.

Lord Varick took Aya's arm and led her away from the thrones. With every step, she tightened her grip around his elbow. Varick must have noticed, but he didn't let on, keeping his face even and greeting the various nobles as they passed. The nerve of King Archon. Sitting high on his throne, taking compliments on his new wife as though she was some sort of trophy. And the way he looked at Aya! If he kept up such piggish behavior, Aya would have no problem setting him up for execution.

Aya tried to temper her breathing by gazing around the room. She saw many noblemen she recognized from working at the Rudder, but she'd never served any of them. She doubted any of them would remember glimpsing her in the hallway or through a cracked door, but even if they did, they could not reveal her identity without exposing themselves as adulterers. She searched the crowd for Lord Collingwood or Lord Derringher to see if she could get a look at their wives to report back to Dellwyn. Unfortunately, she didn't see either of them. Perhaps they had already paid their respects to the queen. She made a mental note to look for them again at the ball—assuming she really did attend.

When they were back in the corner of the room, Lord Varick released her arm. "For a woman, you have quite a strong grip."

Aya shrugged. "I do a lot of clinging in my line of work."

Lord Varick laughed.

"How did I do?"

Lord Varick grinned, his eyes crinkling. "You did quite well, my dear. The king already seems intrigued by you."

"I had forgotten his voice." Aya shuddered. "I thought I

could hear it clearly in my nightmares, but it is much sharper in person. And his eyes, they pierce you."

Lord Varick nudged her. "Some women find piercing eyes appealing."

"And some women find piercing eyes a reminder of the ax that pierces through a man's neck."

Lord Varick smirked. "The more you speak your mind, Miss Aya, the more delightful you become. You really should be more open with your thoughts."

Aya rolled her eyes. "I was taught to be open with nothing but my legs."

"That is it!" Lord Varick clapped. "That fire! Keep that blazing, and King Archon and every other man in this palace will come crawling to you."

Aya blushed. She hadn't meant to be so forward, but seeing King Archon again ignited something in her—something she hadn't been allowed to express when she'd been thrown out of her home and selling off her dresses for bread and washing noblemen's seed off of pillows. She had been good. Mouth shut and legs open. She had allowed Madam Huxley to command her every action and Dellwyn to speak for her. No more.

This was her chance to reclaim her life, to get back her father's shop, and finally attain justice for his death. She was going to take it or die trying.

5

———

"**W**hat's next on the agenda this evening, Varick?" Aya asked as the lord led her away from the throne room.

Lord Varick squinted. "Hmm. How about a quick walking tour to get you in position for your first moment alone with King Archon?"

Aya raised her eyebrows. "We're starting this evening?"

"Of course." Lord Varick tapped his cane. "No time to waste! We want you to stay fresh in his mind, after all."

Aya squeezed Lord Varick's arm. "Good."

They walked until they reached a fork in the hallway. At the fork stood a tall stone statue, immortalizing the broad body and stern face of a queen. A plaque rested at her feet. *Queen Hildegard, the Navigator.* So this was the woman behind the ship's name. Aya admired Queen Hildegard's determined expression. She didn't look as though she would have been so easily duped by King Archon. She looked like a woman who would have laughed the king all the way to Sternville.

"To the left of our beloved Queen Hildegard is the corridor that will take you back to my estate." Lord Varick pointed down the left-hand hallway and crooked his finger to the right. "At the end of the corridor, take a right. My estate will be down the hallway on the right-hand side. You will know it by sight, I'm sure. In case of emergency, there is a stairwell at the end of the corridor that will lead you out of the palace."

Aya repressed a shudder as she thought of the eye painted on Lord Varick's door. "I remember the stairs. We're near the Rudder, then?"

"Very clever, Miss Aya." Lord Varick nodded. "Yes, those are the same stairs my guard led you through last night."

"And the right-hand corridor?" Aya pointed toward it.

"Ah, yes. Down this corridor, our destiny awaits." Lord Varick turned Aya to face it. "This hallway spans nearly the entire length of the ship. There are many offshoots. Some go to libraries or sitting rooms or ballrooms, others to servants' chambers and the many food pantries and kitchens. However, if you follow it all the way to its end, you will find yourself in a rounded area with a large grandfather clock staring back at you."

"A clock," Aya gasped. "Truly?"

Lord Varick laughed. "My goodness, you are the cogsmith's daughter. If I had any doubt, it is erased now."

Aya blushed. "I'm sorry. Please continue."

"On either side of the clock will be a door. The door on the left is the door to King Archon's private chambers."

Aya nodded. "And the door on the right?"

"It doesn't go anywhere." Lord Varick tugged on his glove. "It is simply a diversion to slow down those who may seek to enter the king's chambers uninvited."

"Oh." Aya studied Lord Varick's face. His eyes avoided hers a moment too long, the way men's eyes at the brothel avoided hers when the men claimed they didn't have enough coins left for a tip.

Lord Varick cleared his throat. "I am afraid, my dear Miss Cogsmith, this is where I leave you for the time being. I cannot expect you to succeed in wooing King Archon if I am lingering on your arm, now can I?"

"True." Aya smirked. "You might dampen the mood."

Lord Varick laughed. "There is my girl! Follow the corridor to the end and busy yourself with examining some element of it. There should be plenty of tapestries and old books to fawn over. There should also be a fainting couch in the center to pose on. When King Archon arrives, which should be rather shortly, play the lost, innocent newcomer and inflict your best charm upon him."

Aya swallowed. "What if Queen Zedara is with him?"

"I do not expect her to be. She will likely want to return to her own chambers to dress for dinner, and they are in a separate corridor."

"All right. And if things go well with the king…" Aya paused, trying to formulate modest words. "How far should I let them proceed?"

"Goodness, Miss Aya." Lord Varick wagged a finger. "Not far at all. While I imagine you must be drooling over the opportunity to establish physical intimacy with your father's murderer, trying to do it tonight will get us nowhere. He is not like your clients at the Rudder. He thrives on the chase, and to my knowledge, he has never actually committed adultery. If that were his game, he would still be married to one of his earlier wives, and my sweet daughter would be alive."

"So, the Honest Husband Package?"

Lord Varick cocked his head to the side. "Beg pardon?"

Aya blushed. "At the Rudder, we have this routine for married clients who want to feel desired but who are too scared of breaking the law to actually engage in the adultery. With these men, we use suggestive language and gentle touches, but we go no further."

"That is precisely what you need to do." Lord Varick tapped his cane on the floor again. "Give him a little taste, and leave him wanting more, so that the next time he sees you, he will be the one to instigate the interaction."

"Got it." Aya pushed her shoulders back. "I can do this."

"I know you can. Now, hurry along down the corridor. The nobles will be exiting the throne room, and we need you to be in place to greet our beloved king." Lord Varick gave her a quick kiss on the hand, squeezing her fingers tightly in both fists. "Good luck, my dear."

Aya nodded and turned on her heels. She tried to keep a steady pace down the corridor. If she encountered servants or wandering nobles, she wanted to look confident in her destination but not rushed enough to seem suspicious. One way she tried to temper her pace was by memorizing the different doorways and corridors. However, after the twentieth door, she gave up and settled for simply admiring the ship's craftsmanship.

Even though the palace held so many bad memories for her, she still found it beautiful. The iron arches holding up the ceiling, with their big round rivets and patchy oxidation, were breathtaking. She adored the marble floors and the high ceilings. She would have loved to live in a world where she could have helped build such a vessel.

Eventually, Aya reached a point where the corridor began to narrow. It grew thinner and thinner, until finally, it was about the width of three men standing side by side. After a few feet, it opened abruptly into the rounded room that Lord Varick described, and Aya found herself face to face with the first clock she had ever seen. At nearly eight feet tall, it towered over Aya, and she became mesmerized by its circular white face. She counted the numbers, each written in a thick swirled script, and the little tick marks between them. The body of the clock was made of dark wood, but its belly consisted of glass, with two golden rods hanging down, presumably attached to its face in some way. Aya longed to crack it open and peer inside its brain.

"Admiring my clock, Miss Wellman?"

Aya jumped at the sound of King Archon's gravelly voice. She turned around slowly, making sure to flick her curly hair over her shoulder.

"Is that what it is, Your Majesty?" Aya placed a single finger on her bottom lip. "I have never seen such a contraption before. What does it do?"

"Nothing, I am afraid." King Archon held his hands behind his back. "It has been broken since the *Queen Hildegard* landed in Desertera."

"What a pity." Aya ran her finger from her lips to her collarbone. "Why not throw it out?"

"It is an heirloom." King Archon crossed the room to stand next to her. "My ancestors felt it necessary to safeguard the broken thing, perhaps as an emblem of the world before. Whatever the reason, I am bound by blood and honor to let it rest outside my chambers."

"How noble," Aya whispered, letting her hand slide into her hair. She twirled a curl around her forefinger.

"Now that I have educated you about the clock, Miss Wellman, I am afraid I must ask. What are you doing outside my personal chambers?"

"Oh!" Aya let her curl fall and clasped her hands together in front of her chest. "I had no idea these were your chambers. Lord Varick encouraged me to explore the palace. I had no intention of intruding on my king's privacy."

King Archon's cold eyes appraised her. Aya saw them beginning to harden with suspicion, so she tried a slightly different tactic. She sat down on the fainting couch that Lord Varick had mentioned. Trying to emulate the way Dellwyn sat to greet clients, Aya crossed her legs so her ankles showed and arched her back to accentuate her breasts and hips.

"But since I am already here," Aya began, rubbing her fingertips along the red velvet cushion of the couch, "perhaps I could attain a private audience with His Majesty?"

"Miss Wellman, what could you and I possibly have to

discuss?" King Archon raised his eyebrows and crossed his arms. Aya couldn't tell whether he was being coy or growing irritated. Why did he always have to look so angry?

Aya lingered on the couch for a moment. When King Archon held his ground, she stood and walked over to him. She placed her fingers and thumb on either side of his chin and traced his beard down to its point. "We are intelligent people. Surely we can devise a topic of conversation."

King Archon stepped back. "Miss Wellman, I do not understand your intentions here, but I assure you we have nothing to talk about."

"But, Your Majesty, I—" Aya reached for the king, only to let her hand fall to her side when he snarled.

"No. Whatever your request is, I deny it. If you are unsatisfied with the marquess and want another guardian, or if you want me to secure a noble husband, or feed your family in Sternville; whatever it is, I will not fulfill it."

"But I thought—" Aya didn't know what she thought. She had no idea what to say. All she knew was that she could not reveal her true purpose, and she needed to get out of here quickly, before he figured her out. Assuming, of course, that he hadn't already.

"You thought what, Miss Wellman?" King Archon asked, pointing a ringed finger at her. "That I seemed like a nice man, that we had such a lovely rapport at the ceremony? Well, I assure you, you are not special. I speak to every one of my subjects in the same manner. Whatever favor you thought you had gleaned, it does not exist."

Aya knew that King Archon expected her to apologize and flee. But she couldn't do that. She would not apologize to this man, not for anything. Even though he couldn't know it and wouldn't think it if he did, *he* should be the one apologizing to *her*.

"My mistake." Aya turned away with a soft smile, as if kings chastised her all the time. She felt his eyes on her as she walked away, but she willed herself not to look back. She didn't know what she'd see—surprise, distrust, the same malice that had slain her father? It didn't matter. She wouldn't give him the satisfaction of taking another morsel of her dignity.

~

ONCE AYA REACHED the statue of Queen Hildegard, she allowed herself to glance back over her shoulder. King Archon had not followed her. A laugh echoed through the corridor, and Aya saw a small group of nobles heading toward her from the direction of the throne room. She ducked down the hallway.

Aya walked past Lord Varick's estate, purposefully avoiding meeting the eye on the door, to the doorway that led to the Rudder's stairwell. After a quick look to ensure the hallway was empty, Aya sat down on the floor next to the door and began to cry. She felt stupid for sobbing, but the king's swift rejection made her feel like a child, and being the object of his scorn and stubbornness—again—made her feel like the girl who had watched her father dragged away.

Slumping over, Aya buried her head in her arms. She didn't know what she would say if someone came by, but she hoped a passerby would have the decency to let her cry in anonymity. As the tears slid down her cheeks, Aya tasted salt on her quivering lips.

Salt water, she thought. *We're all filled with salt water.*

After a few moments, Aya took a deep breath and tried to think logically. Yes, the king had scorned her, but all was not lost. By refusing to apologize, she had maintained a scrap of dignity. Surely, a nobleman would respect that. Surely, she had increased her mystique, at least marginally.

As her tears slowed, Aya heard footsteps coming up the stairwell. Knowing she did not have time to avoid an encounter, she shuffled down the hallway a few feet, hoping the stranger wouldn't notice her. She hid her face in her arms again. The door creaked open. The stranger stepped into the corridor, paused, then walked toward her. When the footsteps stopped in front of her, Aya knew she had to look up. To her humiliation, Aya found herself staring up into the eyes of a man—of, frankly, a rather gorgeous young man.

She put her head in her hands. "Shit."

Aya stayed hidden for a few moments. She hoped that, if she kept still, the man would lose interest or begin to feel awkward, the way most men did around women displaying emotions, and walk away.

The young man tapped his foot. "I don't believe I've ever heard a young noblewoman use such vulgar language."

Aya's head snapped up, and she glared at the man. "Maybe you haven't been listening."

The young man laughed. Aya had to admit she liked the sound of it. Deep and sincere.

"Perhaps you're right. Should I start now?" The young man sat down cross-legged in front of her.

Aya looked around the corridor to ensure that no one else was watching them, two grown adults seated in the hallway like insolent children. When she was sure they were alone, she returned her gaze to his face.

From this direct angle, Aya could examine him more closely. He had lightly tanned skin and dark brown hair. His jawline was pronounced but still soft, unlike the king's pointed chin. Tiny black hairs speckled his jawline and cheeks, not enough to make a beard, but enough to create a handsome shadow on his face. His eyebrows were thick, which gave character to even his subtlest facial expression. Then Aya noticed his eyes. They were the color of the desert sand at sunset with rings of gold and green circling the pupil. Aya looked down into the black folds of her dress, wishing that Lord Varick's family colors were more flattering.

The young man touched Aya's chin, tilting it up with his

fingers. It felt as if a lightning bolt had issued from his fingertips, striking in her jaw and crackling down her neck.

"If I may be rude once more," he began, "why are you sobbing on the floor?"

"It's nothing." Aya looked away. "I just—I did something foolish."

The man let his hand drop from Aya's chin to rest on her knee. In other situations, Aya would have recoiled from such an intimate touch from a stranger—from a non-client stranger, anyway. However, after the king's rejection, being comforted by a handsome man reassured Aya that she must be somewhat attractive.

"We all make mistakes. I am sure you can reconcile this one."

Aya shrugged. "I hope you are correct."

"I know I am." The man smiled, pulled his cream pocket square from the front of his jacket, and handed it to her. As Aya wiped the lingering teardrops from her cheeks, the man fiddled with the hem of her skirt. "These are Lord Varick's house colors, are they not? I did not realize he had taken a new wife."

Aya jerked, causing the man's hand to slip from her knee. He didn't replace it, returning it to his own knee. Aya's chest deflated, and she handed his pocket square back to him. "No, absolutely not. I'm his ward, an orphan. Lord Varick took me in off the streets of Sternville."

"My apologies." The man tucked his pocket square back into his jacket. "I didn't mean to offend you."

"Oh, you didn't." Aya bit her lip. "I was more concerned that the potential of a marital attachment to me would offend Lord Varick."

The young man placed his hand back on her knee. "I don't think any man would take offense to the possibility of being married to a beautiful woman, no matter what her status."

Aya's eyes widened. She had never been called beautiful

before, at least, not by anyone other than her father. Her clients had never needed to show kindness, and suitors, well, there hadn't been any. No self-respecting man, not even a wellman, would court a lady from the Rudder.

"Oh, I'm not—"

"Do they have many mirrors in Sternville?"

Aya's brow furrowed.

"Do they?"

Aya shook her head. She'd never seen a mirror in Sternville. They had one at the Rudder in the communal changing room, but the women in the higher-priority rooms, and even Augustus, were given the most time to study their reflections. Aya was lucky to catch a quick glance of herself once a night, and even then, she didn't care to see her self-pitying eyes staring back at her.

"Then in these few short minutes, I have seen you more often and more clearly than you have probably seen yourself in your entire life. And I assure you, you are stunning."

Aya touched her puffy cheeks and the corners of her swollen eyes. The young man was looking at her intently, barely holding back a pleased smile.

"And I assure you," Aya replied, grinning, "you are blind."

He threw his head back and laughed. Aya's grin widened, and her head felt dizzy—the pride of successful flirting. After catching his breath, the young man stood and reached his hand out to help Aya stand. As he pulled her to her feet, she popped up as if she might float to the ceiling.

They stood there for a moment, hands still clasped, before the man shook himself and released his grip. He put his hands behind his back, like a little boy trying not to break anything in a merchant's shop. "Will you be at the ball next week?"

"I don't know." Lord Varick had inquired about the ball when they spoke with the king and queen, but she didn't know whether Varick intended for them to go.

"Well, if you do decide to grace it with your presence, may I reserve a dance?"

Aya thought his formality a bit overblown, but she nodded anyway. "You may." She did her best to imitate his lofty tone.

He bit his bottom lip. "Do I really sound like that?"

Aya rolled her eyes, keeping her smile in place to show she was teasing. "All of you nobles sound like that."

"What makes you think I'm a nobleman?" he balked, equally playful.

"Well, they certainly don't dress the servants this nicely." Aya gestured to his tailored jacket and cream cravat.

The young man nodded and frowned. "I shall try to do better next time."

Aya laughed. "Might I know the name of the man who has secured a dance?"

"I could give you my full title, but in an effort to sound less pompous, I'll have you call me Willem."

Aya extended her hand. "Pleasure to make your acquaintance, Willem. I'm Aya."

"Aya what?" He shook her hand, and her stomach somersaulted.

"In an effort to sound less unimportant, just Aya."

Willem smiled and ran his fingers through his dark hair. "All right. If not before, I will see you at the ball, Aya."

"Lovely."

Willem began to walk away, but after a few steps, he turned back to her. "I feel it is only right to warn you: I am a wonderful dancer."

Something between a laugh and a scoff escaped Aya's open mouth. "I shall do my best to keep up."

"I hope you do." Willem winked. Aya didn't realize a wink could produce the same spark as his touch. But she felt it sizzle all the way down to her core.

6
______

$\mathcal{A}$fter her encounter with Willem, Aya felt as if her whole body were buzzing. She practically floated back to Lord Varick's estate. When Aya arrived, she shut the black door behind her, leaning back against it to close her eyes and breathe. Her chest still hummed, and it felt delightfully swollen.

This is how it must be for normal girls.

"From your silly smile, I assume things went well with the king?"

Lord Varick's voice startled Aya out of her reverie. He stood at the end of the hallway with his arms crossed over his chest.

Aya straightened and patted down her ruffled skirt. "Not exactly." Aya chose her words carefully. She didn't think Lord Varick would be too pleased to know that her pride and girlish joy came from winning the favor of a man other than the king. "King Archon was entirely displeased at my presence near his chambers. He did not have any interest in entertaining me, in any capacity, and he promptly dismissed me."

"I see." Lord Varick turned away. "Come sit down."

Aya followed Lord Varick into the sitting room, her breath

catching in her throat. In an armchair by the fireplace sat Madam Huxley.

"Good evening, Aya." Madam Huxley held herself perfectly straight, a long-stemmed glass of red liquid in her hand. If Aya had been an outsider, she would have thought the madam was the queen.

"Good evening, Madam." Aya positioned herself on the same leather couch she'd occupied that morning. Lord Varick sat across from her and poured her a glass of the red liquid. Aya took it, but she didn't drink.

"Don't look so alarmed, child." Madam Huxley turned the stem of her glass between her fingers. "You are not being punished."

Aya adjusted her hair so that it fell over her exposed collarbones, hiding the flush that threatened to spread across her chest. "I'm sorry, Madam. I am just surprised to find you here."

"Lord Varick thought it wise for the three of us to have a little chat about the terms of your employment."

"Oh?" Aya bit her lip, glancing between the two of them.

"Yes." Lord Varick took a drink from his own glass. "And I thought the wine might help us all get through it with some cheer."

Madam Huxley did not smile. Aya looked down at the drink in her hand. Wine. It must be a fancier version of the crude alcohol the wellmen used to brighten their spirits and get into trouble. She swirled and sniffed it, discovering a strange mix of sweet and bitter.

"You see, Aya," Lord Varick continued, "while you are participating in this mission, we cannot risk your working at the Rudder. Obviously, if one of the noblemen recognized you, that would jeopardize our entire operation."

Aya raised an eyebrow. "Why would the noblemen recognize me now? They've never taken a second look at me before."

"Before, you were just another corset in the brothel, and since you did not serve the nobles, they had no reason to notice you." Lord Varick shifted in his seat. "Now that you have debuted as my ward, you will be a topic of conversation. The nobles will remember your face and study you as one of their own. You would certainly be recognized."

"Of course, we realize that your primary clientele is merchants." Madam Huxley smirked. "The risk of running into a nobleman is significantly reduced if you are confined to your room and chaperoned in and out only when the establishment is empty. However, Lord Varick astutely noted that some merchants do visit the palace to bring their goods, and if one of these men were to recognize you, it would create complications."

As Madam Huxley took another drink, Aya widened her eyes and mouthed a "thank you" to Lord Varick. He nodded. Aya tried a sip of her wine. Like its scent, it tasted part sweet and part sour, and as it slid down her throat, it left a warm, fuzzy feeling on her tongue.

"I agree that postponing my work is the safest option to ensure our uninterrupted progress." Aya forced her tone to remain level. Inside, she beamed.

Lord Varick grinned.

"Postponing?" Madam Huxley wrinkled her nose. "Lord Varick informs me that you wish to permanently abandon your work. He says that the two of you struck a bargain, and in return for your assistance, he is to purchase your father's old shop so you can begin your own cogsmith business."

This time, the look Aya gave Lord Varick was not so grateful. While he did save her from an uncomfortable discussion with Madam, Aya would have preferred to keep her intentions private until she completed the mission. But the secret was out now, and if she wanted to escape Madam Huxley's influence once and for all, Aya couldn't be obedient any longer.

"That is correct." Aya squared her shoulders. "I'd intended

to deliver the news a little more delicately, businesswoman to businesswoman. You understand."

Madam Huxley's eyes burned, their flame directed straight at Aya. It took all of Aya's strength not to look away, but she knew that the woman who averted her eyes first would lose.

"Well, I suppose it is settled, then," Lord Varick rubbed his hands together.

Madam Huxley turned to look at him, and Aya smiled. "I do have one question. Madam Huxley, I realize I will not be a great loss to your establishment, but I have never seen you relinquish a courtesan so easily. What do you stand to gain here?"

Lord Varick's face broke into a grin akin to that of a proud father. Madam Huxley pursed her lips. "As it stands, King Archon strictly enforces the death penalty for adultery, in a way that no other royal leader has. This has left the noblemen, and people all over the kingdom, terrified to transgress. Given that the majority of Desertera's population is married, you can see how this fear might cut down on my client base."

"You believe that, if King Archon is executed, the rules around adultery will once again relax, and more people will feel secure enough to frequent the Rudder?" Aya appraised Madam Huxley over the edge of her wineglass.

"I certainly can't imagine how it would be *bad* for business to have a king like Archon out of the picture," Madam Huxley scoffed.

"And you think Prince Lionel will be more lenient?" Aya thought so. After the way the prince had so easily succumbed to the king's pressure to order the death of Aya's father, Aya knew he was a coward. He wouldn't do a thing to stop people like Madam Huxley.

Madam Huxley smirked. "I think Prince Lionel would quite love adultery to be legal again."

"Why is that?" Aya took another drink, hoping to conceal

the pink tint growing along her neck. Coyness always flushed her skin.

Lord Varick chuckled. "Prince Lionel has a reputation as a charmer. I have seen many a young lady eying him at balls and even more crying into their tea over him. He has certainly inherited his father's love of women. He simply hasn't been foolish enough to bind himself to one yet."

Aya stared into her wine. It figured that such a weak-willed boy would grow into a pig of a man, just like his father. Aya almost pitied the girls who were dumb enough to fall victim to his charms, but if they were not intelligent enough to see a snake in their beds, they probably deserved to be bitten.

"Well then." Lord Varick tapped his cane on the floor, snapping Aya out of her thoughts. "Now that we all understand our motives are harmonious, why don't you tell us more about your attempts to woo the king, Aya?"

Aya took a long drink of her wine. She had not grown accustomed to the dryness it created on her tongue and throat, but she kept swallowing anyway. She had heard from the girls at the Rudder whose clients brought them wine that, if you drank enough of it, you felt warm and happy and didn't care about all the bad things anymore. Aya wondered how much she would have to drink to get to that point. Unfortunately, she reached the end of her glass. She set it down on the table. "As I said when I walked in, my attempts were positively futile."

"Yes, we understand that." Madam Huxley sighed. "But if you explain your actions in more detail, we may be able to figure out exactly what you did wrong."

"And how we can improve for next time." Lord Varick reached over to pat Aya on the knee. His touch brought her mind back to Willem, and she felt her face flush. Aya hoped they would see her reddening as a product of the wine.

"Very well." Aya took a deep breath. "I positioned myself in the round room, and as you instructed, I took interest in one of the objects. My back was to the doorway, and when King Archon came in, I turned around with a flourish."

"What do you mean by *flourish*?" Madam Huxley placed her hand over her mouth.

Aya furrowed her eyebrows. "I flipped my hair and smiled."

Madam Huxley snickered.

Lord Varick glared at the madam. "And next?"

"We talked about the object briefly before he informed me that I was outside his private chambers. I pretended to be lost and innocent, and I sat down on the fainting couch to better position myself. I thought he may sit next to me to visit, but he wanted me gone. I stood up and tried to flirt, but he ordered me to leave."

"How did you position yourself on the couch?" Madam Huxley leaned forward. From the smug smile on her face, Aya knew the madam was dying to pick apart her every mistake.

"The way Dellwyn taught me." Aya hoped bringing up Madam's rising star would gain her some credit. "I arched my back to accentuate my curves. I played with my hair, touched my chest—you know how it goes."

Madam Huxley pursed her lips. "You must have been too exaggerated in your movements. Subtlety is key, Aya."

"Miss Aya does not seem to be one for subtlety," Lord Varick chimed in, mercifully refilling her glass.

"Thank you, Varick, for the *wine*." Aya took a drink, finally feeling warmth spreading from her belly.

"And what did you do upon standing?" Madam Huxley asked.

"Oh." Aya blushed. "I touched his face."

Madam Huxley's eyes bulged, and she placed a hand over her wine-filled mouth. She swallowed hard. "You touched the king's face? When he clearly had no interest in you?"

"I more of, um, stroked his beard." Aya looked down at her feet.

Madam Huxley threw her head back and guffawed. "Oh, Aya, I thought you would have learned *something* over the last ten years."

Lord Varick raised his hand to silence the madam's laughter. "In Miss Aya's defense, there is not much flirting, let alone subtlety, required at your place of business. I'm sure all the Rudder's clients enter wanting more than their beards stroked."

Aya smiled at Lord Varick. Once again, his wit and compassion had come to her rescue.

"Indeed," Madam Huxley conceded. "I suppose any lack of technique is not Aya's fault. She's never desired to move up in rooms, and therefore, I never gave her any proper training."

Lord Varick glanced at Aya, and she shrugged. "I never thought I would need it."

Lord Varick sighed. "There is nothing we can do now. Best not to dwell in the past." He leaned forward. "Anyway, Miss Aya, how did you leave the king?"

"He ordered me to remove myself his private area," Aya replied, straight-faced.

"Did you respond at all?" Lord Varick widened his eyes. "Did you apologize?"

"No." Aya had to pause to rein in her indignation before it contaminated her entire statement. "I simply said, 'My mistake' and left."

"At least you did one thing right." Madam Huxley patted the arm of the couch. "The moment you act weak, he'll be done with you."

Lord Varick tapped a gloved finger against his chin. "It seems that all is not lost. Miss Aya clearly annoyed the king with her intrusion, but she maintained her act of innocence and kept her head held high. However, I think we can all agree that some training is in order."

Aya and Madam Huxley both nodded, the latter much more enthusiastically.

"Madam Huxley, what is your recommendation?"

The madam placed her empty wineglass on the table, leaned back in her chair, and tapped the ends of her fingers together. "Firstly, we shall make sure you receive a bath and are perfectly groomed for next week's ball. This way, the next time King Archon sees you, you will be fresh and radiant."

Aya's mouth dropped open—partly at the prospect of a proper bathing and partly at the notion that Madam Huxley thought Aya could be attractive.

"As for your education," Madam Huxley continued, "I shall have Dellwyn assist us. I assume that you have already informed her of this plan?"

Aya bit her lip. "Yes."

Lord Varick's face hardened, but he didn't say anything.

"Then I shall have Dellwyn show you some basic seduction tactics. She has been successful in wooing several noblemen into blind, genuine affection, so she will be the perfect one to teach you."

Lord Varick leaned back, crossing his arms and squinting at Aya. "And we can be assured of this Dellwyn's discretion?"

"Absolutely," Aya piped. Lord Varick turned to Madam Huxley.

"I'd imagine so." The madam shrugged. "Dellwyn is a fiercely loyal friend, and she despises the way the king treats women. She should not jeopardize us in any way. In fact, I am sure she will be a great asset."

"Fine," Lord Varick conceded, placing his hands on his legs. "Madam Huxley, would you be willing to spare Dellwyn for a few days? I think it would be best if she and Aya were allowed to work uninterrupted and in the safety of my estate."

"Varick?" Aya leaned forward. "Don't you think it would be safer if Dellwyn and I stayed at our own hovel in Sternville? Her clientele consists almost entirely of nobles. Besides, no one in Sternville knows I am acting as your ward, and they may become suspicious if I am away for too long."

"Perhaps. But in my estate, I could—"

"Aya is right." Madam Huxley stood to leave. "Sternville makes for a much less conspicuous location. And I will allow Dellwyn three nights off work, starting tonight, for Aya's training."

"You are sure you would feel safer in Sternville, Miss Aya?" Lord Varick dragged out the question as if Aya were a toddler who needed to be led to the correct answer.

"Yes." Aya rose as well. "Just for a few nights."

Lord Varick inclined his head. "And you are sure no one from the palace will see you?"

"Positive." Aya gave Lord Varick her most reassuring smile.

Lord Varick twirled his cane in his hand. He squeezed his beady eyes shut, but after a moment, he opened them again, letting out a long breath and softening his face. Like Aya, he put on a charming grin. "I suppose it is settled then. My guard will escort you ladies back to the Rudder. Aya, you and Dellwyn will work tonight and two more nights, and I shall see you back on the third sunrise."

Aya nodded, her chest tightening with the movement. "Very well, Varick."

~

THE SAME GUARD who'd led Aya up to Lord Varick's estate the previous night walked Madam Huxley and Aya back down the winding staircase to the Rudder. When he had shut the door behind them and they were standing by Room Z in the Rudder's back hallway, Madam Huxley took Aya by the arm. "Before we are no longer alone, I must speak with you."

"What is it?"

"I am concerned about Lord Varick," Madam Huxley whispered, hovering close to Aya's face. "He is working diligently to keep you dependent upon him and to isolate you from others."

Aya's eyebrows furrowed. "Aren't I dependent upon him by the very nature of my status and this arrangement?"

"Yes, I suppose." Madam Huxley's forehead creased.

"And isn't isolation necessary to an extent?" Aya tilted her head. "We don't want other nobles to figure out what we're doing."

"Yes, Aya, I realize that." Madam Huxley clenched her jaw. "But just a moment ago, you were exactly right in thinking that you and Dellwyn would be safest in Sternville. No one will look twice at you, and even if they were to figure out what you were doing in the palace, they would not care enough to interfere. Not when they have to worry about putting water and food on their own tables." Madam Huxley sighed. "And Lord Varick should have known that, but he was so insistent to persuade you otherwise."

"He was a bit unnerved at my suggestion." Aya shrugged. "But I don't think he was too argumentative."

Madam Huxley released Aya's arm and let her hands fall to her own skirt, patting it down as if it were ruffled by this business with Lord Varick. "Maybe not this time. But trust me, I know men like him. I've worked with them for years. Once they get it in their heads that they own you, it can be difficult to become a free woman again."

"Varick knows he does not own me." Aya straightened. "We've agreed that we will part ways after the mission, and I will return to my father's shop to run a business."

"Yes, you will." Madam Huxley smirked. "And whose badge of patronage will be on your door?"

Aya drew back. She hadn't considered that possibility before, assuming Lord Varick would give her the shop in return for the favor she was currently doing him. Surely he wouldn't try to act as a landlord or hold his assistance over her head. They would be even. Right?

"I don't think our agreement will work that way." Aya shook her head. "We are partners in this endeavor."

Madam Huxley pursed her lips. "That may be so. But you will notice, Aya, there is neither a badge on the propellers outside, nor another person sitting in my office, and I am the longest-standing female business owner in Desertera."

Aya's eyes darted between the madam and the direction of the propellers.

"Be careful," Madam Huxley said. "That is all I am trying to say. Sometimes, the nobles—especially noble*men*—do not see the world the way we do."

It was the first time Madam Huxley had ever shown Aya any true concern, and it was also the first time she'd ever implied Aya could be her equal.

Aya felt a knot forming in her stomach, and she swallowed. "Thank you, Madam. I will."

Madam Huxley nodded and strode down the hallway. "Now, burst into Dellwyn's room and pry Lord Collingwood off of her. You two have a lot of work to do."

7

____

"You did what?" Dellwyn gripped her sides, wincing as her laughing stomach fought against her corset. She had not changed out of her work attire when she and Aya arrived home, insisting she had to hear about Aya's time in the palace immediately.

"I stroked his beard," Aya repeated. She and Dellwyn sat at the table in their common room. They had started a fire in the iron stove to warm up the hovel, but Aya had still gone into her bedroom to fetch a blanket to wrap around her shoulders. She had returned home wearing the garish outfit of Lord Varick's house colors. Her favorite green cloak and her nightdress remained at Lord Varick's estate.

"All right, I'm sorry," Dellwyn wheezed, still clutching her sides. "Whew, we've got a long way to go."

"That's what everyone keeps saying." Aya rolled her eyes. "Over and over."

"I'm sorry, Aya." Dellwyn sat up straighter, wiping her hand in front of her face to indicate that she was ready to be serious. "Why don't we start by figuring out where you are now? Tell me how you interact with clients at the Rudder."

"What do you mean?" Aya shuffled in her seat.

"When they come into the room, what do you do to pique their interest?"

"Well, I generally pose myself on the bed the way you taught me, with my back arched and skirts askew to show off my legs."

"That's a great start." Dellwyn squeezed Aya's hand. "Once they are in the room, what do you do?"

"If they come over to the bed, I just let them begin and have the experience they want." Aya shrugged. "If they linger in the doorway, I will get up, go over to them, and start unfastening my corset. That generally gets things moving."

"I know what your problem is." Dellwyn smiled. "You don't know how to lead the seduction. Of course, I don't blame you. You've only ever been in the Rudder, where clients want instant satisfaction. You've never had an opportunity to be in control."

"Do you think I need to take control with King Archon?" Aya leaned back and crossed her arms.

"Yes." Dellwyn's full lips formed a wicked smile. "In my experience, the more powerful the man, the more he likes to yield to a powerful woman in the bedroom."

Aya furrowed her eyebrows. "So, I should be more aggressive with the king?"

"Not necessarily aggressive." Dellwyn tapped her fingers against her chin. "Power and control do not have to be expressed with action. You hold the power when he comes to you. If you can make the man approach you first, speak to you first, or make a physical move first, that means that *he* wants *you* more than *you* want *him*. Therefore, he is the one who has to work for it, and you are the one who can give and take as you choose."

Aya nodded and stared down at the table. She wondered if she'd had the power in her interaction with Willem. After all, even though she looked pathetic when he stumbled upon her, he did approach her and make the first move—and he did ask her to share a dance. That had made him vulnerable, if only for a moment.

"Aya?" Dellwyn waved her hand in front of Aya's line of vision. "Do you understand?"

"Yes, I do." Aya straightened. "But I still don't get how to make him want me. I mean, how will I gain the power if I can't entice him?"

Dellwyn's gaze drifted to the window. She dipped her head down to see the position of the moon. Aya followed her lead. However, instead of looking for the moon, she searched the palace, wondering which, if any, room Willem lived in. Was Willem a high enough nobleman to live in the palace, or had he been walking through on his way home to Starboardshire?

"It's getting late. Let's end for the night." Dellwyn yawned and stretched her arms. "Tomorrow." She lowered her voice for dramatic effect. "I will teach you everything you need to know to entice your father's murderer into killing his wife to be with you."

"You make it sound so disturbing."

"Isn't it?" Dellwyn laughed.

"Oh, yes, it is." Aya groaned, putting her head in her hands. "I'm just trying not to think about the whole picture. Not when I'm in the moment, anyway."

Dellwyn chuckled and headed to her bedroom.

"Dellwyn?" Aya called. Dellwyn stopped in her doorway and turned around. "Do you think I can do this? Can you really teach me enough in two nights?"

"Aya, by the time I'm through with you, every man in that palace will be crawling on his knees for you."

Aya nodded. The nerves in her stomach told her otherwise, but if anyone could teach Aya to seduce a king, it was Dellwyn.

"Hey, cheer up." Dellwyn winked. "Who knows? Maybe you'll find a nice nobleman to bed. You know, for fun instead of money."

Aya blushed, placing her hand over her chest to hide her

flush. She had not told Dellwyn about Willem yet. For now, he was Aya's alone. "Maybe," Aya whispered. "Maybe."

THE NEXT MORNING, Aya awoke to the sound of knocking. When she answered the hovel door, Lord Varick's gray-haired guard stood before her. The guard placed his fist over his chest and bowed. "Good morning, Miss Aya."

"Good morning." Aya glanced around to see if any of her neighbors had noticed a palace guard at the dwelling of two ladies of the Rudder. The sun had just begun to rise, and as far as Aya could see, the inhabitants of Sternville remained in their hovels.

"Do not worry, Miss Aya." The guard smiled. "If anyone questions my presence, I shall tell them I am delivering a message from my lord to Miss Dellwyn."

Aya raised her chin, not entirely reassured. "And what is your true purpose here?"

"Lord Varick has scheduled an appointment for you at the bathing house. It begins when the sun reaches the starboard railing of the palace." The guard pointed toward Starboard-shire. "The bathing house is beyond—"

"I know where it is." Aya blushed at her rudeness. "Forgive me. I have been there before, but thank you for your assistance."

"Of course." The guard bowed again. "Have a nice day, Miss Aya."

Aya smiled. "Same to you."

When Aya shut the door, she leaned back against it and grinned. Even though one of her rare trips to the bathing house meant being crammed into a tub filled with already soiled, lukewarm water and a few other women, Aya nearly salivated at the prospect of being clean.

In Desertera, it didn't take long to get dirty. The wind

carried a layer of dust that crept into every nook and cranny the body had to offer, whether covered by clothing or not. Aya routinely found dust balled up in the corner of her eyes, nestled in the folds of her armpits, and gooped up between her toes. Her hair was the worst. Luckily, being brown, her hair did not show dirt the way it did for the black-haired or blond women at the Rudder. However, whenever she scratched her scalp, thick clumps of congealed dirt and body oil gathered under her fingernails. But today, the dirt—and everything that came with it—would be washed away. Today, she would be clean.

Aya's excitement carried through the morning, and even as she walked to the bathing house a few hours later, her body still hummed with delight. However, when the building finally came into view, Aya's smile faltered. A small crowd—judging by their varied clothing, a mixture of Starboardshire nobles and Sternville peasants—stood outside the bathing house, surrounding a man. The man perched atop something, making him taller than his onlookers, and he shouted and shook his fist at them.

He wore a loose black shirt and tight black pants, affixed with leather belts that held canteens and tools. On his head rested a flat black cap with a pair of farmers' goggles strapped around its base. All farmers wore goggles to keep the dirt out of their eyes while tending to their plants and animals. Aya had never seen a farmer near the bathing house before. Farming kept them perpetually dirty, and other than their wedding nights, they never bothered with bathing.

The farmer paused in his speech, his chest heaving. He glowered at the crowd with wild, bulging eyes, and Aya noticed that they did not match—one eye was green, the other gray.

"The great rain is coming!" the farmer cried. "I'm telling

you the truth! The Benevolent Queen sent me a vision. Any day now, She will send Her torrential showers upon us and drown us for our sins! She says we must repent! She says we must be loyal lovers to our partners and devoted servants to our Divine Royals!"

Some of the people from Sternville clapped, but every Starboardshire resident stared up at the man with scorn. Aya had seen these fundamentalists from time to time when she lived in Portside. They would stand up tall and preach about the rain, but it would never come. Every now and then, they would excite some lower merchants to close their shops for a day to stand outside the palace and demand propriety and a greater share of the water, but mostly, they simply rambled on before stumbling off their boxes and disappearing in a cloud of dust. Once, Aya had believed in them as prophets, believed in the Gods and the salvation rain, but now, she only believed in what she could see: dirt, murky wells, and a murderous king.

"Please, listen to me!" The farmer clasped his hands together. "I have been given the divine sight from the Benevolent Queen. The salvation rain is coming. If you do not repent, if you do not live well, you will drown. She told me to save you!"

A worker came out of the bathhouse and threw a small bucket of soiled water on the farmer. "There is your rain. Now be gone!"

The crowd erupted into laughter. The farmer stepped down from his perch and walked away, but he kept shouting warnings over his shoulder. "The rains are coming. She told me! Our new queen will bring the rains!"

Aya watched the farmer leave, wondering about his claims. Typically, prophets predicted doom and howled at their audiences, but she had never heard one claim that a mortal monarch would save them. How did he expect Queen Zedara to bring the rains? Surely he was not so delusional as to think that Queen Zedara would survive long enough to prove her fidelity to the Benevolent Queen—not when every other woman paired with King Archon fell victim to adultery, real or invented.

As intrigued as Aya was, she forgot all about the farmer when she walked into the bathing house. The building was divided into two large rooms, one for women and one for men, both with separate entrances. Steam filled the bathing room, radiating from four buckets of water boiling on iron stoves in each corner. In the center of the women's room sat a large tub made of wood and bound with metal rings, where four women shared a bath. Smaller tubs, reserved for those wealthy enough to afford private bathing, lined the edges of the room.

A servant wrapped in a sunset orange toga greeted Aya. "You must be Miss Aya." She gestured toward Aya's dress. Aya still wore the ensemble from Lord Varick. "Please allow me to escort you to your private bath."

Aya's jaw dropped. "Private bath?"

"Absolutely." The servant bowed her head. "Lord Varick has insisted upon it."

"Who am I to argue with Lord Varick?"

The servant smiled. "Right this way, Miss Aya."

Aya followed the servant to a tub positioned against the back wall of the bathing house, between two of the fires. Clear, steaming water filled the tub, and as Aya removed her clothing, she felt the steam caress her bare skin. The servant helped Aya step into the bath. As Aya's muscles slipped beneath the water's surface, they began to relax for the first time in ten years. Even Aya's stomach, which twisted with guilt at so much water being spent on her body, slowly uncurled itself and allowed her to soak peacefully in the hot bath.

The servant held up three vials filled with liquid. The first one contained a rich yellow liquid, which shimmered as she poured it into the bath. "Lemongrass oil, to revitalize and cleanse your pores."

Aya breathed in, her nose crinkling at the strange scent. It smelled of sour and shrubbery and sun.

The servant removed the second cork, which belonged to a pinkish liquid. "Rosewood oil." She poured it into the tub. "For strength."

This one smelled of the wildflower fields and the wood of the barrel.

"Peppermint oil." The servant uncorked the last vial and sprinkled a few drops into the bath. "To sharpen your senses."

The drops from this vial were clear. Aya's nose felt empty aas the odor reached it. The only way she could think to describe it was as the smell of cold.

The servant left Aya to soak in the oils for a long time, until the skin on Aya's fingers and toes began to shrivel. As she relaxed in the tub, Aya wondered if Lord Varick had chosen the oils himself, if he intended for her to gain beauty, strength, and sharpness during this bath. Whether the potion had been intentional or not, Aya hoped it would bring her those gifts. She needed all the help she could get—with King Archon and with Willem.

After a while, the servant returned to wash Aya's hair. She held Aya's head as she dipped it in the water, letting it soak in the soft smells of the bath oils. Aya's head felt light as the servant massaged it, scrubbing away all the dirt and weaving her fingers through it to unwind the tangles. Aya had never had her hair washed by someone else—not since she was a child and her father helped her bathe with a washcloth and well water—and for a moment, she almost believed she was a noblewoman. When the servant finished, she lifted Aya's head and poured a fresh bowl of water over it.

As Aya stepped out of the tub, the servant wrapped her in a red toga. The servant also affixed Aya's hair in a red wrap and draped a red cloak over her shoulders.

Aya touched the soft fabric of the new outfit. "Why so much red?"

"Red is lucky. It makes you fierce." The servant winked. "It makes men's blood boil."

Aya raised her eyebrows. If she had any doubt that Lord Varick had arranged the symbolism behind her bathing experience, the red erased it. However, she still wondered what the servant knew and whether she was one of the little birds Varick mentioned. Aya smiled at her. "Thank you."

The servant shrugged. "It is what you need. Besides, you look lovely in red."

Aya laughed. "I'll trust your word."

The servant shrugged again, handing Aya the clothing she had come in, wrapped up in a black and purple ball. "Now, you walk home fast, and stay all covered. When you go to the palace, you walk faster and cover more. Lord Varick will be mad with me if you get dirty."

"It won't be your fault."

The servant smirked. "Who am I to argue with Lord Varick?"

Aya didn't like her words being turned on her.

She followed the servant's instructions, walking quickly. Once she was outside of the bathing house and into the confined space of the hovel's common room, she could smell the aroma of the oils lingering on her skin and hair. While she still thought it was wasteful, she had to admit, it gave her an enormous boost in confidence to know that she smelled so beautiful. And rich. She wouldn't need to wear Lord Varick's house colors next time—no one would question her place in the palace.

When Dellwyn came home from the grocery merchants in Portside, they shared a simple dinner of cacti meat and wheat bread. Aya was starving. She hadn't realized that she had been at the bathing house all day, missing lunch. After dinner,

Dellwyn showed Aya some basic seduction tactics. Dellwyn started with her best suggestion for helping Aya recover her image in front of King Archon and moved into how Aya should perform her next approach. She also taught Aya how to fend off unwanted advances without offending. And just in case, Dellwyn told her what to do if she encountered a man that she wanted to seduce for real.

"You know," Dellwyn said, once they had finished their lesson, "if you did find someone in the palace to practice on, it would do wonders for your education. And confidence."

Aya blushed. Dellwyn raised an eyebrow. "Is there someone?"

Aya shook her head. "No, no. You're being silly. I have to focus on the king."

"Mhmm. Well, if there *does* happen to be someone, make sure he hasn't been involved in the deaths of innocent people."

Aya laughed. "That isn't a concern."

Dellwyn nodded. "Well then, I think that's enough for tonight. Tomorrow, we'll try roleplaying, and you can practice what you learned on me as if I were the king."

Aya wrinkled her nose. "I really don't want to picture you as that man. You're the only friend I have."

Dellwyn laughed. "Don't worry. My acting skills are even worse than your seduction skills." Aya swatted Dellwyn's arm, and she lunged backward, her face contorted in fake pain. "In any case, there's always your new friend, Varick."

"Indeed." Aya shook her head.

Dellwyn looked at Aya for a long moment. "Are you sure he's trustworthy?" she asked, her voice uneven. "From what you've said, he seems like a creep."

"Yes, he's fine." Aya waved a hand. "He's just a little controlling."

Dellwyn rubbed her wrists. "What nobleman isn't?"

Aya's lips formed a sad, sympathetic smile.

"Are you sure you can handle this?" Dellwyn moved her hands up to rub her arms.

Aya stared into straight into her friend's eyes. "Dellwyn, I have dreamt my entire life of a chance to obtain justice for my father. Now that I know how to do it, nothing can stop me."

8

On the night before her return to the palace, Aya barely slept. Her body tossed and turned in rhythm with her racing mind. In mere hours, she would be back in the palace, equipped with Dellwyn's teachings and the lingering scent of the bath oils. She played out dozens of scenarios in her head—crossing King Archon's path in a hallway, bumping into him on the dance floor at the ball, happening upon a library as he read inside. The possibilities were endless, but each one ended the same way: with his ill-timed profession of lust overheard by the queen's guards or other nobles and with his head lopped off by the executioner.

When sunlight finally peeked through her shabby curtain, Aya leaped out of bed and dressed herself in the red toga and accessories from the bathing house. Before rushing out the door, she grabbed Lord Varick's outfit from her steamer trunk, taking an extra moment to feel around the bottom to ensure that Charlie still rested safely in her blue dress. As her hand landed on his metal head, Aya patted him. "Be good, buddy. I'll see you in a few days. I hope."

Aya arrived at the black door of Lord Varick's estate shortly after sunrise. The purple eye in its center seemed brighter today, and it made her a bit queasy to look at it for too long. She knocked on the door, right in the center of the eye. Before her hand even left the iron, the door swung open. Mrs. Lemot greeted Aya. They exchanged polite smiles, and Aya walked past the maid into the sitting room. She found Lord Varick perched in the armchair, a fire blazing behind him. There was a large breakfast spread on the table: eggs, bacon, and to Aya's delight, more fruit.

"Good morning, Miss Aya." Lord Varick motioned to the platter. "Please, help yourself to some breakfast."

"Thank you, Varick." Aya sat down and filled a plate. She selected one hardboiled egg—she'd never had a boiled egg before; to waste water to harden an egg was considered near blasphemy in Portside and Sternville—along with some bacon and oblong red berries with green tops and little seeds embedded in their skins. Aya held up one of the berries and inspected it. Upon closer examination, she saw little white hairs protruding from the surface.

"A strawberry," Lord Varick said.

"Do you eat all of it?"

"All but the green part."

Aya bit into the fruit. It was even juicier than it was sweet, and the juice dribbled down her chin. She wiped it up with her finger, then popped the rest of the berry into her mouth.

Lord Varick leaned forward, resting his elbows on his knees. "How did your evenings with Dellwyn go?"

"Wonderful." Aya took a bite of bacon. "I believe I know everything I need to now."

"Splendid." Lord Varick grinned. "Judging from your appearance and the heavenly smell that wafted in alongside you, I daresay I need not ask how it went at the bathing house."

Aya touched her soft hair. "It was perfect, Varick. Thank you. I have never felt so alluring, so *clean*. I must admit, I felt guilty at using so much water, but it was lovely."

Varick *tutted* and wagged his finger at her. "Now, now, Miss Aya. If that bath helps in any way to attract the king, that water was not wasted. In fact, it may be the most important use of water in the history of Desertera."

Aya nodded. She liked being important. She hadn't felt important since she'd been the *living* cogsmith's daughter.

They finished their breakfast in companionable silence. Once Aya had scarfed down her fill, she pushed her empty plate away. "Now, please tell me, Varick. When do I begin today?"

Varick smiled. "I am enthralled by your enthusiasm. My little birdies tell me that King Archon will be at the mask maker's this morning to retrieve his mask for the ball."

"Mask?"

"Yes, my dear. It is a masquerade ball. Everyone will be wearing them. Perhaps you also fancy a mask?"

Aya beamed. Thoughts of the ball brought her mind back to Willem. How would she find him at the masquerade? And more importantly, how would he recognize her to claim his dance? She hoped she'd left a strong impression.

"I would love one." Aya crossed her legs. "But I find it strange that the king runs his own errands."

Lord Varick tugged at his lapels. "Well, it seems the king's valet has fallen ill and cannot perform his tasks today. And since the king trusts no one but this valet, he has taken it upon himself to complete his errands."

Aya wondered what this meant. Was the valet a willing cog in Varick's scheme? Or had he fallen ill because someone made him? Aya didn't know if she wanted to know the truth.

"Besides," Lord Varick said, bringing Aya out of her thoughts, "King Archon has quite a passion for masks, wouldn't you say?"

～

Lord Varick had advised Aya to stay in the red outfit from the bathing house for her trip to the mask maker's shop. "Red suits you. I'll have a dress made for the ball."

Aya followed Lord Varick's directions to the shop. He'd told her it was nestled among other stores near the Starboardshire exit. As she made the long trek through the ship, Aya noticed the artwork and relics decorating the hallways. Tapestries depicting once-famous battles hung on the walls, statues of long-dead nobles stood sentry outside doors, and rusted machines rested on platforms and stands. If Aya had not been on a mission, she would have paused to admire these relics, and she promised herself that, if she found time, she would learn more about them and their roles in Desertera's history. She wondered if maybe, just maybe, her actions would earn her a spot in history, too.

When Aya reached the shops, she halted. The row of stores lined the entire length of the wide corridor, and they had been built to look exactly like the metal versions of the Portside shops—complete with awnings to shade the nobles from the sun. Ha! The only light came from the candle chandeliers hanging from the ceiling and the large door at the end of the corridor, which opened to extend a drawbridge to Starboard-shire, much like the Portside entrance the merchants used.

Shaking her head, Aya strolled over to the mask maker's shop. It was easy to spot, with a broad awning in the shape of an eye mask with long, pointed sides. It even had windows so that customers could peer inside. One window displayed the various masks, arranged by color and design, and the other showed a little wooden desk littered with tools—no doubt the mask maker's workshop.

Aya entered the shop to find King Archon sampling the masks. The king sat on a dark blue ottoman in the center of the store, wearing a green mask in the shape of a lizard's head. His blue eyes and pointed beard peeked out from behind the lizard's face, and the sight of them made Aya's skin crawl. The mask maker, a bent-over old man with a long gray beard and warped hands, fluttered around the king, bringing and taking away masks at his request.

When he saw Aya, the mask maker paused to give a small bow. "I'll be with you in a moment, miss. Feel free to browse while I attend to His Majesty."

"Take your time, sir." Aya absorbed herself in examining the many intricate masks. She ignored King Archon's presence, a trick Dellwyn assured her would drive him mad.

"Every man hates being ignored," Dellwyn had said. "And they hate even more to think they are no longer a god in your eyes."

Aya lifted a sparkling golden mask from its peg. It covered the entire face. Even the eye slits were enclosed by a thin white film. Aya heard heavy footsteps coming toward her, and shortly after, she felt a brush against her arm. King Archon had come to stand next to her.

"I figured you would look for something more aquatic, Miss Wellman." King Archon chuckled. "A fish. Or a bucket, perhaps."

"Oh, Your Majesty." Aya kept her tone quiet, aloof. "I didn't notice you standing there."

King Archon huffed. He silent for a moment. Aya heard him inhale deeply and saw him incline his head toward her in her peripheral vision. "How did you like my mask?"

"The lizard?" Aya wrinkled her nose. "It was quite off-putting, not exactly the charming face one would expect of a king."

"Isn't that the point of a masquerade? To be what one is not?"

Aya smirked. "Then perhaps you should keep searching."

Trick number two from Dellwyn: gentle jabs to the ego make men desire the reparation of their manhood. King Archon huffed again, crossing his arms over his chest.

Aya placed the golden mask back on its peg and moved

over to the flower section. One of the masks was designed like a desert wildflower, with its spindly petals fading from lavender to pink, like an inward sunset. Aya did not recognize the flowers on the other masks. There was a bright yellow one with wide, silky petals and red tips. Another was pure white with long, rounded petals circling a yellow center. Aya wondered if these flowers still existed in the palace or if they were inspired by paintings of the world before.

The mask maker attempted to get King Archon's attention, but the king waved him away and followed Aya. "Flowers? A typical choice for a lady."

"Oh, I would never wear one of these." Aya flicked a petal. "Much too showy. But I do like to study the flowers I have never seen in person."

Trick number three: deny any assumptions about your character. Once a man thinks he has you figured out, he will lose interest and move onto the next plaything. Aya guessed this must be especially true of King Archon, given how quickly he disposed of his wives.

Pity. She had actually thought the flower masks to be gorgeous.

"Which ones are you considering, then?" The king stepped closer.

Aya gave a demure smile, placing one of the floral masks over her face. "If I tell you which one I shall wear, won't that defeat the purpose of the masquerade?"

"I suppose you are right. I'll have to identify you by other means." The king returned her smile, letting his cold gaze roam down her figure.

Aya felt a jolt in the center of her chest, and her muscles grew tense. She focused on keeping her face frozen. "You can try."

The mask maker returned with a different mask, and this time, King Archon followed him back to the ottoman. After a few more minutes, the king paid the mask maker and made to leave. "Good luck finding your mask, Miss Wellman." The king's gaze took one final sweep over her. "I hope it suits you."

"I have no doubt that it will, Your Majesty. Good day."

When King Archon turned, Aya rolled her eyes and returned to browsing the masks. That seemed to have gone well—better than last time, at least. She didn't really care to analyze or dwell. She had a mission.

"I apologize for the wait, miss," the mask maker said.

"Not to worry." Aya turned to him and smiled. "I know as well as anyone that we must all yield to our king."

The old man studied Aya, stroking his beard. "I have not dressed your face before. I never forget a face."

"You haven't. I'm new to the palace. Lord Varick recently took me in as his ward." Aya watched the old man's face for some sign of judgment, but he remained only thoughtful and pleasant.

"Ah, that explains it then." He smiled. "What is your name?"

"Aya. Aya Wellman."

"Pleasure to meet you, Miss Wellman. My name is Abrim." Abrim stretched out his arms. "Welcome to my humble shop."

"Thank you." Aya curtsied.

"All right. Now that we have the formalities out of the way," Abrim began, rubbing his hands together, "how would you like a mask for the ball?"

Aya grinned. "I would like one very much."

Abrim took Aya's hand and led her over to the ottoman. She sat down, and he gave it a gentle shove. The ottoman twirled lazily, allowing Aya to take in each section of masks.

"When you see something you like, I shall stop. Of course, if you begin to feel dizzy, do let me know."

Aya nodded. She watched the sections unfold before her—masks of solid colors, masks painted like the sky, masks mirroring real human faces. When the ottoman turned her to the animal section, Aya asked Abrim to stop. Her eyes had spied a friendly face. She pointed to the one she liked, and Abrim brought it to her. He helped her place it over her face and fasten it in the back. He held up a looking glass for her inspection.

Much to Aya's delight, she saw a smiling frog face, much like Charlie's, staring back at her. Her green eyes looked radiant against the bronze, and Aya thought they were the perfect swampy color to imitate the drawings of real frogs her father had shown her.

"It is fun," Abrim said. "But what a shame to cover so much of your pretty face."

Before Aya could answer, another voice cut in. "I agree."

Aya turned around to see Willem leaning against the shop's doorframe. Hidden behind her mask, Aya allowed herself to smirk as she took in the sight of him—his tall, lean frame, sharp gray suit, and warm hazel eyes. If it weren't for the protection of the mask, her entire face would have blushed as red as her toga.

"Good to see you again, Willem."

"And you, Aya." Willem bit his lip as though fighting back a smile.

"You recognize me?" Aya lifted her chin. "Even in the guise of a frog?"

"Of course." Willem chuckled. "I couldn't ever forget those emerald eyes of yours."

Mask or no mask, Aya's skin most certainly matched her toga now.

"I'm glad to see that you are planning to attend the ball." Willem stepped into the shop.

Aya crossed her arms. "Did you fear that I would back out of our agreement?"

"No, I trust you." Willem held up his hands. "Perhaps I should have said that I'm simply glad to see you again. And though I cannot see your whole face, you seem to be in much better spirits this time."

"Yes, I am. Thank you."

Abrim walked over to Willem, taking a long look up at his face. Aya assumed the old man must be growing hard of sight, or maybe he simply wanted a better look at Willem's face to outfit it for a mask.

"I'll be right with you, Mr. Willem." Abrim stretched out his name, making it three syllables instead of two.

"Thank you, Abrim. Thank you."

The mask maker waved his hand. "How are Lord Collingwood's bakeries doing? I hear they are dealing with the overflow of pastries that the palace chefs cannot handle."

"They're managing quite well." Willem tugged at his jacket sleeves. "I believe they're happy to have the extra income."

Abrim nodded. Aya glanced between the two men, wondering why Abrim would care about the bakers in Portside. For her part, Aya cared about gathering whatever insight she could into Dellwyn's most loyal customer. Before Aya could formulate an appropriate question, Abrim had turned back to her. "Now, Miss Wellman, you have a fondness for the animals, yes?"

"Most definitely."

The mask maker looked between Aya and Willem. He untied Aya's frog mask and lifted it off her face. "Would you allow me to make you a special mask? I wouldn't charge Lord Varick a cent over the regular price. I simply think that a face as beautiful as yours should be accented, not hidden, by one of these animal faces."

"Oh, that's not necessary." Aya placed a hand over her heart. "Truly, I am honored just to wear one of your artful designs. I require nothing special."

"Nonsense." Abrim shook his head. "I want to do this. You have inspired me."

Aya looked at Willem for assistance. He chuckled. "I have known Abrim a long time. There is no talking him out of this."

Aya sighed. "Fine then. But please, don't go to too much trouble."

"It will be no trouble at all. In fact, I shall begin work right now." Abrim tottered over to his workshop, the frog mask still in his hand. "I trust you can select your own mask, Wil-le-em?"

Willem nodded. With that, Abrim closed the door to his workshop, leaving Aya and Willem alone amongst the masks.

"I'm sorry Abrim abandoned you." Aya frowned. "I have no clue what got into him."

"I do." Willem sat down next to Aya. "As he said, you inspired him."

"I'm sure." Aya rolled her eyes. "Are you this much of a flirt with all the ladies?"

It was Willem's turn to blush. He looked down at his feet like a boy chastised for spilling a cup of water. "Is my flirting with you a problem?"

"No." Aya nudged his arm. "I'm just trying to figure you out."

"And maybe my silver tongue is trying to loosen yours." Willem smiled.

Aya sucked in an audible breath, letting it out in a laugh. "You have a line for everything, don't you?"

"Yes," Willem stated, deadpan.

"Then tell me this," Aya began, allowing her face to turn serious. "Why did Abrim say your name so oddly?"

"What do you mean?"

"He stretched it out. Wil-le-em," Aya mimicked, watching Willem's hazel eyes travel to the exaggerated flicks of her tongue.

"Oh, that." Willem rubbed the back of his neck. "It's an old joke of his. He finds my name strange, because it is 'Willem' instead of 'William.' He's always said it that way."

His answer seemed odd to Aya, but she nodded anyway. As she did, the aroma of the bath oils wafted from her curls. Willem leaned in closer and inhaled. "You smell heavenly."

"I know." Aya's eyes widened, and she put her hand over her mouth. "I'm sorry. That was arrogant of me. It's just…I haven't felt this clean and pretty in a long time."

Willem brushed a curl over her shoulder. "It shows. You are much more confident than the last time I saw you. It's very becoming."

Aya tilted her head. "I do feel changed. Though, I don't think the bath oils should get all the credit."

"What else has happened in such a short time?" Willem squinted at her.

"A lot. A lot can happen in two days."

Willem gaze flitted between her eyes and lips. Aya wanted to close the distance between them, but the possibility of passerby outside the shop kept her in place.

Instead, she returned to her unspoken musing. "Why did Abrim ask you about Lord Collingwood's bakeries?"

Willem froze, his brow furrowing. "Oh, um, I help oversee the management of many of the merchants' shops."

"But why did he ask about those specifically?" Aya wondered if Willem had some sort of familial connection with Lord Collingwood. Somehow, the thought made her feel proud, to know that she could attract an equal caliber of man as Dellwyn.

"Lord Collingwood and I are rather close. I pay a bit more attention to his businesses than the others, which is probably unjust of me. So don't tell anyone." Willem whispered the last sentence, leaning in closer.

Aya would not be deterred. "How close? Are you family?"

"I think the better question is, 'which nobles are not family?'" Willem laughed. Aya kept her face sincere, and Willem's gay expression slowly faded. "Why are you so curious?"

"I'm trying to loosen that silver tongue of yours," Aya joked. She looked down, fiddling with the fabric of her toga. "I like you."

Willem placed his hand over hers. "I like you, too, Aya."

With his other hand, he placed a finger under her chin, lifting her gaze to his. For a moment, Aya thought he would kiss her. "But if you keep asking questions, you're going to ruin my man-of-mystery act."

Aya squinted and scrunched her nose.

"He's my uncle." Willem squeezed her hand. "As he has no sons, I am legally his heir."

Aya smirked, feeling a petty pride at the fact that the younger, future patriarch of the Collingwood family found her so alluring. Of course, if Willem met Dellwyn, he would probably drop Aya like a poisonous toad. She pushed the thought from her mind, enjoying his attention while she held it. "Was that so difficult?"

"I suppose not." Willem removed his hand from hers. "Well, Aya, I guess I should select my mask before Abrim comes back in here and throws me out of his shop."

Aya's heart fell. She hoped he wasn't upset that she had pried. The last thing she wanted was for him to think she only cared for his title or wealth. "I suppose you should."

"But I will see you at the masquerade?"

Aya beamed. At least he was still interested in his reserved dance. "If you can find me through my magic mask."

Willem laughed. "I told you. Those eyes won't let you escape. I will find them for my dance."

"I hope so." Aya stood, adjusting the skirt of her toga. "I shall see you then."

Willem rose as well, taking her hand in his and placing a light kiss on her knuckles. "In two days." He looked up at her with his hazel eyes. The hint of green was back, burning through the brown.

Aya sighed, feeling as though her body were full of warm air. "In two days."

9

"*V*arick, slow down!"

Aya stumbled, her body lurching forward as Lord Varick pulled her through the busy corridor. She glanced down to the floor, where the hem of her dress had been torn by a hurried misstep of her toe. Luckily, she was only wearing the hideous ensemble of Lord Varick's house colors and not her beautiful toga from the bathhouse.

"I'm sorry, Aya, but we have to hurry. King Archon will be livid if we are late!"

Apparently, Varick wasn't the only noble concerned about the king's temper. Anxious nobles surrounded Aya and Lord Varick, all caught in a rough gait, going as fast as possible without breaking propriety to run. Together, in their dark house colors, they looked like a murder of crows flying through a strong wind.

Murder.

Aya wondered if she would see a murder today. She had been in the stern estate's kitchen, learning how to make meat pies with Mrs. Lemot, when Lord Varick had burst through the doorway. His face had been bright red, his beady eyes entirely black, as he tapped his walking staff on the floor. He had informed Aya to change into the house uniform immediately. As they left the estate, Aya had managed to squeeze out one sentence, and one alone, from the rushed nobleman.

"King Archon is conducting a trial."

The words made Aya shiver, and she had been as eager as Lord Varick to hurry to the courtroom. However, after the first few flights of stairs, Aya's heels had begun to pinch her feet, and she could barely keep up the pace without stepping on her dress.

Just as Aya was about to complain again, the nobles in front of them stopped walking. Over the tops of their hats and coiffed hair, Aya spied a set of wooden doors. As she and Lord Varick filtered through behind the rest of the crowd, the courtroom came into sight. The room was entirely round with a throne on a raised platform in the center and two tables with chairs placed before the royal seat. High walls with rows of benches at the top encircled the furniture. Lord Varick led Aya up to these benches, and they seated themselves near the entrance with a direct view of the throne. Other nobles filed in until the benches were filled.

As the nobles' chatter grew louder, Lord Varick leaned in close to Aya. "I know this is going to be difficult for you, my dear. However, I want you to remember, what happens today will be much like what happened to your father—and almost identical to what will happen to us, should our plot be revealed."

Under the protection of the crowd's volume, Aya allowed herself to speak plainly. "My father's trial took place in this room?"

Varick nodded.

Aya swallowed. "Did you see it?"

"Yes."

"Did he get a chance to plead his case?" Aya placed a hand over her upset stomach. "Did anyone come to his defense?"

Before Varick could answer, the crowd fell silent. Three

nobles entered the courtroom, two of them escorted by palace guards. One of the persons, a middle-aged man with an upturned gray mustache, went to the table to Aya's right. The other two individuals, a younger man with a bald head, and a young woman with waist-length black hair, were escorted by the guards to sit together at the table on Aya's left.

Aya felt Varick's hot breath on her cheek.

"Left is for guilty," he informed her. "Right is for innocent."

Aya cocked her head toward Varick. "Don't you mean for accused and accuser?"

"One and the same."

The nobles rose, and Lord Varick grabbed Aya's elbow to pull her upright. The short bishop from Queen Zedara's greeting ceremony entered the room. He opened his arms wide, his white robes hanging limp from his scrawny arms, and bowed. "My lords and ladies."

Aya jumped at the strength of his voice booming throughout the courtroom, and she wondered how so much sound emitted from such a little man.

"You have been summoned here today to witness the trial of Lady Jauntley and her alleged lover, Lord Pottsmore." The bishop clapped his hands together twice. The clinking of his many rings echoed through the courtroom. "I call to the Throne of Judgment His Majesty, King Archon Lionel Monashe, ruler of Desertera."

King Archon entered from a doorway behind the throne. He wore his signature cog-embroidered top hat and a black suit. Aya imagined his white cravat was a noose, and she smiled at the thought of it tightening around his neck. As King Archon reached the center of the room, the bishop bowed again and exited. The king bowed to the nobles and took his seat on the throne. As he did, the nobles sat down on their benches. The three individuals on trial, however, remained standing.

"It begins," Varick whispered.

King Archon cleared his throat, and Aya felt goose bumps rise on her skin as his gravelly voice issued throughout the room. "Lady Katlyn Jauntley, you have been accused of adultery. How do you plead?"

"Innocent, Your Majesty." To Aya's surprise, Lady Jauntley's voice did not shake. It was defiant.

"Very well. Lord Aron Pottsmore, you have been accused of aiding Lady Jauntley's adultery. How do you plead?"

"Innocent, Your Majesty." Lord Pottsmore's voice, Aya noticed, did quiver.

"I see. Lord Enok Jauntley, you accuse your wife and Lord Pottsmore of these crimes. Is that correct?"

Lord Jauntley cast a cold glance at the accused lovers. "Yes, Your Majesty."

King Archon nodded. "The accused may sit. Please make your case, Lord Jauntley."

As Lord Jauntley waited for his wife and her alleged lover to settle, Varick leaned into Aya again. "Listen and watch carefully, my dear. King Archon will do most of the talking, and it will be over before you know it."

Aya's nostrils flared. "How is that possible?"

"*Shh.*" Lord Varick patted her knee. "Watch."

Aya's mouth went slack, a dozen question unspoken. What about the finer details of the case? What about witnesses? Surely King Archon would have to call on witnesses, the same way the merchants in Portside always asked for bystanders when someone was accused of stealing. And what about deliberation? Everyone knew the king was the sole judge of crimes of this caliber—unlike in civil crimes when a group of merchants or farmers would decide the punishment—but did he not need time to think?

Aya nearly laughed at her naivety. Of course he didn't. The king had his mind made up about her father before he even walked into Prince Lionel's room that day. Papa's trial had been an inconvenient formality, political theatre.

Lord Jauntley bowed to the nobles. "My lords and ladies, please forgive this intrusion on your lives. However, I simply could not let our fine nation's laws be so violated once I found out the truth." Lord Jauntley paused, shaking his head as he stared at the accused. "My wife, Lady Jauntley, intends to divorce me so that she can be with her *true love*, Lord Pottsmore." Lord Jauntley could not have said "true love" more sarcastically if his life had depended upon it.

"Divorce is not a crime," Aya whispered. "As scandalous as it may be, people have divorced to avoid adultery. The king can't have her killed for that, can he?"

"Just watch."

King Archon straightened on his throne. "She may divorce you if she wishes." King Archon turned his cold eyes on Lady Jauntley, and Aya saw within them the same manipulative malice as when he had questioned Papa.

"Lady Jauntley, since your husband will not be direct, you tell me. Have you had sex with Lord Pottsmore while engaged in matrimony with Lord Jauntley?"

Lady Jauntley stood, her head high and voice steady. "I do not believe Lord Jauntley and I are properly married, Your Majesty."

King Archon guffawed. "Lady Jauntley, I attended your marriage ceremony. I blessed your union myself."

Lady Jauntley glanced in her husband's direction before staring down at the table. "Yes, Your Majesty. However, Lord Jauntley and I, even after a year, we have never…"

"Spit it out, Katlyn."

"We never consummated our marriage, Your Majesty." Lady Jauntley looked up at the king, and Aya noticed the sad catch in the lady's voice. "Enok won't touch me."

King Archon's eyes widened, and he turned them on Lord Jauntley, who looked down at his feet. The courtroom was silent for a moment. Then King Archon burst out in laughter. He carried on until tears streamed down his face.

While the king laughed, Lord Varick nudged Aya. She tore her eyes away from the trial to follow Lord Varick's pointed finger.

"There's the prince. He came in late, of course, but he's sitting in the back. If you look past the throne, you can see him."

Aya craned her neck. "What does he look like?"

"He has a top hat. There is an ugly little redhead with him."

Aya shifted to her left, and she finally saw the prince. For some reason, his appearance surprised her. He did not look as she remembered, but then again, she had only seen him once and on the worst day of her life. He wore a plain black top hat with a large black feather sticking out of a satin band. The only features he shared with his father seemed to be his sharp nose and an affinity for pointed beards. He leaned into whisper to the girl seated next to him. She was pretty, of course, but she looked far too young to be courted. Then again, if the prince took after his father, as the rumors indicated, Aya knew better than to be shocked.

When Aya's eyes landed on the girl's other side, her heart leaped. Seated next to the childish redhead was Willem. He was fussing with his hair, which kept flopping defiantly over one eye. As he did so, the top hat resting in his lap threatened to fall to the floor, and he had to scramble to grab it before it fell. Aya pressed her lips together and repressed a giggle. He was adorable when he was flustered.

As much as Aya would have loved to watch Willem for the rest of the trial, her attention was taken away by a sudden silence. King Archon had stopped laughing, and now that he had decided to compose himself, he had done it so quickly that his laughter still echoed throughout the court as he delivered his judgment.

"So your argument, Lady Jauntley, is that you are not truly married to your husband because he refuses to bed you?"

"Yes, Your Majesty."

King Archon raised his eyebrows. "And therefore, your bedding of Lord Pottsmore is innocent?"

Lady Jauntley gathered her long, black hair between her hands and fidgeted with it. "I never said that we—"

King Archon held up his hand. "But you implied it. Whether you did or not, you have led me to believe that you have had a sexual affair."

Lord Pottsmore stood up. The sun from the skylight glinted against his bald head. "Your Majesty, I swear to you that Lady Jauntley's honor is intact."

King Archon glowered at the interruption. "Lord Pottsmore, did I address you?"

Lord Pottsmore fell silent.

"Lady Jauntley," King Archon continued, "intercourse or no, under our divine law, you are your husband's property, as he is yours. I believe that you were too impatient to wait for your husband to exercise your bodily rights and turned to fulfill your lustful desires elsewhere. I sentence you to execution."

If Aya hadn't been sitting, her knees would have buckled right alongside Lady Jauntley's. The lady fell to the floor, weeping. Lord Pottsmore bent down and held her in his arms.

"And there is my proof." King Archon pointed at the couple. "Lord Pottsmore, your loving actions support my suspicions. I charge you with aiding Lady Jauntley in adultery and sentence you to execution."

Somewhere at the surface of her consciousness, Aya felt her mouth hanging open and her head shaking slowly back and forth—but her mind no longer lingered in the courtroom. King Archon's pronouncements had sent her back to that day with her father, when Prince Lionel had said the words that would end her Papa's life. Her vision blurred, and she could not tell whether she merely cried or was about to faint. She heard the prince's words echo in her head, over and over. *We execute them.*

And that was just the past. What would happen to *her* if she took a misstep with the king? Would he execute her for merely flirting with him? How far would Queen Zedara let their flirtation go before she accused Aya of attempting adultery? Aya imagined herself in Lady Jauntley's place, giving a one-sentence plea before the king snapped his fingers and sent her out the door to execution.

Lord Varick shook Aya's shoulder, and she felt herself lurch back into reality. Aya quickly became aware of two facts: her hand was clutched around her neck, and someone in the courtroom was screaming. Aya released her grip and looked down. The guards had returned, and they were attempting to separate Lady Jauntley and Lord Pottsmore. The couple clung to each other. As the guards ripped them apart, their fingernails left slender, red trails on each other's pale arms. Aya could not make out the words they shouted to each other, but she understood them. She, too, had said such words.

When the guards finally dragged the couple out separate doors, the courtroom once again fell silent. Lord Jauntley still stood behind his table, staring at the doorway through which his wife had vanished. Aya could guess his thoughts. Lord Jauntley was imagining his wife's head being lopped off by the executioner, seeing it flop to the floor, watching the blood spurt from her open neck. Aya did not think a noble could go a year without intercourse, and she wondered if perhaps Lord Jauntley were as guilty as his wife, only choosing a more devious route to secure his innocence. From his furrowed brow and agape mouth, Aya could not tell whether Lord Jauntley faced the gravity of what he had done to two people or the gravity of his newfound freedom.

King Archon broke the silence. "Lord Jauntley." The soon-to-be widower turned to the king, holding out his hands as if he carried a body draped over his arms. "I proclaim you innocent. However, I strongly advise you to put your pecker in your next wife the moment you get her home from the wedding."

Lord Jauntley nodded, his eyes looking past the king into another space. King Archon returned the gesture with a curt nod of his own before rising from his throne and striding out of the courtroom. With the king departed, the nobles began to file out of the benches, chattering about the excitement of the trial. Aya and Lord Varick stayed seated, the nobles parting around them like a sand slide slipping around an unmovable boulder.

Aya had no words for what had transpired. She knew now what her father's trial must have been like—Prince Lionel standing at the right-hand table, saying one sentence to condemn the cogsmith, and her father standing at the other, speaking to deaf ears. Part of her wished she would have been there to support her father, but the smarter part knew that her young mouth probably would have gotten her executed alongside him. No, it was better this way. Aya needed to see this trial now so it would be sharp in her mind, so the memory would still throb like a fresh wound the next time she saw the king, so it would keep her from stepping out of line and losing her own head.

No statements. No witnesses. No council of peers.

Varick turned to Aya and placed his hand on hers. "Did that answer your questions?"

10

———

*A*ya spent the entire next day distracting herself from anything related to a trial—be it the one she witnessed or the ones she imagined. Lord Varick thought it best for Aya to stay within the estate while she processed her emotions, and although she did not like being confined, she did appreciate the excuse to delay her next encounter with King Archon. After their meeting at Abrim's shop, Aya knew the king was interested in her. However, now that she seen King Archon's brutality again, Aya needed time to recuperate before she could convincingly feign desire for him.

Lord Varick was out on business. Aya did not know what business the noblemen had, especially since they were all born into rich families and didn't seem to have any productive role in Desertera society—other than bossing around commoners—but she was grateful for the time alone. She amused herself by browsing through the books in Lord Varick's small library.

Aya did not have much experience with books. Like water, wood was a rare commodity in Desertera, and most of the existing books were survivors from the world before. Someone had once told Aya that the palace's bookbinder still had pages of blank parchment from the old world, which could be sewn into the backs of existing books to extend them. Someone else had told her that the bookbinder had resorted to using new materials to create parchment, specifically skin from dead livestock, but she didn't know if she believed either tale.

As Aya scanned Lord Varick's library, she found a book entitled *The Monarchy*. She opened it to find an entire lineage of the royal family. It began with rulers from the world before, names that Aya had never heard. Toward the back of the book, the paper protruded from the edges. These were the pages that the first Desertera bookbinder had added. They began with Queen Hildegard and her husband, who was executed for adultery, and went all the way down the line to King Archon, his first wife, the late Queen Lisandra, and their son, Prince Lionel. The book had not been updated to include Queen Lisandra's death or any of the king's subsequent wives. Aya thought this was wise, considering it would have been a huge waste of a scarce resource to chronicle King Archon's exploits.

Aya remembered when Queen Lisandra died. Aya had been around seven years old, and her father had had a difficult time explaining to her what it meant that the queen had taken her own life. King Archon had ordered the entire kingdom to wear black to mourn his wife. Aya had hated the black dress her father had bought for her; it attracted the sun's rays as animal dung attracted flies. She'd had a sunburn for the entire mourning period.

At the time, her father had told her to feel sorry for the royal family. After all, Aya and her father knew their pain— Aya's own mother had died attempting to birth Aya's younger brother, who did not survive either. However, Aya couldn't help feeling jealous of Prince Lionel. He got to know his mother for nearly a decade, and when she did die, the entire kingdom mourned alongside him and his father. When Aya's mother died, Aya and her father simply received a cake from one of the bakers and pitiful looks in the street.

Now, Aya couldn't muster any sympathy for Prince Lionel. After the way he'd ordered her father's execution so easily—and then shown up at poor Lady Jauntley's trial yesterday with that young girl—Aya hoped he grieved his mother's death and every death of every stepmother. It wasn't so surprising that Queen Lisandra took her own life. With a monster for a husband and a compassionless coward for a son, Aya might have done the same.

When evening came, Aya received a dance lesson from Mrs. Lemot and a visit from the dressmaker. Lord Varick had insisted that Aya learn the noble dances, as simply following a man's lead would not do. She had to be perfect, he had said, the most desirable creature at the masquerade, to keep the king's interest. Aya didn't mind dancing, and the maid was a good teacher, so the exercise was a happy distraction.

Her visit with the dressmaker was not nearly as entertaining. The old woman came in, took measurements of Aya's entire body, and left without saying more than "Raise arm. Lower arm." Her unsociability had Aya rather worried about how her dress would turn out. But anything had to be better than the ugly black and purple ensemble.

THE NEXT EVENING, Aya and Lord Varick dined on a platter of fruit, vegetables, goat cheese, and thin crispy slabs of wheat he called crackers. Lord Varick insisted Aya sample all the foods she had missed out on throughout her life. Aya felt guilty about the extra expense Lord Varick was doubtless accruing to obtain such a variety of foods for her, but instead of insisting he stop, she ensured he did not waste a single coin—by devouring everything she was given.

"I apologize for the lack of protein. But I felt it best to keep the meal light this evening. We don't need your corset straining as you dance."

Aya glanced between the cracker in her hand and her stomach as if they were conducting a conspiracy of their own. While she was used to clients and her fellow courtesans commenting on her body—a necessity of her occupation—she had never been told to watch her figure. She was one of the smallest girls at the Rudder, and based on the few noblewomen she had seen wandering the palace, she held her waistline in even higher esteem. If anything, most of her coworkers told her to eat more to fill out her bosom and hips.

Aya looked Lord Varick in his dark eyes as she placed a square of cheese on her cracker and popped both into her mouth. "My corset is the one thing about tonight that does not trouble me. Nor should it you."

Lord Varick opened his mouth to speak, but he was interrupted by Mrs. Lemot entering the room. She had a long black bag draped over both her arms. A smaller bag, this one made of red silk, perched on top of the black one.

"Miss Aya, your dress and mask have arrived."

"Well then." Aya stood up and dusted cracker crumbs off her skirt. "I think it is time to put that corset to work."

Aya followed Mrs. Lemot into her bedroom. Mrs. Lemot untied the garment bag to reveal a floor-length satin dress. The color struck Aya first—a rich, blood red that made her heart throb. She loved it.

As she put the dress on, Aya traced her fingers along the fabric, feeling the boning of a corset constructed into the bodice. Criss-crossing black laces adorned the front of the bodice, woven through silver eyelets. The dress had a high collar, but the chest was cut open to reveal Aya's entire décolletage. The neckline, lined in black lace, swooped low, a bit lower than Aya thought was proper. At the hips, the dress expanded out into the shape of a bell.

With Mrs. Lemot's help, Aya put on black silk stockings and low black heels. Once the maid had arranged Aya's brown curls into a sophisticated bun, she unveiled Aya's mask. The mask looked like bird wings. The feathers around Aya's eyes were black, and they gradually faded into maroon then scarlet toward the tips of the wings. It covered the area around Aya's eyes and cheeks, but the crown of her head and the tip of her nose down to her chin remained visible. The maid held up a looking glass for her. Aya knew that King Archon—and of course, Willem—would still be able to identify her, but the mask added a touch of mystery.

When Aya emerged from her room, Lord Varick was also dressed. He wore the same amethyst velvet suit he had worn the night he came to the Rudder. His mask contained two parts. Covering his eyes were a pair of black goggles. A metal plate adorned with bronze and silver cogs concealed his mouth and chin. Only his forehead and cheekbones remained exposed. He looked like a mechanical monster.

"Miss Aya, you are absolutely ravishing!" Lord Varick's voice was muffled behind his mask, making his exclamation throaty and deep.

"Thank you." Aya forced herself to smile. "Your mask is interesting. I've never seen one in two pieces before."

Lord Varick tapped his chin. "This way, my expressions are entirely my own."

Aya repressed a shudder. "Shall we go?"

"So anxious, Miss Aya." Lord Varick held out his arm. She took it, making a point to stare into the dark panes of glass over his eyes.

"Yes, yes, let us go," he continued. "I would hate to keep the king waiting on his destiny."

When Aya and Lord Varick arrived outside of the ballroom, noblemen and women already filled the room. The short bishop greeted Aya and Lord Varick. Aya wondered if he were the only religious figure in the palace and why exactly he was involved in every noble gathering.

The bishop held a large, steel scepter with a golden cog as its topper. As Aya and Lord Varick passed through the doors, the bishop banged his staff against the marble floor three times. "Lord Varick, Marquess of the Stern, and Miss Aya Wellman, his ward."

Some nobles stopped dancing to peer through the crowd, no doubt trying to glimpse Lord Varick and his new ward. However, most of the nobles kept dancing and drinking, too caught up in the merrymaking to pay attention to who came in with whom.

Lord Varick led Aya behind the procession of other newly arrived nobles to greet the royal family, who perched atop a platform in the middle of the room. King Archon sat in the middle throne, raised an extra step. Queen Zedara sat to his left, but the throne to his right was empty. At the sight of the empty throne, Aya scoffed. No doubt Prince Lionel was off with his little redhead.

The dancers twirled around the royal family's raised platform in couples and quartets. They weaved in and around the line of waiting nobles, the ladies' skirts brushing up against the standers' ankles as they twirled by. Aya couldn't help looking around at these fine people in their fine clothes with their elaborate masks and full cups and think how wasteful it all was. People in Sternville would kill for the drops of water mixed in with the nobles' juices and alcohol.

When King Archon motioned for Aya and Lord Varick to step forward, Aya put on her most neutral face. Dellwyn had told Aya to keep playing uninterested until the king came to her, which was about all the civility Aya could manage after the trial. Dellwyn had assured Aya, over and over again, that the king's curiosity and ego would overcome his pride.

"Your Highness." Lord Varick bowed. "You make the most adorable bunny rabbit."

It was true. Queen Zedara looked fetching in her white bunny mask with its long, pointed ears—one sticking straight up toward the sky, the other coyly cocked. She reminded Aya of the talking animal fairy tales Papa used to tell her.

Queen Zedara smiled. "Lord Varick, with that silver tongue of yours, you should have dressed as a fox."

Lord Varick chuckled before turning his attention to King Archon. "Your Majesty, you, on the other hand, look as vicious as any lion in the mythical savanna."

King Archon chuckled and stroked his mask's whiskers.

Once again, Lord Varick was spot on. King Archon's snarling lion mask looked menacing. Aya had heard stories about lions, ancient creatures associated with royalty, and it seemed so cruel to her that nature might once have taken something as sweet and companionable as a cat and turned it into a ferocious monarch. The king's mask covered his entire face—a mane of horsehair concealed his head, and a fang-filled sneer hid his mouth. Only King Archon's blue eyes protruded, but they were enough to chill her blood.

Aya took a deep breath before speaking. "Your Highness, you are as gorgeous as ever. You make every woman in this ballroom bubble over with envy."

Queen Zedara shifted, crossing her ankles. "You scrub up well yourself, Miss Wellman. Enjoy the party."

"Thank you." Aya breathed deeply to contain the blush the queen's curtness threatened to create. She turned to the king, using every ounce of her willpower to look him in the eyes. "Your Majesty, you look well. Will Prince Lionel be joining us this evening?"

"Oh, he is out there in the crowd." King Archon waved his hand over the gathered nobles. "I'm sure he's already found a lovely lady to court for the evening."

"To be young and unattached, eh, Your Majesty?" Lord Varick wiggled his eyebrows.

"Humph." King Archon shrugged and turned back to Aya. "Miss Wellman, how do you like my final mask selection?"

"It's fitting. A kingly pride animal for a proud king."

King Archon cocked his head. "Better than the lizard?"

Queen Zedara's head snapped to face her husband before slowly turning to stare down at Aya. Aya did her best to avoid the queen's glare. If the queen began to suspect something was brewing between Aya and the king, the entire operation could be compromised. Personally, Aya hoped Queen Zedara would jump to conclusions, fill with rage, and kill King Archon in his sleep. Then Aya wouldn't have to put up with the torture of letting him grope her—with his eyes or his hands.

Aya dared a smirk. "I think the lion is much more representative of the face you want your kingdom to see."

"Good. As my wife said, you are stunning tonight, Miss Wellman. Please, enjoy your evening, and perhaps we shall meet on the dance floor."

Aya's eyes widened. "I hope not too soon."

"Oh?" King Archon sat up straighter.

"My first dance has been claimed." Aya batted her eyelashes. "I am bound to my partner by my womanly honor, and I would hate to have to deny my king."

King Archon leaned forward on his throne, as if he might ask who had reserved Aya's dance, but Queen Zedara set her hand on his, and he reclined. "You heard Miss Wellman, darling. Best let her find her dance partner."

King Archon nodded, his blue eyes narrowed behind his mask. "Indeed."

Aya curtsied, Lord Varick bowed, and they wove their way through the throng of dancers to the drink table. Once they each had a glass of wine in hand, Aya turned to Varick. "You were quiet back there."

"I was happy to let you lead. And you were *brilliant*. That bit about your first dance being reserved was genius. I thought

Archon would jump from his seat with jealousy. Now you just have to find a lucky chap to play your suitor."

"That part wasn't a lie." Aya lifted her glass, examining the color of the wine to avoid Varick's gaze. "I met a nice man in the mask shop after the king left. He asked for a dance, and I thought it might make the king jealous."

Lord Varick took a sip of his wine. Aya wished she could see through his goggles to discern whether his eyes shone with pride or irritation. "Clever thinking, Miss Aya. But do not let yourself get distracted from the mission. You can do all the fraternizing you like once it is finished. In the meantime, you are claimed by the king."

It was Aya's turn to stall her response with a drink. "Yes, I know. As I said, this man is merely a convenient device to aid our plan."

Lord Varick took Aya's glass from her hand. "Well then, you'd better go find your shiny new cog and get him turning in our machine."

11

Aya had no idea how to begin searching for Willem in the bustling crowd of nobles, but she welcomed the opportunity to escape the gaze of Lord Varick's un-seeable eyes. Those beady black orbs were intimidating enough on their own without the dark, thick-paned goggles to add to their obscurity.

As she wandered away from Lord Varick, Aya decided the best tactic for finding Willem would be to circulate on the periphery of the dance floor. She moved slowly, avoiding the swirl of dancers, taking great pains to seem occupied with observing the intricate patterns of the dances. No one stopped to talk to her or ask her for a dance. This was fine with Aya, as she truly did like observing the colorful crowd.

The orchestra music wafted through the ballroom, and Aya stepped in time with it. Musicians stood against the back wall playing ancient instruments—some with metal bodies and brassy sounds, others with wooden bodies and long whines. Up to this point, Aya's only experience with music had been the small parties thrown in Portside, where merchants would beat on makeshift drums and the brewer would pour his bitterest batches, the ones he couldn't sell to the nobles, and everyone would drink and dance a jig. As joyful as this night looked, in comparison to the gatherings at Portside, the masquerade felt foolish, forced.

Once Aya had made her way halfway around the room, behind the thrones but in front of the band, someone tapped her shoulder. Aya turned to see Willem's warm hazel eyes, peering out at her from behind the golden frog mask she'd admired in Abrim's shop.

"Aya." Willem took her hand and placed it against the frog's lips. His voice sounded deeper behind the frog mask, but the change in tone was softer, unlike the hollow rasps produced behind Varick and King Archon's disguises.

"Willem." Aya smiled.

"I am surprised to find you alive and well."

Aya pulled her hand out of his grasp. "Why would you say such a thing?"

"Because," he said, gently retaking her hand, "I cannot believe Queen Zedara would allow a woman whose beauty so vastly outshines hers to breathe in her presence."

Aya rolled her eyes. "I see you are as ridiculous as ever this evening."

Willem smirked. "I believe you mean as astute as ever."

Aya laughed. "I take it you're ready to claim your dance?"

"Ah, so we are both astute." Willem lifted the hand he already held to shoulder height, took her other hand, and placed it on his shoulder. He wrapped his free arm around her waist, pulling her a bit closer to him than was proper. Aya glanced at the other dancers, who were executing a synchronized rendition of the Hildegard waltz.

"We're supposed to be waltzing," Aya hissed. Willem was leading them through a slow, close dance—one that Lord Varick's maid had not taught her. He released her waist, sending her into a single spin then clutching her back to his body.

Aya felt her face pale. "Willem, people are staring."

He kept his eyes on hers. "I don't see anyone else."

Aya knew he meant to be charming, but the attention they attracted made her nervous. The more people noticed her, the more likely it became that someone would recognize her—either now, as the cogsmith's daughter, or later, as King Archon's latest pursuit.

"Stop staring back at them." Willem squeezed her hand. "You're giving them too much satisfaction."

Aya forced herself to look up at Willem.

"How do you like the mask Abrim made for you?"

"It's gorgeous." Aya wrinkled her nose. "Strange but gorgeous."

"Do you know what you are?"

Aya shrugged. "A bird?"

Willem chuckled. "You, love, are not just any bird. You are a phoenix." He placed a finger on the bridge of her nose, where the mask was black. He traced it upward to the tip of the wings. "Rising from your own ashes to bring your fire to a new life."

"That's beautiful," Aya whispered.

Willem winked, returning his hand to her back.

"And I see you have chosen my frog mask. What is the symbolism in that?"

"I was hoping you could tell me." Willem spun her again, and Aya watched the crowd of onlookers and other dancers flash before her eyes in a blur of color and distorted faces.

"What do you mean?" she asked when she returned to Willem's arms.

"Why did you want this mask? Did it mean something to you?"

Aya sighed. "When I was growing up, I had a mechanical frog toy. I adored it dearly, as if it were a real pet. My father had to remind me not to feed it sometimes."

"What happened to him?" Willem traced his fingers along her spine.

Aya paused, trying to keep from shivering beneath his touch. She doubted Willem shared the king's interest in the vortric cog, but she did not know him well enough to trust him with any information about Charlie.

"Oh, I don't know. I hid him away somewhere and never found him again." As the lie slipped through her lips, Aya's stomach twisted. She liked Willem. He had been a good friend —if that's what he was—but she couldn't risk divulging anything too close to the truth.

"No, your father." Willem shook his head. "I'm sorry. That was rude. It's not my business to know how you came into Lord Varick's care."

"It's fine." A heavy weight settled in Aya's chest. "My father died when I was thirteen. I've been laboring to get by ever since. Lord Varick took pity on me, maybe because I remind him of his own daughter."

Willem pursed his lips. "Is that a good thing?"

"Why wouldn't it be?" Aya quirked an eyebrow. "Lord Varick loved his daughter, and now he is showing me kindness in her honor."

Willem's eyes scanned Aya's face, but he didn't say anything more. They danced in silence for a few moments.

"May I ask about your mother?" Willem's voice was soft, and he rubbed Aya's back.

Aya bit her lip. "She died giving birth to my younger brother. He died then, too. I don't remember her well, but my father used to tell me stories. He said I was growing up to look just like her."

Willem smiled. "That's nice. It must make you feel connected to her somehow, to know that whenever you stare into a mirror, a face like hers stares back."

"I never really thought about it." Aya looked down to their feet. "It made my father sad to think about my mother, so I tried to forget about her too."

Willem didn't reply, but when Aya dared to glance up, she saw compassion in his eyes.

Aya took a deep breath. If Willem asked her such personal questions, surely Aya could do the same. "What about your parents? Am I right to assume they are nobility like your uncle?"

"Yes, regrettably." Willem's eyes squinted, as though he were wincing behind his mask. "I'm sorry. That was insensitive. I know I'm lucky to have been born to advantage."

Aya smirked. "Not *everyone* envies the nobles as much as you all think we do."

"You should tell them that." Willem inclined his head toward the onlookers. "To answer your question, my mother died when I was a child. She was murdered."

Aya gasped. "I'm so sorry, Willem." She reached up to place her hand on his cheek. Unlike Charlie's metal face, the side of the mask was warm against her hand.

"And your father?" Aya sucked in her lower lip, hoping the question would not elicit another sad answer.

"He's alive." Willem's eyes showed no emotion.

"What is he like?"

Willem scoffed. "You don't want to know."

Before Aya could respond, she saw a thin finger tap Willem on the shoulder. The couple turned to see Lord Varick's blank glass stare.

"Might I have a dance with my dear ward?"

"Of course, Lord Varick." Willem moved to put Aya's hand to the lips of his mask, but instead, she stretched up on her tiptoes and placed a gentle kiss on its nose. His hazel eyes glowed behind his mask, and Aya felt the heat all the way from her own eyes down to her thighs.

Aya smiled. "Until we meet again."

"I shall count the seconds, Aya." Willem smiled at her, before bowing to Lord Varick. "Good evening."

With that, Willem disappeared into the crowd, and Lord Varick took his place.

"That is some high company you are keeping, my dear." Lord Varick led them in the same dance the other nobles performed. Aya did not know the name or the steps, but it did not seem to require much finesse from the ladies.

"Oh, Willem?" Aya glanced over her shoulder in the direction Willem had gone. "Yes, I know. He told me he is the heir to Lord Collingwood's estate. Dellwyn would never believe it if I told her I had danced with him."

Lord Varick raised his eyebrows. "Is that so?"

Aya cocked her head to the side. "Yes. Why? Is he not someone I should associate with?"

A muffled chuckle emitted from behind Lord Varick's mask. He shook his head and took a few deep breaths through his nose to compose himself.

"What?" Aya stopped dancing, staring up into Lord Varick's goggles.

Lord Varick shook his head again and pulled Aya back into the dance. "Nothing, Miss Aya. It's just..." Lord Varick chuckled again. "Comical. Leave it to the worst seductress in the Rudder to find a highborn suitor when she should be courting the king. I trust that you will be more discreet in the future?"

Aya blushed. "I will. I'm sorry. I told Willem not to dance like that."

Lord Varick shrugged. "You were out of the king's sight. I do not think it did any harm. As long as you are careful from now on, all will be well. I am anxious to watch this unfold."

"Same." Aya wished she had dark goggles to conceal the distrust in her eyes.

"I don't think we will have to wait much longer."

"Why is that?"

Lord Varick inclined his head to Aya's left. She glanced over her shoulder to see that they were dancing in front of the king and queen. She hadn't realized that Lord Varick had already led her halfway around the dancing circle. Aya noticed that King Archon's gaze was fixed on them.

"The king has been watching you ever since we entered his line of sight."

The thought of the king spying on her made Aya's stomach tumble—partially out of disgust and partially out of delight, for his attention meant their plan was working.

Aya and Lord Varick danced in silence for a few more minutes. However, Aya knew this silence was not empty. Varick strategically turned them to and fro, giving the king a view of Aya from every angle and making sure her face showed in his direction whenever she smiled. After a few more turns, Aya glanced up to find the king's throne vacant. She peered through the crowd, and sure enough, King Archon strolled toward them.

"He's coming." Aya's pulse quickened.

Lord Varick's mask prevented her from seeing his mouth, but his raised cheekbones told her he was smiling. Right before the king came into earshot, Lord Varick pulled Aya in for a hug. "Best of luck, my dear," he whispered into her hair.

Aya nodded.

"Lord Varick," King Archon said. "I would like to take a turn with your ward."

Before Lord Varick could respond, Aya piped up. "Should you not ask the ward herself, Your Majesty? Or is Lord Varick to be my voice now?"

Lord Varick's goggles shifted upward. "Your Majesty, please forgive her imprudence. Miss Wellman is not yet versed in ballroom etiquette."

King Archon held up a hand. "That is quite all right. Miss Wellman, I did not mean to offend you. It is merely customary to ask the gentleman to yield his partner. Might I have a dance?"

"You may." Aya smirked and took his outstretched hand.

Like Willem, King Archon led Aya to a dance of his own design.

"Are you sure Queen Zedara will not mind you taking another woman to the dance floor when she has sat all evening?"

King Archon looked up at his wife. Queen Zedara perched on her throne with her arms crossed, her eyes purposefully examining every aspect of the room *except* where Aya and the king danced.

"My wife does not like to dance." King Archon grinned. "I am sure she would thank you for taking the tedious task off her hands."

Aya frowned, not blaming Queen Zedara one bit. "I hope she does not find all her queenly duties so odious."

Aya could not be sure, given the muffling effect of the king's mask, but she swore she heard a purr escape through the lion's fangs.

"And how are you finding palace life, Miss Wellman?"

"Please, Your Majesty." Aya swallowed hard. "Call me Aya."

"All right then. How do you like palace life, Miss Aya?"

Aya glanced up, batting her eyelashes. "I must agree with your wife that some of it is tedious. Most days, I simply sit around in Lord Varick's estate with the maid and his sparse library as my only companions."

"What a shame." King Archon pulled Aya closer. "A lovely girl like yourself should not be hidden away in some lord's dwelling. You should get out and tour the palace, make some female friends with whom you can socialize."

"Oh, I'm sure I will." Aya gave her best innocent smile. "I believe Lord Varick just wants me to adjust slowly. The palace ways are so strange compared to what I am used to."

"I hope they are better."

Aya squeezed King Archon's large arm. "Certain aspects are exceptionally better."

The king took her forwardness as permission to slide his hand down to her lower back. Aya's skin crawled beneath his caress, and she said a silent thanks to the dressmaker for using so many layers of fabric. She managed a tight-lipped smile, hoping her expression appeared pleasant.

"Did dancing with Lord Varick bore you?"

Aya furrowed her brow, uncertain of the king's intentions. "A little."

King Archon made a show of spinning Aya and pulling her back in smoothly. He kept her locked in his arms for an uncomfortable moment before dipping her down so that she was forced to stare up at him over her breasts. After a few seconds, he straightened her and put his arms back around her. A few onlookers clapped. Queen Zedara glared.

"Better?" The king cocked his head.

Aya blinked against her dizziness. "Exceptionally better."

The king laughed, tapping his fingers against the top of her bum. As they continued their dance, King Archon strategically led them away from Queen Zedara's line of vision. Once they were safely out of her sight, the king allowed his hand more liberty, tracing it up Aya's spine then down the curve of her back and over her hips. He repeated this process several times, and Aya thought her skeleton might lurch out of her skin and run away. It took all of her strength to keep smiling up at him with a semblance of warmth in her eyes. She wished Abrim had crafted her a more concealing mask.

"Would you like to see more of the palace, Aya?" The king's gravelly voice jarred her from her thoughts. While they grated on Aya's ears, at least his words offered a distraction from the activities of his hand.

"I would love to." Aya beamed.

"How about a tour? Tomorrow, perhaps?"

Aya's brow furrowed again. Was King Archon asking to spend the day with her?

"A tour would be lovely." Aya squinted. "But I doubt Lord Varick has the time."

King Archon scoffed. "Nonsense. I would give you the tour myself. And before you protest, I assure you, you would not be inconveniencing me. It would be my pleasure."

"Your Majesty, please do not think me rude, but, I must ask." Aya spoke slowly, letting her eyes widen with every word. "Is it appropriate for a married nobleman to give an unmarried peasant girl a private tour of the palace?"

King Archon puffed out his chest. "Please do not think me rude, Aya, but you forget—I am the king." He paused, his blue eyes boring into Aya, as if making sure she understood. "I hardly have to stand upon propriety, especially in a circumstance that is truly innocent."

"Are you certain, Your Majesty?" Aya thought of Willem's touch to make herself blush. "I would hate if my actions were to damage your reputation."

"Aya, it will be fine." King Archon rubbed her back. "If anything, my kindness to a ward of the palace will make me look like a gracious leader, don't you think?"

Aya smiled. A genuine smile. She had him. It was only a matter of time.

"I know I find you to be the kindest and most gracious king I have ever known." Aya neglected to mention that she had been born after King Archon succeeded his father on the throne.

"Then it is settled. I shall come to Lord Varick's estate and retrieve you after your morning meal."

Aya bowed her head. "Very well."

King Archon stopped their dance and took both of Aya's hands in his own. "For now, I should return to my station. I will see you tomorrow."

As she had done with Willem, Aya stretched up on her toes to place a soft kiss on the king's mask, on the lion's whiskered cheek. Of course, unlike with Willem, the act and the glittering result it produced in King Archon's eyes made bile rise in her throat.

When she pulled away, Aya noticed the gazes of several nobles studiously avoiding her and the king. The kiss was a bold move, but a polite kiss on the cheek was not scandalous. A young woman could give affection to an older man, a patriarchal figure, after he showed her a kindness. And even if such a thing were taboo in the palace, how was Aya to know? She was merely an uneducated ward.

"Tomorrow," Aya said.

This time, it was her turn to disappear into the crowd.

12

———

$\mathcal{A}$s Aya weaved through the crowd, she scanned it for signs of Willem's golden frog mask or Lord Varick's dark goggles. She did not see either of them. Her head throbbed from the rising volume of the orchestra, and she felt dizzy from the drinking and twirling. Deciding it best to call it a night, Aya headed to the exit. As she departed, the bishop gave her a stiff bow, but otherwise, she left undisturbed.

Aya followed the long hallway back toward Lord Varick's estate at the stern. As she walked away from the ballroom, the music became fainter, and she felt her head depressurize with every step. After a few minutes, she saw the end of the hallway with the statue of Queen Hildegard. However, the statue was not the only queen waiting for her. Standing directly in front of it, right in the center of the hallway's fork, was Queen Zedara. She had removed her rabbit mask and held her hands on her hips as Aya approached her.

Aya made a conscious effort not to slow her gait. To change her speed in any manner would be to imply her guilt. Instead, she straightened her shoulders and strolled up to the queen. "Your Highness." Aya curtsied. "Did you tire of the merry-making as well?"

Queen Zedara crossed her arms. In the dimly lit hallway, her pale skin glowed the same color as desert sand in moonlight. "I had enough of watching you dance with my husband."

Aya shifted her eyes around the area, ensuring no one else was present. She did not need any other nobles, or worse, the queen's guards, hearing this conversation. "My apologies. If I had known you desired time with the king on the dance floor, I gladly would have surrendered my position."

Queen Zedara shook her head. She turned around and looked up at the statue of Queen Hildegard, both women's eyes fierce and unblinking. As she stood at Queen Zedara's side, the hairs on Aya's arms struggled to rise against the fabric of her sleeves.

"It's not that." Queen Zedara turned her gaze to Aya. "I know what you're doing."

Aya's body went rigid. "Excuse me, Your Highness?"

"Don't play the innocent little ward with me." Queen Zedara rolled her eyes. "I *know* what you're doing."

"I-I'm sorry, Your Highness." Aya took a step back. "I really don't know what you're referring to."

"You're trying to seduce my husband so he will want to get rid of me."

Once again, Aya wished that her mask covered her entire face. She felt the blood rising to flush her chest and neck, and she placed a hand at the base of her throat, hoping the queen would take her actions as signs of her shock, not guilt. "I'm doing no such thing!"

"Yes, you are," Queen Zedara huffed. "And frankly, you're not doing a good enough job."

Aya's heart skipped a beat. "Pardon?"

"Aya, I *know*." Queen Zedara put her hands on her hips again. "I helped Varick come up with this scheme, for goodness sake."

Aya glanced around, making sure that no one was lurking

in the three corridors. When she was certain the coast was clear, she said, "Explain."

This time, Queen Zedara also scanned the room, shuffling her feet ever so slightly. She motioned for Aya to come in closer so they could pretend to admire Queen Hildegard's statue together. Aya scooted in until her shoulder touched the queen's. Queen Zedara did not speak directly to Aya but rather toward the statue. "The late Queen Isadona, Lord Varick's daughter, was my best friend. She was my world. I was closer to her than anyone, even my own sisters. Do you know what that is like?"

Aya thought of Dellwyn, who was probably wrapped around a drunken nobleman at that moment, and nodded.

"Isadona didn't intend to attract the attention of King Archon. She was in love with—" The queen paused, touching the locket hanging around her neck. "Isadona loved someone else. But Varick didn't care who she loved. He wanted her to be queen and himself to have the prestige and power of being the king's father-in-law. He pushed her on King Archon, and eventually, the king took the bait."

Aya crossed her arms. "And then the previous queen found herself in bed with one of her guards."

"A terrible shock for His Majesty." Queen Zedara pressed her lips together. "Isadona saw the pattern as clearly as we all do. She didn't want to marry King Archon. I don't know why she did. My best guess is that he threatened her—or her lover, maybe—so she consented to protect them both. Of course, the pressure from her father didn't help anything."

Aya's brow furrowed. "What do you mean?"

Queen Zedara scoffed. "Lord Varick was thrilled when King Archon asked for Isadona's hand. As if the act of the king having to *ask* Varick for *permission* didn't get his tiny pecker hard enough, the idea of securing his family's place in the royal lineage certainly did."

Aya tilted her head. "That's not what Varick told me." She paused, trying to remember Lord Varick's exact words. "He said that Isadona was madly in love with the king. That she was blinded by his charm and neither she nor Varick realized the king's scheme until it was too late. In fact, Varick said he only figured King Archon out because he knew Isadona never would have betrayed him."

Queen Zedara's hands tightened into fists. "That's ridiculous. Isadona begged Varick not to make her marry the king. Sure, once Varick forced her into it, she put on a good act. She had to. But everyone knew it was a loveless marriage, the same as mine."

Queen Zedara bit her thumbnail and studied the statue of Queen Hildegard. "Varick must have told you that to make himself sound better. He probably didn't want to risk telling you that Isadona's death is on his hands."

"Maybe." Aya glanced over her shoulder. Still empty. "Your Highness, if you knew all of this, how did you end up married to the king?"

Queen Zedara clenched her jaw. "At Isadona's funeral, King Archon approached me with the grieving widower act. He said that I was the only one who could understand his pain. After the funeral, Lord Varick propositioned me. He told me how guilty he felt about forcing Isadona to marry King Archon. He claimed that he had truly believed she would keep the king's interest, and he had never meant for her to die. I do believe him about the last part. Isadona died too early to put Varick's blood in the royal line."

"That's revolting." Aya shook her head, her face forming into a grimace. "Why would you agree to do this, knowing everything you know?"

Queen Zedara turned to stare at Aya directly. "Look, Varick may be slime for carelessly putting his daughter at risk the way he did, but I do think he regrets it, even if for his own selfish reasons."

Aya looked down and bit her lip. "Lord Varick was right to

lie to me. I never would have agreed to this if I'd known he betrayed his daughter for a chance at the crown."

"Yes, you would have."

Aya grabbed the sides of her dress to keep herself from slapping Queen Zedara. "What in the Benevolent Queen's name would make you think that?"

"Because I did." The queen sighed. "Varick gave me the same deal he gave you. Put yourself in the path of a madman, risk your life, and maybe, just maybe, we'll be able to stop him, kill him, and save the kingdom."

Aya touched her cheek, the skin hot beneath her palm. What did it say about her that Queen Zedara was right? Or that she had fallen for Varick's lies? She had thought Varick needed her, the same way she needed a father. But she was no more than a pawn to him.

"Don't be ashamed." Queen Zedara placed a hand on Aya's shoulder. "Regardless of how you came here, you're doing the right thing. King Archon must be brought to justice. No matter the cost."

Aya nodded. She examined Queen Zedara, a blond ball of rage who Aya didn't know from any other noblewoman, and for some reason, when she looked into the queen's dark blue eyes, she believed every word.

"King Archon killed my father."

Queen Zedara raised her eyebrows. "Your father? Varick told me you lost someone to the king. I'm sorry."

Aya smiled, her lips tight. "I'm sorry for your loss as well."

"Thank you." Queen Zedara blinked several times, as if trying to hold back tears. Aya studied the queen's features, her pursed lips, the way she held herself upright like someone constantly in defiance. Aya wondered if she would have been so torn up about Dellwyn's death. She wondered exactly how close Zedara and Isadona were.

Queen Zedara sighed. "Look, Varick is a lying sack of filth, but he is our ally. He may not share our motives, but he does want the king dead, and that's what matters."

"Agreed."

"Good. Now, we're running out of time." Queen Zedara glanced over her shoulder. "The masquerade will start winding down any moment, and I haven't even gotten to the reason why I met you here yet."

Aya bit her lip. "And that is?"

"I need you to work faster with the king."

Aya let out a sound between a choke and a chuckle. "I can't. I tried working fast when I first met him, and he practically laughed me out of the palace."

"Yes, Varick told me." Queen Zedara shook her head. "But you're doing better now. You've created some serious interest. He hasn't visited my bedchambers since the day at the mask maker's shop."

Aya felt her eyes widen. Exactly how much did the queen know? "And you think that is my influence?"

Queen Zedara smiled. "Yes, judging from the stories Isadona told me about his courtship."

"What do you expect me to do?"

Zedara ran a hand through her hair. "I don't know. But you're doing so much better, and I cannot stand many more days of being married to this monster. Every time I look at him, I see Isadona's head fall to ground. Do you know what that's like?"

Aya nodded. She did.

"Yes, of course you do!" Queen Zedara grimaced. "Surely you don't want to spend any more time waltzing with him or feeling his hands crawl all over you. Not when you see your father's face reflected in his empty blue eyes."

"I see my father's back." Aya stared up at Queen Hildegard's statue. "I see his back as he is dragged to execution. I hear his screams."

Queen Zedara returned her hand to Aya's shoulder and

squeezed it. "Then let's speed this up. Let's put ourselves and the entire kingdom out of our misery."

"How?"

The queen smirked. "King Archon had several drinks before you arrived at the party, and now that you've left and he doesn't have to keep himself steady to waltz with you, I guarantee he's drinking more. The alcohol and memory of you will drag him to my bedchambers. When he comes, I will pretend to be hurt that he danced with you, and I will reject him."

Aya raised her eyebrows. "Will he allow that?"

"My guards will throw him out."

Aya crossed her arms. "Your guards aren't supposed to protect you from His Majesty."

"Trust me." Queen Zedara imitated the gesture. "They will do as I say."

Queen Zedara's tone made Aya's bones cold.

"When you see him next, King Archon will still be stinging from my rejection. It will make him desire you, the sweet obedient ward, even more. If you show the slightest interest in him, he will seize the opportunity to have you."

"And then? I can't let him take me. I refuse to bed my father's murderer."

Queen Zedara huffed. "How lucky for you."

Aya's mouth slammed shut. She couldn't imagine what it must be like for Queen Zedara. It had to be worse than bedding all of the merchants who came to the Rudder. Aya took a deep breath. "I'm sorry. But you know I can't bed him. I'd be executed."

"Yes, I know. I wouldn't ask you to do that." Queen Zedara shuddered. "All I'm asking is that you let him get a little physical with you. Not enough to commit a crime, just enough to secure his attraction. Once he has a little taste, his palate will be only for you, and he'll be ready to cast me aside."

"And then, Your Highness?"

"And then, the next time you meet, he will do as he did

with Isadona. He will pledge his undying love for you, and he will ask you if you will have him, if only he can get his wife out of the way."

Aya smirked. "That's when we'll get him."

Zedara smiled a slow smile that spread over her face like a snake slipping across the sand. "Yes, Aya. That's when we bring him to justice."

13

———

As the nobles poured out of the ballroom in boisterous groups, Aya and Queen Zedara went their separate ways. Instead of going back to Lord Varick's estate as she had planned, Aya decided to wander around the palace. She needed to process what Queen Zedara had told her.

If she'd been outside, Aya would have spit in the dirt. After everything her own father did to keep her taken care of and safe—after he was unfairly ripped away from her—to know that Lord Varick hadn't protected his daughter, hadn't even cared that his child had been killed, infuriated Aya. It was unfair that such an unloving, worthless father was allowed to live when hers had been killed. Of course, Aya knew that life wasn't fair, but it didn't lessen the acid churning in her gut.

Aya stopped to lean against the statue of some forgotten poet and breathe. She tried to be rational, to think logically. She had to admit it was possible that Lord Varick had loved Isadona more than Queen Zedara believed. After all, Isadona was his child. Surely a father had to love his daughter for more than her breeding potential. Maybe he simply hadn't realized the depth of his love until Isadona was executed. Maybe he still tried to hide his affections because it hurt too much to admit

143

his own guilt in her death. If anyone understood that kind of guilt, it was Aya.

She kept walking, wending her way through the palace's winding corridors, smiling pleasantly at drunken and jovial nobles as they passed. Thankfully, she did not spy Lord Varick amongst the merrymakers. However, she did finally see Lord Collingwood, stumbling down the hallway supported by a tall, thin woman—the mysterious Lady Collingwood at last.

Aya stepped aside to allow the Collingwoods more space in the narrow corridor. She had seen Lord Collingwood in passing at the Rudder, but watching him in his proper place made her heart skip, as if she had been caught peeking through his windows at night. Lord Collingwood's hair had long turned gray, but it was thick. Like Willem's, she thought. Aya also noticed Lord Collingwood had hazel eyes under his wiry eyebrows. She didn't know much about the lord's personality. Dellwyn had only told her that he was kind, generous in his gifts to her, and quite sprightly in bed for a man of his age. Aya already knew that Willem was a kind man, and she couldn't help wondering if the vitality was a family trait.

Before she flushed any deeper, Aya distracted herself by examining Lady Collingwood. As the couple stepped around Aya, she observed that Lady Collingwood was over a head taller than her and had translucent white skin that revealed the veins in her hands. Admittedly, Lady Collingwood had a regal handsomeness to her. However, she was the absolute antithesis of the dark-skinned, curvy Dellwyn. Aya imagined that Lord Collingwood had taken up with her friend for that exact reason. She made a mental note to report her findings the next time she saw Dellwyn.

After almost an hour of wandering, Aya found herself back at the statue of Queen Hildegard. She must have walked in a circle. Aya stood there, looking up at the immortalized queen for guidance and wondering how someone so fierce would have handled the night's revelations.

Aya groaned. "Why are your descendants so idiotic?"

She hated the palace game. It was exhausting, never knowing if you could trust your allies enough to be honest with them. In Sternville, people were open with one another. Sure, you could get your feelings hurt that way, but at least you always knew where you stood with your neighbors. These palace politics—with the lies and manipulations and backhanded compliments—disgusted her. Madam Huxley had tried to warn Aya from the beginning, and Aya had ignored her. She wouldn't repeat the mistake with Queen Zedara's warning. Aya was finished.

She took a deep breath, her eyes still on Queen Hildegard. "Fine," Aya whispered. "I have to play the game with Lord Varick. But I don't have to play by his rules."

Aya pulled off her mask and marched toward Lord Varick's estate. The corridor seemed to close in around her as she walked. As she passed each candle and lantern, the flames flickered with the breeze created by her movement, and she swore the light had a tint of red.

WHEN SHE REACHED the black and purple door of Lord Varick's estate, Aya didn't bother to stand on ceremony. She let herself in, not caring for Mrs. Lemot to interrupt her mission. She followed the short hallway to Lord Varick's sitting room, and sure enough, the lord perched on the edge of the armchair. His mask sat on the table, but he still wore his top hat and his walking staff lay across his lap. A fire blazed behind him, and when he noticed Aya's entrance, she swore the flames blazed in his eyes, too.

"There you are, Miss Aya. I've been worried sick." Lord Varick *tutted*. "Please tell me this means you spent time with our noble King Archon after the ball."

Aya sat on the couch facing the balcony and looked out

into the night sky. "Funny you should say that. It was quite the opposite. After I left the masquerade, I had a rather lengthy discussion with the queen."

Lord Varick's entire body stiffened. He straightened and put the end of his staff on the floor, as if it would keep him anchored upright. He followed Aya's gaze out to the sky. "Did you? Whatever could she have had to discuss with you? Surely she is not bold enough to accuse you of flirting with the king. After all, he is the one who made advances on you tonight."

Aya snickered. "Actually, she accused me of not working fast enough to seduce him."

Lord Varick stared at Aya. She glared back, wondering if the eyes really were the gateway to the soul, and if so, if Varick's soul were truly that black. "Queen Zedara told me everything, Varick. She told me that Isadona was her best friend and that you approached her with your vengeful plot after King Archon flirted with her at Isadona's funeral."

Lord Varick stayed silent. Aya guessed he wanted to wait for all of her information so that he wouldn't unnecessarily divulge any secrets.

"She also told me a very different story about Isadona and King Archon's relationship."

"Oh? What did she say?" Lord Varick fiddled with his staff, spinning it in a circle the way the old drills must have dug the wells, back when there was still enough water to run the steam machines.

Aya crossed her arms. "She said that Isadona did not fancy King Archon, but rather, she loved someone else. She told me that you forced Isadona to marry the king so you could connect your family line to the crown."

"Is that so?"

"Yes." Aya scoffed. "Though, I think Zedara is a little short-sighted there. After all, knowing the king's pattern, betting on Isadona to last nine months was obviously a stretch on your part. And even if she had lived long enough to bear a child, you would have had to get Prince Lionel out of the way before your grandchild could have ruled."

"Indeed." Lord Varick smirked. "And did Queen Zedara tell you the identity of Isadona's great love?"

"No." Aya pursed her lips. "But I can't see how that matters now."

Lord Varick raised his eyebrows. "Humph. And do you believe Queen Zedara's claims?"

Aya let her head fall back against the couch and closed her eyes. "I'm not sure who to believe. You tell me that you want vengeance for your beloved daughter, who was head over heels for that monster. Zedara tells me that you want vengeance for losing your ties to the crown. You have been so kind to me, taking me in, helping me escape my life of poverty, giving me a chance at my own revenge. Zedara is a stranger, but she has also lost a loved one, and like me, she is actually doing work to execute this plan." Aya let out a long breath. "I'm conflicted, Varick. And you don't deny a thing."

"Why should I?" Lord Varick widened his eyes. "It is not up to me to defend my case. You can judge for yourself. Either you will believe me, your benefactor, or you will believe Zedara, your unhappy queen."

Aya opened her eyes and sat up. She put her hands on her knees and leaned forward. "I choose to believe neither of you."

Lord Varick's lips twisted up into the faintest smile. "Well, that is probably the safest decision, Miss Aya."

Aya nodded. "If Zedara and you can hate each other and still work together, I see no reason why you and I cannot feel nothing toward each other and still work together."

Lord Varick leaned back in his chair. "True. However, our friendship did bring you certain perks that Zedara would not have received if she were of your status. After all, you realize, if you are not my friend, I will not return your father's shop to you when this is all over."

"And of course, you realize, that we are all in this together."

Aya smiled. "Even after King Archon is dead, if I go to Prince Lionel and tell him that it was your plot all along, won't that spell trouble for you?"

"You would never, Miss Aya." Lord Varick laughed. "The prince would have you and Zedara executed right along with me."

"Yes, but if you're not giving me my shop, what do I have to lose?" Aya licked her lips. "You forget, Varick. You live in an illustrious estate, have all the fruit and wine you can ingest, and receive every pampering from your staff. I live in a dirt-floored hovel, trudge miles for water, and let disgusting men penetrate me for the smallest coins in our currency. Do you really think death wouldn't be a relief?"

Lord Varick frowned. He had to know Aya spoke the truth. He would have to honor their agreement and give her father's shop back to her, whether he liked it or not. She held all the cards.

Lord Varick sighed. "So where do we go from here, Miss Aya?"

"I'm sure we both agree we can't trust each other anymore. Therefore, I will not be staying at your estate any longer."

"That is probably the safest arrangement."

"Indeed." Aya tilted her head. "Can I expect your guards to remain stationed at the stern for the duration of our mission? I would hate to be caught coming and going from the palace, and as I've already said, if the worst should happen, I have no qualms about sending you to the executioner along with me."

Lord Varick huffed. "Very well. Though, you know, I cannot guarantee whether nobles or peasant passersby linger near the stern."

"I assure you, I will not be noticed by them." Aya wrinkled her nose. "Now then, seeing as you have successfully introduced me into noble society and will continue to ensure my safe passage to and fro, I see no reason for you to be involved any longer. I will do my part to seduce the king, as Zedara does hers. I will not report to you. You may enjoy the show from afar."

"And when it is almost done?" Lord Varick raised his eyebrows.

"When it is time to catch the king revealing his plot to me, I shall send word to both you and Zedara. You will both bring witnesses to hear the king's treachery. Once he speaks it, you can reveal yourselves, and we'll all take him to execution."

Lord Varick chuckled. "You have it all figured out, don't you, Miss Aya?"

"I certainly hope so." Aya stood to leave, and Lord Varick followed suit.

"Very well, then. We shall remain business partners, and I will wait to hear from you when it is time to end this."

"Good." Aya extended her hand, and Lord Varick shook it stiffly. "I will collect my things from your guest room and be gone within minutes."

Lord Varick's lips twisted again, ever so slightly, and as Aya withdrew her hand, her heart beat unevenly in her chest.

"Good luck, Miss Aya. You'll need it."

14

___

*A*s Lord Varick's door slammed behind her, Aya placed a hand over her chest, sensing a hollowness lurking beneath her fingertips. She hadn't felt this alone since the day her father had been killed. Yet, for the first time in ten years, Aya held no worries about her future. Unlike when Papa died, Aya was no longer a helpless little girl. She had a mission, a tangible way to obtain justice for her father. She had a friend in Dellwyn and potentially more than a friend in Willem. She had secured the repossession of her father's shop and, consequently, a future without the Rudder. No matter what happened, she would be fine. She would pick herself up and take care of herself the way she always had. She didn't need some lying, self-absorbed lord to hold her hand.

Aya strutted away from Lord Varick's estate and headed toward the stairwell that led to the Rudder. She considered staying in her room there—assuming Madam Huxley had not reassigned it to another girl—because it would prevent Aya from being spotted outside the palace and save her a long walk. However, if Aya were being honest with herself, she knew that she was far more likely to run into nobles at the Rudder than anywhere else. Therefore, she resolved to simply sneak in the back entrance, pop into Dellwyn's room between clients, and have Dellwyn watch for the corridor and lobby to be empty so she could make her way back to their hovel unnoticed.

In her hands, Aya carried her phoenix mask, her night-dress, and her green cloak. She had left the masquerade dress and the ugly house ensemble in her empty guest room, as she did not want Lord Varick to believe that she owed him for anything. However, she had elected to keep the red toga and wraps from the bathhouse. She couldn't risk being caught in the corridor in her bedclothes, and at least the outfit had been a complimentary gift from the bathhouse and not something that Lord Varick had purchased directly. As for the mask, Aya remembered that Abrim had put it on Lord Varick's account, but she didn't care. She considered it her tip for being lied to.

As she walked, Aya stroked the mask's feathers, the rhythmic motion easing the tension in her chest. She wondered if phoenixes had ever existed, if they really could have burned to a crisp and emerged from their own ashes. She hoped they had. It was comforting to think that the world had once held such beauty and life, even if it couldn't anymore.

Aya was so absorbed in her thoughts that she didn't see the person coming toward her. Just before she ran into him, the person reached out his arms and grabbed her by the shoulders to prevent their collision. Aya gasped, nearly dropping her mask, and looked up into warm hazel eyes. "Oh, Willem, I'm sorry. I wasn't paying attention."

Willem laughed, allowing his hands to slip down from her shoulders to her elbows before dropping back to his side. "My apologies for startling you."

Aya nodded. "Right. Well, have a good night." She moved past Willem, her shoulder brushing against his. Before she had taken even ten steps, Willem darted after her.

He grabbed her arm. "Aya? It's terribly late. Where are you going?"

Aya stopped, turning to face him. "Home."

"Isn't home that way?" Willem asked, releasing her and pointing in the direction he had originally been walking. Aya gazed past him, back toward the estate.

She shook her head. "Lord Varick's may be, but mine is not. Please, don't ask. It's been a long evening."

Willem sighed, his brow furrowing. "Aya, I have to. Where is home?"

Aya clenched her jaw. As she craned her neck to look up at him, she felt like a defiant child. "Sternville. As it always has been."

"Do you think it's safe for a young lady to walk the streets of Sternville this late at night?"

Aya shrugged. "As safe as it is to walk the corridors of the palace."

Willem gaped. "But at any moment a man could—"

"Appear out of nowhere and accost me with questions?"

"Among other things, yes." Willem blushed. "I'm sorry for being overprotective, but I would feel better if you stayed here."

Aya stared up at his eyes—so inviting, so sincere. She knew that he truly was concerned for her—unlike Lord Varick, who seemed to care for no one, or Queen Zedara, who prioritized her own safety. Not that Aya blamed *her*.

Aya allowed her gaze to fall to the floor in what must have looked like innocent thought. In truth, she was admiring Willem's frame, the patch of skin peeking out from behind the laces of his shirt, the slight bulge under the buttons of his trousers.

Just as her eyes lingered a second too long, Willem took her hand. Aya inhaled sharply, feeling the lightning shock from his fingertips sizzle its way through her flesh. She felt a rising heat in her chest and a matching one between her thighs. His touch triggered reactions in her body that no touch from any client, from any other person, had ever created.

Maybe it was because she was too tired to walk all the way

to Sternville. Maybe it was because he was the only attractive man who had ever shown genuine interest in her. Maybe it was because she was in a slightly vulnerable position combined with newfound confidence and indignation. And then again, maybe it was simply that she had known too much pain and never enough pleasure. Whatever it was, she let her tongue get the best of her. "And where exactly should I stay, Willem? With you?"

Aya watched in delight as Willem's jaw dropped. His cheeks turned a delicious shade of pink, and his hand twitched ever so slightly in hers. He closed his eyes for a moment, taking deep breaths. Aya smiled, waiting for his answer. When his eyes opened again, the green in them had cut through the gold, and they practically smoldered. "Yes."

The word lit Aya's body on fire. Willem clenched her hand tighter and pulled her down the corridor in silence. Aya's heart pounded so hard she could barely hear their footsteps. At every corner, Willem stopped to check that the hallways were empty before continuing onward. He led her past Lord Varick's estate, all the way down the corridor to the statue of Queen Hildegard. At the statue, he veered left then took a quick right down the next hallway. This corridor was unlit with no paintings or tapestries lining the wall, and it ended in a single green door.

As they reached the door, Willem dug under his shirt for a chain. Hanging from it was a spindly golden key. One end of the key was cone-shaped; the other end had three prongs extending from it.

Willem opened the door and pulled Aya inside. He wasted no time in slamming the door shut behind her and pushing her up against it. Holding Aya there, he pressed his body against hers and stared down into her eyes. Aya didn't know what he was waiting for, but she knew she would explode if he stalled another second. She reached up and grabbed Willem's neck, pulling him into a deep kiss. Willem slid his hands down to her hips, his fingers gripping her flesh so tightly she felt the pressure to her bones. He sucked her bottom lip lightly, bringing it in between his teeth for a gentle nibble. Aya gasped, dropping her phoenix mask and bundled nightclothes, and she felt him smile into the kiss.

Aya wove one hand into Willem's dark hair and let her other one roam his body. Even after all her years at the Rudder, she had never taken the time to properly explore a man's physique. Tracing her fingers across Willem's broad shoulders, Aya felt his muscles contract as his hands wandered. As Willem arched his body into hers, Aya slid her palms down his back to his bum. She gave it a playful squeeze, relishing the tightness of it under her fingers, which earned her back a squeeze from both of Willem's hands.

Willem broke their kiss and feathered his lips across her jawline down to her neck. As he kissed and nipped at the curve of her neck and collarbone, Aya clutched his shoulder for support with one hand and slipped the other to the growing hardness under his trousers. Groaning at her touch, Willem moved his mouth back to Aya's, enveloping her in another wet kiss.

Untangling herself from Willem's embrace, Aya clenched his shirt with her fists. She used all her strength to push him backward, where she hoped a bed or chair or other cushion would be waiting. As if he could read her mind, Willem pulled Aya into his arms and wrapped her legs around his waist. Her shoes fell off her feet. Willem took a few wobbly steps, still kissing her, before turning them around and tossing Aya onto the most luxurious feather bed she had ever encountered.

Above them hovered a royal blue canopy supported by four golden posts. Blue pillows with gold fringe, nearly as long as Aya's body and twice as full, cradled her head. As Aya relaxed into the bed, the softness enveloped her, making her feel weightless in its embrace. Willem smiled at her from the end of the bed before climbing onto it and crawling over her.

It was all Aya could do to keep from squirming as Willem

fidgeted with the fabric of her toga. After a few seconds, he found the master knot. After a few more seconds, he had it undone and pulled the fabric off Aya's body.

As she lay naked under him, Aya realized that her skin was entirely flushed—except, this time, she was not reddened from embarrassment or nervousness or pain. Instead, she glowed pink with heat, excitement, and anticipation. As Willem's hands traced her bare skin from her neck to her breasts to her thighs, Aya couldn't help thinking that Dellwyn was right. Everything was completely different—wonderful—when you did it for you. When you wanted it.

Aya tugged at Willem's shirt, and he stopped his exploration of her body long enough to pull it over his head and toss it onto the floor. As he straddled her, Willem simultaneously tugged off his boots and bent down to take her nipple into his mouth. As his tongue licked and played with her breast, Aya thanked the Benevolent Queen for Willem's ability to multitask.

Unable to control herself any longer, Aya reached down and gently scratched at Willem's stomach, trying to grasp his trousers. Willem removed his mouth from Aya's breast, kissed her nose, and smiled. "Not yet."

"Please." The word came out faint. Aya could barely breathe for the rush of blood shooting through her head and the pulsating between her legs. In all her life, she had never felt this yearning. She wanted him inside her. She wanted to know what it felt like when her body craved the man on top of her.

To her embarrassment, Willem chuckled. "Be patient."

Before Aya could argue, Willem started kissing her neck again, working his way down to her chest then stomach then lower. Aya looked down at him with wide eyes. What in the world was he doing? As his lips reached the lowest part of her torso, Aya bit her lip—both confused and more excited than she had ever been. As Willem's tongue slowly licked her center, she finally understood.

Aya began to tremble—first from her womanhood and then from her entire body. His kiss felt so good, and with every movement of his tongue, her body grew hotter. Stories from the other women at the Rudder flashed through her mind, about the heat and the shaking and the pleasure, and Aya knew she was finally experiencing what they had. As her pleasure reached its peak, Aya quivered in the core of her center and sparks shot out through her entire body. Her hips began to thrust, but Willem grabbed them with both hands and held her in place. As her tremors built, Willem increased the focus and intensity with which he worked, until finally, Aya felt as if her very core had exploded. She let out a loud, long moan, one that she must have been keeping inside her entire life. As it escaped her lips, Willem slowed the movement of his mouth, but he didn't stop, rather keeping himself in rhythm with the slow, circular motion of her hips. As they moved together, Aya felt the energy trickle out from between her thighs.

When she was still, Willem rolled off of her and wiped his mouth with the back of his hand. "Now, wasn't that worth your patience?"

Aya laughed, sliding down the bed to Willem and kissing his neck. His skin tasted salty, holy. She sat on top of his stomach, straddling him, and reached behind herself to unfasten his trousers. At least one skill from her previous life came in handy tonight. Aya stared down into his hazel eyes as her hand finally reached its prize.

"Yes." Aya stroked his length behind her. "But now I need more."

Willem smiled and granted her wish—into the darkest hours of the night.

15

*A*ya dreamed she floated in the ocean. While she had never known the sensation of floating, in her dream, she felt light, as if her body could rest forever on the infinite drops of water. At the same time, her heart pounded, alerting her that, at any moment, her body could become heavy and slip under the water until she could no longer feel the warmth of, nor see the light from, the sun above her. Aya shivered as her feet dipped below the water's surface, then her ankles, then knees. Before she could slide any further, she opened her eyes.

At first, Aya thought she might truly be drowning. All around her lay waves of blue, her feet tangled in their softness. But something else wrapped around her, too—Willem's arm, draped over her midsection. With that realization, Aya smiled, the lightness returning.

As Willem's fingers flexed against Aya's stomach, she realized that she had never slept with a man before. Aya snuggled closer into Willem, relishing the peace of having another person breathe in rhythm with her. She wanted to drown in his embrace forever.

The previous night, Aya had been too caught up in

enjoying Willem to pay much attention to his room. Now, however, she fought off her waking haze by examining her surroundings. Willem's room was in the interior of the palace, so it did not have any windows. Aya squinted in the dim light. Candles burned throughout the room, some affixed above electric lanterns that no longer worked without steam to power the palace. On the wall to the right of the bed stood a grand wardrobe with an oval mirror hanging next to it. The left-hand wall contained four tall bookshelves filled with books. In between the two pairs of bookshelves sat a plush couch, which Willem must have used for a reading area. Across from the bed stood the door, and next to it, a grandfather clock.

If Aya had any doubt about the wealth of the Collingwood family, it had vanished. To have so many books, to have a *clock*, meant money—and lots of it. Aya tried to relax in bed for a while longer, but the clock on the other side of the room called to her. She hadn't had time to investigate the one near King Archon's chambers, but if she were quiet, she might be able to sneak a look inside Willem's.

Aya gently lifted Willem's arm, slid out from under it, and replaced it on the bed. She did not bother to gather a sheet to wrap around herself or put her toga back on. With any luck, she could examine the clock and slip back into bed before Willem awoke.

Aya tiptoed over to the grandfather clock. It stood slightly taller than her and was made of wood that matched Willem's wardrobe. Like the one outside King Archon's chambers, it had a plain white face with intricate black numbers. However, Willem's clock had golden hands. The shorter one had stopped on the five and the longer one had stopped on the eleven.

The trunk of the clock had a glass panel in the front to show the long golden limbs of the mechanism hanging from the clock's core. Aya wondered what exactly these did—her father had never told her about them. From her best guess, it looked like they would swing back and forth, perhaps keeping momentum so the clock would run for a long time. Obviously, the clocks in the palace had lost their pace at some point.

What fascinated Aya even more than the golden limbs was the glasswork behind which they hung. Unlike the glass pane in King Archon's clock, which was perfectly clear, the glass on Willem's clock contained carvings. Etchings of an intricate network of cogs and gears covered the glass. Aya wondered whether this were simply an artistic addition to the timepiece or a map of its inner workings.

Aya reached up to the clock's face and felt around the edges. There were no latches or keyholes to help her open it. She peered into it, wondering if maybe keyholes or other crank holes hid there. None. Aya crouched to examine the glass pane again. She ran her hands down the side of the clock's body. About halfway down on the left side, her fingers caught a latch. Aya unhooked it, swinging open the front of the clock's trunk.

At the bottom of the clock's insides rested a mess of cogs and gears, made in all different sizes and kinds of metals. There were also two large golden pieces, smooth and curved, and a silver winder. Aya wondered if they were part of the clock's mechanics, if it were meant to be wound somewhere like the music boxes her father had repaired. She left the pieces in place and reached her hand inside to stroke the round orb hanging from the clock's longest limb. Moving her fingers up to the shorter limbs, she rubbed the dangling chains between her fingers. She gave one of the chains a slight pull, delighted to hear the clock's mechanism clicking as she did so.

"I could grow accustomed to waking up to this sight."

Aya froze at the sound of Willem's groggy voice. She realized that, from her position bent over the clock, all of her most womanly assets must be on display. Feeling the blood rush to her cheeks, Aya straightened and fastened the clock's door.

"I'm sorry." Aya bit her lip. "I've never seen a grandfather clock this close before. I had to get a better look at it."

Willem propped himself up on his elbows, staring at her as

if he saw her for the first time. His brown hair stuck up in all directions, and Aya noticed that his chin stubble had darkened overnight. His messy hair, along with his sleep-kissed eyes and lopsided smile, made something in Aya's chest pang, and she blushed deeper under his scrutiny. Shaking his head, Willem patted the empty space beside him. Aya crossed the room and crawled back into bed. Once she was under the covers, Willem lifted his arm so Aya could curl up against him and rest her head on his chest.

"Did you discover anything about the clock?" Willem tucked a curl behind her ear.

"I might have an idea how to wind it." Aya tapped her fingers on his chest. "But I'm not sure if it would be a permanent fix or if there is something else broken in the mechanism. I've never seen a working one before to know what to do."

"I had no idea you were so fascinated by mechanics." Willem chuckled. "A wellman's daughter with a mechanical frog and a clock fetish. Whoever heard of such a thing?"

Aya's breath hitched. In her most casual tone, she managed, "Oh, well, I don't know much of anything. I just think the old machines are interesting." A bit of venom crept into her voice. "Just because I come from Sternville, that doesn't mean I'm an imbecile."

Willem squeezed her shoulders. "I'm sorry. I didn't mean to imply that you were uneducated. Clearly, I'm the ignorant one for making assumptions."

Aya nodded, her pride still aching. "It's fine. Tell me more about the clock."

"Hmm." Willem ran his fingers through her hair. "Well, it used to work. It never kept the proper time, but it at least ticked, and the hands spun around the face. The other ones in the palace haven't worked in decades."

"When did yours quit working?"

Willem rubbed at the scruff on his chin. "Oh, ten years ago, maybe. It's been broken since I was a child."

Aya glanced back over at the lifeless clock. "I know how it feels," she whispered.

"None of that." Willem kissed the crown of her head. "Speaking of clocks," he continued, "What time do you think it is? Do you want me to call for breakfast?"

"Breakfast!" Aya jumped out of bed and scrambled for her toga. Out of the corner of her eye, Aya saw Willem push the flung-aside covers out of his face. "Willem, I'm so sorry. I forgot. I have an important meeting after breakfast. I can't miss it."

Willem untangled himself the rest of way and moved to help Aya gather her clothing. "It's fine. Slow down. We don't even know what time it is. It's probably not even sunrise yet."

"No, no." Aya shoved her feet into her shoes. "I shouldn't have stayed here. If anyone sees me, it'll ruin everything."

Her fingers fumbled with the fabric of her toga. Willem took it from her, helping her drape it around her shoulders. "Aya, neither of us is married. Your reputation as a lady won't be ruined if someone spies you leaving my room."

"It's not that." Aya wrapped her hair up in the headscarf and patted her toga as if she had forgotten something. She looked down at the red fabric then over to her crumpled nightdress in horror. "Shit!"

Aya didn't have anything else to wear. She *might* have a spare ensemble tucked away in her room at the Rudder—that was, if Madam Huxley hadn't cleaned it out. But, even if there were an outfit there, it would never be appropriate for a day with the king. Maybe one of the other women had something she could borrow.

"What?" Willem grabbed her shoulders and gave her a gentle shake. "Aya, seriously, what is the matter?"

"I don't have any other clothes." Aya's eyes widened, her panic increasing as she spoke her problem. "I can't wear these to my meeting, and everything else I own is at my house in Sternville."

Willem's brow furrowed. "What about Lord Varick's estate? Surely he clothes you."

Aya bit her lip, unsure how to explain. "I'm not his ward anymore. Not exactly."

Willem frowned. "What does that mean?"

"Willem, please. I begged you not to ask last night. Don't ask now." Aya took Willem's face in her hands and kissed him. He reached around her back to pull her closer, but she pushed him away before he could deepen the kiss. "I'm sorry. I have to go."

"No." Willem kept her locked in his arms.

"I must." Aya pushed on his chest. "I have to go home and change."

"No, you don't." Willem released her, smiling. "I can help."

Willem went over to the wardrobe and opened the bottom drawer. Aya craned her neck to see what he searched for. Inside lay rows of bright fabric in every color Aya could imagine. Willem glanced over his shoulder at her and appraised her figure before removing two handfuls of the fabric. He shook them out to reveal two floor-length dresses. "Yellow or blue?"

Aya admired both dresses. The yellow one reminded Aya of the sun—vibrant, warm—with long sleeves and loose layers of fabric that stretched like rays from the corseted bodice. The blue dress matched Willem's bedding and consisted of a thicker, more structured fabric. Its neckline was wide and scooping, and paired with its brown leather external corset, Aya knew it would accentuate the few curves she had. And, she loved the way the blue looked next to Willem's golden eyes.

"Blue."

Willem draped the dress across the bed and replaced the yellow one in the drawer.

"Where did you get all of these dresses?"

He walked to the other side of the bed and picked up his own clothing. "They were my mother's."

Aya touched her hand to her chest. "Willem, I can't wear your moth—"

"Yes, you can." Willem smiled, his eyes watery as he stared at her. "They are mine now, and I want you to."

Aya wanted to dispute further, but she was desperate. She went to the bed and removed her toga. They dressed in silence.

At first, Aya held her breath, fearing that the silence would be uncomfortable, but eventually, she relaxed, finding it nice to simply exist alongside Willem. They moved fluidly around each other, each going about their own business. Aya fastened the brass buckles in the front of the corset herself, but when it came time to lace up the back, Willem stepped behind her and tightened and tied it for her as if he had done it every day of his life. The corset was a bit too tight the way he fixed it, but Aya guessed it would make her waist look tiny and push up her small breasts. She took the liberty of checking her reflection in the looking glass. She was right.

Willem came up behind her and kissed her on the neck. "You are divine."

Aya smiled. She began smoothing her hair and untangling her mess of curls. She didn't have the right tools to fix it properly, but she hoped the king would find her slightly wild hair inviting. Willem's reflection disappeared from the looking glass. It reappeared a moment later, a black velvet box in its hands. Aya turned around as he opened it.

Inside rested a golden barrette in the shape of a flower, with petals filled with rubies and leaves made of emeralds.

"Pull your hair back."

Aya put her hands up in protest, but Willem widened his eyes and pursed his lips. Knowing an argument would be useless, Aya did as he commanded, gathering the top half of her hair behind her head. Willem reached up and fastened the barrette in place then gently fluffed up her curls around it. He loosened a lock of hair by her hairline so that a single curl dangled to the side of her face. "Perfect."

"It's too much, Willem." Aya shook her head. "I can't accept this."

Willem rubbed Aya's arms. "My mother would be proud to know you are wearing her jewels."

A lump swelled in Aya's throat. If Willem knew that she were about to go from his bed to King Archon's side, he would not be lavishing her with these gifts. "You can't say that. We barely know each other."

"We may not know each other's histories, but I know your character, and you know mine." Willem took Aya's hand, placing a gentle kiss on her knuckles. "You're a good woman, Aya. My mother would have liked you."

As Aya stared into Willem's eyes, her heart thumped in her stomach. Even after only a few encounters, Aya felt more comfortable with Willem than anyone she had ever known, save her father and Dellwyn. Somehow, she knew he was a good man. But she—a believed traitor's daughter, a courtesan, a hopeful traitor herself—couldn't consider herself a good woman anymore, not by a nobleman's standards.

"I will return the barrette and the dress, too." Aya squeezed Willem's hand. "I promise."

Willem shook his head. "You keep them."

"No, Willem." Aya crossed her arms. "They were your mother's. Please, let me return them."

Willem sighed. "Will it really make you feel better to give them back?"

"Yes." Aya stood straighter.

"Fine. When I am ready to have them back, I will ask."

"Willem." Aya clenched her jaw.

"Aya, I'm not budging." Willem made a show of mimicking her by crossing his arms. "They were my mother's, yes. And they are special to me. However, they are also mine now, and you are special to me, too. This is the best deal you're getting."

Aya blushed. "I'm special to you?"

Willem threw his arms up in the air. "After the hours we spent in bed last night, do you seriously doubt that?"

Aya bit her lip and blushed even redder at the memory. If anyone knew that sex and affection were separate, it was her, but hearing him place them together made her heart flutter. "When you put it that way, I suppose I believe you."

"Good." Willem grinned and rolled his eyes. "Now then, are you well enough prepared for your meeting?"

"Yes." Aya let her arms fall to her side.

"If I check the time with the staff and it's early enough, will you please eat breakfast with me?"

Aya laughed. "I didn't know 'please' was in the noble vocabulary."

Willem inhaled sharply, his jaw tightening. "Aya."

"Yes." Aya poked his chest. "But don't tell anyone I'm here."

"Yes, yes, woman of mystery." Willem waved her hand away. "Stay put. I'll be right back."

Willem left the room, and Aya seated herself on his bed. She smiled as she noticed a few of her brown hairs lingering on the pillows, and she hoped that they would find a way to stay in his room, even after she could not. Aya knew that if Willem found out about her occupational history, or worse, her involvement with the king, he would never invite her back into his life. Likewise, even once the king was executed, when Aya officially left Lord Varick's care and took up residency in Portside, the Collingwood family would never entertain the idea of their heir taking up with a merchant woman.

For all of these reasons, Aya thought about sneaking out before Willem returned. After all, they were both bound to get hurt, and it was better they end their short affair on the blissful note of the previous night.

Aya fingered the barrette nestled in her hair, feeling once again Willem's gentle touch as he fastened it there, his firm pull on the corset strings, his soft lips on her neck.

Even though it was dangerous, even though it was foolish, even though it only drowned her deeper in her hopeless desires, when Willem told her the sun had yet to rise, Aya stayed for breakfast.

16

After a quick breakfast of fruit and a creamy substance Willem introduced as yogurt, Aya had to leave to meet King Archon for her tour of the palace. As she headed out the door, Aya gave Willem a soft kiss on the lips. He held onto her a little longer than she'd planned, but she didn't mind. If she could have had her way, she would have stayed hidden in his room for eternity.

Aya tiptoed through the corridor outside Willem's room. When she reached the end, she peeked her head out to glance down both sides of the main hallway. Empty. Aya sighed with relief and headed back toward Lord Varick's estate, deciding she would meet the king outside the door to avoid any run-ins with her now-estranged benefactor.

Bright light streamed in through the circular windows in the corridor. Realizing it must have been past breakfast time, Aya hastened, holding up Willem's mother's dress to avoid stepping on it. She rounded the statue of Queen Hildegard without a second glance, darting down the hallway to the stern.

When Lord Varick's estate came into view, Aya saw that King Archon already stood outside the door. It appeared that he had not knocked yet, as he was whispering to a man in a plain gray suit next to him, no doubt his trusted valet. Aya took a deep breath to brace herself then waved her arm to catch the king's attention. He looked up from under his illustrious cog-embroidered top hat to smile at Aya. Even from this distance, the king's smile was chilling. It exaggerated his pointed beard and lit up his cold blue eyes. Aya had to force herself to return his grin, and she knew her face looked stiff. She needed to steel herself—retreating would mean returning to the Rudder, and failing would mean a repeat of Lady Jauntley's trial, with Aya as the star.

Think of Papa to keep your feet moving. Think of Willem to smile.

Aya took another breath and remembered the way that Willem's lips traveled down her body. She felt her face form a demure smile. *There you go.*

"Miss Aya." King Archon took her hand and kissed it. "You look lovely this morning."

Aya patted her curls, hoping her cheeks had not flushed in her haste. "Thank you, Your Majesty."

King Archon squinted, his mouth forming a playful smile. "I hope your presence outside the estate does not mean you were trying to avoid our day together."

"Quite the contrary." Aya bit her lip. "I found myself restless with anticipation and took a walk to pass the time. I am pleased that you've arrived just as I returned to receive you."

King Archon's smile widened. "This is my valet, Eldric. Eldric, this is Miss Aya Wellman."

Eldric bowed to Aya, but he did not speak. Aya curtsied. "Pleasure to meet you."

King Archon he held out his arm. "Shall we begin? Or do you need to notify Lord Varick of your departure?"

"No, no." Aya wrinkled her nose. "He is aware of my plans." Aya took the king's outstretched arm. From this position, her shoulder and upper arm rubbed against the king's torso, and she felt her skirts brushing against the side of his trousers as they walked. The scent of his cologne stung her nostrils. There was no going back now.

Again, Aya tried to strengthen herself by thinking of her motivations. She thought of her father as he was dragged away. She thought of Lady Jauntley and Lord Pottsmore clinging to each other. She thought of all the vile men *she* had clung to in the depths of the Rudder. All these memories made her stomach churn, but they also kept her moving forward. The sooner she got this over with, the sooner she could avenge her father's death, reclaim his shop in Portside, and entertain possibilities for keeping Willem in her life. Until then, she must charm the snake on her arm.

"What parts of the palace will you be showing me today, Your Majesty?"

"Well, considering how interested you were in my clock, I thought you might enjoy seeing more of the ship's mechanics." King Archon raised his eyebrows. "The old engine room, perhaps?"

Aya had already seen the engine room—when Alfred gave her a tour of the palace the day her father died. She swallowed hard before speaking. "How thoughtful of you. That sounds fascinating."

"Good. Later, I will show you around some of the shops and areas where the ladies like to socialize. After all, you need to start integrating yourself into noble society."

"Another considerate idea, Your Majesty."

"I'm glad you think so." King Archon squeezed her arm. "For the end of our tour, I have arranged for us to have lunch on the deck of the palace."

Aya beamed. "That sounds delightful."

"Wonderful."

As King Archon spoke this last word, he stopped in front of a large set of double doors. Being already in the stern, it hadn't taken them more than a few minutes to walk to the engine room. Aya noticed that Eldric had followed them. However, he lingered a respectful distance behind, probably just within earshot. King Archon opened the double doors, which led to a wide staircase. Aya remembered these stairs. She had been so anxious to see the engine room last time that she had tripped on her dress.

The wide staircase ended on a red-carpeted platform where the nobles could stand to observe the work of the engineers and crewmen. Lanterns lit along the platform allowed Aya to see across the wide room. A rickety, iron staircase led down from the platform, and Aya remembered that Alfred had not let her climb down it before. At the time, Aya had been annoyed with Alfred for treating her like a child. However, now she could see that it would have been a terrible idea to let her run loose in the engine room. It was a massive maze of machinery. Undoubtedly, if she had been allowed to run free within it, she either would have become lost or gotten an appendage caught in one of the giant machines.

These machines filled almost the entire space, except for a few pathways to allow the workmen to pass between them. A row of long machines lined one side of the room, limb-like with their round bottoms—a hip or a shoulder—and long rods —a leg or an arm—protruding from them. These rods connected to others that extended from the ceiling or walls, and Aya imagined they must move in some kind of circular motion to pump water or steam through the rest of the engine.

Even with some mechanical training from her father, Aya couldn't begin to understand how the rest of the machinery might work. It was an interwoven system of pipes and cogs, of gears and levers. She wished that she could go back in time to see how each piece flowed into the next to spin the propellers and lurch the ship forward.

King Archon came to stand next to her at the railing, his arm brushing against hers. He pointed his other arm out and leaned in closer to Aya. "Do you see those doors on the back wall?"

Aya followed the line of his arm. Frowning, she leaned into the king to see exactly where he pointed. "Yes, I think so."

"That's where they used to put the coal."

"The coal?" Aya's brow furrowed.

"Yes." King Archon rested his hand in the center of her back. Aya shuddered. "They would shovel heaps of coal into the furnaces. The fires would heat the water and create steam to help the ship run."

"What exactly is coal?" Aya looked up at the king, her eyes wide.

King Archon rubbed his chin. "You know, I'm not sure. I believe it looked like a black rock but not as hard. If you tried to smash it, it could crumble and leave ash everywhere."

"Is there any left?" Aya took a step to the side, as if examining another part of the room. King Archon's hand fell to his side. Her back felt cold where it had been.

"There might be, in the engine furnaces or a storeroom back there. I've never bothered to have anyone look, honestly."

"Why not?"

King Archon shrugged. "There's no use for coal to run the ship without any water for it to sail on, is there?"

Aya glanced back at the engine room and did her best not to scoff. If coal really did burn, and if there were piles of it heaped behind those doors, they needed to retrieve it. Having coal to create warmth in the night and cook food would be far superior to tumbleweeds, crop stalks, and dried cacti. It could vastly improve the lives of the poor. More than that, Aya wanted to tell the king that knowing these things wasn't just a matter of functionality. It was a matter of historicity, of preserving the collective past of Desertera. If the monarchy allowed all of this knowledge to be lost, what would they do if one of the so-called prophets turned out to be right and the rain came again?

Instead, she smiled and pushed herself back from the railing. "How silly of me. Of course you don't need any coal."

King Archon took Aya's chin in between his thumb and forefinger. "Curiosity suits you, Miss Wellman."

Aya's face flushed, and she clenched her fist behind her back to avoid smacking him. King Archon smiled, no doubt taking her reddening as a maiden's blush.

"Did you notice this?" King Archon walked to the other side of the platform, motioning to a bronze statue of some sort. It had a white face like a clock. However, instead of numbers, words extended out from the middle with a lever that pivoted around them. King Archon grabbed the lever and pushed it to the other side of the device. As he did so, the two brass bars around the word "Full" moved to surround "Two Thirds" then "Half" then "Stop."

King Archon waved Aya over. "Come try it."

Aya moved to stand by the device, placing her hand on the lever. As she did, King Archon set his hand atop hers. He gripped her fingers around the lever and pulled it back to "Full."

"What does it do?" Aya tried to remove her hand, but he held it against the lever.

"It used to tell the crewmen how hard to run the ship." King Archon's fingers traced hers. "There is one up in the captain's cockpit on the deck, and it is linked to this one. The head engineer down here would use this to reply to the captain and signal the change in speed to the workmen."

"How clever." Aya went to remove her hand again, but King Archon still wouldn't budge. She felt his other hand brush her hair. He touched the barrette. Aya closed her eyes and imagined that it was Willem fastening the barrette into place.

"These jewels are beautiful. May I ask where you got them?"

Aya shrugged. "A friend gave them to me to wear today."

"What a generous friend." King Archon emphasized the last word, and Aya guessed he suspected she had a male suitor.

Aya smirked. "A friend who understood that I must look my best today."

King Archon smiled down at Aya, gently removing his hand from hers. Aya kept hold of the lever for a second longer, half clinging to the ship's history and half needing it to keep herself upright. The king's presence was overbearing, suffocating. Had she been a real mistress, she would have loved the attention.

"Shall we move on? I want you to see the shops as they open, before the corridor is too crowded with gossipy noblewomen." King Archon took her arm and wove it through his. He led her back up the staircase. Eldric waited at the top. It took all of her strength not to jerk her arm away.

For Papa. For Papa. For Papa.

"Are you worried we may become a topic of gossip, Your Majesty?"

King Archon motioned for Eldric to close the doors behind them. The valet complied, and Aya watched them shut with a heavy feeling in her chest. She felt compelled to stare at the closed doors, but King Archon turned her away and guided her toward the shops.

"Trust me. After our dance at the masquerade ball, I am sure we are already a topic of intense conversation."

This time, Aya did not need to act. Her eyes widened, and her jaw dropped slightly. She wondered how palace gossip could spread so quickly. The ball had been last night. But then again, every single noble had been in attendance, and many had brazenly watched her dances with the king and with Willem.

Aya wondered if palace gossip would be her ally or her foe. Gossip about her and the king could add legitimacy to her case when she exposed the king's plot to get rid of Queen Zedara. After all, if the nobles believed that King Archon had already primed Aya to be his next wife, they were more likely to believe that he wanted to relieve himself of his current one. However, gossip could also make the nobles dislike or distrust her, and it could put her at risk for being accused of adultery—even when the plan she had hatched with Lord Varick and Queen Zedara left her innocent.

"Should we be worried?" Aya's voice cracked.

King Archon laughed, patting Aya's arm as if she were a mother fretting over her child's bonnet. "My dear, perhaps you forget, but I am the king. My word outweighs the gossip of every person in Desertera."

"Of course, Your Majesty." *Which is why I have to ensure that others hear and see your treachery firsthand.*

Aya spoke with an authority that closed the subject. She saw a smirk cross King Archon's face, and she assumed that her ready acknowledgement of his power pleased him. They walked in silence for the majority of the distance between the stern and the center of the ship, the only sounds those of their shoes hitting the marble floors and Eldric humming behind them.

Aya was thankful for the king's quietness and the rhythmic sounds of their small party. They gave her time to think and to calm herself. So far, the tour had been a success. The king showed his interest by his careful planning, and he had already made great efforts to start conversation and create physical contact. Surely, after a few more hours of the same, and after the spurning he should have received from Queen Zedara last night, he would be putty in her hands by the end of the day.

"We're almost there," King Archon announced, pulling Aya out of her thoughts.

The king continued talking, explaining the various kinds of shops in the palace and which noble families shopped at which ones. This spawned a detailed explanation of the history of the various noble lines and how they were all disgustingly inbred from centuries of confining themselves to the limited supply of other nobles.

"Breeding must have been so much easier when one had

other nations of people to choose from." King Archon squeezed Aya's arm. "Of course, the noble families are reaching the point now where we admit that it may be necessary to introduce some fresh blood into our lines."

"Oh?"

Aya wasn't really listening. The common people knew of the lineage and happenings of the royal family, but they didn't really care about the other nobles at all—excepting, of course, their patrons. Aya remembered discussions between her father and other merchants, where they would laugh at the nobles for their lack of a trade, their utter uselessness, as her father would say.

King Archon stopped walking and turned Aya to look at him. "That's why introducing wards like you into our society is so important. Despite your bad blood, you have still managed to display finer qualities than the common peasant. A handful of women like you would make sturdy breeders without tainting the bloodlines too much."

Aya couldn't decide whether to feel insulted that she might taint the bloodlines, terrified that King Archon considered her a viable breeding candidate, or hopeful that maybe Willem's family would feel the same way about accepting a little bad blood into the Collingwood lineage.

"I'm honored you think me worthy of such a noble cause."

"You honor yourself by proving that civility can still blossom in such wretched surroundings, Miss Wellman. What was it like growing up out there? I can't even fathom it."

Aya's eyebrows raised. She had never seen the king show genuine interest in another person before. "It was not so bad when I was a child." Aya spoke slowly, carefully. "My mother died when I was little. My father raised me through my childhood, then he died at work."

"Did he fall in a well?"

Aya looked the king dead in his eyes. "More like he was pushed."

The king's forehead creased. "Do you have any proof of foul play? If so, I can help you bring his attacker to justice."

Aya pursed her lips. If only he knew. "No, I do not. It was not as simple as that. And even if I did, I would not want you to involve yourself in that way, Your Majesty. You would not either, if you understood the circumstances."

King Archon nodded and cupped her cheek with his hand. "I'm so sorry, my dear."

Aya gently brushed his hand away from her face, feigning nonchalance. "It's all right. A kind woman took me in. She tried to teach me her craft, but I was never good at it. Then one day, Lord Varick came to her establishment and made me his ward. While I can never consider myself his equal, I am ever grateful for the opportunities he has given me."

King Archon lifted Aya's hands to his lips and kissed her knuckles. His pointed beard scratched her fingers. "I am sorry you had to live through that, Aya. I promise you that your new life will be better, the life you deserve."

"Yes." Aya smiled. "I believe it will be just."

As they approached the shops, Aya observed that the corridor was relatively empty, and she let out a long breath. All of the shopkeepers were out, opening their doors and attending to their displays, but only a few customers—two elderly noblewomen waiting outside the cobbler's shop and three young women clustered outside the tea room—lingered in the corridor. When both groups of ladies caught sight of King Archon with Aya on his arm, they leaned their heads in together and whispered, not even bothering to be discreet. Aya smiled and attempted to widen her eyes with wonder and innocence.

"See?" King Archon whispered. "We are already the topic of conversation."

Aya nodded but chose not to comment further out of concern for how the ladies would interpret any words they overheard. Instead, Aya gazed out across the shops. One of the shopkeepers swept the marble floor in front of his store in the same manner that the Portside merchants smoothed out the dirt that accumulated at their doorsteps overnight. Aya shook her head. "Why do these shops exist?"

King Archon scowled and cocked his head. "What do you mean?"

"There is an entire section of the kingdom devoted to merchants and shopping. Why do the royals do their shopping in the palace instead of Portside?"

"Oh, the shops in Portside are good for basic needs, but they cater to the villagers. Their goods are not nearly as fine, and there are many items offered here that commoners do not want." King Archon waved his hand as if dismissing them. "Besides, no respectable noblewoman wants to go out into the desert to shop, not when she can do it in a clean environment."

Aya scrunched her face. "What kinds of special goods are sold here?"

They turned down the main hallway and walked along the storefronts. As they passed each shop, its shopkeeper came out to bow to the king. King Archon did not acknowledge them. "All kinds of things. Masks, as you already know, bespoke clothing, furniture, bath oils, teas. Everything, really."

With such an eclectic selection of specialty stores, Aya could not help wondering why her father's shop had not been inside the palace. Surely, as the only cogsmith, his services would have been extremely attractive to the nobles, who kept the old machines as relics in their shrines to the old world ways.

"Is there any place that could fix your clock?"

King Archon laughed. "I knew you were interested in that old beast. No. Unfortunately, none of the shopkeepers here can help with it. The last cogsmith in Desertera died almost ten years ago. Clockwork, and many other crafts, died with him."

Aya felt her stomach drop. To hear King Archon speak about her father's death, in almost a respectful way, made her sick. If she didn't know better, she would have thought the king regretted the death of the last cogsmith.

"He didn't have any apprentices?" Aya tried to keep her voice level.

"He had a daughter. I believe he must have intended to teach her his craft, but I do not know how successful he was."

Not successful enough.

"Where is she now?" Aya turned away from the king, hiding her face with feigned interest in her surroundings. "Does she have a shop in Portside?"

"What a humanitarian you are, Aya." King Archon grinned, shaking his head as if Aya's sympathy were novel. "I have no idea. Perhaps she was taken in by another merchant. Perhaps she fell to less honorable means. Perhaps she died. I cannot concern myself with what happened to one orphaned girl when I am entrusted with the wellbeing of my entire kingdom."

More like the wellbeing of your pecker.

"Oh, yes, I know, Your Majesty." Aya winced. "I was simply thinking aloud. Please forgive me."

King Archon patted her arm. "No need to apologize, my dear. I find your wonder refreshing. So many noblewomen, our beloved queen included, have become so accustomed to this life that they do not have any intellectual spark left in them. Their entire lives are one script after another."

Aya looked down at her feet. "That's so sad."

For once, Aya meant what she said to the king. She thought that sounded like a horrible, boring life. All she had ever wanted was to reclaim her father's shop, to learn cogsmithing, to *work*. To live a life devoid of usefulness had to be soul crushing. Aya promised herself that, when this was all over, if she did manage to continue her courtship with Willem, she would never allow herself to become another golden shell of a woman. She would always put her craft and herself before whatever expectations the Collingwood line had of their women.

King Archon tucked a curl behind her ear. "Would you like to sample a cup of tea? I am sure it will put your spirits right."

Aya nodded. King Archon led her into the tearoom, a shop in which every surface was either white or pink. Inside, sat five white, round tables with pink flowers and vines painted on them. Each table had four chairs around it. King Archon led her to the table nearest the windows. Aya didn't know whether this was so she could have the best view of the street, or so the street could have the best view of her. Two of the other tables were filled with women. A server came over to take their order. The king asked for two cups of their best brew.

"It is a lovely day, isn't it, Your Majesty?" one of the women asked from behind them. She was young, around Aya's age, with skin so smooth and pale that Aya wondered if she had ever seen the sun. While the woman had a pretty smile, her eyes were a bit abnormal, a little crossed and cloudy. Aya wondered if this was a cosmetic effect of the inbreeding King Archon talked so passionately about.

"Why it certainly is, Miss Collingwood." King Archon inclined his head. "Pray tell, how are Lord Collingwood's farms faring with this excessive heat?"

"Father's farms are doing quite well, thank you, Your Majesty." Miss Collingwood placed a hand on her chest. "He had to abandon one, though. The heat has scrambled the farmer's brains."

So Lord and Lady Collingwood had a daughter. Willem had a cousin and was heir to farms, not just merchant shops. Aya should have expected a *Miss* Collingwood, given that Willem had only said Lord Collingwood had no sons, but it was still odd to see his child in the flesh—especially knowing that the girl was around the same age as Aya and Dellwyn. Now Aya had another finding about Dellwyn's best customer to report.

"Pity." King Archon shook his head. "I'm sure he will find another willing farmer to replace him."

"Yes, I'm sure he will." Miss Collingwood turned to Aya. "Miss Wellman, you look beautiful today."

Gossip must be spreading if a lady as high up the noble tree as Miss Collingwood knew her name. Aya touched her chest. "Thank you. As do you, Miss Collingwood."

"I mean it. That dress is divine—fit for a queen! Lord Varick must have paid handsomely for it. You must tell me who made it for you."

From the smirk on Miss Collingwood's face, Aya could tell that she was only partially sincere. What she really wanted to say was, "How does a poor ward like you have finer clothing than me?" Then again, with her use of the word "queen," Miss Collingwood may have been asking, "How many times did you have to bed the king before he gave you that?"

"Unfortunately, I cannot." Aya smiled. "It was not made for me but rather loaned to me by a friend."

Miss Collingwood lifted her chin. "Ah, I suppose that makes sense. How are you enjoying your new life in the palace?"

Aya withheld a chuckle. "It has been quite educational. And everyone is so welcoming. I am delighted to be here."

"Good. You will have to join us for tea some time." Miss Collingwood glanced at King Archon. "The society of so many men must grow tiresome."

Now Aya really wanted to laugh. Miss Collingwood was insinuating that Aya was a loose woman. Aya bit her cheek. If only the prudish society lady knew!

"It does. I would love some female company."

"It's settled then." Miss Collingwood clapped. "The next time we take tea, we shall send you an invitation."

"That would be lovely. Thank you."

Miss Collingwood bowed her head, and the discussion was closed. Aya turned back to watch the street. There were more and more nobles visiting the shops, and many of them stole a glimpse at her and the king. The server came back with their tea, brown and steaming inside white porcelain cups with flowers painted on to match the tables.

"Why look at that," King Archon whispered, his eyes sparkling with delight. "You're making friends already."

Aya twisted her lips and glanced back at the table of ladies. "I highly doubt Miss Collingwood wants to be my friend so much as she wants the enjoyment of having someone to feel above."

King Archon chuckled. "You have everyone in the palace figured out, don't you?"

Aya let her eyes trace the lines of his face. "Almost everyone."

King Archon took a sip of his tea. Aya stirred a silver spoon in hers before doing the same. She'd never had tea before, but the moment it washed over her tongue, she nearly gagged. It tasted like dirty water mixed with the bath oils she'd been given at the bathing house—grainy, lemony, minty, with some kind of plant extract. She forced herself to keep a straight face.

"How do you like the tea?"

The king seemed to appreciate her candor, so she kept it coming. "It's vile. But I'm willing to try to acquire the taste."

King Archon laughed. "You will do well here, Aya. You really will."

17

———————

After they finished their tea—even by the end of her cup, Aya still had not acquired a taste for it—the king insisted they visit some of the other shops. "It is a show of goodwill."

Aya did not want to browse the stores, but she had to admit, it was nice to have distractions to keep King Archon from staying so close by her side. She could scurry from display to display in the shops, pretending that a hat or ottoman or vial had caught her eye, to escape the king's clutches. After she had repeated this process at a few different shops, King Archon finally learned to stand in the center of the shop with his arms folded and chat with the shopkeeper. His eyes still followed Aya's every move, staring at her like a child who had caught his first sand beetle, but at least his hands stayed off her.

Once a couple hours had passed this way, they reached the end of the shops. Aya nearly bounced on her heels, anxious to get away from the pushy shopkeepers and the nosy society ladies and into some fresh air. She didn't know how much longer she could stand to be cooped up amongst all the excess and wealth.

"Your Majesty?"

King Archon was conversing with the palace's painter and did not notice her at first. She called after the king again, and it became apparent that he was ignoring her. Aya sighed. Knowing he wanted attention, she stood beside him and tapped his shoulder. "Your Majesty?"

He looked at her with exaggerated surprise. "Oh, Aya. Are you done?"

"These paintings are exquisite. I'm sure I could gaze at them forever." Aya smiled at the painter, hoping she would not think Aya rude. "However, I am growing rather hungry for our lunch."

"Me too, my dear. Let us head up to the deck. Good day, Piero."

The painter bowed as they left. King Archon took Aya's arm in his again. As they strolled away from the shops, Aya swore she heard a ripple of whispers in their wake. She could not make out any of the words, but she hoped they were more about how King Archon's pattern was emerging again and less about how she should be detained for socializing with a married man.

As they traversed the palace's passages and stairwells, King Archon tried to engage Aya in more polite conversation. Looking away from the king, Aya rolled her eyes and prayed he would quit talking. A quick glance behind showed her that Eldric still followed them, and Aya repressed a sigh. When would he leave them alone so she could reel in the king and get the day over with?

King Archon cleared his throat. "Which shop was your favorite?"

Aya released her pent-up sigh. "Oh, that is difficult. They were all so lovely." Aya tapped her bottom lip with her finger. Unlike the first time she attempted to woo the king, he responded to her physical cues. His gaze fell to her lips, flitting between them and her eyes.

"I think I liked the bookbinder best. The act of repairing

books is incredibly noble. She is literally holding together our ancestral culture and history."

"Hmm. I never thought of it that way." King Archon slipped his arm out of Aya's and around to her waist. "Your creativity continues to amaze me."

"Thank you, Your Majesty." Aya took a few quick steps to break free from his arm. The king's brow furrowed, but she played it off with an innocent shrug and a smile. He had to know that any woman he socialized with would fear such intimate contact. After all, he was a married man. Or was he already living as if his queen were gone? That would make Aya's task much easier.

Aya and King Archon arrived at the top of the palace. They climbed a grand staircase with red velvet carpeting to a set of double glass doors framed in gold. The extravagance of the ship washed over Aya again. If it were built for the purpose of survival, why expend so many resources on decorations? They could have been put toward extra rooms, food, or fuel to support more people. How many citizens were left behind because of the nobles' greed?

A maid waited at the doors, holding a dark green headscarf. When Aya reached her, the maid curtsied and extended the scarf. "To protect your lovely hair, Miss Wellman."

"Thank you."

Before Aya could take the scarf, King Archon had already snatched it from the maid and was wrapping it around Aya's hair. Once he had tightened the scar, King Archon tucked a stray curl behind the fabric. His fingertips brushed against Aya's neck, and she shivered, imagining the executioner's blade in their place.

King Archon rested his hands on her shoulders. "Something about you seems familiar. I feel like I've known you for longer than I have."

It took all of Aya's self-control not to roll her eyes. The king was finally flirting with her—and in the most foolish possible way. Aya imagined those words coming from Willem's smooth voice, instead of the King Archon's gravelly one, and she smiled. "I feel like I know you well, too, Your Majesty."

She did. Aya knew his cruelty better than most. She had seen his true nature ten years ago and received a fresh taste only a few days back. She could not wait for the moment of his undoing, when she could reveal her true self to him, when those blue eyes would finally show horrified, glorious recognition. Knowing the king as she did now, she thought he might even be proud that his new pet was capable of deception of the same caliber as he. Of course, the difference was that her deception was just, retributive, and not merely for her own sick pleasure.

Once Aya's headscarf securely sheathed every brown curl, King Archon motioned for the maid to open the doors. She pushed them back at the same time, allowing a gust of wind to blow into the palace. Aya hustled out to the deck, anxious to take in the warm air. She raised her arms, allowing the breeze to envelop her frame and swirl around her limbs. It was the closest she had ever been to swimming.

"I'm glad you are enjoying the fresh air," King Archon said.

"It is divine."

Divine. Aya remembered the word on Willem's lips, and her face flushed.

"Shall we take a walk around the deck while our lunch is brought up?"

"Sure." As soon as she spoke, King Archon once again extended his arm for her to hang on. Aya sighed, wondering whether all noblemen pulled their ladies around like farm animals.

King Archon led her over to the railing. They had emerged at the northern side of the palace, and Aya looked down to see Bowtown's curved rows of farmhouses. From the deck, the people looked the size of lizards, the larger animals like beetles, and the smallest ones like ants. It made Aya's knees quiver to be so high, and she unthinkingly clutched the king's arm tighter.

"Are you scared of heights?"

Aya looked down at her hand to see four white knuckles and a hooked thumb. Blushing, she loosened her grip. "I'm not accustomed to them, Your Majesty."

King Archon gripped the railing and tugged. "There is no need to fear. The railings are as sturdy as the day they were built. You would have to want to go over them."

Aya nodded, thinking that she would love for the king to go over them and solve all of her problems himself.

King Archon pulled her closer to his side and began turning her toward Starboardshire.

"Wait." Aya slipped out of his grasp. "I want to see Portside."

The king frowned. "Whatever for?"

In truth, Aya wanted to look for her father's shop and see if she could view its condition. She did not make many trips into Portside, except to pick up food or get a dress mended, and she had purposely avoided her childhood home. However, now that she knew it would be hers again, she wanted to see it. She did not know whether another merchant had occupied it or if it simply sat empty and falling to disrepair.

"I want to save Starboardshire for last. I want to look at how far I've come and gaze upon my new home at the end."

King Archon chuckled. "As you wish."

Aya didn't reply. She walked over to the Portside railing and clutched the steel bar with both hands. Shading her eyes with her hand, she counted the rows of merchant shops until she found her childhood street then scanned the stores for her home.

The shop was still standing, a good sign. Aya squinted. A woman exited the shop with something in her arms, and a man entered after her. So it was occupied. She hoped the owner had kept it in good shape. It would be a shame if Aya had to hire a carpenter to fix it up for her, especially considering she would be starting her father's business back up on only the few coins hidden in his urn.

"What are you looking for?" King Archon placed one hand on Aya's lower back and the other over one of hers on the railing. Aya couldn't decide whether he wanted an excuse to touch her or was worried she would tip over the railing. She made the mistake of looking down at his hand, and her eyes found a direct line to the ground below. The guards stood in the shade of the palace, but instead of looking like tall sentinels, from this angle, they looked like black dots. Aya stepped back from the railing. It was much more terrifying to look down than it was outward.

"I…" Aya bit her lip, searching for a believable lie. "I thought I recognized a friend. But it's so difficult to see from up here. I suppose it wasn't her."

King Archon smiled. "Forget about her. Try to focus on the present."

"Of course." Aya closed her eyes and took a deep breath, knowing the king's advice wise for both situations. King Archon slid the hand on her back around to her side and pulled her onward to Sternville. They walked in silence to the southernmost point of the palace. After touring the palace, the shabby tents and rundown hovels of Sternville looked even sadder than she remembered. Aya quickly spotted her hovel, one of the village's more house-like structures.

"Can you see where you lived in Sternville?" King Archon leaned down to align himself with Aya's line of sight.

Her breathing hitched. "Yes."

"Show me."

Aya shook her head. "I'm sorry, Your Majesty, but I won't. I wouldn't want you to think of me there."

Or make inquiries and figure out the truth.

King Archon stood and rubbed Aya's shoulder. "You must

know by now that I would never think less of you because of your origins."

Yes, because, for a poor lass, I sure would make a fine breeder.

"I do, Your Majesty." Aya sighed. "But you must know by now that I am grateful and anxious to bury the memories of my life in Sternville in its dust."

King Archon pressed his lips together. "Very well. On to better sights, then?"

"Please."

Once again, the king kept ahold of Aya as he led her to the final village of Desertera. Starboardshire looked just as Aya remembered from her first visit to the palace—artisan-crafted, wooden homes surrounded by wildflower pastures spotted with sleek horses. Aya bit her tongue to avoid saying anything out of character. Starboardshire was gorgeous, disgustingly so. The acid of envy pooled in her gut.

"How do you like the view from this side of the palace?" King Archon's chest puffed up, as if he were personally responsible for every green blade of grass between the houses.

Aya barely concealed a scoff. "It is the most aesthetically pleasing of the villages."

"You do not sound as enraptured as I expected."

"Don't get me wrong, Your Majesty. Starboardshire is clearly the most beautiful village and by far the cleanest." Aya paused, knitting her brows together. "However, I feel like it lacks the character of the others. It is *too* perfect."

King Archon took Aya's hand in his. "If there is one thing you will learn in your palace life, it is that nothing can ever be *too* perfect."

Aya saw it in his face: the arrogance, the self-awareness, the boldness. The king's head tilted slightly, and she knew he meant to kiss her. But she couldn't stand it. Not yet. Not after seeing her father's shop and the hovel she shared with Dellwyn —not when her stomach churned with jealousy and indignation.

"But don't you ever get sick of it?"

King Archon straightened and tugged at his jacket. "What is there to tire of? We have everything we could ever want in Starboardshire and the palace."

"Yes, I realize that." Aya waved her hand over Starboardshire. "But, this life—the gossip, the monitoring of the bloodlines, the always having to impress one another and exist without a single hair out of place—is it not tiring to you? I'm new to it, and I'm already exhausted."

The king crossed his arms and gazed out over Starboardshire. "Well," he finally began, "I suppose I would rather be mentally drained from keeping pace with noble politics than physically drained from a life of labor."

Aya shrugged one shoulder. She had to admit, she did prefer an unwanted conversation with a man she hated to an unwanted bedding from a man she didn't know. Of course, that could have been because she knew the satisfaction from the end of her mission would be so much sweeter.

"I suppose that is fair. I guess I miss the authenticity of the villagers. When people don't have what they need to survive, they don't have time to put on masks. You know exactly who everyone is and what everyone is thinking."

King Archon shook his head. "I believe you are not giving your people enough credit, Aya. Maybe they put on a mask of honesty to hide their vanity, the way we put on vanity to hide our honesty."

For once, Aya took in the depth of King Archon's words. "Maybe you're right."

"Now that's a sentence I never thought would escape your lips." King Archon laughed and retook her arm. "Come, let us eat."

Aya took a final glance at Starboardshire over her shoulder. Maybe the king was right. Maybe the nobles and the commoners weren't so different after all.

18

———

King Archon led Aya to the middle of the palace's deck, where a table for two had been arranged between the center smokestacks. The greenhouse stood nearby, a few yards outside of the smokestacks' shadows, but this time, Aya did not have to wonder about the fruits inside. As they moved closer to the table, King Archon weaved to avoid part of the deck, and Aya glanced down at a wide pane of thick glass on his other side. She realized it must lead to the ballroom or courtroom beneath, and she shuddered as her mind calculated the distance to the floor below.

When she looked up again, Aya noticed the maid from the doorway standing a few feet away from the table with a carafe of red wine in her hands. Eldric stood an arm's length away from her. There was another man present, and from his crisp white apron, Aya guessed that he was the palace chef or perhaps King Archon's personal chef. As they reached the table, the chef opened his arms. "Your Majesty. You have picked the perfect day for a luncheon!"

"I do hope so, Stefan. What have you prepared for us?" The king pulled one of the chairs away from the table and motioned for Aya to seat herself.

"Thank you," she said.

The king scooted the chair in so that Aya sat close to the table, the folds of her blue gown lost under the white table-cloth. As King Archon seated himself across from her, Stefan moved to stand between them. The table was filled with all kinds of food and more silverware than Aya had seen in her life. She couldn't imagine what each utensil was used for.

"Well, for your entrée, I have prepared a loaf of bread from Bowtown's finest wheat fields. It is, of course, seasoned with garlic, rosemary, and other herbs for your palatal pleasure. There are plenty of spreads—goat butter, strawberry jam, et cetera—for you to enrich it."

Aya had never seen such round and full bread before. The rolls and loaves from Portside were half as large and not nearly as fluffy. She looked at each of the spreads in turn, finding it fascinating that anyone would need something to enrich bread. Wasn't a hot slice of bread a treat enough in itself?

"For your main dish, I have prepared a succulent pork roast from the largest pig in Bowtown. I flavored it with my secret sauce, and I am sure it will make your mouths water."

"Secret sauce?" Aya asked.

King Archon tapped his nose. "Oh yes, Stefan's secret sauce is legendary in the palace. He has never told his recipe to another person."

Stefan winked. "My mother passed it to me on her deathbed, and I shall do the same."

Aya's eyes widened. "What if you don't get the chance to tell someone before you die?"

King Archon cleared his throat. "Don't be morbid."

"No, no, the lady makes a good point." Stefan clasped his hands. "Luckily, there is a written recipe for such an occasion." An artificial secret then. "For dessert, I have prepared an ice cream made from goat milk and fresh fruit picked just one hour ago from the greenhouse."

Aya's mouth fell open. "Ice cream?"

"Certainly." Stefan grinned. "It is on ice whenever you are ready."

"On actual ice?" Aya had never seen ice. She hadn't even realized anyone still had the technology, or the excess water, to make it. No wonder the water levels in the wells sank so much lower every year.

Stefan laughed again. Aya liked his laugh. It was soft and kind.

"Of course, Miss Wellman. Now, if there are no more questions, I shall leave you to your meal. Please send the maid if there is anything else you require."

"Thank you, Stefan," King Archon said.

Aya's jaw remained slack as she shook her head. While she digested her shock, King Archon slathered a red spread—the strawberry jam, Aya guessed—on a piece of bread. Taking a deep breath, Aya pushed past her emotions and reached for the goat butter, hoping it would not enrich the already-seasoned bread too much. As the buttered bread hit her tongue, Aya's mouth began to water, melting the creamy spread and fluffy slice together. She closed her eyes to savor the appetizer. After everything she had tasted at the palace, Aya did not know how she would ever go back to the food in the villages.

"How do you like it?"

"It is sensational." Aya covered her mouth with her hand. "I have never tasted bread so full and rich, and the butter, it's incredibly sweet."

"It must be nice," the king began, scooping a piece of pork roast onto his plate, "to be so easily pleased."

"How are you not pleased? As you said yourself, you want for nothing here." Aya took a piece of meat for herself. She watched King Archon's movements carefully and used a new knife and the long-tonged fork. The meat was so tender that it nearly fell apart in her mouth; she hardly had to chew it.

"True. All my needs are met in one way or another." King Archon twirled a piece of pork on his fork as he spoke.

"But when you are born with the best, you grow accustomed to it, and once that happens, you want something better. When there is no better, it is easy to become bored and disgruntled."

Aya looked up. The moment her eyes met his, she knew that they were no longer discussing food. The way the king watched her raise each bite to her mouth, the way he licked the corner of his lips, the way he leaned toward her, told her everything she needed to know. He was finally dancing around the concept of obtaining new wives.

"I simply cannot believe it." Aya sipped her wine, allowing a tiny drop to dribble down her chin. She wiped the liquid with her finger and sucked the juice off her fingertip. "You are the most powerful man in Desertera. You have wealth and…" Aya paused, swallowing to loosen her throat. "…a handsome demeanor, a palace, an heir, a gorgeous wife. What more could you possibly want?"

King Archon shrugged, picking up his wine. He swirled the red liquid around and sniffed the top of the glass. "Is it wrong to want more than the superficial? Yes, I have money. I have a son to replace me in death and a beautiful wife to entertain me in life. But that is not all I want. Can I not want substance with it all?"

Aya leaned back and crossed her arms. "What kind of substance?"

"Oh, I don't know. I want to be challenged, to have genuine conversations with a woman who is clever and curious and honest, not one who just tells me what I want to hear and relies on her pretty face to nod."

And so the battle began—Aya versus Queen Zedara. Aya made a show of sitting up straight and nodding as high and low as her head would bobble. King Archon chuckled. Other than her initial slip up, Aya had seemed to full all of the king's desires. She wondered how far she could push the limits of propriety.

"Forgive me if I am being too bold, Your Majesty, but are you saying that you are unhappy with the queen?"

King Archon took a deliberate drink of his wine. "Oh, no, no. The queen is a lovely woman. I just wish she wasn't so much like all the other noblewomen. I wish she had more substance."

If only Queen Hildegard's statue could clue poor Archon in.

"Again, Your Majesty, I apologize for being so blunt, but—what did you expect when you married a noblewoman? Does society allow them to be anything other than what you describe?"

The king stared at Aya for a long moment. "I suppose you are right."

Aya decided to let the subject drop. She had made her point and implied what she needed to imply. Now she had to wait to see if the king would take the bait.

King Archon set his wine glass down and rubbed his stomach. "I think I am ready for some ice cream. How about you?"

The king waved his hand at the maid, and she hustled off to fetch the ice cream. Aya looked down at the table. Three-quarters of the bread loaf and over half of the pork roast remained uneaten. Images of the thin children in Sternville flashed through her mind, and Aya's stomach knotted.

"Will all of this go to waste?"

King Archon glanced at the leftover food as if he did not realize they were at a meal. "Oh, well, I imagine the servants will finish it off."

Aya clenched her fists in her lap. The king had never even thought of what to do with the excess food. And his solution? Feed it to the servants. He viewed food in the same way he viewed women. If he became bored or they could not be of use to him, get them off of his plate, and let someone else clean up the mess. And the loved ones left over? What leftovers?

The maid returned with two glass bowls, each containing three pink scoops of ice cream. Aya waited for King Archon to select a utensil, and when he picked up a spoon, Aya did the same. She dipped her spoon into the ice cream. It was the strangest texture—soft enough that the spoon sliced through it easily but firm enough to hold its shape. It reminded her of the yogurt she had eaten with Willem, only thicker. She balanced a small bit of the ice cream on her spoon and took a bite.

Aya had never experienced real cold. Sure, she had walked through the streets of Desertera on crisp mornings to fetch cool water, but she had never experienced something *frozen*. The cold spread through her entire mouth, and strangely, the place on her tongue where the ice cream rested felt as though it was burning. She tried to chew, but a sharp pain hit her teeth like a hammer. Desperate for an escape, she swallowed, feeling the ice cream slide down her throat and plop into her stomach.

King Archon chortled, scooping a large spoonful of ice cream into his mouth. "Your senses will adjust. Keep taking little bites. Don't eat too quickly, or it will make your head hurt."

Aya did as he suggested, and eventually, the sting of the cold lessened, and she was able to enjoy the creamy texture and fruity flavor of the ice cream. She wondered how Stefan manufactured the ice to make the dessert and keep it cold. Aya's father had told her that the nobles used to have machines and metal boxes to make and store ice, but she thought those had lost function, along with most other machines, when the bulk of the water dried up. She hoped the nobles were not using water to power their machines. The thirsty commoners would riot if that were true.

They ate their dessert in silence. King Archon appeared content to watch Aya. She felt his eyes on her and did not know what to do with her face. She settled for alternating between surprise and contentment. Apparently, these expressions pleased the king, as he smiled and stared at her.

When they were finished, the king scooted her chair away from the table and took her arm again.

"Thank you for lunch." Aya smiled. "It was delightful."

"It was entirely my pleasure, my dear. Now, would you like to move on to the grand finale?"

"Please."

King Archon motioned for Eldric to come over. The valet leaned into him, the king whispered a few words, then Eldric departed, taking the maid with him. As the valet strolled away, Aya's heart thumped. With him gone, Aya could better complete her mission to acquire the king's affections. However, that also meant Aya had to be alone with the king, a thought that sent her thumping heart into her throat.

King Archon and Aya walked back through the double doors and down the grand stairwell. Before they reentered the hallway, King Archon stopped and turned to face a large portrait hanging on the wall. The portrait began at the floor and stretched at least six feet high and three feet wide. From its canvas stared Queen Hildegard, standing at the helm of the ship and steering it through the great rains.

"Aya, can you keep a secret?"

Aya grinned. *Oh, can I ever.* "Of course, Your Majesty. Anything for you."

She swore she saw a little pink dance across the king's cheeks.

"Good. I want to show you something, and you must swear never to tell another living soul what you have seen."

"I promise." Aya took her finger and drew an X over her heart. King Archon nodded, reached up to the portrait, and pushed. Instead of falling or clattering against the wall, the painting slid to the side, revealing a dark passageway with a sloping floor. The king stepped aside and motioned for Aya to enter the tunnel. She held her breath for a moment, wondering if she could trust the king. While she was almost positive he had no notion of her true identity and her quest to have him executed, she did not like the idea of crawling into a hole with a snake. However, to deny him would be to show her distrust, and he had been nothing but doting and kind to Miss Aya Wellman. Miss Aya Cogsmith would have to sit this one out.

As Aya entered the darkness, her knees trembled and her ankles grew weak. Once she was inside, King Archon came into the passageway. He turned around to pull the portrait shut behind them, and the corridor became pitch black. The king moved around Aya, taking advantage of the close quarters to brush the full front of his body against hers. He reached down and grasped Aya's shaking hand, giving it a squeeze before leading her down the tunnel. "The passageway becomes a bit steep, but it is entirely straight, so you do not have to worry about running into any walls."

Despite his reassurance, Aya still pulled back on his hand, insisting they walk slowly. The king did not seem to mind, and he used the extra time to rub his thumb over her knuckles and wrist. Aya shivered at the realization that he could feel her pulse, that he had a direct connection to her heart, which he probably thought he would own shortly—if he didn't already.

"Where are we going?" Aya's voice quivered.

"Patience, my dear. It's a surprise."

Aya heard the smile in his voice. Her jaw clenched. "I don't like surprises."

King Archon laughed. "You have not seemed too opposed to the rest of today's surprises."

"Well, I don't like ones I can't see coming."

"Aya, if you could see them coming, they wouldn't be called surprises."

She huffed. He chuckled again. *We'll see who likes surprises.*

Aya reached her free hand out to touch the wall. It was cold and smooth, no doubt made of the same metal as the rest of the ship, and as her hand explored the surface, it found a seam and a series of bumps—rivets. Judging by the feeling under her shoes and the quick glimpse she got at the entrance to the tunnel, she believed the floors to be made of wooden planks. Each step felt a bit rough and unlevel, and she thought she felt a few pokes where a nail head might have stuck out from the wood.

"Almost there."

The slope grew steeper, and Aya took short, hard steps to steady her feet. She was actually grateful to have the king anchoring her, so she could dip her weight backward to keep herself from toppling forward. Granted, the king probably would have loved for her to fall into him.

King Archon stopped and released Aya from his grasp. She heard his fist knock against something. It sounded hollow.

"Here we are."

The end of the passageway erupted into light. Aya shielded her eyes as the king slid the door open the rest of the way. Like the previous entrance, this one was obscured by a piece of decoration. King Archon stepped into the room, and Aya followed. They were in the round area outside King Archon's chambers.

Glancing behind her, Aya saw that one of the king's book-shelves hid the tunnel's exit. The king pushed it back into place with ease—the books must have been for show. Aya looked to the grandfather clock and the mysterious door beside it. "I would have thought we would have come through that door."

King Archon followed her gaze. "No, no. That door doesn't go anywhere."

"What do you mean?" Aya raised her eyebrows. "All doors go somewhere."

"Not that one." King Archon sighed. "I have tried to open it. It has been locked for decades, and none of my guards are able to break it down."

"How curious."

Before Aya could examine the door further, she felt King Archon's presence behind her. His chest pressed against her back, and his large hands slid up her arms to sit on her shoulders. The king rested his chin next to his hands, and Aya felt his pointed beard poke her naked clavicle.

"Just like you. Always so curious."

Aya took a long, slow breath and closed her eyes. This was the moment. The king had gone out of his way to spoil her, had complimented her wit, had maintained physical contact—and now he had raised the level of intimacy. All of her training, waiting, and tolerating had come down to this. If she could not secure the king's affections now, the entire mission would be compromised, Lord Varick and Queen Zedara would have to start over with a new seductress, and Aya would be back in her room at the Rudder with her father unavenged.

Aya reached her hand up to the back of King Archon's neck. He exhaled sharply at her touch, and she felt his lips brush her shoulder. She shivered, which encouraged him to continue kissing, all the way up to her neck. She kept quivering, shaking—she couldn't pull herself together. She tried to think of Willem's lips on her, of her father's screams as the guards dragged him away, of her own head being chopped off if she messed this up—anything to motivate herself.

Okay. One. Two. Three.

Turning around, Aya grabbed King Archon's head with both hands and smashed her lips into his. She kept her eyes shut tight, but she forced her lips to move against his. She opened her mouth a fraction of an inch, and the king took the bait, licking her bottom lip before pushing his tongue into her mouth. He shoved it around her mouth furiously, as if he wanted to turn her inside out. Even though it was small comfort, she couldn't help thinking that Willem was a much better kisser.

King Archon wove one hand through Aya's curly hair and slid the other down her back to grab her bum. Aya jumped against his touch, which only made him squeeze her harder. It felt as if his fingers would pierce her skin. With every movement she made, he held her tighter, pulling her body against his until she felt her spine would crack. She wondered if all the royals had been like this, if they all were so forceful and greedy and relentless in their lovemaking. If so, she probably could have learned a thing or two from Queen Hildegard to take back to the Rudder.

After a few more moments of suffocation, Aya pulled King Archon away from her by his hair. He growled but broke the kiss, staring down at her with a mixture of pain and delight in his blue eyes. Aya caught her breath and wiped her mouth with the back of her hand. "Your Majesty, while I am flattered by your—"

"Then just be flattered, Aya." He grabbed her by the waist and pushed her up against the wall. Using his hips and legs to pin her into place, the king explored Aya's body with his hands, sliding them up her sides, across her stomach, over her breasts. His lips kept her head locked back against the wall as they placed little kisses all over her face and deeper kisses down her neck and shoulders. All Aya could do was claw at his back and moan—which served the dual purpose of expressing her agony and furthering his deception. As the king's head dipped down toward her breasts and his hand began to search through the folds of her dress, Aya pushed him away.

"Your Majesty. We must stop."

"My dear, we don't have to—"

Aya pressed both her palms against his chest. "Yes. We do."

King Archon's eyes flared with anger, and he backed away from her. Aya took a breath and closed the distance between them. She affixed her face with a sad smile and returned her hands to the king's chest. "Your Majesty, as much as I want to —and trust me, I do—we cannot continue this. If we go any further, we will be in breach of the adultery law, and I will not risk your life for the little satisfaction a night with me will bring you."

"I assure you, I will be quite satisfied." The king's hands moved back to Aya's waist.

She let hers run up and down his chest, hoping her unwillingness to meet his eyes made her appear more vulnerable than disgusted. "No, Your Majesty. I cannot sacrifice your kingdom for my own selfish pleasure. Desertera needs your noble leadership. Without you, the kingdom would fall to pieces."

"I'm the king." King Archon cupped her cheek. "No one will find out about us, and even if they do, no one will dare speak against us or harm us."

Aya clutched his shirt in her fists and unleashed the full force of her eyes on him. "*You* have the safety of being king. I'm a ward. Before that, I was nothing. As your mistress, I will never have security. I will always live in fear of being discovered, of being the downfall of your kingdom. I couldn't bear it."

King Archon craned his neck down and kissed Aya's nose. He rested his forehead against hers. "Aya, you are the most curious, passionate, fiery woman I've ever met. I cannot live without you for a moment longer."

Aya sighed. "And I cannot live with the thought of my actions removing you from this world, Your Majesty."

"And what if they didn't have to?"

Aya felt her eyes light up in genuine shock. She didn't think it would come so easily, but here it was. King Archon straightened, wrapping his arms around Aya. She let herself sink into his embrace, literally hanging on his every word. "What do you mean?"

King Archon took her chin between his thumb and forefinger. "What if I weren't married? What if I were free to be with you as I pleased? Would you have me?"

Aya bit her lips to keep from breaking into a premature grin. "Have you as what? My lover?"

"For a while, yes." King Archon tilted his head. "And then as more, as your husband, if you could?"

Aya had not smiled this widely since the day her father had opened his hands to reveal Charlie's golden frame. If the king hadn't been holding her, she was sure she would have floated up to the ceiling. It was done. All she had to do was get him to say it, one more time, with Lord Varick and company within earshot.

"Yes. A million times yes."

King Archon took Aya's face in her hands and kissed her. She smiled into his kiss, not caring that his beard scratched her neck, his lips were rough, and his hands were clammy. She had done it. It was only a matter of time now. She wanted to kiss him—she truly did—for presenting her wildest dream on a silver platter.

The king broke the kiss and wiped Aya's cheek with his thumb. She hadn't even realized she was crying, but there it was, the holy salt water slipping down her face. King Archon beamed at her.

"But how, Your Majesty?" Aya whispered. "Is there truly a way for us to be together?"

"Yes, my dearest. But you must give me a few days to make the arrangements."

"What do you have to do?" Aya prayed he would say it.

King Archon wiped another tear from her cheek. "Do not worry yourself with the details. I will take care of everything. You simply stay quiet and safe, and I will send word for you to come to me in a few days."

"Promise?" Aya widened her eyes.

King Archon grinned. "Cross my heart."

Aya bounced on her heels, stretching up to kiss the king again. In just a few days, she would complete her mission and finally know the taste of justice, which, she hoped, wouldn't be so salty.

"Now, hurry back to Lord Varick's estate." King Archon rubbed her shoulders. "My valet will be returning soon, and I don't want anyone to see you coming from my chambers."

"Yes, Your Majesty."

King Archon wrinkled his nose. "I think Archon will do now, dear."

Aya batted her eyelashes. "Yes, Archon."

She wished she could see herself in a looking glass now. She knew she must be radiant.

King Archon kissed her again, before wrapping her in his arms and burying his face in her hair. He took a deep breath, which left Aya's neck cold. She hugged him back just as tightly, wishing she could thank him for what he was truly doing.

"I cannot hold you any longer, or I won't be able to let you go. Hurry now, and I shall see you in a few days."

"I will count the seconds."

As they parted, Aya took the king's hands and kissed them. He smiled at her and returned the gesture, then released her. She scurried off down the hallway, stopping outside the round room's narrow entrance to take one final look at him.

There he stood, her father's murderer, straight and proud with his tall top hat and pointy beard. His blue eyes watered, the softest she had ever seen them. For a moment, just a moment, her heart fluttered at his beaming white smile and the crinkles it created around his lips. If someone else were planted in her body, they would see a man in love, staring longingly after the object of his affection. But Aya knew better. Behind this handsome, regal exterior slept a monster, one that would devour everything she gave him before spitting her out and moving onto the next bright-eyed girl—no doubt taking a few other innocent lives along the way.

As she turned away, Aya felt the heat of the king's desire radiating out of the room after her. She did not take another look back. Like the first night she had left this room, she kept walking forward, her back straight and steps purposeful. Let him sleep with a light heart and easy mind tonight. It would be one of his last.

*A*ya kept her pace steady and determined. While her nerves were on fire and every muscle in her body wanted to leap for joy, she knew that she had to remain as inconspicuous as possible. Before, she'd had the excuse of naïveté. But after her public dance with the king at the masquerade and their outing to the shops today, her presence near his chambers would invite extreme suspicion.

Aya kept her eyes forward, unsure of where to go. Undoubtedly, Lord Varick would want to know of her success and the nearing end of their mission. However, it was close to dinnertime, and the idea of being trapped through a meal with him, assuming he still felt so hospitable, made her stomach churn. No, Aya would go to her hovel in Sternville, visit with Dellwyn before she headed to her shift at the Rudder, and get some much-needed sleep in her own room. As much as she adored the two lavish rooms she had slumbered in at the palace, Aya missed having a space that didn't come with another person and a sense of obligation.

Just as the statue of Queen Hildegard came into view, someone grabbed Aya's arm. She went to scream, but a hand covered her mouth and pulled her into a dark hallway. Aya beat against her attacker's chest with her free arm. He pushed her up against a wall, pinning her body so she could not move, and Aya looked up. Her heart rate slowed, and she sighed. Willem. Maybe she wouldn't be returning to Sternville yet.

Aya smiled against Willem's hand. He responded by removing his hand from her mouth and relaxing his grip on her side. He did not, however, release her from the wall. Smiling even wider, Aya gently rocked her hips against his. "If you wanted to get my heart racing, you didn't have to scare me. A kiss would have done the trick."

Willem grimaced. "I thought you would have had enough kissing today."

"From you?" Aya smirked. "Never."

"Obviously, I have failed you, Aya." Willem's hands squeezed her sides again. "After all, if I had satisfied you, maybe you wouldn't have felt the need to kiss the king."

Aya's eyes widened, and she felt the blood drain from her face. She stared up at Willem, who glowered down at her with a mixture of hurt and anger in his hazel eyes. "I don't know what you're talking about."

Willem scoffed. "I saw you with King Archon. His Majesty had you pinned up against the wall, just like this, and with the way you were moaning—"

"Stop." Aya tried to make her voice firm, but it wavered. "You don't know what you saw. You don't understand."

Willem shook his head. "No, you don't understand. I thought you liked me. I thought you cared about me the way I care about you. That I meant more to you than my title."

Aya clenched her fists. "And am I anything more to you than a nice bedding?"

"Excuse me?" Willem looked as if he would spit the words. A single vein bulged in his forehead.

"What? Both times I ran into you near the stern, you were coming from the staircase that leads to the Rudder." Aya mockingly put her hand on her chest. "Whatever could you have been doing down there?"

Willem's brow furrowed. "I wasn't…I was retrieving my uncle…I…" He stopped mid-sentence, his eyebrows lifting. "How do you know those stairs go to the Rudder?"

Aya flushed, her mind scrambling for an answer. "Lord Varick told me when I moved into his estate."

"Is that so?" Willem said the words slowly, clearly unbelieving.

"Stop it," Aya hissed. "The point is, how can I know I'm more than your whore?"

Willem squared his jaw. "And how can I know I'm more than your next rung on the noble ladder?"

Aya let out a long breath. "It's not about wealth or title. Not with you or the king."

"Then what is it about, Aya?" Willem ran his fingers through his hair. "Explain it to me."

Aya glanced down the hallway. No one passed by the entrance. Her head ached with all the secrets banging around in it. She longed to tell Willem the truth, to be done with the lies. He might have even understood. He had told Aya that his mother had been murdered. Surely he could empathize with Aya's motives. But dragging Willem into her scheme, whether he understood or not, would put him in too much danger. Aya's heart panged at the thought. She said the only honest thing she could say.

"Willem, I swear to you on my father's ashes that I do not care about the king—not about his money or title or personality." Aya took a deep breath before looking up, hoping her eyes could communicate what she could not. "But I do care about you, and that is why I cannot tell you about my involvement with King Archon."

"That's not good enough." Willem pursed his lips, stepping away from Aya. "I believe that you have no affection for the king. That coldness in your eyes…" Willem shook his head.

"I'm even arrogant enough to believe that you do feel something for me. But none of this makes sense. The king is married. What you're doing, it's—"

"Adulterous?" Aya whispered.

Willem rubbed his forehead. "Exactly. What could possibly be worth risking your life?"

Aya's jaw tightened. "Trust me. It's worth it."

"Look, I don't know what you're doing. But even if you do not commit adultery, you are still in danger. King Archon, he uses people." Willem glanced over his shoulder, as if someone might be eavesdropping. "He's not a good man. He's not safe to be around."

Aya raised her eyebrows. "What makes you say that?"

"I've lived in the palace my entire life." Willem's jaw clenched. "It's difficult not to notice things."

"What things?"

Willem rolled his eyes. "Don't act innocent with me. Whoever you're working with—and yes, I don't think this is something a wellman's daughter would have cooked up on her own—they must know what the king is like. All the nobles know. What I can't figure out is who would be stupid enough to play games with the king and what exactly constitutes winning."

Aya bit her lip. She couldn't say anything more, not without overtly lying or revealing the truth. As she stared up at Willem, she saw the anger drain from his eyes. His forehead crinkled with confusion and concern. Knowing this may be her only chance to secure his sympathies, Aya reached for his hand. Willem didn't pull away.

"Please don't tell anyone," Aya whispered. "I'm sorry that I've hurt you, and I'm sorry that I can't tell you the truth. But if you truly care about me, you won't turn me in to the guards."

Willem swallowed hard. "Let me help you. Whatever

you're doing, I can get you out of it. My family has connections, I can—"

"*Shh.*" Aya squeezed Willem's hand. "Your life isn't worth risking."

"And yours is?"

The corner of Aya's lip tugged up in a sad smile. "It has to be. Now, will you please leave this alone?"

Willem shook his head. "There must be a way I can help. Please, I've seen what the king can do firsthand. You have to let me save you."

"I don't need you to save me, Willem." Aya squared her shoulders. "I'm saving myself."

Before Willem could retort, Aya grabbed his neck and pulled him into a soft kiss. His lips moved against hers slowly but with great pressure, as if he needed her to feel his urgency. After a moment, Aya pulled away and cupped his face.

"I won't say anything." He sighed. "Not because I support whatever it is you're doing, but because I do care about you, and I don't want to see anyone else get hurt."

"Thank you."

"But if you need anything—"

Aya pecked his lips again. "I know. But I won't."

Aya turned and walked away. Other than a quick glance to check for passersby at the end of the corridor, she did not stop. It took every ounce of her self-control not to look back to see if Willem would follow her, but she didn't. As she had said to him, this was something she had to do for herself. Aya merely hoped his hazel eyes would still gaze down at her warmly after Willem learned the truth about who she was and what she had done.

20

———————

*E*ven though Willem had agreed not to tell anyone about Aya's involvement with the king, her heart still pounded unevenly. What if he changed his mind and informed the royal guard? What if Willem told someone in confidence, his uncle perhaps, and that person turned Aya in? What if Willem tried to intervene after all, getting both of them hurt?

With every step Aya took, the beating of her heart grew louder, pulsating in her ears, until she felt out of breath. As she reached the statue of Queen Hildegard, Aya stopped in the fork of the three corridors and placed her hands on her hips. Inhaling deeply, she stared up at the stern, unflinching Queen. In every image Aya had seen of her, Queen Hildegard appeared calm and determined, as if she knew exactly how to handle every challenge with grace and precision. Even etched into marble, the queen looked as if she was merely allowing herself to be adored until she was ready to move her stone arms and take back the palace.

"How did you do it? How did you save all of us without one moment of weakness?"

"The weakness never makes it into the history books. It dampens the story."

Aya turned around to find Queen Zedara standing behind her. The queen was dressed in an elaborate lavender gown. Undoubtedly, she was on her way to dinner with the royal family.

"I'm sorry, Your Highness. I did not see you standing there."

"It's fine. And you can call me Zedara, please." Zedara waved her hand. "With any luck, this title is temporary."

Aya smiled. Running into the queen reminded her that this would all be over soon. She would complete her mission, reclaim her father's shop, and give Willem the explanation he so desired. If he truly cared about her the way she cared about him, he would find a way to forgive her, and they could take their relationship from there. And if not, she would still have her business.

"I think your time as the queen is nearly at an end."

Zedara beamed and crossed the distance between herself and Aya. Her blond hair glowed in the candlelight, and her pale skin had the faintest golden cast. "I don't have much time —King Archon is expecting me—but please, tell me what's happened."

"The king and I spent the entire day together. He planned the whole affair around my personal interests and spent an inappropriate amount of time explaining how those of poor birth would actually do wonders for the stale noble bloodlines."

Zedara rolled her eyes. "What a swine."

Aya returned the gesture. "Anyway, when the evening came to a close, he took me back to the round room outside of his chambers and kissed me."

Zedara raised an eyebrow.

"A lot. All over." Aya shivered. "And then he asked me to be his mistress, and I refused."

"How did he respond to that?"

Aya straightened, a triumphant smile on her lips. "Exactly as we hoped."

Zedara grabbed both of Aya's hands in hers. Aya felt as if her bones would snap under Zedara's joyful squeeze. "He wants me gone?"

"Yes." Aya tightened her grip on Zedara's hands. "He asked if I would be with him if he were not married, and I said that I would. He told me to wait a few days while he made arrangements and that he would summon me when it was time."

Zedara bounced with excitement. "This is brilliant. Absolutely fantastic!"

Aya jerked Zedara's arms, and the queen stood still. "We have to be careful now. I haven't told Lord Varick yet, but I will in the morning. Stay away from any attractive men and anything that could kill you. You never know when the king is going to strike."

Zedara smirked. "Trust me, attractive men are the last thing on my mind. I know the king's games. I'll stay alive until the deed is done. And I'll be extraordinarily unpleasant tonight at dinner so he will want to speed up his arrangements."

"Wonderful. I will let you know when I hear from the king."

Zedara released Aya's hands to pat down her ruffled skirt and hair. Then, she cocked her head and frowned at Aya. "If everything went so well with His Majesty, why did you look so troubled? I thought you would faint at Old Hildy's feet."

Aya used Zedara's reference to Queen Hildegard as an excuse to turn away and look back at the statue while she formulated a response. "I suppose I'm anxious. I mean, I have spent the last ten years grieving my father's death and fantasizing about avenging him, and now that the moment is only a few days away, all that sadness and all these nerves are bubbling up inside of me."

Zedara squinted. "If you say so."

"What?" Aya crossed her arms.

"No, nothing. I believe you." Zedara sighed. "I was just making sure you weren't backing out on us."

Aya chuckled. "I would never. I'm sorry, but of the three of us, I think I have the most on the line here."

Zedara shrugged, a smile creeping over her face. "You're probably right about that. Then again, my head was just added to the stakes."

As Aya laughed, a door opened down the hallway that led to King Archon's chambers. A line of maids and butlers filed out, carrying silver food trays.

"Oh, splendid. I'm late. Thank you for the update." Zedara gathered her skirts and rushed down the corridor.

"Stay safe, Zedara."

The queen smiled back at Aya over her shoulder. "You, too, Aya."

WHILE AYA APPRECIATED Zedara's sentiment, it was unnecessary. She had every intention of keeping herself safe and out of sight until the king summoned her again. She continued on her way to Sternville, down the corridor that housed Lord Varick's estate. For a minute, Aya considered stopping in to inform Lord Varick that their mission was coming to end, especially since the king would probably be sending word for her at Lord Varick's home. However, the thought of speaking to Lord Varick sent inexplicable shivers down her spine, and Aya decided she felt more secure keeping the knowledge between her and Zedara. Besides, King Archon had claimed it would take a while to arrange everything. Tonight, Zedara could play the despicable wife and secure the king's intentions, and Aya could return to her hovel and rest. Lord Varick could wait until morning.

Aya hurried down the corridor. It was not crowded, but every few minutes a butler carrying a tray of food or finely dressed nobles would pass her on the way to their dinners. The servants would not acknowledge her at all—no doubt they were trained to act as if they did not exist—but the nobles nodded and greeted her. She replied in kind, wondering whether they remembered her as Lord Varick's ward or if she passed as a normal lady in Willem's mother's finery. A few of them erupted into whispers once she passed, and she suspected these nobles had seen her with King Archon at the shops—or worse, heard about it secondhand.

As Aya caught sight of Lord Varick's doorway, she held her breath and tried to tread as lightly as possible. The moment she did so, she blushed, cursing her foolishness. After all, it wasn't as if Lord Varick would be leaning his ear against the door, waiting to hear her specific footsteps and pounce on her. Still, better safe than sorry. Aya passed the door as quietly as she could, craning her neck to keep it in view until she was down the hallway. When she looked up, Aya had to jump to the side to avoid running into a butler with his hands full of wine bottles.

"Oh, excuse me," she said.

The butler gave a curt nod and kept walking.

The stairwell to the Rudder came into view. Aya scanned the corridor. Empty. Darting down the stairwell, Aya allowed herself to move faster now that she no longer risked encountering any nobles—at least, not any nobles who could admit to spying her in this part of the palace.

Running down the winding stairwell made Aya dizzy, and she took a moment to steady herself at the bottom. She opened the Rudder's back door slowly, peeking into the courtesans' hallway before stepping inside. A woman she didn't recognize led a merchant into Room V, but once they shut its door, the hallway was empty. If Aya had any doubt that her position at the Rudder was no longer available, the sight of the new girl quashed it. On one hand, the knowledge that she could not go back to her old life made Aya's chest swell with joy. On the other hand, if she failed her mission and managed to live through it, or if Lord Varick found a way to worm out their deal, Aya would have no way to make a living. The thought sent the air rushing out of her lungs.

Keeping her gaze straight ahead, Aya dashed up the hallway. At the end, she flattened herself against the wall, glancing around the corner to see if anyone was in the front room. Madam Huxley leaned on her podium, and a man—a well-man, judging from his muddy work clothes—stood on the other side, holding out his palm. Three bronze coins sat in his hand.

Madam Huxley raised her arms, shaking them for a second, before pointing to the door. Aya could not make out Madam Huxley's exact words, but she could guess what they were. If there was one thing Aya could say for Madam Huxley, she did not negotiate price. This resulted in great profits for the Rudder, which, of course, the courtesans never saw.

After a few more moments, Madam Huxley broke out into a yell. "Get out of my establishment, you filthy peasant!"

The man clenched the coins in his fist and raised his hand as if to punch Madam Huxley. However, after a trembling moment and a few words Aya couldn't hear, the man lowered his fist and walked out of the Rudder. Madam Huxley patted her red hair then shook out her hands.

"You know what I've always admired about you, Madam?" Aya asked, stepping out from the hallway.

Madam Huxley started, turned around, and appraised Aya's noble appearance. "Aya, I'm surprised to see you. What are you talking about?"

"You have never let men push you around. Or women, either. No matter how rich or poor they are, you control every relationship."

Madam Huxley stared past Aya's shoulder to the courtesans' hallway. "Trust me; it was not always this way." Madam

Huxley pursed her lips. "But we grow, we learn, and we improve ourselves. As you have been doing."

Aya smiled. "I am certainly trying."

"No, you're there. I can see it already. Remember, I knew you as the shivering child who had just lost her father. And now look at you, pretty and clean from the palace, seducing the king and a few other noblemen, no doubt."

Aya blushed and moved to stand next to Madam Huxley behind the podium. "Perhaps."

"Ah, perhaps. Still retaining that illusion of innocence." Madam Huxley touched Aya's pink cheek. "Smart, Aya, really. It's charming."

Aya decided not to mention that her blushing was as natural and uncontrollable as her heartbeat. "Thank you."

"How is Lord Varick treating you? I hope you're not still squirming under his thumb."

"I took your warning seriously. I also learned some information about Lord Varick that proved his character false. I've been able to leverage our arrangement to my advantage, and I believe that he is trapped into keeping his word, whether he wants to throw me out on the streets or not."

Madam Huxley raised her eyebrows. "So you will be back in Portside soon? The first lady cogsmith in the history of Desertera, maybe even in the whole world."

Aya nodded. "That's the plan."

"Good for you. I mean it." Madam Huxley tapped her fingers on the podium. "Though, I hope you remember the Rudder when you are making connections with merchants. I would be happy to give you a small commission from the transactions of those you refer here. A little favor from you would be a little favor to me and would help us both make lasting business relationships."

Aya guffawed. "Madam Huxley, I would as soon tell the merchants to fuck the next queen."

Madam Huxley's jaw dropped. After a moment of stunned

silence, she tilted her head back and laughed. "Oh, sweet Aya, you really have grown a brain after all."

"So it seems." Aya glanced down the courtesans' corridor. "Is Dellwyn in already? Or is she working later?"

"Later, of course. Her clients never start rolling in until after they've stuffed themselves at dinner and played house with the wife."

Aya cringed. *And the children, the grown children near the age of the women they bed here.*

"I'm going to go visit with Dellwyn before her shift begins. If I don't see you the next time I pass through, we may not cross paths again." Aya paused, her watery eyes surprising her. "I want to say thank you. I loathed this job and the status it brought, but you clothed and fed me. You kept me off the streets where I would have died or suffered worse fates, and I will always be grateful for it."

Madam Huxley took Aya's hand. "You're welcome. As much as I would have liked to keep you as a steady courtesan, I am truly happy to see you move on. But I'll survive." Madam Huxley dropped her hand. "You barely made me any money anyway."

Aya chuckled. "Goodbye, Madam."

"Goodbye, Aya."

21

———

*A*ya scurried through the streets of Sternville, shading her hand with her face, both to keep the setting sun out of her eyes and lessen her chances of being noticed. Now that she was dressed in palace finery, being seen by her Sternville neighbors would raise suspicion. As she hastened between the hovels, Aya's stomach churned with guilt—partly that she wore such a fancy dress among such poverty and partly that, as every gust of wind blew, dust clung to Willem's mother's dress.

When she reached her hovel, Aya paused outside the door. Should she knock? It seemed ridiculous to do so, given that this was still her dwelling. However, so much had happened in the last week. The hovel didn't feel like home anymore—not that it ever really had. Plus, Dellwyn wouldn't be expecting her, and Aya didn't want to barge in on her unannounced. Aya raised her hand and placed her knuckles against the wood, before lowering her hand and opening the door.

Dellwyn sat at the table in the common room, a meager dinner in front of her, and she jumped at the sound of the door.

"It's just me." Aya closed the door behind her. "I didn't

mean to startle you. I thought about knocking, but it just seemed so—"

"Strange and unnecessary?" Dellwyn raised her eyebrows, her eyes scanning Aya from head to foot.

Aya wiped some dust from her skirt. "Yes. Exactly."

"Well, do come in, madam." Dellwyn gave a half bow from her chair. "Like it or not, you technically still live here, too."

Aya smiled and sat down at the table.

"I'm surprised to see you. I mean, not really, since I figured you'd come back eventually." Dellwyn took a drink of water, then tilted her cup at Aya. "But isn't it a bit late for a noble-woman to be out without a chaperone?"

Aya rolled her eyes. "Very funny. Actually, I spent the day with his royal monstrosity, and I could not stand to be in that place any longer."

Dellwyn laughed. "You poor thing. You must tell me every-thing—every disgusting detail." She looked down at her plate and then at the space in front of Aya. "Are you hungry?"

"No, you eat." Aya patted her stomach. "I had a big lunch."

"Are you sure?"

"Yes, it was obscene. The king had a whole pig prepared for the two of us."

Dellwyn's eyes bulged. She glanced at her plate again, plucking a chunk of bread from her small slice. She pointed it at Aya and traced her finger up and down in the air. "At least seducing the murderer comes with perks."

Aya touched the neckline of her dress. "Oh, this? It's not from King Archon."

A smile spread across Dellwyn's face, slowly and deliber-ately, and Aya watched her eyes brighten. "From Lord Varick?"

"No." Aya felt herself blush.

Dellwyn clapped her hands. "Ah, ha! I knew you had someone on the hook when you came back here for lessons. Forget the king, tell me about *him*."

Aya raised her eyebrows, and Dellwyn let out an exasperated breath. "Fine. I want to know about the king, too. Just make it quick."

Aya chuckled. "No disgusting details?"

Dellwyn crossed her arms. "Stop stalling."

"Very well." Aya straightened herself. "After I left here, I went to the mask maker's shop while the king was selecting his mask. I used a few of your tips and got him interested. At the masquerade, he danced with me and invited me on our date today."

"Date, huh?" Dellwyn wrinkled her nose. "Did that go well?"

"Yes." Aya beamed. "Perfectly, in fact. He gave me a tour of the palace, we had lunch on the deck, and he fell right into the trap."

"So the queen's days are numbered then?"

"If he has his way, which, of course, won't happen. We'll stop him before then."

Dellwyn shook her head. "I can't believe you actually did this. I can't decide whether to be proud or scared of you."

Aya swallowed and looked down at her lap. She didn't know whether to laugh or look ashamed. She determined to change the topic instead. "Oh! Guess who I finally saw?"

Dellwyn leaned forward. "Who?"

"Lord Collingwood—and dear Benevolent Queen, is he richer than I thought. He owns merchant shops in Portside and multiple farms in Bowtown."

Dellwyn's jaw dropped. "Wow. Well I guess the next time I fancy a glass of goat milk, I know how to get it."

Aya twirled a curl between her fingers. "Guess who else I found? Lady Collingwood, herself, and her daughter, Miss Collingwood."

Dellwyn bit her lip, failing to suppress a grin. "Really? Is she hideous? And a daughter? Damn. I didn't know he had any children. How old is she?"

"His wife is the anti-you in every possible way." Aya smiled, proud of her information gathering. "Old, incredibly tall, skinny as a rail, and so sickly pale that you can see her veins through her skin."

"Ew." Dellwyn shuddered. "Is it bad that I love that?"

Aya laughed. She wanted to say that it was bad, that Dellwyn shouldn't delight in the nobles' physical imperfections but rather pity them for their uselessness and perpetual boredom. But she didn't. When she first saw Lady Collingwood, she too had delighted in her unattractiveness, and Dellwyn was still at that stage in her knowledge.

"His daughter is quite pretty, a little cross-eyed though. The weirdest part is how old she is. She's maybe a year younger than I am. And she invited me to tea."

"Did she? Strange." Dellwyn wrinkled her nose. "Well, that's a bit disgusting, that she's near my age. But at least she's not a baby. I don't know why I care, but I always feel gross when I find out my clients are impregnating their wives after a night with me."

"You are not the gross one."

"You know what I mean."

Aya nodded. She did. The fact that these people committed adultery—out of their own free will and not out of necessity— was reprehensible enough. But the fact that they would create a child at the same time was shameful.

"So is that all the gossip?" Dellwyn's face brightened again. "Any sign of Lord Derringher and his wife?"

"Nope. I did not have the pleasure. I was only there a few days, and my attention has been rather occupied."

"Oh, yes," Dellwyn cooed. "By your mysterious lover."

Aya blushed and let out a laugh. "Dellwyn Rutt, don't even—"

"Oh, no. Don't you full name me. You're not my mother. Tell me all about him."

Aya sighed, blowing a stray lock away from her cheek. As

she tried to think of what to tell Dellwyn about Willem, her brow furrowed. What did she really know about him? Sure, she knew the basics of his family history, what he was like in bed, and that he was charming and kind. But she knew nothing of his childhood or how he spent his days. And wasn't it strange that she almost always saw him alone? On the two occasions Aya encountered Willem in public, Abrim had acted oddly, the nobles had stared, and Lord Varick had been stranger than anyone. Aya's stomach knotted. Maybe she should ask Zedara about Willem the next time she and Aya crossed paths.

"Well, he's obviously rich." Dellwyn gestured to Aya's dress, interrupting her thoughts. "Unless he stole those clothes from his employer. Now that would show devotion."

"He's a nobleman." She fingered the barrette still clipped in her hair. "Actually, he's your Lord Collingwood's nephew. This dress belonged to his mother."

Dellwyn burst into laughter, barely covering her mouth before her dinner escaped. Aya frowned. She had expected Dellwyn to be jealous or irritated, not amused.

"Wow." Tears pooled in Dellwyn's eyes, and she clutched her corseted stomach. "By bedroom logic, I'm practically your aunt!"

Aya narrowed her eyes. "Practically."

"And what does the lady mother think of her son taking up with a harlot?"

Aya wished she had something to throw at Dellwyn, and she indicated as much by faking a toss at her. Dellwyn pretended to dodge, and Aya stuck out her tongue. "She doesn't think anything about it. She's dead."

Dellwyn sat up straight and pursed her lips. "I'm sorry."

"You don't have to apologize to me. She wasn't my mother."

"I know, but—"

Aya held up her hand. Almost everyone they knew had at least one dead parent. There was no reason to tiptoe around it.

"His name is Willem. And, before you ask, yes, he is gorgeous. He's at least six feet tall, lean but still muscular. Beautiful, thick brown hair that flops over his forehead in an endearing curl. And his eyes, don't even get me started on his eyes."

Dellwyn leaned forward, cradling her face in her hands. She stared across the table with moony eyes that grew consistently more mischievous. "And is he well-endowed? Outside of the wallet, I mean."

Aya took an even breath, hoping to stop her blush before it spread over her chest and face. She looked Dellwyn straight in her dark eyes and matched them with a wicked smile. "Now, now, Miss Rutt. A lady does not bed and tell."

Dellwyn leaped up from the table and ran around it, then crushed Aya in a hug. Aya hugged her back, laughing so hard she thought her ribs would crack. Or maybe that was Dellwyn's embrace.

"I'm so happy for you! Screw that. I'm so proud of you! How was it?"

"Wonderful. It's everything I knew it should have been all along and everything I never want to have with a client."

Dellwyn sat back down in her chair and crossed her legs. "So was he just a buckle in your corset? Or is he more?"

Aya fiddled with the laces on the dress' exterior corset. "I'm not sure yet. He's a good man, but we haven't known each other very long, and I don't know what will happen with the rest of my time in the palace."

"That's fair. If you do think he might be something more once this is all sorted out, be careful."

"Why?"

"It messes with your head. When you share something that intimate with another person, sometimes they get this hold over you." Dellwyn smiled toward the window. "Make sure you keep him at arm's length until you figure out what to do with yourselves."

Aya sighed. "I don't think that's going to be an issue after the truth comes out."

"What do you mean?"

"Well, first of all, Willem's a nobleman. And even if Lord Varick honors our arrangement, I'll still be merely a Portside merchant. Willem's father is alive, and I cannot imagine a nobleman would allow his son to wed a merchant, let alone a former lady of the Rudder. And even if he does, I'm not keen to give up my father's shop, not after everything I'm doing to get it."

Dellwyn gave an understanding nod.

"Besides, even if Willem's family would agree to our being together with me as a working cogsmith, I'm not sure what he will think of me after what I've done with the king. I think he will understand, but I'm not sure."

"You haven't told him?"

Aya shook her head.

"Once you explain things to him, he has to accept it. The king is a monster, and he ruined your life. Avenging your father and saving the queen, and any future queens, and the entire monarchy at that, is pretty damn heroic."

Aya bit her lip. "I hope he sees it that way."

"If he doesn't, he doesn't deserve you anyway." A smirk crept across Dellwyn's face. "And if he's mean about it, I'll castrate him."

"Dellwyn!" Aya swatted her friend's arm.

"What?" Dellwyn held up her palms. "Just offering."

Aya laughed. Even though she had only been away from Dellwyn for a few days, Aya had missed her. She doubted she could ever have this close or comfortable of a friendship with any of the noblewomen. She wondered, if she and Willem were to explore a relationship, how he and his family would feel about her staying friends with Dellwyn. After a split second of pondering, Aya decided she didn't care about his family's opinion. And if Willem didn't accept it, as Dellwyn said, Aya shouldn't be with him anyway.

"So what happens now?" Dellwyn asked.

"I wait for the king to summon me, and when he does, I get him to confess to his plans to get rid of Queen Zedara. A group of nobles will be waiting to overhear his confession, and when they do, we've got him."

"That simple?"

Aya shrugged. "That simple."

"Huh, wow." Dellwyn took her empty plate and brushed it off with a cloth from the stove before placing it back in the trunk. Aya cringed. After all the water the nobles wasted—in their wine, their baths, their frozen desserts—it nearly brought tears to her eyes to remember that the people of Sternville couldn't even afford to use water to rinse their plates.

Dellwyn turned back around, and Aya pulled her expression together. "I almost forgot. A man came by asking about you."

"What?" Aya sat up straighter. "When?"

"Early this morning. He wouldn't say who he was; though, judging by his clothing, he was a servant from the palace. Or at least from Starboardshire."

Aya crossed her arms. "Why was he looking for me?"

"Well, not you *you*." Dellwyn gestured toward Aya. "Not at first. First, he asked me about Aya Wellman."

"What did you say?"

Dellwyn shrugged. "I said that you were the orphaned daughter of a wellman and had been taken ward by some lord or other in the palace."

"Did he believe you?"

"I don't think so. He seemed shocked when I said that. He said that every other person he had talked to said they'd never heard of an Aya Wellman."

"Shit." Aya rubbed her forehead. "What else?"

"He said that a few other people, from both Portside and

Sternville, said that the only Aya they knew of was Aya Cogsmith, and they all directed him here."

Aya ran her fingers through her hair. Why would some manservant be looking for her? Did the king suspect something? Was Lord Varick investigating her, trying to find a weakness or a way out of their deal? Or maybe it was Queen Zedara, attempting to figure out who Lord Varick had entrusted her life with? Could it be Lord Collingwood or Willem, curious about the ward who'd bedded the family heir?

"What did you tell him? About the real me."

"I couldn't admit that you didn't live here, not when so many people had told him that. I told him you've been working double shifts at the Rudder and sleeping there the past week."

Aya bit her cheek. "Do you know if he checked your story with Madam Huxley?"

"No, I couldn't risk going to tell her." Dellwyn tilted her head. "But she knows everything right? She'd lie for you?"

"Yes, I believe so. I saw her on my way here, but she didn't mention it to me either way."

"I hope I did the right thing." Dellwyn shuffled her feet. "I didn't know what else to say."

Aya reached out her hand. Dellwyn took it, and Aya squeezed. "I'm certain it will be fine. Whoever he was and whatever he wanted, it won't matter in a few days anyway."

"Yeah, I'm sure you're right." Dellwyn glanced at the door. "Look, I need to get to work, but if you want me to stay, just in case—"

"No, it's fine." Aya withdrew her hand. "You don't need to miss pay on my account. Go."

Dellwyn raised her eyebrows. "Are you sure?"

"I am. Please, go make Lord Collingwood forget all about his ugly old wife."

Dellwyn chuckled. "I wish I could say something about her, but I know it would give too much away."

"Me too. I bet he picked you simply because you are the exact opposite of her."

"Probably. Poor lady. It would suck to be married to the man. I mean, he's fun to bed, especially for his age, but he can be so uptight."

Aya didn't know how to respond. She wished she could feel so flippant about Willem.

"I'll see you in the morning." Dellwyn grabbed her cloak off the wall. "And please, don't get the water. We can't have you seen, and I still owe you from last week."

"Trust me, I won't."

"Good. Have a nice night."

"Dellwyn?" Aya stared up at her friend, silhouetted in the dusky light from the doorway. "I love you."

Dellwyn grinned, one foot out the door. "I love you, too."

As Dellwyn closed the door behind her, Aya took a long, deep breath. Her eyes fell on her father's urn, still sitting in its place in the center of the table. A shiver slipped down Aya's spine. One of the nobles wanted to know more about her, and whether they were smart enough to realize it or not, the commoners had led them to her dwelling, her best friend, and her true name. If anyone put the pieces together, the entire plan would be ruined, and she would end up dead for treason —just like her father who wouldn't give up the vortric cog for Prince Lionel's bird.

The cog. Charlie!

Aya bolted up and rushed to her room. Her mind reeled with the memory of her upturned house the day Prince Lionel called for her father's execution. What if the man were after the vortric cog? She flipped open the lid of her trunk, which left a small dent in the wall where it slammed against it. Holding her breath to keep from gasping, Aya rifled through her clothing and other belongings. Her old dress remained at the bottom of the trunk. She unfolded it and breathed a long sigh of relief. Charlie was safe.

Her heart rate slowed back to a normal pace. Aya scooped up Charlie in the palms of her hands. She turned him to peer through his side into his center. The vortric cog was still in place, its nine golden teeth dug into other parts of Charlie's mechanism. Aya stared at the cog for a while, willing it to move, to reveal to her why it was so special, why her father would be willing to die to keep it out of King Archon's hands.

Aya set Charlie down in her lap and searched the bottom of her trunk for something else she had not had the heart to sell after her father's death. Her fingers found the old leather, and she pulled out her father's tool kit. The case did not hold all of her father's tools, only the most basic ones for cogsmithing, the ones that had been in their family for several generations. Aya removed two screwdrivers and examined their tips for the right size. She selected one and put the other back in its slot. She held up the tool in one hand and Charlie in the other.

"I'm sorry, buddy. It's just for a few days. Until we're safe again."

For the next hour, Aya carefully dissected Charlie, stopping only once to light some candles. She unscrewed each of his legs, unwound his winder all the way, and pulled apart gears and cogs smaller than her thumbnail. When she reached his center, she took out the vortric cog. She set it on top of her father's tool kit for safekeeping, and proceeded to reassemble Charlie. Despite the cool air wafting through her window, beads of sweat formed along Aya's forehead as she concentrated. The task of reassembling Charlie without the cog was like trying to build an eggshell without white or yoke inside. After another few hours, Aya had Charlie put back together. Unless she stared through exactly the right gap, she couldn't tell a piece was missing.

Aya wrapped her hands around Charlie to support his frame and walked him over to his place by her bed. She set him on the wooden floor in a beam of moonlight from the window. He looked exactly as he had before, if not a little sad. Aya returned his sad smile before going back over to her chest and hiding away her father's tool kit. She took the vortric cog in her hand and lay down in her bed.

Sighing, Aya turned Charlie so that he faced her. Since there was no risk of his jumping on her in the morning, she liked the idea of letting him stand sentinel by her bedside. She hadn't changed into her spare nightgown, but she did unclasp the barrette and place it next to Charlie. She wanted these pieces of Willem, the dress and barrette, to surround her.

Opening her hand, Aya examined the vortric cog in the moonlight, puzzling over it one last time. She sighed again. It was just a cog. No one knew she had it. She was probably being paranoid. Still, she slipped it inside her dress, tucking it between her breast and the corset.

Blushing, she looked at Charlie. "I know it's odd, but it will be safe here."

Charlie, of course, did not reply. But Aya liked to think that he looked a little less troubled.

"Besides, what better place for your heart than next to mine?"

22

ya awoke to profound, painful silence. Before anything else, her eyes landed on Charlie, still watching over her, still motionless. She reached her hand into Willem's mother's dress and pressed the vortric cog between her fingers. She knew it was childish, but a small part of her had hoped that Charlie could still croak without the vortric cog so that she could just destroy the thing and never have to worry about it again. But of course, Aya knew better.

Reluctantly, Aya rolled out of bed and changed into her simple brown dress, keeping the cog on her person. She headed into the common room and leaned her ear against Dellwyn's door. She waited until Dellwyn emitted a soft snore. Aya let out a long breath—she hadn't realized that she had been holding it. At least Dellwyn's return and slumber meant that she hadn't had another run in with the strange man.

Aya moved to the trunk they kept in the common room and searched for a writing implement and parchment. Sometimes, Dellwyn's clients would give her rare trinkets like these as gifts. Apparently they were out or had not had any to begin with—Aya couldn't be sure anymore—so she knew she must deliver her message by word of mouth. Her cloak still lay on

Willem's bedroom floor, so Aya grabbed Dellwyn's off the wall. She wrapped it tightly around her shoulders and went out into the bright Desertera morning.

Aya was greeted by a hot gust of dusty wind and a swarm of grubby children. Delightful. She walked slowly to the palace, using the trip to formulate her message exactly. She wanted it to be vague enough that a guard would not comprehend its meaning but clear enough that Lord Varick would understand her without the need for further conversation.

As she reached the palace, Aya surveyed the guards near the stern. As promised, Lord Varick had about half a dozen guards stationed outside the ship. Near the propeller blades, Aya spied the graying guard who had led her to Lord Varick's chambers when she'd first agreed to help with the mission. If Lord Varick had trusted him with information that first night, he must be good enough for her purposes today. Aya approached him and curtsied. "Good day, sir."

"Good morning, m'lady." The guard bowed. "How may I help you?"

Aya stepped in closer so she could lower her voice. The guards were spaced far enough apart that she did not think the others would hear her, but she did not want to take any chances. "Do you remember me?"

The guard nodded.

Aya pulled her cloak close to her cheek. "Can you deliver a message to Lord Varick?"

"Certainly."

"It is very important." Aya widened her eyes. "It needs to reach him as soon as possible."

The guard chuckled and spat on the ground. "I'm sure the fine people of Sternville will resist the urge to storm the palace if I step out of line for a moment."

Aya smiled. "Tell him I have done what he asked. Tell him that I am waiting on instruction from a higher power and that I expect him to contact me immediately if he hears anything. I shall do the same."

The guard bowed again. "Right away, miss."

Aya curtsied again then turned to leave. The guard cleared his throat, and she looked back at him over her shoulder.

"You know, you seem like a smart girl, but apparently you need told. Those higher powers you're praying to, they haven't been listening for decades. You need to put your faith in someone else."

"Thank you, but I already have." Aya strutted away, allowing a smirk to creep over her face. *I've put my faith in me.*

Aya spent most of the day waiting: waiting for Dellwyn to wake up, waiting to hear back from Lord Varick, waiting for Charlie to perform a miracle and jump. Now that the villagers were awake—she heard their heavy footsteps and long dresses sweeping across the dirt streets—she couldn't go outside. She did not want to deal with explaining her absence or the manservant's inquiries to her neighbors, and she couldn't risk being seen by anyone who might visit the palace. So, she passed the morning wiping down the common room and beating out rag after rag full of dust out the window.

Around the middle of the afternoon, Dellwyn finally woke, only to leave shortly after to fetch water. Dellwyn's departure left Aya by herself again, so she continued her cleaning in her room. About an hour after Dellwyn left, Aya heard a knock at the door. She grabbed one of her father's tools, a sharp metal chisel he had used to engrave the softer metals, and clutched it behind her in case the strange man had returned with more than questions.

"Who is it?" Aya called, attempting to keep her voice level and pleasant.

"I am a guard of the palace."

"And what is your purpose here?"

"To deliver a message from Lord Varick."

Aya opened the door a crack. Once her eyes adjusted to the brightness of the sun, she saw that the visitor was the guard she'd spoken to this morning. "And what is your message?"

The guard bowed. "Lord Varick responds that he understands. He will anxiously await further news and send it to you the moment it passes his ears. He also would like me to inform you that Miss Collingwood's butler stopped by on her behalf to invite you to have tea with her and some other ladies tomorrow morning. While Lord Varick understands your feelings about such matters, he encourages you to attend to keep up appearances."

Aya cocked her head. "Is that all?"

"Yes, miss."

Aya raised her eyebrow. "How much do you know?"

The guard ran his hand through his thinning, gray hair. "More than Lord Varick thinks, less than is dangerous, but still more than I'd like."

"I thought so." Aya squinted. "I'm sorry you've ended up in the middle of all this secrecy. It will be over soon."

The guard shook his head. "Miss, as much as you think that, trust me, it won't be. It never is in the palace."

Aya smiled. Knowing the nobles' lives as she did now, she figured he was right. "Thank you. You may tell Lord Varick that I will consider going to tea if a more enticing invitation does not present itself."

The guard nodded. "Will do, miss."

Aya thanked him again and closed the door. She rested her back against it and let out a long breath. The message from Lord Varick seemed civil enough, respectful of her newly claimed independence, but still as scheming as ever. He would always play the game.

Straightening up, Aya looked around the hovel. Once she cleaned Dellwyn's room, she would officially be out of dusting unless, of course, she opened the door a crack and let some more dust filter in for her to clean tomorrow. She could try making some curtains again, see if her seamstress skills had somehow improved. Or she could try to patch some of the slivers in the ceiling, in case it ever rained more than a few drops.

Aya tossed her head back in defeat. She stomped over to her trunk to see if she had anything other than Willem's mother's dress to wear to tea.

23

The next morning, Aya arrived outside of the tearoom right as it opened. She was one of a few ladies there, but Miss Collingwood had not yet arrived. Aya wondered if any of the other women were a part of Miss Collingwood's party, but she did not care to ask. The ladies had been talking amongst themselves ever since they reached the tearoom, and given their carefully non-synchronized glances in her direction, Aya suspected they were either talking about her connection to the king, her shabby dress, or both.

A waiter walked up to the inside of the door, pulling a large bronze key out of his apron. He unlocked the door and opened it wide. "Good morning, ladies. Step right in. We have a brilliant brew waiting for you today."

The other women didn't move. Rather, they looked everywhere but at Aya and the door. Rolling her eyes, Aya entered the tearoom first and seated herself at the table where Miss Collingwood had perched the other day. Her compatriots chose the table furthest from hers. Aya's table proved to be strategically located—close enough to the window to see out but not always be seen and close enough to the counter to have the servers within earshot. Aya understood why Miss Collingwood had chosen it.

"Good day, Miss Wellman. What can I get for you?" A server stood over her with bright, expectant eyes. Aya blushed, suddenly realizing that she had forgotten to fish a few coins from her father's urn to pay for her tea. "Oh, I'm sorry. I did not bring any coins. I am simply here to meet Miss Collingwood."

The server touched her shoulder with one hand and twirled the end of his mustache with the other. "Miss Wellman, you must know by now that palace ladies do not carry money. We will put your purchase on tab, of course."

Aya raised her eyebrows. "On whose tab?"

"Lord Varick's, if you like. Or His Majesty's again—if you are sure he will not mind."

Aya didn't want to owe Lord Varick another cent. And perhaps using the king's account would reassure him of her confidence in their relationship.

"The king's, please. I know he will allow it."

"Yes, Miss Wellman." The server grinned. "Now, what can I get for you?"

"Do you have anything sweeter than what I had the other day?" Aya grimaced at the memory of the tea. "And something to eat, a scone, maybe?"

"Leave it to me." The server patted her shoulder and went behind the counter. Aya watched him approach another server and whisper something to her—probably news of Aya's financial decision—which resulted in her taking a peek at Aya over her shoulder. Undisturbed, Aya looked back out the window. Let them talk about her affair with the king and even her worn pink dress. In a few days, she would be a hero and escape the palace forever.

"Miss Wellman, you are the punctual one, aren't you?"

Aya looked up to see Miss Collingwood and two other ladies standing over the table. Miss Collingwood's brown hair was pulled back into a low braid with loose tendrils hanging around her face. Aya wondered if the comparative wildness of her hair was to distract from her eyes. The other two ladies, one plump with red hair and one rail-thin with black hair, stood silent. Aya gave her cheeriest smile. "I think punctuality is a virtue, don't you, Miss Collingwood?"

"Yes, of course."

Miss Collingwood's companions sat down at the table on either side of Aya. Miss Collingwood stayed standing a moment longer, staring at her. Aya realized that Miss Collingwood wanted the seat Aya had chosen. It was the one in which she had been sitting when Aya first met her.

Aya smirked. "Miss Collingwood, you look a little pale. Why don't you have a seat?"

Miss Collingwood opened her mouth to speak but then closed it and sat in the chair across from Aya. She busied herself with tugging off her white gloves and placing them in her lap. When she finally looked up, her face was smooth and untroubled, as if she had never wanted to sit anywhere else. Aya struggled not to chuckle.

Three servers came to the table, each attending to a different lady. The women placed their orders, each confidently naming an account for her beverage to be charged to.

Before her server walked away, Miss Collingwood glanced across the table at Aya. "Oh, Miss Wellman, how rude of us." She placed a hand over her heart. "Would you like me to place an order for you on my father's account?"

Before Aya could answer, her server reappeared with a steaming mug of dark brown liquid and a fluffy yellow pastry. "Miss Wellman is covered. Thank you, Miss Collingwood."

Miss Collingwood shooed her server away and fiddled with the tablecloth.

"Thank you." Aya widened her eyes at the server to show her sincerity.

Her server nodded, giving his mustache another elaborate

twirl. "A mug of hot cocoa, from the palace greenhouse's private beans, and a wedge of lemon cake made from fresh lemons and Bowtown's finest field crops."

Miss Collingwood's eyes bulged, and the other two ladies shared skeptical glances.

"Thank you," Aya repeated. "You have chosen wonderfully."

In truth, she had no idea if she would like this hot cocoa —though it couldn't be any worse than tea—and she had only ever experienced lemons in her bath oil. But she wasn't about to let Miss Collingwood and her entourage know all of that.

"Only the best for you, Miss Wellman." The server bowed. "Please let me know if you desire anything else."

Aya replied that she would, and the server left.

"My, my, Miss Wellman." Miss Collingwood *tutted*. "Lord Varick's purse will be quite stretched. I would have felt much better if you had put those treats on my father's account."

Aya smiled, thinking back to all the times she had used Dellwyn's name to dip into Lord Collingwood's pocket. "Lord Varick's purse shall survive. And I would never dream of using a prestigious name such as Lord Collingwood's to my advantage."

Miss Collingwood squinted.

"Speaking of names," Aya continued, "you have not introduced me to your friends."

Miss Collingwood straightened in her seat. "How rude of me! The lady to your left is Miss Aster, daughter of Lord Aster, Duke of the Starboard."

Miss Aster inclined her head to Aya, and she returned the gesture. Even though she knew nothing about this Miss Aster, Aya liked the look of her. She had a bright smile nestled in a face smattered with brown freckles. The spots could have been inherited, but Aya liked to think that Miss Aster might have spent time in the sun—even if only for recreation.

"The lady on your right is Miss Frieson, daughter of Lord Frieson, Viscount of the Crow's Nest."

Unlike Miss Aster, Miss Frieson did not look warm. She held herself rigidly with a cold detachment to those around her. She barely gave Aya a nod, which Aya chose not to return.

Aya wondered if the palace ladies ever grew exhausted of being defined by their fathers' titles. She knew from experience that being linked to one's father could bring a distinct kind of pride, but if fortunes turned awry, as hers had, it could also bring sadness and shame. Being a woman was difficult enough without having one's fate inextricably linked to the man who'd helped create her, even after his death.

"It is my pleasure to meet you both," Aya offered. She did not know what palace ladies were supposed to discuss over tea, other than what titles their fathers held, and she hoped that this statement would invite someone to open a topic of conversation.

"I am sure I speak for Miss Frieson and myself when I say that is also our pleasure to meet you," Miss Aster replied.

That was not terribly helpful.

"Yes," Miss Frieson added. "After all we have heard of you around the palace, it is nice to put a face to the name."

"And what have you heard?" Aya took her first sip of the hot cocoa, finding it sweet, warm, and nothing like the wretched plant water of the tea. She followed it with a tiny bite of the lemon cake. Like the chocolate, it was sweet, but it also had a delightful tang to it, a refreshing contrast to the richness of the beverage. She would have to thank the server again for his fine selection.

"Oh, you know how people talk around the palace." Miss Collingwood put her hand over her mouth. "I'm sorry. You're new. I suppose you do not know."

"Gossiping is not unique to the rich." Aya dabbed at her mouth with a napkin. "Though you seem to have more time for it than any people I've ever met."

Miss Aster chuckled, and Miss Frieson simply watched Aya.

Miss Collingwood smiled demurely. Aya could imagine her practicing the expression in the mirror. "Either way, people talk. At first, everyone simply discussed you because you are a ward. You see, nobles do not usually take in wards unless they cannot have children of their own. Therefore, Lord Varick taking you in, especially after the loss of his own daughter, was quite a surprise."

Aya licked a dab of lemon cream off her fork. "You said at first. What does everyone say about me now?"

Miss Collingwood blushed. "Well, I hate to repeat such rubbish. You seem like a respectable young lady to me."

Miss Frieson cleared her throat. "They say you have made many friends in the palace."

Aya raised her eyebrows? "Like whom?"

"The king, of course." Miss Aster said. The other ladies glared at her. "What? Don't look at me like that. No use beating around the bush when Miss Wellman clearly knows what we're hinting at."

Aya smiled. Yes, she liked Miss Aster. Shrugging, Aya allowed her voice to float, light and carefree, from her lips. "I had not thought about it before, but I suppose I could call the king my friend. So, yes, I guess that rumor is true."

"Might I ask why you have begun a friendship with His Majesty?" Miss Frieson wrinkled her nose. "It's an unusual relationship."

"It was not my doing." Aya waved her hand to dismiss the idea. "Lord Varick suggested it, actually. You see, they do not share it in public now that the late queen Isadona has gone to the next world, but the king and Lord Varick grew close while the king and Isadona were married. This friendship has remained, but they believe it would be in poor taste to continue it in plain sight now that they are no longer kin. Anyway, when I came to the palace, Lord Varick thought it would be nice for the king to help introduce me to noble society. After all, who knows the palace better than its ruler?"

Miss Aster nodded, but Miss Collingwood and Miss Frieson glanced at each other. Their servers arrived with their orders, placed the saucers and plates on the table with perfect synchronization, then left. The ladies stirred their tea, blew across the cups, and took dainty sips. Aya's brows furrowed at the continued synchronization, and she wondered whether the ritual was learned or born out of habit.

Miss Aster bounced in her seat, obviously uncomfortable with the silence. "Did the king's education prove to be instructional?"

"I believe so. I feel that I have my bearings when I walk around the palace, both geographically and socially." Aya waited for another question or some backhanded comment, but none came. She lifted her hot cocoa to her lips and drank, not bothering to cool it with her breath.

"So…" Miss Collingwood stirred her tea. "How do you like His Majesty?"

There it was, just as Aya expected. She was surprised the ladies had waited this long. "I cannot say I know him well enough to place sound judgment on his character, but he seems to be a kind man and a smart ruler."

"Surely you must have gleaned more from him than that." Miss Frieson tapped her spoon on the edge of her cup.

Aya tilted her head, pursing her lips to keep from smiling. "I don't know what you're implying."

The ladies wanted her to slip up, to show too much affection or admiration, to divulge her undying love for King Archon. Aya did not expect them to think highly of her, given her lowly background, but she had to admit that she was insulted. If they only knew how intelligent a poor girl could be, they would be terrified.

"It's just that," Miss Aster began, intertwining her fingers, "none of us have ever had much opportunity to speak with the king. And he is our ruler. Is that not strange? We simply want to know more about him, and you know him well already. It is not as if we can, in good taste, interview the king's valet or the prince."

Aya shrugged and took another bite of her cake. That was a logical point. At least one of them had some tact. "True, Eldric is a man of few words, and the prince seems to be elusive."

"To some of us, maybe." Miss Collingwood licked her lips.

So Miss Collingwood and the prince were courting. That would explain her eagerness to speak with the king the other day and some of her arrogance. Then again, Aya had just seen the prince at the trial a few days ago, and he hadn't been with Miss Collingwood.

"Do you know the prince well, Miss Collingwood?" Aya asked.

"Oh, yes. Lionel and I have been close since childhood. In fact, I would not be surprised if we become even closer very soon." Miss Collingwood waggled her left-hand ring finger, and Miss Aster and Miss Frieson pointedly sipped their tea.

"Really?" Aya brushed a curl away from her face. "From what I have gathered of the prince's reputation, the idea of him binding himself in marriage seems unlikely."

Miss Collingwood giggled. "All men have their wild oats to sow. I would rather Lionel get them out of his system now, so he does not end up under the executioner's ax."

Aya could not believe that Miss Collingwood, who seemed territorial in all respects—tables, chairs, conversations—would be so cavalier about letting her potential husband sleep his way through Desertera. Of course, as long as she claimed the title of princess and future queen, why should anything else matter? After all, she could not inherit her father's estate, but she could marry her way into a better one. Aya tried to figure out a way to bring Willem, Lord Collingwood's heir and Miss Collingwood's cousin, into the conversation without revealing her connection to him.

However, before Aya could devise a strategy, Miss Aster spoke. "Speaking of the monarchy…" She inclined her head toward the tearoom's window.

Aya saw King Archon and Queen Zedara strolling past the shops, arm in arm. The sight of the king and queen walking so closely together made Aya's chest tighten. For a split second, she thought that Queen Zedara had changed her mind and decided to keep her title. However, after a quick sip of cocoa, Aya came to her senses, realizing that King Archon was putting on a show, making the public's last glimpse of him and the queen that of a loving pair.

As the royal couple reached the tearoom, Queen Zedara motioned that she would like to go inside. King Archon glanced in at the tables, and when his eyes landed on Aya, he tugged the queen's arm and spoke to her. The queen turned to look over her shoulder, and when she saw Aya sitting in the cafe, she smirked. If any of Aya's unfounded doubts lingered, they were dismissed with that small action. At the same time, King Archon looked past the queen's shoulder and smiled softly. Luckily, Miss Collingwood had no way to see this inter-action, and the other two ladies were not bold enough to stare at the royal couple through the window.

"Are they coming in?" Miss Collingwood whispered.

Aya shook her head. "They've moved on."

"That is so strange," Miss Aster said. "I wonder why they did not come inside. This is the king's favorite shop."

"Maybe the queen lost her appetite." Miss Frieson narrowed her eyes at Aya.

Aya smiled. "Well, I certainly haven't." She took her last bite of lemon cake, making sure to savor every crumb. The other ladies watched her with a mixture of pity and envy—oh, how rotten to be poor, but how lucky to taste everything in life for the first time.

Miss Collingwood and her entourage kept Aya captive for another two hours. To hear them tell it, they wanted to get to know the newest palace lady their age and to introduce her to the ways of noble life. They recounted their childhoods in Starboardshire and their introduction to noble society, should Lord Varick decide Aya needed a "coming out" party. They explained which dressmaker was most skilled and how to direct her to best accentuate your prettiest features. They outlined the social convention involved in courting—just in case a nobleman would be willing to take on a ward as his wife—and Miss Collingwood told Aya exactly the type of husband she could expect.

"Only widowers take on wards as wives. But don't worry. After you see their purses, it will be easy for you to get over their round bellies and balding heads."

When Miss Collingwood finally announced that teatime was over, Aya stood straight up, gave each lady a curtsy and word of farewell, and bolted. As she emerged into the busy shopping corridor, Aya breathed in deeply as if she had entered fresh air. Anything felt refreshing after being cooped up in the tearoom with those bratty women for so long.

As the nobles ambled around her, Aya's heart lurched at the possibility that Willem might be among them—partly out of hope to see him again and ensure his silence continued and partly out of dread of what would surely be an awkward, stilted encounter. To avoid either, Aya kept her eyes forward and strode toward the exit. She focused so intently on leaving that she did not notice someone falling into step behind her. When that person grabbed her waist and pulled her into a narrow alleyway between two of the storefronts, Aya shrieked, her noise quickly met with a hand over her mouth. Aya took a calming breath through her nose, assuming that Willem had once again whisked her out of sight for a confrontation. As she turned around to look at him, Aya's eyes widened. "Your Majesty." Aya forced herself to smile. "You gave me such a fright!"

King Archon grinned and touched each corner of her mouth. "You do not seem to be too shaken up."

"Well, I suppose I had my hopes that my attacker would be devastatingly handsome."

King Archon wrapped his arms around Aya's lower back and leaned down for a kiss. She placed her hand in front of her face, gently pushing his chin back. "Oh, no you don't. Not until you explain yourself to me."

"What do you mean, my dear?"

Aya stuck out her bottom lip and placed both of her hands firmly on the king's chest. Her palms made a quiet slapping sound when they hit his jacket. "You know I saw you with her."

"With whom?" King Archon's brow furrowed. "Zedara?"

"Yes. And weren't you the dutiful husband?" Aya poked his chest. "With your arm intertwined with hers so lovingly as you perused the shops together."

"Aya, dear," the king began, sweeping a stray curl behind her ear, "you know I want you and only you. I simply must put on a good show with Zedara. If I am not a doting husband in public, the people will suspect when…" The king stopped talking and glanced at the opening of the alley. Eldric stood there, keeping watch.

"When what?" Aya tilted her head.

"You mustn't worry about such things." King Archon touched her nose. "It is not safe."

"No, Archon." Aya wrinkled her nose and stepped away from him. "You must tell me. What will happen? How will we be together?"

"My dear, you must wait."

"No. I'm tired of waiting." Aya took a deep breath. "I have waited an eternity. You must tell me now."

King Archon squeezed her shoulders. He looked to his

valet again, and Eldric's hand tightened into a fist. "It is not safe to talk here. If you must know, come to my chambers tomorrow night after dinner. The preparations will be finished by then, and I will be able to tell you everything at once."

Aya could barely contain her grin. "And you promise you will tell me everything?"

King Archon nodded.

"You swear it?"

"Yes. On my honor as the king."

As if you *have honor to swear on.*

"I shall see you tomorrow night." Aya pushed down the retching feeling in her gut and put her hand on the nape of King Archon's neck, embracing him in a deep kiss. She opened her mouth, encouraging his tongue to explore hers, which it did, eagerly. Just as the king's hands began to wander down her backside, Eldric coughed, and King Archon broke away.

"I'm sorry. I must go. Tomorrow night, my dear, we shall have everything."

Aya wiped her lip with a single finger. "Yes, we will. Until then, Your Majesty."

As she watched the king walk away, Aya leaned back against the wall, letting her head rest against the cool metal. One more day. In only one more day, her entire life would change. She would avenge her father's death, reclaim his shop as her own, rid Desertera of its horrid king, and maybe, just maybe, have her chance with Willem.

All she had to do was wait. And tell Lord Varick.

24

---

*A*ya knocked on Lord Varick's door three times. When the last knock's echo faded from the corridor, she began counting. Once she hit ten, she would leave and send a message via the gray-haired guard; she would not stay a second longer. Aya thought about the first time she had knocked on this door, how enraged and desperate she had felt. It was incomprehensible to think that her mission was nearly complete. She had to give Lord Varick credit. He knew people, and he knew how to play them.

As Aya's count reached eight, she stepped away from the door. She stared at the purple eye, daring it to blink. On the count of nine, the door opened. Aya smiled, expecting to be greeted by Mrs. Lemot. However, she looked up into the beady eyes of Lord Varick himself. He returned her smile and made a show of bowing to her. "Miss Aya. To what do I owe the honor of your presence?"

"Lord Varick." Aya curtsied. "To what do I owe the honor of your opening your own door?"

Lord Varick straightened and laughed. Sarcastic but civil, as always. "The maid is busy, and the butler is out on errands.

But when I saw it was you through the peephole, I knew I had to answer."

Aya glanced at the black door. She did not see a peephole, but perhaps the color helped to obscure it. "I hate to admit it, but I'm glad you did. May I come in? I have exciting news."

Lord Varick's black eyes sparkled. "I expected nothing less at your arrival. Please, let us retire to the sitting room."

He held the door wide open and gestured for Aya to enter, pointing his cane down the hallway. She walked past him into the estate and seated herself in the armchair in front of the fireplace. Despite not having staff on hand, Lord Varick still had a blazing fire and an assortment of fruit and cheese laid out on the table. Aya felt better knowing that all the excess wasn't about her; but then again, as she thought about all the water the palace had to invest to make the spread, she felt even worse.

Lord Varick sat in his usual place on the couch facing the wall of windows and the balcony. He twirled his upright cane between his fingertips. "What is your grand news?"

"I took your advice and had tea with Miss Collingwood and her friends this morning."

Before she could explain further, Lord Varick tapped his cane on the floor and interrupted. "While I am happy to know your newfound pride has not dampened your intelligence, that is hardly newsworthy."

"If you would let me finish—"

"Please, go on." Lord Varick waved his hands as if telling her to hurry.

Perhaps Aya had been wrong. Maybe he was going for sarcasm and piggishness today. "While we were having tea, I saw King Archon and Queen Zedara browsing the shops, and they saw me. As I was leaving, King Archon pulled me aside into an alleyway. I challenged him about his affections for his wife, and he asked me to meet him outside his chambers tomorrow night so he can explain everything that is happening."

"Tomorrow night, eh? My, my, you have been a busy girl."

"That was the intention, was it not?"

Lord Varick held up his palms. "No judgment. I am simply impressed at your vast improvements. Are you positive that King Archon is going to confess to plotting Queen Zedara's death?"

Aya smirked. "Absolutely."

"I hate to sound doubtful, but certainty is paramount. If Queen Zedara and I arrange for people to hear this, and the king does not confess, you will be tried as an adulteress and sentenced to death, and the queen and I will likely lose our own heads for treasonous activity." Lord Varick leaned forward. "You must be sure. For all our sakes."

Aya scooted to the edge of her seat. "Lord Varick, I can make the king say anything I want at this point."

Lord Varick raised his eyebrows and tapped his staff on the floor again. "You have become quite the cocky one. You'd best be careful. Not everyone appreciates your confidence and candor the way I do."

Aya leaned back in the chair, running her fingernails up its upholstered arms. "Do you, Lord Varick? Appreciate my confidence and candor?"

"Let me just say, you are not the same girl you were when I came to you with this proposition." Lord Varick squinted. "And even though this new you is much less easy to…to work with, I can respect that you have used the opportunity I presented you to grow. I know how alluring power can be, especially when you start without much."

Aya smiled. "Thank you. And while I think you were a rotten father and are likely still a horrid excuse for a person, I appreciate your ability to mix revenge and charity."

Lord Varick chuckled. "You're most welcome, Miss Cogsmith. Now, is there anything else I need to know?"

"There is. Have you been to the staircase that leads to the deck's bow end?"

"Many times, yes."

"Do you remember the portrait of Queen Hildegard? The one where she is steering the ship through the storm?"

"That monstrosity? I do not think I could forget it if I tried. Why?"

Aya straightened. "The king showed me that it is a door. It conceals a secret pathway, which leads directly to the round room outside King Archon's chambers. The doorway on the other side is a bookshelf filled with fake books."

"How interesting." Lord Varick raised his eyebrows. "And you believe this would be a good place to view your show with the king?"

"I do." Aya winked. "I thought it would be best for you to stumble upon the passage with some friends and end up witnessing our exchange. Queen Zedara could come in from the regular entrance, as if she were merely on her way to visit her beloved husband."

Lord Varick tapped his chin. "Good thinking."

Aya grinned. "Thank you."

"Now, if that is all, I assume you will want to go home to your hovel for the evening." Lord Varick tilted his head. "However, if you would like, I can have the maid make up your room when she returns. If you want to keep up appearances, that is."

"No, thank you." Aya waved her hand. "That will not be necessary."

"Of course."

Lord Varick stood, and Aya did the same. She followed him down the hallway, past the aforementioned room, and to the door. As she walked past the bedroom, Aya noticed that the door was ajar, and she saw the bed already made, as if she had never slept there or as if it waited for her. On top of the bed lay a white gown.

"The room I stayed in," Aya began, "it was Isadona's, wasn't it?"

Varick nodded, and Aya wondered if it was the staff who loved Isadona enough to make her room a shrine or Lord Varick. Moreover, Aya wondered why Lord Varick would disturb the room to have her sleep there. She doubted it was the only spare room in Lord Varick's estate. After all, she had only seen a tiny portion of his living quarters, and as a marquess, he was sure to have a large section of the palace to himself.

"Why didn't you put me somewhere else? Surely you have other rooms?"

"I do." Lord Varick shrugged. "But I wanted to remind myself."

Aya's brow furrowed. "Of what?"

Lord Varick sighed. "Of the way I treated my daughter. Of my failure in using her as a pawn and all the pain it brought me. Of the fact that you are the closest thing I have to her now."

Aya bit her lip. "You are the closest thing I have to my father now."

"And we will always disappoint each other."

It wasn't a question. Aya opened the door and stepped into the hallway. Without looking back, she said, "Yes. Yes, we will."

25

s Aya walked down the corridor to King Archon's chambers, the hallway grew narrower, and her chest tightened. She had not slept the night before, and she had spent all day lying in her bed with Charlie standing watch as she tossed and turned and tangled herself in the blankets. When the sun had begun to lower over the horizon, Aya had put on Willem's mother's dress and placed the barrette in her hair for luck. She hide the vortric cog between her left ribs and corset and strapped one of her father's screwdrivers to her inner thigh. She took a deep breath, hoping she had everything she needed to face the king.

Aya noticed that her footsteps sounded louder and faster as she neared the king's chambers. The metal of the screwdriver had been cold against her leg at first, but now it had warmed to her body temperature. The only reminder of its presence was the garter squeezing her thigh to keep it in place. The vortric cog had also warmed against her flesh, but she could still feel its teeth biting into her side. Despite the physical discomfort they caused, Aya liked carrying these tools with her. They reminded her of her father and her capabilities. She might not have been a noblewoman, but she was a cogsmith's daughter, and that was far more useful.

When Aya arrived at the narrowest part of the corridor, which opened into the king's round sitting area, she spied King Archon standing before the motionless grandfather clock. His intricate top hat blocked the clock's face, and Aya saw the cogs and gears embroidered onto it as a glimpse into the clock's brain. She stopped walking and placed her hand on the wall, inhaling a long, deep breath. With any luck, Lord Varick and his witnesses were already stationed behind the bookshelf, and Queen Zedara would shortly be standing with her guards where Aya now stood. This was it: the final act for revenge.

"Good evening, Your Majesty."

King Archon turned around, a smile already on his face. His blue eyes sparkled. He crossed the room and scooped Aya up in his arms, twirling her around before setting her back down on the floor. Before she could shake off the dizziness, King Archon grabbed her face and melded his lips with hers. She waited a few moments before she pushed him away.

"Perhaps I should have said 'Jubilant evening, Your Majesty.'" Aya laughed.

King Archon beamed. "It is the perfect evening, Aya."

"What has gotten into you? I have never seen you so over-joyed." Aya imagined all the women before her, all the dumb young girls who wanted to be queen and all the smart society ladies who knew what was happening but could not figure out how to stop it. *This is for you, ladies—you and Papa.*

"It is all set in place." King Archon rubbed her shoulders. "You do not have to worry about a thing, my dear. By this time tomorrow, I will no longer be married, and we can be together."

Aya took a step back, mindful of her audience and wanting to maintain as much of her innocence as possible. "Your Majesty, I still do not understand. How can your marriage end? Surely you do not have grounds for divorce? That would be a horrible scandal, one your family line may never recover from."

"No, of course not." The king waved his hand. "I would never put my reputation in such a position, especially not when it would harm yours and my son's as well."

"Then, I am afraid I do not understand you." Aya cocked her head to the side. "You told me you would explain everything to me."

The king sat down on the fainting couch, patting the cushion beside him. Aya seated herself next to him, and he took both her hands in his. He rubbed his thumbs in circles over the tops of her hands. She watched his thumbs move as if hypnotized, praying to the Benevolent Queen, or any other deity who would listen, to give her the strength to be patient and carry through with the plan.

"Aya, if I tell you this, it will put us both in grave danger. You must promise me that you will never tell another living soul."

Aya swallowed. "I swear."

The king squeezed her hands and looked down at the floor. "Aya, Queen Zedara does not love me. She never has."

The surprise on Aya's face was genuine. This was not how she expected King Archon to begin this conversation. "What?" Aya squinted. "Then why would she marry you?"

"For the money or the power, maybe." King Archon shrugged. "Regardless, she does not love me, nor could she love any man."

Aya raised her eyebrows and turned her head ever so slightly toward the entrance to the room, where she expected the queen to be standing just out of sight. "What do you mean?"

King Archon sighed and cupped Aya's cheek with one hand. "I did not realize it before, but Zedara and Isadona were in love. I knew that Isadona was committing adultery, but she would never say with whom. I've learned Zedara is doing the same, with a new woman."

Aya frowned. She thought back to her conversations with Queen Zedara. The queen had said she was closer to Isadona than anyone, that she loved her, that she knew for sure that Isadona was in love with someone else. At the time, Aya had wondered if she would have been equally distraught if Dellwyn were in Isadona's place. Now she had her answer.

"Are you certain?"

"Yes." King Archon squeezed her hand. "And you must be, too."

Aya did not know what to say, but the churning in her gut told her to be careful. Aya knew King Archon was lying. Perhaps Zedara and Isadona had continued their romance while Isadona was married to the king—but Zedara was too haunted by Isadona's memory to move on. The king had taken half the truth and crafted the perfect way to make him appear the jilted lover, entirely innocent, worthy of the public's sympathy. His watery blue eyes stared at Aya expectantly, and she stumbled through the only sentence she could formulate.

"Forgive me, Your Majesty." Aya looked down at her lap. "But were not your last four wives, before Zedara that is, adulteresses also?"

"Yes, they were."

"Again, forgive me, Your Majesty, but—is that not a strange pattern?" Aya wrinkled her nose. "It cannot possibly be that not a single one of them loved you, that each of them merely wanted to be queen and bed other men—people—on the side."

The king scowled before covering it with a smile. He released Aya's hand and tapped her forehead. "Always so curious, so clever. You never let me slip a single thing past you."

Aya glanced up at the king, her eyes wide, alert. "What do you mean?"

"You do not believe me when I say that my last five wives have all been heartless adulteresses and betrayed me, do you?"

"If you tell me it is true, I will believe you, Your Majesty." Aya pursed her lips. "But it does seem highly unlikely that you would have such continuously poor judgment of character. I know you to be a much smarter man than that."

The king grinned wider and reclaimed Aya's hand. "I suppose I reveal myself then. No, Aya, not all of my past wives committed adultery. One of them truly did, my second wife, the first woman I married after Queen Lisandra died. She served as my inspiration for the rest of them, Zedara included, of course."

"Your inspiration?" Aya did not know how long she should play dumb.

"Yes, Aya. Think."

Aya sucked in her breath, holding it for a moment to redden her face, before letting it out in a quiet gasp. "If the other wives did not commit adultery, they must have been framed."

King Archon tapped the end of her nose. "There's my clever girl."

"You framed them?" Aya stood up from the fainting couch and backed away from the king. She took a deep breath to repeat herself louder, so every member of her unseen audience could hear her. "You framed the last three queens, and soon Queen Zedara, in adultery?"

"Yes. Isn't it brilliant?"

Aya did not say anything. She expected the bookshelf to slide away from the passageway's opening, expected Lord Varick, Queen Zedara, and their witnesses to come bursting through the entrances, expected to hear declarations of the king's arrest and impending execution echoing down the corridor.

Nothing happened.

"Aya? Dear?" The king adjusted his top hat. "You have

turned as white as the clock."

Aya realized that she had backed up against the grandfather clock, her arms wrapping around its body for support. The king stood up and stepped toward her. She glanced between the entrances. Maybe her allies were waiting for her to clear herself, just to be safe.

"But you have never committed adultery yourself, Your Majesty?" Aya nearly shouted the words. "Not with me. Not with anyone."

"No, never." King Archon chuckled. "I'm not stupid enough to commit the crime for which I frame them. In fact, I've never even had to consider adultery."

There. The king admitted to arranging four murders and committing treason against the queens, and he cleared Aya of adultery. Now Lord Varick and Queen Zedara could burst in.

Aya held her breath. Still, nothing happened.

Maybe her allies needed more proof. Or perhaps they had arrived late and missed the first confession.

"But, Your Majesty, what you are doing is wrong. To escape your own adulterous urges, you frame your wives in one of the worst betrayals—worst crimes—and then you have them *murdered*. That is treason in itself!"

The passageways remained silent. Tightness encircled Aya's heart, squeezing it as it tried to beat out of her chest. They weren't coming. Lord Varick and Queen Zedara had lied. Aya wasn't making it out of this alive.

"None of them would have been queens without me. And none of them were wholly innocent. Each had her own sins, as does Queen Zedara." King Archon took another step. "All I do is make room for a new queen, a better queen, a queen like you."

"Me? Queen?"

"Where did you think this was going? Of course you will be the next queen."

Aya gulped. The king had reached her, towering over her,

close enough that she could feel his breath against her face.

"And what happens when you get bored with me? Will you find some cute, clever girl to replace me and have me killed, too?"

As she described this possibility, Aya remembered the king's accusation of her father. In a split-second decision, King Archon and Prince Lionel condemned her father to death. She began to cry, anger and loneliness rising as bile in her throat.

King Archon grabbed Aya and hugged her to his chest. "No, my dear, never. I told you when we had lunch—you are the smartest, wittiest, most challenging woman I have ever met. Every moment with you is a new adventure." He stroked her hair. "I could never grow tired of you. I would never, ever need to replace you."

Aya did not know what to do. Her father was not there to show her how to unwind the king like a mechanical animal. Dellwyn was not there to teach her a move to escape. Madam Huxley was not there to shelter her. She was entirely, hopelessly on her own, trapped against the will of the man she hated most in the world.

"I can't believe you," Aya whispered.

"Yes, you can." King Archon kissed her forehead. "Please, my dear, you must know how I feel about you."

"I know what you can do." Aya shook her head. "I will never believe you."

"I will make you believe me." The king's hands raced over her body, running down her arms, passing over her backside, caressing her breasts. His lips found her neck and sucked the breath out of her. Aya shoved his chest, but he pinned her back against the clock. She thought she heard the glass of the clock's body crack under their combined weight, but it did not shatter. She tried harder to push the king away, but she was not strong enough. This left her without another choice.

No matter what Lord Varick and Queen Zedara had planned together, Aya would not take the fall for them, not without a fight. Aya stretched her hand down to the folds of her dress and tugged at them, trying to get her hand underneath to reach the screwdriver.

King Archon noticed the movement and pushed Aya away, holding her at arm's length. She was somewhat curved in front of him, her hand under her dress at her knee. The king stared down at Aya's hand beneath her dress, and a wicked smile spread across his face. "I knew you'd come around."

Aya wanted to scream, to lash out and hit the king, but her voice caught in her throat, and he picked her up in his arms. King Archon carried Aya over to the fainting couch and threw her down on top of it. She tried to push herself up, but the king flopped down on top of her.

"Sorry, darling. I like to be on top."

Before she could retort, the king pressed his lips against Aya's, stealing the sound of her voice in his mouth. He used his left hand to hold her right one above her head, and with his own right hand, he began unbuttoning his trousers. Aya squirmed beneath him, trying to break the kiss, but this only encouraged King Archon to kiss her harder and work faster at his buttons.

As the king pushed his trousers below his hips, Aya's free hand desperately groped the folds of her dress for her father's screwdriver. She felt it beneath the fabric, but she could not get her fingers around the metal. The king began to help, unknowingly, pushing the fabric of her dress aside so that he could reach her flesh. For the first time, Aya was thankful for the king's lips on hers—his head blocked her vision so that she couldn't watch what was about to unfold.

More than any other time in her life, Aya begged the Benevolent Queen to send her back in time. Back to her father's house on the morning they went to the palace, so she could make him stay home or take the vortric cog with her to pacify the king. Back to her hovel with Dellwyn, where she could feel safe and loved for the person she truly was. Back to the Rudder, to the night when Lord Varick came to her, so she could persuade him to assassinate the king instead. Back to any rough client who took from her without kissing, without talking, without further desire. Aya knew it would be useless—she could not change time—but she would have rather relived any moment of her life than be in her body for what was about to happen.

As he prepared to enter her, the king's hand landed on the screwdriver. He froze, stopped kissing Aya, and pulled back the last layer of fabric to reveal the metal tool. His blue eyes grew wide, and he threw Aya back on the couch, gripping her neck in his hand. "What is this?"

Aya had never known the absence of air. Time seemed to stop, and the world grew quiet. She felt the king's hand around her neck, felt her windpipe compressed, but nothing else. She saw in more detail than ever before—the vein bulging from King Archon's forehead, the spittle in his pointed beard, the black specks in his pores. It was as if all of life had paused to allow her to witness it in its most vicious form, one last time.

"I'd like to ask you the same thing, *husband*."

Aya looked over the king's shoulder to see Queen Zedara and six guards standing in the entryway. In his shock, King Archon released Aya, and she was able to scramble up from the couch and grasp at her neck, the screwdriver still strapped to her thigh, now covered by her dress. She took several deep breaths, wincing against her aching throat.

"Zedara!" Aya gasped. A wave of relief washed over her. Zedara had come through, after all. "Thank goodness you're here!"

Queen Zedara glared at Aya. "You, peasant, will never address your queen that way again. Guards, seize them!"

Three guards ran to King Archon, two grabbing his arms and one grabbing him by the cravat. Two guards ran over to Aya, each grabbing one of her arms. The final guard stayed by Zedara's side. Aya was too stunned to thrash against them. She looked at Queen Zedara with wide eyes, her jaw hanging slack. She had been right about the queen. Zedara had planned this, waiting to barge in until Aya looked guilty of adultery.

"Zedara, my love." King Archon tugged against the guards to stand straighter. "Please, I can explain."

"Quiet!" Zedara pointed at him. "You lost the right to speak the moment I caught you with this peasant whore. You are lucky my guards did not behead you while you still lay between her thighs."

"You cannot have me executed. I am the king. I am the law!" King Archon no longer needed the lion mask. His top hat had fallen to the ground, leaving an untamed mane of gray hair around his reddened face. His blue eyes bulged wider than Aya thought possible, and his mouth warped into a snarl.

"Yes, and you broke it." Zedara smirked. "Desertera has never had to execute a king before, but my darling Archon, it looks like you will be the first."

"You cannot do that. I am the king!" King Archon lurched toward Zedara, but the guards held him back. "I decide who to execute."

Queen Zedara cackled. "Well, I suppose it is time for a new system then. Maybe one you and all the future kings can't cheat." She snapped her fingers at the guards. "Take him away."

King Archon struggled against the guards, kicking his legs and swinging his arms. When that did not work, he allowed his legs to go limp and attempted to pull the guards to the floor. His flailing proved to be ineffective, and the guards strengthened their grip and dragged the king out of the room. Despite the strong hands digging into her own arms, Aya smiled at the sight of the king being pulled away. He looked exactly as her father had. No matter what happened next, at least she had her justice.

Aya turned her attention to Queen Zedara, who still watched the retreating figure of King Archon. As her anger coiled in her stomach, Aya clenched her fists and jerked her arms. One of the guards let her slip out of his grasp, but the other held her firm, doubling the strength of his grip. Instinctively, Aya groaned, and the sound made Queen Zedara's glare turn to her.

"This was the plan all along," Aya hissed through gritted teeth. "Bring in the poor little whore, blind her with her lust for revenge, and catch her in the king's embrace."

Queen Zedara tilted her head and walked over to Aya. She leaned in close to Aya's face and studied her. For a second, Aya saw a flicker of sympathy in her eyes, then it was gone, as quick as a bolt of heat lightning over the desert.

"I'm sorry, Aya, but I don't know what you are talking about." Queen Zedara widened her eyes at her guards and shook her head. "Lord Varick showed you a great kindness by taking you in. I welcomed you into my palace, tried to be a gracious queen. And this is how you repay us both? By bedding my husband?"

"Stop with the lies." Aya twisted her neck to look at the guards. "Zedara planned this. She and Lord Varick both did. They wanted King Archon to be caught in adultery, to be executed. They are traitors."

The guards remained silent, but their fingers tightened around Aya's arms again.

Queen Zedara stuck out her bottom lip, mocking Aya. "It's over, Aya. Lord Varick and I cannot let you go back to your life. If anyone else finds out about this, we would all be in too much danger."

Aya scoffed. "And *I'm* the one who will tell? *I'm* the one the public will believe? You and Varick are a much bigger threat to each other than I am."

"You are the cogsmith's daughter, a traitor's daughter." Queen Zedara scrunched her eyebrows, something between pity and contempt in her eyes. "I cannot let you live. I'm sorry. I simply can't."

Aya felt the blood drain from her face. She had not realized that Queen Zedara knew her true identity, but after everything she had learned tonight, Aya cursed herself for being so naïve. She struggled against the guards, screaming at them to let her go, but they were too strong for her to break free. Aya settled for what she could do. She spat in the queen's face. "You lying bitch."

Queen Zedara did not wipe Aya's saliva from her face. Her eyes watered, and she leaned in closer to Aya, her voice almost inaudible. "I'm sorry. It was me or you. I had to choose me."

With that, the queen turned away and pointed to the entrance. Like the prince before her, she had condemned an innocent person to death out of fear and selfishness, too cowardly to say what needed to be said, to even try to find another option. The guards began dragging Aya out of the room, but she fought. She knew she would not break free, but she wanted to make their trek as slow and difficult as possible. Aya thought back to her father being dragged away, seeing her younger self through his eyes. She might die, but she would get in one final punch.

"You are a coward, Zedara!" Aya shouted. "You are no better than Varick or Archon or Lionel! Isadona would be ashamed."

As the guards reached the entryway, where the corridor narrowed, they turned sideways to shimmy through the tight space. Aya looked back over her shoulder to see whether Queen Zedara still stood there pointing or if she had moved to follow them. As Aya expected, the queen remained in place, her arm limp at her side. Aya felt a wave of pleasure knowing that her words had stung Zedara. However, that feeling evaporated as Aya's gaze landed on the other side of the room.

Lord Varick emerged from the hidden tunnel behind the bookcase, a smug smile plastered on his face. And next to him, wearing a cog-embroidered top hat, stood Willem.

26

If it were possible to die of shock, Aya's heart would have stopped. Willem was the prince.

Willem, the man who had been her only friend in the palace, who had been her first enjoyable bedding, who had offered to help her escape from King Archon, was the same boy who had ordered her father's execution. And now, he was working with Lord Varick to execute his own father and frame her.

How could she have been so stupid? Her entire time in the palace, Prince Lionel had been right in front of her—in her arms, maybe even in her heart. Had she really been so blinded by his wit and charm, so distracted by her own desire, so flattered by her first taste of true intimacy that she had overlooked all the clues staring her in the face? She had, and it was about to cost her her head.

Aya's knees buckled, and she bent over, feeling as if she might be sick. The guards tugged on her arms, trying to coerce her into moving again. After a few deep breaths, Aya rose and continued. The guards led her to a staircase, slowly winding their way toward the bottom level of the palace. As Aya watched her feet plop onto each step, realizations popped into her mind—Abrim's odd pronunciation of Willem's name, the nobles' stares at the ball, Lord Varick's fit of hysterics after Aya danced with Willem.

Understanding the irony, Aya began to laugh. Her cackles grew louder, until her stomach shook and tears pricked her eyes. She wondered, briefly, whether she'd gone mad, and decided she didn't care. The guards stopped walking, both of them staring down at her. The stronger one slapped Aya across the face, but when that did not stop her laughter, they grunted and resumed their course.

As they reached the bottom level of the palace, Aya caught her breath and let out a long sigh. Her cheek stung, but she ignored the pain, lifting her head to take in her surroundings. The corridors were narrow, lined with even narrower doorways, each one about two feet away from its neighbor. The doors consisted of metal, and they each had two small windows covered with iron bars, one near the top of the door and one near the bottom. Aya realized the guards had brought her to the dungeon.

At the end of the hallway sat another guard in a wooden rocking chair, sharpening a long knife. He didn't look up at them. "Put her in thirty-seven."

"Yes, sir," the guards replied in unison.

They pulled Aya down the corridor to cell number thirty-seven. The key was waiting in the keyhole. They turned it and opened the door. The larger guard pushed Aya into the doorway, grabbing her hands and placing them on either side of the frame. He ran his hands over her arms and torso, taking his time inspecting her breasts. Bending down, he motioned for her to widen her feet. Aya closed her eyes and did as instructed, praying that his fingers would not brush the screwdriver. The guard lifted her feet from her shoes, glanced inside, then replaced them. His hands slid up her calves and around the backs of her thighs. Aya let out a breath, only to suck it back in as the guard's hand pressed roughly between her legs, fortunately still on the outside of her dress.

"Nothing," the guard said.

Before Aya could straighten herself, the guard pushed her into the cell. She stumbled forward, catching herself against the wall. The guards slammed the door closed behind her, and she heard the lock click into place. Aya stood up on her tiptoes to peer out the top window. From her cell, she could only see that the guards went in the direction of the guard on watch duty. They must have given him the key.

The guards turned around and walked past Aya's cell. She beat on the door. "Let me out! This is a mistake! I'm innocent!"

The guards did not turn to look at her. They disappeared from her view.

Aya kept banging on the door and screaming for the guard on duty to release. With the large number of cells in the dungeon, Aya imagined that King Archon had to be among them and maybe other prisoners as well. If she kept hollering, kept fighting, kept up hope, maybe she could inspire them to rally with her. She tried—hitting the door and yelling until her hands became sore and her voice began to crack. "Please! I didn't do anything."

A hand reached between the bars and grabbed a hunk of Aya's curls, slamming her head against the metal door. Aya whimpered, stretching to make herself taller so the pull on her scalp would not hurt as much.

"Quiet down, you filthy whore. I ain't havin' no more of yer yelling."

Aya twisted her neck as best she could to look at the guard. His hair and beard were so bushy that all she could make out was a pair of dark brown eyes and a bulbous nose. She was tempted to spit in his face, but she thought better of it. Apparently, no one else could hear her scream down here, and if they could, they were not at all inspired.

"Fine," Aya said, willing to rest and regroup. "Let me go."

The guard slipped his knife through the bars, sliced off a lock of Aya's hair, then shoved her head away from the door. Aya stumbled to the floor of her cell, grasping her scalp with both hands. The cell was about four feet by four feet, and she was lucky to be short enough that she could stretch her legs out comfortably.

The guard dangled her hair inside the window and sniffed it. "You smell pretty good for a whore. Might have to see what the rest of you smells like."

Aya glared up at him. Let him try. The guard who had searched her had been too busy exploring her womanly assets to find anything. Aya imagined he had seen no reason to take the search seriously. After all, she was just a whore. She smiled, knowing the vortric cog and her father's screwdriver remained in place. She might only get in one stab with the screwdriver before the guard gave her one better with his knife, but she would not allow him to violate her without a fight.

There was a knocking sound further down the corridor, and the guard went to investigate. Aya breathed a sigh of relief and leaned her head back against the wall. The entire cell was made of metal, so the only way out was through the door. Even if she could miraculously make the iron bars disappear, the windows were still too narrow for her to shimmy through. She would have to exit through the door itself.

The screwdriver would be small defense if she faced more than one guard, and even so, the chances of her making it all the way back to Sternville without being caught were slim to none. And once in Sternville, what would she do? She couldn't put Dellwyn in danger, and Desertera was too small. There was not a big enough population to get lost in. She would have to take her chances in the desert beyond the city. She wondered which would be worse, public decapitation or private dehydration.

The guard came back, slamming his fist against Aya's door. "You have a visitor, whore."

Aya stayed seated, waiting for her visitor's face to be revealed in the window. The sound of footsteps alternating with the tapping of a staff gave his identity away. Lord Varick.

His beady eyes appeared in the window, as he was not tall enough for his nose and mouth to show. Without the rest of his face, Aya could not discern whether his eyes were crinkled with concern, cruelty, or calculation.

"Oh, Miss Aya, it breaks my heart to see you like this."

His words were too thick—full of false sympathy to the point the vowels were nearly all she could hear. Aya jumped up and put her face close to the window. She wanted Lord Varick to feel her sour breath on his face. "You lying sack of filth."

"Now, now, Miss Aya." Lord Varick *tutted*. "There is no need for name-calling."

Aya glowered. "Why?"

Lord Varick rolled his eyes. "I'm sorry, my dear. You're going to have to be more specific."

"Why are you framing me?" Aya shouted as loudly as her cracking voice would allow. She wanted the guard to hear, to know Lord Varick was guilty and throw him in the cell next to her. "There is no need for this. We had a plan."

Lord Varick blushed and turned his head to the guard, shaking it. "Poor girl. It seems her mind has slipped already."

The guard grunted. From the faintness of the sound, Aya could tell he must have returned to his chair. Lord Varick turned back to Aya and lowered his voice. "You said it yourself. We *had* a plan. Plans change, my dear. I believe this one will be safest for everyone."

"For you." Aya spat.

Lord Varick sighed. "I cannot leave any loose strings behind. If the other nobles ever found out that *I* orchestrated this, even with the king's crimes exposed, I could still be tried for treason. I must protect myself."

"You selfish bastard. You used me, just as you used Isadona."

"An unfortunate coincidence, yes. But what more are daughters good for?"

Aya took slow, deep breaths, using every muscle in her body to restrain herself from reaching through the bars and poking out Lord Varick's beady eyes.

"And what about Queen Zedara?" Aya raised her eyebrows. "She's something of a loose end, is she not?"

"Oh, certainly." Lord Varick winked. "Do not worry. Zedara will be next."

"So you kill us, and then what? You have taken your revenge, your secret is safe, and you go on with your life like it never happened?"

"Miss Aya, for such a clever girl, you do have trouble seeing the big picture." Lord Varick shook his head. "Trust me. Your death is not in vain. You and Zedara are making noble sacrifices to rid Desertera of a gluttonous and irresponsible royal line. This is only the first step. When it is all done, you ladies shall be revered as saints."

Aya almost laughed. "You want to be king. You, a mid-rank nobleman, think you can kill your way to the crown?"

Lord Varick squinted, wrapping his fingers around one of the iron bars. "I would never say such a thing. Now, if it were to happen, I do think I would be a great king. But as you say, I am so far down in the line."

The consequences of Lord Varick's plan filtered into Aya's mind, and her heart panged—with joy and fear—when she realized that Lord Varick would have to kill Prince Lionel. Willem.

"Where does Prince Lionel fit into your plans?"

Lord Varick's eyes brightened. "I wondered when you would ask about him. Willem is the name he gave you, correct?" He chuckled. "I certainly cannot rule with Willem around."

Aya pursed her lips. Maybe Willem—Lionel—had not known Aya would be hurt. Perhaps he regretted what he had done to Aya's father and had joined with Lord Varick to redeem himself. "Then he is like Zedara and me, another pawn in your scheme."

"Actually, the prince was not involved in our little plot to oust King Archon. Not originally."

A lump rose in Aya's throat, and she fingered the jeweled barrette—Queen Lisandra's barrette—still clipped in her hair. "When did he become involved?"

"Only a night or two ago." Lord Varick released the iron bar, leaning closer to the window. "He was quite upset when he caught you with King Archon. So upset, in fact, that when he confronted me about your behavior, and I told him of my plans to spy on you and the king, he leaped at the chance to send you and his father to the executioner."

Aya recoiled from the door, hoping the shadows in the cell would hide the pain in her eyes. Willem might have cared for her once, but now he only cared about getting rid of her.

Aya bit her lip, feeling foolish for her moment of hope. "You'll never get away with it. The other nobles may be stupid enough to overlook my and Zedara and Archon's corpses, but once others start piling up at your feet, someone will figure you out."

"Miss Aya, please. Give me some credit. It doesn't have to be all bloodshed and cruelty." Lord Varick rolled his eyes. "Besides, King Archon orchestrated the deaths of four wives before someone took action against him. And that someone was me. Without me in the way, I think I can make it further than he did before anyone tries to stop me."

Aya shook her head. "You're an idiot. Or insane. This is hopeless."

"Says the woman behind bars."

Aya glowered. He had her there. As far-fetched as Lord

Varick's plan seemed, he had successfully finished step one, complete with Aya's head on the chopping block.

"You were never going to give me my father's shop back." Aya clenched her fists. "You always planned for it to end this way."

"You are clever. Just never quick enough." Lord Varick cleared his throat and raised his voice for the guard's benefit. "Well, my dear, it breaks my heart to see you like this. If I'd known you would turn out to be an adulteress, I never would have taken you under my care. It hurts me to lose a second daughter to temptation. Though you do not deserve it, I will pray to the Benevolent Queen to forgive your soul."

Aya turned her back to Lord Varick. If by some miracle she got out of this, she never wanted to see him again, unless it was to watch his head fall from the executioner's ax. Aya heard the guard's heavy footsteps. They stopped in front of her cell door, then they were joined by Lord Varick's soft footsteps and the clacking of his cane. As the guard shut the dungeon door behind Lord Varick, it sent a clanging echo throughout the corridor.

Aya sat down and hugged her knees to her chest. "I'm sorry, Papa. I'm so sorry."

27

———

*A*ya didn't realize that she had fallen asleep until pounding on the dungeon door startled her awake. Within seconds, the guard on duty—no longer the hairy man —flung open her door and hauled her up by her arm. Aya stumbled, still fighting through her waking haze, and the guard passed her to two larger guards, who each grasped one of her elbows. As the guards pulled Aya forward, a sharp pain shot through her neck and shoulders, sore from her hunched sleeping position.

Unlike her trip to the dungeon, Aya walked of her own accord, doing her best to hide her aching muscles and the fear in her eyes. The screwdriver was still nestled in her garter, and for a moment, she considered again trying to grab for it and make an escape, but the rippling biceps of the guards dashed her foolishness. If she were going to die, she might as well face it with dignity. Papa would have wanted her to.

The guards led Aya back up to the middle of the palace to a room she did not recognize. At the doors stood another guard and the bishop who'd presided over Queen Zedara's greeting ceremony and Lady Jauntley's trial. Once again, the bishop wore loose white robes and rings on every finger. He signaled to his attendant guard to open the doors. The guard did as directed, flinging open the double doors and stepping aside to allow Aya a view into the room or, more accurately, the room a view of her.

"Miss Aya Cogsmith," the bishop announced. "Accused adulteress."

Aya could only see a small portion of the room, but she knew immediately that it was the same courtroom in which Lady Jauntley had been on trial. The guards led Aya into the courtroom, and once she emerged from the short passage, she found herself surrounded by nobles. They were seated a level above where she stood, in rows upon rows of benches that surrounded the entire circular room. Now Aya knew how small and scared Lady Jauntley must have felt.

Like last time, the main floor of the courtroom contained two tables and a throne on an elevated platform. At the left-hand table sat King Archon, an empty chair beside him. At the right-hand table sat Queen Zedara, the six guards behind her. The throne was empty, but Aya remembered that another short hallway like the one she'd passed through was directly behind it. The guards escorted Aya to the empty chair next to King Archon. She sat down, refusing to look at the queen or the king.

The bishop strode up to the throne and stood before it. He raised his hands to the nobles, his robes once again hanging limply from his thin arms. Aya felt as if she had lived this moment before, only she knew that for her, there would be no lover to clutch before execution—only her last few breaths before the ax.

The bishop cleared his throat. "My lords and ladies, you are here to witness the trial of King Archon and his alleged mistress, Aya Cogsmith. The king normally presides over criminal trials, but as the accused today is the king, we cannot allow that to happen. This is the first time in the history of Desertera that a king has been put on trial, and as such, a council met all night to discuss how to handle this situation. We believe the fairest option is to have the next in line to the throne, Prince Lionel, preside over this trial. If there are any objections to His Highness serving as judge, please air them now."

The blood drained from Aya's face. Prince Lionel—Willem—the man who had once cared dearly for her, who now, according to Lord Varick, despised her and the king, would decide her fate. In this courtroom, the prince was the true scorned lover, not Queen Zedara, and he had all the power.

The nobles' whispers descended upon Aya like a nest of hornets, their buzzing heightening her panic. Aya rose to object, ready to confess her involvement with Prince Lionel in hopes of having another noble—the bishop, perhaps—preside over the trial, but before she could speak, the guard pushed her back into her chair.

The bishop raised his hands, and the nobles quieted. "Hearing no objections, let us begin. I call to the Throne of Judgment, His Highness, Prince Lionel Willem Monashe, heir to the throne of Desertera."

Lionel Willem. At least he'd only lied about part of his name.

Aya waited, breath held, to see the prince. She did not know how to feel about him, let alone how her instincts would react to his presence. Would her blood boil with thoughts of her father? Would her heart flutter as she recalled Willem's caresses? Would her stomach retch at his contempt and the power he held over her? As Prince Lionel entered from the short corridor, wearing a cog-embroidered top hat exactly like the king's, Aya's body did all three.

Prince Lionel bowed to the crowd of nobles before taking his seat. Once situated on the throne, he scanned the three people before him. He gave a short nod to Queen Zedara, showed no emotion to King Archon, and pursed his lips at Aya. Her knees trembled. If Lord Varick had not revealed Aya's true identity to the prince, he knew it now. She could imagine Prince Lionel's thoughts as he stared down at her from his throne: traitor, like father like daughter.

"King Archon Lionel Monashe," Prince Lionel began, "you have been accused of adultery. How do you plead?"

King Archon rose. "Innocent."

"Very well." The prince remained emotionless. "Aya Cogsmith, you have also been accused of adultery as well as falsehood. How do you plead?"

Aya could not stand. The guard seized her under the arm and wrenched her to her feet. She managed, through a tight throat, to croak her plea. "Innocent."

"Very well." Lionel turned to the queen, his face finally forming a kind smile. "Queen Zedara, do you levy these accusations?"

Zedara rose. "I do, Your Highness."

Prince Lionel straightened in his throne. "And do you have any other accusations to add before we proceed?"

Queen Zedara looked at Aya out of the corner of her eye and winked. Aya's veins filled with ice, and she glowered at the queen. Zedara had already betrayed Aya, but to mock her now was incomprehensibly cruel.

"I do, Your Highness." Queen Zedara clenched her jaw. "I accuse King Archon Lionel Monashe of four counts of conspiracy to commit murder and high treason."

The noble audience gasped and erupted into whispers. Prince Lionel nodded. Aya's eyes drifted between Zedara and the prince. They were working together to reveal the truth about King Archon. Aya scanned the crowd for Lord Varick, but she could not find him. Was this part of Varick's plan, too?

The bishop stepped forward and clapped his hands to reclaim the nobles' attentions. "The accused may sit."

Aya and King Archon sat back down.

Prince Lionel waved his hand, and the last of the whisperers fell silent. "Queen Zedara, these are very serious accusations. Please explain."

"It is as I told you before, Your Highness." Zedara tucked a strand of blond hair behind her ear. "Last night, I went to my husband's chambers to share his bed for the evening, as is a wife's duty. I took my guards with me, because I had noticed a strange man following me earlier in the day, and it made me nervous. When I arrived at the king's chambers, he was speaking with Miss Cogsmith."

The prince's brow furrowed. "What were they saying?"

"The king was confessing his love for her." Zedara blushed, looking every bit the embarrassed wife. "Miss Cogsmith was obviously distressed by his affections and worried about committing adultery. The king informed her that adultery would not be an issue, as he was intending to frame me for the crime and have me executed."

"You're a lying whore, Zedara!" King Archon slammed his fist against the table. "She's making it all up, son. Don't believe a word she says."

"King Archon, please wait your turn to speak." Prince Lionel paused to ensure that the king would stay silent before motioning to Zedara. "Go on, Your Highness."

"After the king promised to have me executed, Miss Cogsmith seemed doubtful. To reassure her, he told her that he had performed this exact scheme with his last three wives, and he had not been caught yet."

"His last three wives?" Prince Lionel raised his eyebrows a bit too high. "What about his first and second wives?"

"The king did not mention his first wife, Queen Lisandra." Zedara shook her head. "However, he did say that his second wife was truly guilty of adultery and that she served as his inspiration to entrap his future wives in the crime when he tired of them. Myself included."

Queen Zedara's words became increasingly difficult to hear as the nobles in the stands erupted into fierce whispers. Prince Lionel held up his hand, and the courtroom quieted, but did not fall silent. A lump swelled in Aya's throat, and her heart beat unevenly as she imagined where Zedara's testimony would lead.

"What happened after that?"

Zedara fidgeted with the sleeve of her gown. "The king began to make physical advances on Miss Cogsmith. She appeared to struggle, but she was no match for his strength. Seeing her in distress, I made my presence known."

"And when you entered the room, had King Archon and Miss Cogsmith completed the act of adultery?"

Aya held her breath. Whatever Queen Zedara said next would determine her fate. Even though she had fought against the king, if Zedara claimed the act had been done, Aya would be guilty—willing or not.

"No, Your Highness. The act was yet done."

Aya's jaw dropped, and her breath came out in a shaky *whoosh*. The guard behind her smacked her shoulder to quiet her. Tremors racked her body, and she gripped the edge of her chair to steady herself. Closing her eyes, Aya prayed that she'd heard Queen Zedara correctly. But it wasn't over yet. Even cleared of adultery, Aya could still be imprisoned for falsehood —or treason, if Zedara chose to expose Aya's true purpose in the palace.

"Did King Archon or Miss Cogsmith say anything to you when you entered?"

Zedara frowned. "Both of them denied the adultery. However, Miss Cogsmith also thanked me for stopping the king."

"Is that so?" Prince Lionel rubbed his chin. Aya wondered whether this was part of his act, or if he and Lord Varick had actually arrived after she and the king were separated. "And members of the queen's guard, your statements are the same?"

One of the guards stepped forward. "They are, Your Highness."

"Thank you." Prince Lionel turned to face the accused. "King Archon, you may now speak to your defense."

King Archon stood, fists clenched and quivering. "Everything Queen Zedara has said is a lie. Miss Cogsmith and I were merely talking. It is no crime to have friends of the opposite sex. As to the queen's other accusations, she has taken a series of sad, coincidental betrayals and turned them against me. It is not my fault that my wives betrayed me. I am the victim."

"Do you have any evidence or witnesses to support your claim?"

King Archon's jaw tightened, and he shook his head. Aya's eyes widened. In the trial King Archon presided over, he had never even considered bringing in third-party testimony. Maybe Prince Lionel was not as vicious as his father after all.

"I see. Well, let us try to find you some." Prince Lionel smirked. "Lords and ladies, will anyone support the king's defense?"

Aya watched the nobles squirm, glancing between the king and Prince Lionel, trying to decide where the balance of power would be when the trial ended. A few nobles brazenly crossed their arms or shook their heads, but most kept to shifting their eyes.

As Prince Lionel opened his mouth to close the argument, a lady stood up in the back of the crowd. "I will support the king."

Aya craned her neck to see past the throne. It was Miss Collingwood. Prince Lionel's face reddened, and a vein bulged in his temple. Despite everything that was happening, Aya's nose wrinkled, and her mind raced to connect the pieces. Were Miss Collingwood and the prince cousins, as Willem had said, or potential marriage partners, as Miss Collingwood had implied? Or as King Archon had stated, with the inbreeding problem, were they both? Aya shook her head to banish the images the thought conjured from her mind.

Prince Lionel took a deep breath. "And what have you to say, Miss Collingwood?"

"I had tea with Miss Cogsmith—of course, I knew her to

be Miss Aya Wellman at the time—along with Miss Aster and Miss Frieson. We asked Miss Cogsmith about her relationship with the king, and she denied anything improper. She said that her benefactor, Lord Varick, was friends with the king and wanted him to help Aya adjust to palace life. I believe the king when he claims his innocence."

If Miss Collingwood's testimony had not helped her as well, Aya would have leaped from her seat and called the lady out for what she was—a power-hungry tramp. With Queen Zedara out of the way, Miss Collingwood must have assumed that her saving testimony would make her the next queen. At least Miss Collingwood and King Archon were not related by blood. Aya withheld an eye roll.

Prince Lionel's voice shook Aya from her thoughts. "And can you speak to the accusations of conspiracy and treason?"

Miss Collingwood looked down and intertwined her fingers. "No, I cannot. But Miss Cogsmith is most assuredly guilty of falsehood and should be prosecuted to the highest extent of your power, Your Highness."

Prince Lionel turned away from the lady and raised his eyes to the ceiling. "Thank you, Miss Collingwood. Miss Aster and Miss Frieson?"

The two ladies stood in opposite sides of the courtroom. Miss Aster was instantly noticeable, with her bright red hair, but Miss Frieson's dark appearance blended into the crowd, and it took the prince a moment to locate her.

"Do you both corroborate Miss Collingwood's story?"

"Yes," Miss Frieson replied.

"Yes," Miss Aster began, "but I do not take issue with Miss Cogsmith's falsehood. If my father were a traitor—"

Miss Aster was pulled down to her seat by a gray-haired man Aya guessed was her father.

The prince acted as if he did not notice. "Would anyone else like to speak for the king?"

When the room remained silent, King Archon sat, and

Prince Lionel turned his gaze to Aya. She met his eyes for a moment, but she had to look away. She did not know how to feel about him anymore. That spark still shot through her every time his gaze hit her body, but now it was met with a churning stomach and heat in the wrong places. He had hurt her twice in her life, and she knew she had hurt him, too.

"Miss Cogsmith, please make your case."

Aya rose on shaky legs, clutching the edge of the table for support. She took a deep breath and stared straight at the prince. "As for the matter of adultery, everything Queen Zedara says is true. I have never, and will never, lay with the king." Aya paused, her eyes boring into the prince's, hoping he understood. "Likewise, Queen Zedara's accusations of conspiracy and treason are valid. King Archon did confess to orchestrating the executions of his previous three wives, as well as preparing to have Queen Zedara framed and executed."

Prince Lionel inclined his head. "And to the matter of falsehood?"

"I will admit that I came to the palace under the auspice of Miss Aya Wellman. However, I did not do it with malicious intent." Aya took a breath to try and control the flush that threatened to burn her cheeks. "Lord Varick and I decided I should take the name so that the noble people would give me a fair shot and judge me by my own merits instead of my father's."

"Lord Varick?" Prince Lionel called, searching the crowd for him. "Can you attest to the truth of Miss Cogsmith's statement?"

Lord Varick rose from his place in the audience. From Aya's position, it appeared as if he were seated on top of Queen Zedara's head. He glanced between King Archon and the prince several times, and Aya could practically see the gears turning behind his beady black eyes. He was weighing his options, trying to calculate which royal would win the debate. As she gripped the table, Aya's knuckles turned white. What was he waiting for? He couldn't deny her statement—not without revealing the conspiracy that led to this moment.

When Lord Varick finally opened his mouth to speak, Aya could barely hear his words over the beating of her heart. "My ward speaks the truth. I did not want anyone to know that she was the cogsmith's daughter."

With that, Lord Varick glared at Aya and sat down. Aya closed her eyes and smiled. Lord Varick had told just enough truth, as she knew he had to. Even though there was still more to the trial, Aya's chest began to swell with hope.

Prince Lionel nodded. "Would anyone else like to speak on Miss Cogsmith's behalf?"

Aya held her breath, praying to the Benevolent Queen that the nobles would stay silent. One of them could bring up her work at the Rudder as testimony to her adulterous ways, but of course, then the accuser would be found out as well. Alternatively, and even less likely, one of them could also speak the truth, tell everyone what a good man her father had been, that his murder should be added to the king's list of crimes—and Prince Lionel's, too. Aya felt the vortric cog's teeth bite into her ribs. She wondered what King Archon would say if he knew that the vortric cog were less than a yard away from him, nestled in a place he had been groping last night.

"All right then. I would like to speak." Prince Lionel stood. "I know Queen Zedara to be an honest woman, and I am inclined to believe her. Likewise, I know Miss Cogsmith to be an upstanding young lady, in spite of dire circumstances, which I commend. King Archon, however, he is another matter."

Prince Lionel crossed the room, stopping at Aya and the king's table. He placed his hands on the tabletop and leaned over the king. "Would you like to tell them yourself, Father? Or should I?"

The king clamped his mouth shut and glared at his son.

"Very well. I believe the treasonous accusations against

King Archon, because I have grown up witness to them. When I was a boy, I watched him kill my mother."

The nobles gasped and began talking furiously. Queen Zedara, too, looked shocked, her hand flying up to cover her gaping mouth. Blushing, Aya cursed herself for not putting the pieces together sooner. Willem had said his mother was murdered. Aya glanced around the room, desperate to look anywhere but at the prince. She knew that pain, and she couldn't meet it in his face.

King Archon looked up at his son, tears forming in his eyes. "You don't know what you're talking about, Lionel."

"Oh, really?" The prince scoffed. "You thought I was too young to remember, Father, but I do. I watched as the two of you argued. My mother tipped right over the railing, her hands reaching out to you, and you didn't even try to save her. I heard her body break against the ground." Prince Lionel paused, his voice catching in his throat. "And then you lied to the guards. You told them she was sick, that you had no idea what had driven her to the edge."

Aya touched the barrette still clipped in her hair. The jewels felt cold against her fingertips.

"Your mother *was* sick." King Archon's lips quivered. "She killed herself because she was unhappy. It wasn't anyone's fault."

"It was your fault." Lionel squared his shoulders. "You flirted with every woman within reach. You made Mother feel unloved. She killed herself because of you."

King Archon stood, smacking his hand against the table and making Aya jump. "I loved your mother. I have regretted the way I treated her every day since she died. Blame me if you must, but never say I did not love her."

A tear dripped down King Archon's face. Aya stared at him with wide eyes, feeling as if she saw him for the first time. The courtroom had fallen completely silent. Prince Lionel gaped at his father, mouth slightly open, before turning away and shaking his head. "But after Mother. What about the others?"

King Archon pursed his lips and lowered himself to his chair.

"For argument's sake, let's say you didn't kill my mother." Prince Lionel's brow furrowed. His hazel eyes squinted. Aya could tell that Lionel had not expected his speech to take this turn and was floundering to get the trial back on track. "Still, you trapped wife after wife into adultery. You manipulated them into marriage then cast them aside the moment you grew bored. That is still treason and orchestrated execution. Murder." The prince paused, gazing out into the crowd of nobles. "But my father's tyranny does not stop there."

Prince Lionel moved to stand over Aya. He reached down and placed his hand over hers. She met his eyes and saw tears glistening in them.

"Ten years ago, I let my father manipulate me into his crimes. At his urging, I ordered Master Cogsmith to be tried for treason, simply because he did not have the tools necessary to fix my pet bird. At the trial, my father did not let Master Cogsmith say a single word in his defense. He had an innocent man executed and destroyed Aya's life out of his own greed and pride. What kind of ruler does that? What kind of son lets his father do that?"

The prince gave Aya's hand a squeeze before walking back to his throne. Aya watched his back as he went. His shoulders slumped, and his head hung. She did not know what she should feel at Prince Lionel's confession—anger, justice, gratitude? The nobles finally knew the truth about her father. The prince had showed remorse for what he had done. But all Aya felt was sadness balled up in the pit of her stomach.

Prince Lionel plopped down onto the throne, pulling off his top hat and placing it in his lap. "I'm sorry I never said anything before today. I was too afraid. When the king was the judge of law, the upholder of morality, and my own father, how could I have spoken against him? Especially when I knew what he was capable of? But today, the council voted to give me the power, so I have had my say."

He motioned for Queen Zedara to stand. She did.

"Queen Zedara, you are the main accuser, so I give you the recommendation of punishment. What do you believe is just?"

Aya held her breath, too afraid to look at the queen, let alone breathe. Queen Zedara was in league with Lord Varick, and as far as Aya knew, Zedara had no idea that Lord Varick planned to betray her. If she kept this alliance, she would recommend Aya's death. However, Queen Zedara had obviously conspired with Prince Lionel—her *stepson*—as well and appeared to be on his side throughout the trial. If she were loyal to him, she might spare Aya.

"As for King Archon," Queen Zedara began, "I recommend he be freed of adultery."

Aya saw the king smile from the corner of her vision, his eyes now dry.

"But given your and Miss Cogsmith's testimonies, Your Highness, I recommend he be sentenced to execution for four counts of conspiracy to commit murder against his past wives, myself included, and five counts of treason, for his crimes against his innocent queens and Master Cogsmith."

King Archon moved to stand, but one guard restrained him. The other bound his mouth with a cloth gag.

"As for Miss Cogsmith..." Queen Zedara took a deep breath. "I recommend her freedom. I believe we nobles have punished her enough with our politics."

Aya began to cry, her entire body rocking with the force of her sobs. Waves of relief—and of shame for doubting her friend—washed over her. She could not form words, but she looked at Queen Zedara and mouthed, "Thank you."

The queen walked over and knelt before Aya, wrapping her arms around her waist. Aya bent down over Zedara and hugged her back as hard as she could. She knew there was noise in the background—the king's muffled protests, the nobles' incessant chatter, footsteps echoing off the metal walls as everyone left the courtroom—but it all seemed muted behind the veil of Zedara's golden hair.

"I can't believe…" Aya gulped, shaking her head. "I thought you were on Varick's side. I thought you were going to have me—I'm so sorry for doubting you."

"Aya, you have nothing to apologize for." Zedara wiped at her own tears. "I'm sorry for putting you through this. Lord Varick was watching behind the bookcase. I had to act as if I had betrayed you, or I knew he would come after us both."

"I understand. I—I forgive you." Aya took a quavery breath. "But you should know, Lord Varick was planning to kill you anyway."

"I know." Zedara squeezed Aya tighter. "But now that we are both free and safe, he can't hurt us any more."

Aya nodded against Zedara's shoulder. She knew it was inappropriate to hold onto the queen like a frightened child, but she didn't care. The two of them did not know each other well, but they shared a bond no one else did. They'd survived the wrath of Lord Varick, suffered the physical affections of the person they most despised, and barely avoided their own deaths, all in the name of avenging the ones they loved most.

"The king wasn't lying about Isadona, was he?" Aya whispered. "You loved her."

Zedara sighed, her breath hot on Aya's tear-soaked shoulder. "I did. She was my one. As Lionel is yours."

Aya did not know how to respond, not after everything that had happened. "How did you know?" Her voice cracked. "About Willem—I mean, Lionel—and me?"

Zedara pulled away and looked around the courtroom. Her guards still stood sentry, but Prince Lionel and most of the other nobles had left. King Archon, no doubt, was on his way to the executioner, if not already there.

"I planned to ask Lionel to come with me to catch you and

the king. I knew he despised his father, and regardless, I thought he would be an honest witness. But before I did, he approached me about you. He told me that you were lying about your name, that you were caught up in some mess involving the king, but that you were innocent, and he wanted to help you. So I told him everything and had him go to Lord Varick to play the scorned lover. I knew he could help set you free and Lord Varick couldn't stop him."

Aya sighed. "Thank you."

"Am I right, though?" Zedara tilted her head. "Do you love him?"

Aya looked up to the ceiling, and her fingers found their way to Queen Lisandra's barrette. "I don't know. I think that I could have loved Willem, in time." She bit her lip, holding back the tears that welled in her eyes again. "I don't know if I can love Prince Lionel."

Zedara smiled and rose. She reached out her hands and helped Aya out of her chair. Aya glanced around the room. All of the nobles had now left, and Zedara's guards had moved a respectful distance away. No one could hear their conversation.

"I know it was deceitful of Lionel not to tell you his identity, and I know that what he did as a boy hurt you." Zedara squeezed Aya's hands. "But trust me when I say, the man you care for is who he really is. The prince is just a formality."

28

———

*Z*edara left Aya alone in the courtroom to ponder her next move. A lump swelled in Aya's throat as she realized that she had nowhere meaningful to go. Lord Varick's betrayal meant that she could not go back to his estate, nor return to her father's shop. Aya had said her goodbyes to Madam Huxley and the Rudder. Her only choice was to return to her hovel and decide how to proceed from there.

A creaking noise startled Aya, and her head snapped toward the sound. The door behind the throne opened, and Prince Lionel entered the room. He walked up to the throne and stopped, as if Aya were a puddle of water he did not want to ripple.

"I'm sorry to intrude." The prince removed his top hat and set it on the throne. "May I speak with you?"

Aya wiped her tear-stained cheeks. "It's your palace."

Prince Lionel glanced down at his hat. "Not for another few hours."

Aya shrugged, and the prince approached her, his gait cautious. For the first time since she'd learned the truth, Aya allowed herself to really look at Prince Lionel. He carried himself differently today, a bit taller, his shoulders seeming broader, but his lips still twisted into a soft smile, and his hazel eyes still glowed with golden warmth.

"Are you okay?" Lionel asked. "I know the trial must have been frightening."

"Yes." Aya glanced down at her feet. "Are you okay? Your mother…"

"I don't know. I want to believe my father when he says he loved her." Lionel frowned. "Regardless, he deserved to be brought to justice for his other crimes. But it's difficult. I spent years blaming him for my mother's death, and now everything has changed in one day."

Aya tilted her head. "I know exactly what that is like."

Prince Lionel stopped a few steps away from her. "Aya, I'm so sorry." He sighed. "For lying to you, for accusing you of being after my title, for—for what happened to your father."

"Will—Lion—Your High—I don't even know what to call you." Aya ran both hands through her tangled curls.

"Call me anything you like." The prince took a step forward. "Just keep talking to me."

Aya took a deep breath. "You know why I lied about my name. But why did you lie about yours?"

Prince Lionel rubbed his forehead. "I began with bad intentions. You were—are—gorgeous, and I wanted you. I thought that if you knew I was the prince, you would only be interested in me for my title. I wanted to win you with my charm." He chuckled. "If only I had known revealing myself would have increased the challenge."

Aya smiled, but she did not laugh.

"Once I realized that you weren't like the other noble ladies, it was too late." Lionel shook his head. "I had to keep up the charade. I know it was wrong, and I'm sorry."

Aya bit her lip. "If anyone understands not wanting to be judged by their title, it's me."

The prince nodded. "I know."

"How long have you known my true name?" Aya crossed her arms.

"A few days. There were hints—your interest in the clocks, your mechanical frog, your speech and wit." Lionel looked down at his feet, blushing. "I sent my valet out to question Sternville residents about Aya Wellman. When only Aya Cogsmith turned up, I figured it out."

Aya pursed her lips, angry at his snooping but relieved that Dellwyn was not in danger. "And what do you think of me? Now that you know I'm a lady of the Rudder and conspired to commit treason against the monarchy?"

"What do you think of me?"

Aya narrowed her eyes. "I asked you first."

Lionel stepped forward, closing the distance between them. "I think you are strong for taking care of yourself all these years. I think you are brave for seeking justice for your father. And I think you are still the cleverest, most beautiful woman I've ever met."

Despite the storm of emotions brewing under her skin, Aya flushed. She stood up straighter. "I understand why you did not stand up to your father before now, but I am still angry with you for it. I think you were my dearest friend in the palace and someone I could have grown to love. But now? I don't know what to think of you now."

Lionel took Aya's hands in his, and she resisted the urge to jerk them away. "I'm still that man, Aya. I'm still Willem." He paused, rubbing his thumb along her knuckles. "Do you think you can forgive me one day? I know it may take a while, and I'm willing to wait. But eventually, do you think we could try again—for real, as ourselves?"

Aya's heart thumped unevenly, and she remembered a pair of crooked eyes. "Are you going to marry Miss Collingwood?"

Lionel's nose crinkled. "What? No. Where in Desertera did that come from?"

"Tea." Aya's brow furrowed. "When I had tea with her, she told me she and the prince were to be wed."

"She's my cousin." Lionel emphasized each word, widening his eyes.

"I know." Aya shook her head. "It's what she said."

Lionel sighed. "No, Aya. I'm not going to marry my cousin." He squeezed her hands.

Another unseemly notion popped into Aya's mind, and she shuddered. "And what about other women?"

"What other women? Aya, you have to know that I'm only interested in you."

Aya pursed her lips. "When I asked you about why you were near the Rudder, were you telling the truth?"

"Yes. I was fetching my uncle." Lionel's feet shifted. "To be honest, I have been a patron of the Rudder before. When I came of age, my friends encouraged me to go. It didn't feel right to me—too fake, too transactional—but I can understand why it appeals to some. It is much easier than courting."

Aya stared down at the floor. Her stomach lurched at the thought of Lionel in one of her fellow courtesan's beds, but he had gone as a single man, and at least he had not found it pleasurable. She could not explain why, but she felt as if she might cry again.

Lionel shook his head. "I'm sorry. I cannot even imagine how painful working at the Rudder was for you, and I regret being that pain for one of the other women."

"It's fine. I am in no position to be anyone's judge." Aya looked up, the faintest smile on her lips. "And trust me, you could not have been a pain for anyone."

"Thank you." Lionel pressed his lips together. His forehead creased in thought. "You haven't answered my original questions. Can you forgive me, knowing what you know now?"

Aya scrunched her nose. "I think I can forgive you. Eventually."

Lionel grinned. "And would you be willing to allow me to court you? Properly?"

Aya squinted. "I wasn't just another one of your conquests?"

"Do you listen to anything I say?" Lionel chuckled, but when Aya held his gaze, he sighed. "You are not just another conquest. You are my final conquest."

And if his conquest ended in success, Aya would be queen. The thought sent a shiver down her spine, and she pulled her hands out of Lionel's. Even though her aching heart told her she still cared for Lionel, Aya's stomach churned at the idea of joining the royal family. All she had ever wanted was to follow in her father's footsteps as a cogsmith.

"My father's shop," Aya whispered.

Lionel flexed his empty fingers at his side. "What about it?"

"Lord Varick promised to return it to me in exchange for helping bring the king to justice." Aya touched her fingers to her temple. "It's as if I've lost it all over again."

Lionel smiled. "I'll give it back to you."

Aya frowned. "Lionel, I can't ask you to do that."

"You were willing to ask Lord Varick."

"That was a fair exchange." Aya crossed her arms. "I don't want to feel any obligation to you, nor do I want to be bound to a patron."

Lionel ran his fingers through his hair. "What if it were restitution? Now that the truth about your father's innocence has come to light, surely you, as his only heir, are entitled to your proper inheritance?"

Aya's brow furrowed. "But what about the current tenants?"

Lionel retook Aya's hands. "I will make sure they receive a new shop of equal value."

"That seems fair." Aya bit her lip, a twinge of guilt circling in her gut. "And what about my father's tools? The king seized them when…"

"I will have them sent over once the current tenants have been relocated."

Aya's eyes stung. It wasn't how she had planned, but she was finally getting the rest of her justice. "Thank you."

"You're welcome." Lionel moved to kiss her, but she turned her head so his lips landed on her cheek.

"Lord Varick is after your throne," Aya whispered.

Lionel pulled back, looking down at her with troubled eyes. "Are you sure?"

"Positive. He came to visit me in the dungeon. He said that getting King Archon out of the way was only the first step in his plan."

Lionel pursed his lips. "I can't do anything without other evidence, but I will watch him closely. Thank you."

"Of course." Aya pulled her hands away. If she held onto him any longer, if he tried to kiss her again, she did not know what she would do, and she was too scared to find out. "I should go. You should go, Your Majesty."

Lionel recoiled at the title. "Aya, don't call me that."

"It's who you are now." Aya rplaced a hand on his cheek. "We both need to stop living in the past. We need to be who we are."

Lionel put his hand over hers. "And can't we do that together?"

Aya stared up at him. Lionel's hazel eyes pleaded with her in a way his words couldn't. She thought about all the colors within them, about the way his lips felt on her skin, about how safe and perfect she had felt in his bed. But it wasn't enough. Not right now.

Aya sighed. "No, we can't."

With one last, sad smile, she turned and walked out the door.

Aya did not know how to get out of the palace from the courtroom, but she strode through the corridors anyway, keeping her eyes straight ahead and ignoring the hopeful glances and greetings from the nobles she passed. She'd had enough of them, and they'd certainly had enough of her.

Just as Aya's temples began to pulse, she spied the statue of Queen Hildegard. Aya stopped at the statue's feet, allowing herself to breathe now that she had her bearings. She fluffed her curls to create a breeze for her hot neck, and her fingers landed on a hard spot. Queen Lisandra's barrette was still clipped in her hair.

Aya glanced down at her body, clothed in Queen Lisandra's dress, and sighed. She unfastened the barrette, placing it in her palm and staring down at it. Should she return them? If she went back to her hovel, she would have to send them back to the palace by messenger, and she did not know who she would use now that Lord Varick's guard was no longer at her disposal. As Aya's thumb passed over the emeralds, she felt compelled to give back the queen's belongings now. After all

Lionel had done for her, and after all the news he'd received today, Aya knew he deserved that kindness.

When Aya reached the prince's room, she cursed under her breath. She had not thought about how to get into his chambers. Leaning down, Aya examined the space between the door and the floor. It did not look wide enough to slide the items through, but even if it were, she did not want to risk scratching the barrette or having Lionel step on the dress. As Aya straightened, the screwdriver poked her thigh, and she cursed herself again.

After a few quick jimmies, Aya heard a loud click. She opened Lionel's door, and as the room came into view, her skin flushed at the memory of their night together. He had been so gentle, so caring, so attentive to her desires. Aya thought back to the trial, how he had placed his hand over hers as he confessed, how he had spoken so softly afterward. He was the same man. She knew it in her bones.

Placing the barrette on the bed, Aya noticed her nightdress, cloak, and bathing house ensemble folded on top of a pillow. Her pillow. She allowed her fingers to trace the fabric of the bedspread again, and goose bumps speckled her skin. A lump swelled in her throat, and Aya knew that she still cared for Lionel, that no matter where their lives took them, part of her always would.

Aya removed Queen Lisandra's dress, put on the bathing house outfit, and gathered her nightdress and cloak under her arm. As she turned to leave the room, she noticed again the impressive grandfather clock. She remembered the pile of cogs and gears at the bottom. She recalled a silver winder and the strange, cone-shaped key Lionel wore around his neck. A leg and beak soldered together. Penelope.

Aya closed her eyes and told herself there was no time. She made it as far as the door before her hand tightened around the screwdriver she carried. As she stared down at her father's tool, Aya's mind whirled back to the day she and Lionel first met, and she finally put herself in his place. She imagined the hope of having a broken Charlie fixed, of the king she blamed for her parent's death throwing Charlie against the wall, of picking up Charlie's shattered pieces and placing him in the bottom of a broken clock.

She forgave Lionel.

Not knowing when Lionel would return to his room, or exactly how to fix Penelope, only that she had to try, Aya kneeled before the grandfather clock and pulled out the bird's pieces. When they all lay before her, Aya fished the vortric cog out from its hiding place between her ribs and corset. The cog glittered in the lantern light. Aya still did not know why it had been worth her father's life, to her father or King Archon, but she knew that Lionel would never use it for ill.

Her eyes watered, and she placed a single kiss on the cog. "I'm sorry, Charlie."

When her work was done, Aya wiped the sweat from her brow with the fabric of her toga. Atop her pillow, she set the chirping Penelope, beakless and one-legged, on her side next to Queen Lisandra's barrette and folded dress. After a quick rummage through Lionel's drawers, Aya found the last pieces to her gift. She scrawled her message, scratched out a couple words, and replaced the pen. Smiling to herself, Aya tucked the note beneath Penelope's wing.

My ~~Prince~~ King,
I did the best that I could. You have the key to the rest.
Yours,
The Cogsmith's ~~Daughter~~

THANKS FOR READING!

Ready for the next adventure? Join Dellwyn in *The Courtesan's Avenger (Desertera #2)*.

Want to know what happens to Aya next?
Get a FREE short story when you join Kate's reader list:
http://www.katemcolby.com/newsletter

If you enjoyed *The Cogsmith's Daughter*, please leave a review on websites of your choice.

ACKNOWLEDGMENTS

For me, coming up with novel ideas is the easy part. Putting those ideas into writing and later into a published novel is incredibly difficult. *The Cogsmith's Daughter* would not have been possible without the following individuals and many more who I will undoubtedly be embarrassed to not have named.

Thanks to my husband, Daniel, who introduced me to independent publishing and who has shown unwavering support for my indie author journey. My extended family, who has never once told me that wanting to be a novelist is an unrealistic life goal. Mrs. Sherri Cram, who ignited my love of writing in the second grade. Shelby, my first reader. Jess, who read this novel at every stage of writing and revising—you are a saint. My friends, Sam and Devin, who encourage my creativity. The indie author community that surrounds me—Jonas, Kara, Zach, Amanda, Brittany, Angelika, Galit, Amrita, Whitney, Margarita, Ben, and so many more. To those of you who were also my beta readers, thank you for helping me squeeze this lump of coal into a diamond. And of course, my editing team at Red Adept Editing and the design team at Damonza.com for helping make this novel as gorgeous as I imagined it could be.

Last, I want to thank the indie author trailblazers who have come before me. Without your shining examples, plethora of free resources, and transparency, I would be waiting on a call-back from an agent or still stuck in the drafting phase. I never would have been brave enough to do this on my own, so thank you for lighting the way.

ABOUT THE AUTHOR

Kate M. Colby writes paranormal fantasy novels that feature female anti-heroes, dark magic, seductive monsters, and spooky locales. She has also written a steampunk dystopian series and dabbles in creative nonfiction and poetry.

Kate is pursuing a Master of Liberal Arts in Creative Writing and Literature from Harvard Extension School. She has won local awards for her short fiction, and her first novel, *The Cogsmith's Daughter*, has been taught in college courses.

When not writing or studying, Kate enjoys traveling, wine tasting, playing video games, and giving amateur tarot readings. She lives in the United States with her husband and their feline familiars.

You can learn more about Kate and her books on her website: www.KateMColby.com.

facebook.com/authorKateMColby

instagram.com/katemcolby

goodreads.com/KateMColby

www.ingramcontent.com/pod-product-compliance
Lightning Source LLC
Chambersburg PA
CBHW020939120726
47905CB00008B/2586